## Praise for Patrick Sanchez and

"A witty tale about single women s... unconditional love and the perfect desse...

"Laugh-out-loud funny, a true gem."—Deirdre Martin, author of *Total Rush*

"Lots of drama and truly hilarious moments make this a fast, enjoyable read that readers will devour!"      —*Romatic Times*

"Outrageous! Don't miss it!"     —*Dangerously Curvy Novels*

"Sweet and funny. *The Way It Is* is a good-time book for girlfriends of all sizes."      —Leslie Stella, author of *The Easy Hour*

"A heavy dose of fun."        —*Southern Maryland Weekend*

### And outstanding praise for his debut novel, GIRLFRIENDS!

"Clearly taking his cue from Candice Bushnell and Helen Fielding, Sanchez's style is light and entertaining."
—*Publishers Weekly*

"Grab your girlfriends and read *Girlfriends*. Who knows what will happen!"
—Rita Mae Brown, *New York Times* bestselling author

"If Armistead Maupin and Terry McMillan collaborated on a novel, *Girlfriends* would be the result . . . It is a fast, funny and surprisingly moving romp through the urban singles scene . . . Patrick Sanchez has written a wildly entertaining first novel."
—Todd D. Brown, author of *Entries from a Hot Pink Notebook*

"Imagine *Friends* without the Prozac, as likely to have a group bitch as a group hug, and living in Washington, D.C., and you'll have some idea of where Patrick Sanchez is coming from in *Girlfriends*. Wickedly funny and blisteringly vengeful, this debut marks the start of what I hope is a long career."
—Stephen Stark, author of *The Outskirts* and *Second Son*

"Straight girls, gay girls and all the people who muck up their lives! What a great thrill ride of a book for all the girls—immensely readable—you'll pass this one around."
—Suzanne Westenhoefer, HBO comedy star and author of *Nothing In My Closet But My Clothes*

"*Valley of the Dolls* meets *Bridget Jones* via *Three Coins in the Fountain!*"        —Michael Musto, *The Village Voice*

**Books by Patrick Sanchez**

GIRLFRIENDS

THE WAY IT IS

TIGHT

Published by Kensington Publishing Corporation

# PATRICK SANCHEZ

# TIGHT

*Strapless*

KENSINGTON BOOKS
www.kensingtonbooks.com

KENSINGTON BOOKS are published by

Kensington Publishing Corp.
850 Third Avenue
New York, NY 10022

All Kensington titles, imprints, and distributed lines are available at special quantity discounts for bulk purchases for sales promotion, premiums, fund raising, educational or institutional use.

Special book excerpts or customized printings can also be created to fit specific needs. For details, write or phone the office of the Kensington Special Sales Manager: Attn. Special Sales Department. Kensington Publishing Corp., 850 Third Avenue, New York, NY 10022. Phone: 1-800-221-2647.

Strapless and the Strapless logo are trademarks of Kensington Publishing Corp.
Kensington and the K logo Reg. U.S. Pat. & TM Off.

ISBN 0-7582-1000-0

First Kensington Trade Paperback Printing: February 2006
10 9 8 7 6 5 4 3 2 1

Printed in the United States of America

In loving memory of:

**Bertha Herbert**
God had no idea who he was taking on when he ended your time with us. Heaven should be completely reorganized by now, and I suspect all the angels are now aware of how fat they've gotten. We'll always love you and miss you dearly.

and

**Whitney Clark**
Your husband said it best: "Whitney wasn't a saint, but she'll always be an angel."

# ACKNOWLEDGMENTS

So once again, I've finished a book. And, just as I did when I finished my first two novels, I wonder how the hell a guy with a complete lack of anything resembling an attention span got from a blank computer screen to a four-hundred-page manuscript. I guess I did it through a lot of late nights clicking away at the keyboard, having the will-power to turn off *The Young and Restless* to focus on my writing (except for the episodes when Katherine and Jill really go at it!), and refusing to get up from my desk until I had written something remotely "keepable." But it isn't my hard work alone that's responsible for the completion of *Tight* and the success of my first two books. There are so many people to thank for supporting me through the writing of *Tight* and also for helping with the promotion of *Girlfriends* and *The Way It Is*.

First and foremost, I have to thank all the folks who took a chance on me and bought my books, told your friends and family about my work, wrote reviews on the Web, and sent me e-mails with support and positive feedback (and yes, the occasional constructive criticism). I'll be forever grateful for your support. I love hearing from you by e-mail at *AuthorPatrick@yahoo.com*, and please visit my Web page at *www.patrick-sanchez.com*.

I also need to thank all the bookstore associates who enthusiastically welcomed me into your stores for book signings and presentations, recommended my books to your customers, and generally helped me spread the word about *Girlfriends* and *The Way It Is*.

Additionally, much gratitude goes to my partner, Brian Reid, for seeing a temperamental writer through yet another book, proofing the manuscript for *Tight*, and helping me brainstorm ideas. And to my family, Guillermo and Patricia Sanchez, The Fialkowskis (Donna, Paul, Tom, Geri, Allison, Helen, and Tommy), The Weirichs (Maria, Cal, Freda, Caroline, CJ, Anna Maria, and William), and, last but never least, my little sister, Laurie Sanchez (and Evan), for always offering support and enthusiasm for my books.

There are so many other people I'd like to thank, including the following:

My editor, John Scognamiglio, for always being patient with me, promptly answering all my questions, and willingly playing tour guide when I visit New York City.

The many Puerto Rican women who answered my ad on the Internet, for helping me develop Nora Perez into a true Nuyorican. Special thanks to Jennifer Santiago, Lucy Aponte, Priscilla Colon, and Vannessa (double N).

Stewart Neill and Camilla Ericksson, for drafting the most amazing artwork for my Web promotions. Please visit their Web sites and check out their work at: *www.thecartoonist.com* and *www.millan.net*.

Jacob Reid, for developing the awesome Flash promo for *The Way It Is* and patiently putting up with me and my many changes.

My agent, Deborah Schneider, for always advocating for me and sharing stories about her rescued greyhounds. Kristine Mills Noble for putting the finishing touches on my novel by developing a fantastic cover. Libba Bray for writing super jacket copy. Cara Muller for doing a bang-up job with the copyediting.

Finally, I'd like to express my appreciation to all my friends who support me in so many ways (e.g., helping out at my book events—or just showing up to them—watching my vindictive little dachshund when I travel to conferences, talking up my books to your own friends and family, the list goes on and on). And a special "thank you" goes out to those of you who shared your personal plastic surgery experiences with me when I was writing this book. All the best to the following:

Jennifer Amato, Dorothy Barry, Jennifer Carroll, Susie Chalmers, Yvette and Richard Chisholm, Tony Curtis and Dan Dycus, Dave Elliott and Mark Podrazik, Lucia Ferguson, Jennifer Gauntt and Janet Glazier, Teresa Glaze (and Kelly), Mike and Kerri Gray (and Joey and Katie), James and Mindy Harrington, Barry Hirsch and Rick Leichtweis, Michelle Kulp, Lyn Laparan, Jimmy and Pat Long, Karla Mahoney, Mary McDonald, Tim McDonald and Sandy Wells, Lynette Mitchell, Vondell Morgan, Andrea Newsome, Hope Norton, Cindy Ostrowski, Michael Pfeifer, Jim Palumbo, Angela Perri and Kristin Leitch, Rob Pilaud and Jeff Yake, Pam Dodson (and Jim), Joe Russell, Scott Sexton and Michael Connell, Tony Smith and Rudy Buenaventura, Steve Stark, Martha Stevens, Shayne Thompson and Damien Elford, Tasha Tillman, Holly Tracy, Jenny Veax-Meyer, Alev Weidman, and Stacy Williams.

# 1

## Brenda

I feel lucky. There is something about these harsh winter mornings that always makes me feel lucky. I hear the wind swirling
outside the window and felt the sting of the freezing air when I
was out walking Helga before bed last night. But now, lying
next to my husband (and Helga) under the warmth of my goose
down duvet, hearing the heat click on yet again, I feel lucky—
lucky to be in a nice warm comfortable home when it's so bitter
cold outside. The feeling won't last; of that, I am sure. It's hard
to feel lucky when you suspect your husband is cheating on
you . . . when you suspect your sixteen-year-old daughter is a
lesbian . . . when there's a defiant seventy-pound dog named
Helga taking up so much room on your mattress that your ass is
hanging off the side of the bed.

I look at the clock. It reads 5:27. I have three more minutes
until the alarm will sound and decide to beat it to the punch and
click it off before it has a chance to go off. I hate to be awoken
by those stupid morning DJs jabbering about their weekend or
some dumb story about their kids. What on earth makes radio
producers think we want to hear about these people's lives every
morning? Why can't they just play some music?

I sit up in bed really wanting a cigarette, but, since Jim quit
smoking a few years ago, I've agreed to smoke only downstairs
in the den by a cracked window. Can you believe that? In my
own home I've been banished to one room to smoke my

Marlboro Lights, like an addict or something. As I rustle from underneath the covers, Helga turns her head, her wet nose skimming my forearm, and offers me a snarl as if to say, "Can't you exit the bed with less motion? I'm trying to sleep." I hate that dog. Now don't get me wrong: I don't hate dogs in general. Growing up, I had a dachshund that I adored, and the neighbors have some sort of poodle-looking thing that's sweet as pie. I love *most* dogs. It's just Helga I hate. That bitch.

I shove my feet into my slippers and throw on my robe. I stop by the thermostat on the way downstairs and turn it up another notch or two. As I start the coffee maker, I have the same conversation I have with myself every morning: "Why on earth did I agree to move to Sterling?" I ask myself. "Because you wanted an affordable home with a yard and some space . . . and a decent school for Jodie," I answer back. I do like it here—the newness of everything—the houses, the shopping centers . . . the relative lack of derelicts, but when I'm up at five-thirty in the morning, getting ready for my hour-and-a-half commute into the city, I begin to question living here. Sterling, Virginia is only thirty miles or so west of Washington, D.C., but, in rush-hour traffic and on a parking lot called Leesburg Pike, it may as well be a hundred.

When the coffee's done, I pour myself a cup, leave the machine on for Jim, take my java into the den, and settle into the lounge chair by the window. It's one of those hideous La-Z-Boy recliners from the '80s. It has a lever on the side and everything. I'd never have it in any other part of the house, but it's comfortable, so I keep it around as my smoking chair. I crack the window a hint, strike the pack of Marlboro Lights against my palm, and pull out a cigarette. I ignite it with the gold-plated lighter Nora, my best friend and colleague, gave me for Christmas last year. She doesn't smoke, but she's one of the few people in my life who never pesters me about quitting. I take a drag off the cigarette—nothing like coffee and a cigarette first thing in the morning. If I could just get rid of mornings, I might actually be able to quit. I lean back in the chair and feel the draft of cold air coming through the crack in the window. I hate getting up so early, but once I'm actually out of bed and have my coffee and a cigarette burning in the ashtray on the windowsill, all is well with the world. At least it's peaceful. Jim and Jodie won't be up for another hour. This is my time—my time without Jim looking so lost trying to match a shirt with a pair of pants that I have to go over and help him, without Jodie badgering me about my smoking and rattling off something about the oppression of women in our country, without that damn dog barking non-stop out the front window.

As I inhale the cigarette for a second time, I think I hear Jim stumbling around upstairs, which is odd as he usually sleeps soundly until his alarm goes off at six-thirty. I picture him walking into the bathroom in his underwear, which probably has a tear (or two) in it somewhere, which reminds me that it's about time I go through his underwear drawer and clear out all the ripped or stained items—Lord knows he'll keep wearing whatever is in there, regardless of condition, until I do. On more than one occasion he's put his leg through a tear in his drawers, thinking it was the leg hole, not noticed a thing, and gone ahead and put his pants on over the debilitated briefs.

I expect Jim's especially tired this morning as he came in after midnight last night. He's been working long hours lately—or so he says. At first I believed him. I didn't have any reason not to. He's been with his company for almost ten years and has always had to work the occasional late night or weekend, so it isn't that unusual. But this is the only time that I can remember the late nights at work continuing for such a long stretch. It's January now, and I seem to remember these ongoing late nights starting some time before Thanksgiving. I laugh to myself as I think of Jim having an affair. The idea just seems ridiculous. I can't imagine there are women lining up to sleep with him. He's not a bad-looking man, but he's put on the pounds since we got married (as have I) more than fifteen years ago, has a small bald spot at the crown of his head, and God, how I wish he'd get those eyebrows trimmed. Like me, he's thirty-six years old. Yes, we're the same age. In fact, we were in the same class in high school. We've known each other since we were kids, but didn't really start hanging out together until we were seniors at Robinson. Just before graduation we started dating and were sort of "on-again, off-again" after high school. I think we really were in love, but I'm not sure either one of us planned on marrying the other; however, it seemed like the thing to do when I found out I was pregnant during my sophomore year at George Mason University. We were so young and *so* stupid. "Oh, this one time without a condom? What will it really matter?" I remember one of us saying during one of our "on again" periods. I'm really not sure if it was me or him, but obviously it *did* matter. I should have been on the pill, but at the time, I was still living on my parents' dime and their health insurance and couldn't bear broaching the subject with them. I didn't even tell them I was pregnant until after the wedding, although I'm sure they figured it out when I expressed the importance of making the wedding happen sooner rather than later. To this day neither my mother nor my father has said a word about Jodie being born only six months after our wedding, like she was a seven-pound preemie or something. Not a word! How ridiculous is that? Welcome to my world of Wasp dysfunction.

After a few more drags I smash the cigarette into the ashtray, shut the window, take a last sip of coffee, and head back upstairs to take a shower. I go through my morning ritual with easy efficiency—getting showered, dressed, and groomed in time to be out the door by six-thirty.

"Up, up, up!" I say in a chipper voice as I poke my head inside Jodie's door on my way out of the house. "It's six-thirty, sweetie. Get moving," I prod. She looks so innocent first thing in the morning. At least when she's first getting up she's too tired to pontificate about vegetarianism or explain why we (as in me, her father, and all Americans) are personally responsible for all that ails the world. When I look at her first thing in the morning, struggling to wake up and get out of bed, I can still see the little girl in her. I miss that little girl.

"Okay," she replies through her grogginess. "I'll be up in a minute."

"Have a good day, sweetie," I say and head down the hall,

knowing that Jim will make sure she's up and moving before he heads downstairs. It's not much, but I at least like to have some form of contact with my daughter before I leave the house. I hate the idea of her getting up in the morning and her mother just being *gone*. Otherwise, I'd just let Jim nudge her out of bed every morning. Lucky for him, he works fairly close to home in Reston, Virginia and doesn't have to leave as early for work as I do. "Love you," I add before I head down the stairs, grab a bottle of water and a banana (breakfast) to have on the way to work, and walk out into the January cold to really start my day.

# 2

## Brenda

"Oh, come on and go with me, Brenda. I don't want to have to go alone and sit in a room with a bunch of crusty old hags looking to have their chins lifted and their soggy breasts heaped up to their shoulders," Nora blurts out at me from across my desk.

"Nora, what on earth am I going to do at a seminar about plastic surgery? I'm a wife and mother. My days of trying to turn heads are long over . . . not that I ever did anyway."

"Just come for some moral support. You can help me decide if I really want to go through with this."

"I've already told you my thoughts. You don't need to have anything done. You're beautiful," I say and mean it. She is beautiful. Maybe not as beautiful as she was when she was twenty-five, but she's still one of the most attractive women I know.

"I'm not so sure about that. I was looking in the mirror this morning, and I was thinking 'Maybe forty isn't too early for a full facelift.' And maybe cheek implants wouldn't be such a bad idea."

"Nora. . . ." I'm about to protest her detailed ambitions when Jill Hancock, our boss, pokes her head into my office. "Yes, we should get on that right away," I say to Nora, trying to sound as if we are discussing business instead face lifts and boob jobs.

"Nora?" Jill asks, taking a couple steps into my office. "How's the Verizon presentation going?"

I quickly shut my Web browser so Jill won't see my bank account up on the screen if she gets too close to my desk. I was trying to balance my checkbook before Nora stopped in to say hello, and Jill doesn't take kindly to employees using our Internet access for personal use.

"Good . . . great," Nora replies, and from the look on her face I can tell that it is not going "good" or "great."

"Okay. Make sure I get a draft to review by the end of the day."

"Sure," Nora says. She watches Jill nod at her and then head back to her office. She gives Jill a few seconds to make her way down the hall. "Shit, shit," she mutters. "What Verizon presentation?"

"The one Jill assigned to you last week at the staff meeting."

"What? Why didn't you remind me? You know I never pay attention during those meetings. And I really start zoning when she begins talking about her stupid baby."

"Nora, she gave birth to her first child three months ago. Of course she's going to talk about him."

"Why? When I got a new cat last year, I didn't yack about it to everyone . . . people and their stupid kids."

"Oh yeah. A *cat*. A *baby*. I can see the similarity," I reply, doing a weighing gesture with my hands.

"And I'm so tired of everyone complimenting her on how good she looks," Nora sighs. Nora doesn't like anyone being complimented other than herself.

"She does look good. It's only been three months, and she's so thin. Who would know she just had a baby?"

"Look at her stretched out vagina, and I bet you'll know she just had a baby."

"I think I'll pass, but thanks," I say, grimacing.

"Well I'm up shit's creek," Nora says, getting up from her chair. "Jill wants to see a draft of the Verizon presentation today, and I haven't even started on it."

"Don't worry about it. I'll e-mail you a presentation I did for

Citigroup last month. Just replace Citigroup with Verizon, take out the financial services industry stuff, and add some crap about telecom. It shouldn't take you more than an hour."

"Perfect! Thanks so much," Nora says. "I guess I'd better get back to my desk and get started on it then. Can you send it now?"

"Sure."

"Now come on and go with me to the seminar, Chica," she adds. "We can grab dinner afterward—girls' night out."

"All right, but let me make sure Jim isn't working late that night. I hate for Jodie to eat dinner alone. What time should I be ready to go?"

"It starts at seven-thirty, so we should head over there about seven."

"Hmm . . . what does one wear to a plastic surgery seminar?"

"I don't think there's a dress code for learning about nose jobs and vaginal rejuvenation."

"Vaginal rejuvenation? Eew!"

"Hey, don't knock it. It may be you on the operating table one day getting your coochie all tightened up."

"Nora!" I reprimand. "This is a place of business." I feel my face starting to blush. Nora and I have been great friends since she joined the company two years ago, but I still haven't gotten used to her mouth, which has been known to curse like a wet hen. I'm your quintessential Wasp, born and raised in Fairfax County, an upper-middle-class and generally white (at least back when I was a kid) suburb of Washington, D.C. Nora Perez, on the other hand, is a New York Puerto Rican (a "Nuyorican" I think I heard her call herself a time or two) and grew up in the Bronx. For the longest time I thought she had a Spanish accent. It was months after I met her that I realized it wasn't so much a Spanish accent as a New York/Bronx thing she has going on. Her accent sounds kind of harsh to me—the way she says *Noo Yawk* instead of New York, or *tawk* instead of talk, or *hahd* instead of hard. Her voice, and often her choice of words, do not match the way she looks. She's very petite and quite beautiful with soft features. When you see her, looking demure in one of her lavender pantsuits or silk blouses with perfectly styled hair, you expect her to be very lady-like and maybe even speak in a refined southern accent. Instead she talks to you about "getting your coochie all tightened up."

Nora and I are worlds apart, but for some reason we hit it off. We are both graphic artists for Saunders and Kraff, a national consulting firm headquartered in D.C. Our jobs mostly consist of developing marketing materials and presentations for the sales vice-presidents, who travel around the country selling all sorts of worthless consulting services to major corporations and government agencies. We regularly work on presentations selling Saunders and Kraff's ability to assist companies in "re-engineering" their operations, or instituting "change management" or "total quality management." Whatever trumped-up buzz word we use, it all translates to the same thing: *let Saunders and Kraff come into your organization, charge you barrels of money, and, after a few cursory meetings with each of your departments, hand select masses of employees for you to lay off.*

I had been with the company for a few years before Nora was brought in to replace one of my former co-workers, who went to lunch one day and simply never came back. We were introduced on her first day, but it wasn't until we were both in a meeting presenting some of our latest work to Jack Turner, one of the leading sales vice-presidents, that we started to have any real interaction. I showcased two presentations I had developed for him for Microsoft and 3M. I had worked with Jack several times and already knew what he liked, so he only had some minor edits for me to make to the presentations. Nora also presented her work to Jack—a presentation for a new Internet company called LifeByDesign, which apparently was a Web site that provided some kind of on-line life-coaching sort of nonsense. As Nora went over the PowerPoint slides with Jack, I could see her annoyance growing as he critiqued each one and made numerous edits to her work. He kept nit-picking at little things like the fonts she had chosen (Jack only liked Times New Roman), the colors (Jack liked red), and the overall organization of the presentation. With every criticism, I could hear the irritation growing in Nora's voice. She'd respond every now and then with "okay, no problem," or "sure," or "yes, of course," but there was an edge in her tone, and this thing she did with her eyes, that made it clear Jack was royally getting on her nerves. After going over the more detailed edits, Jack got into this whole thing about how LifeByDesign was a new cutting-edge company, and he really wanted the presentation to be innovative and "sexy."

"Okay. I can add some stock photos of young beautiful people with martinis or something," Nora said.

"Yeah," Jack replied. "And give the presentation a sexy title."

I could see it in Nora's eyes—sexy title? Huh? "How about *Saunders and Kraff: Taking LifeByDesign to the Next Level?*" she offered.

"No, not sexy enough. I want it to be hip and catchy."

"How about *Saunders and Kraff: We got the Magic Stick!*" I'm sure Nora was joking, but Jack took her seriously.

"No, still not sexy enough. I really want to knock their socks off."

"Hmm," Nora said, pausing for effect, her exasperation really showing. "We could always just call it *Cunt.* Would that be sexy enough?"

I'm certain my mouth dropped to the floor as soon as the c-word had escaped her lips. I'm not sure I'd ever heard that word said out loud before and certainly not by a woman. I felt compelled to look away from Nora and Jack even though I wanted to watch—like when you're a kid, and your friend is about to get a spanking. I was sure Jack was going to fire her on the spot. He wasn't her direct supervisor but, still, I was sure he was going to fire her right then and there. But he didn't. He just widened his eyes, trying to hide his own shock and laughed. "Not *that* sexy," he said. It was shortly after the c-word incident that he and Nora started sleeping together. Their affair didn't last—none of Nora's affairs do. As with most men, Nora tired of him and gave him the boot after a few weeks.

I think I was still sitting there in shock when Jack and Nora finally wrapped up, and he left the conference room.

"What a pompous ass," she said to me after he had walked out, looking for me to agree. I did think that Jack was a pompous ass, but I just smiled at her and started collecting my things.

"I bet he's got a dick the size of my little finger," she added, making a fist and sticking out her pinky. I smiled at her again. What was I supposed to say? I grew up in a prudish Episcopalian home. I don't talk about the size of men's . . . well . . . you know, and I certainly don't use the c-word. I allow myself the occasional "bitch" and say "crap" all the time, and every now and then a "shit" escapes from my mouth, but that's as far I take it.

I let out a quick laugh, and I think my face went red—the first of many times (*many, many* times) that Nora would make me blush. She loved doing it the first time, and she still loves doing it now.

"Guess I should go get started on these edits," she said.

"Yeah, me too, but think I'll go smoke a cigarette first."

"You smoke?" Nora asked, a look of surprise coming across her face—I'd seen the look many times before. People are always surprised to learn that I smoke. For whatever reason, I seem to give off a "goody-two-shoes" vibe and have some sort of motherly aura about me. People don't expect someone like me to smoke. I think that's why I started in the first place—to try and give myself some sort of an edge. Even in high school other students saw me as prudish and uptight. Not that I wasn't popular—I was. I had lots of friends and was sort of the mother hen of my class. Everyone came to me with their problems and looked up to me. It was just that I was never someone other people thought of as sexy or hip. And I guess it didn't help that I spent half of my student life in crewneck sweaters and those turtlenecks with the little kelly green whales on them that were so big in the '80s. One day when I was a junior at Robinson, I got fed up with my girl-next-door image and bummed a cigarette off my friend, Stacia, and have been a smoker ever since. In the end, nothing else about me changed. I was still considered prudish and uptight, only now I had a nicotine addiction on top of it.

"Yeah, bad habit," I said.

"We all have them. If it wasn't smoking, it'd just be something else."

"So what's yours?" I asked.

"Men," Nora answered with conviction. And boy, would I find out how true her response was.

# 3

## Brenda

"Hi, sweetie. How was school?" I say as I come through the door. It's about seven-thirty, and I'm tired from a long day at work and the lengthy drive home. Jodie's sitting on the sofa watching a *Xena: Warrior Princess* episode, one I'm sure she's seen a few dozen times. She owns the entire DVD collection and always seems to have one of them running on the TV. I wish she wouldn't watch that show so much. I tried to view it with her once (I'm desperate to share something in common with her), but I couldn't get into it—all the scantily clad women attacking Ancient Greek warriors and mythical creatures. It just seemed like nonsense to me.

"Fine," she says, barely acknowledging my presence in the room.

"Can you turn that off?" I say. "I don't like you watching all that violence." And I don't like her watching all that violence, but the real reason I want it off is because it makes me uncomfortable. I read something in *Entertainment Weekly* about how the show is filled with lesbian sub-text, and how Xena and Gabrielle are actually lovers. I even happened upon Jodie pausing a scene where they were bathing together in a river. The whole thing just creeps me out. I can't explain exactly why—I'm not homophobic or anything, but her watching that kind of stuff just gets under my skin.

"It's almost over," she replies.

"What's it matter? You've seen them all a hundred times."

"Jesus!" she yells at me all of a sudden. "I'm just watching the damn TV." She clicks the television off with the remote and stomps out of the room and up the steps.

Oh, just great, I think to myself. She's in one of her moods. I never know with her—some days I get home, and she's reasonably pleasant, and others days she spits fire at me for no apparent reason. She recently turned sixteen and, for the past few years, we just haven't been able to relate to each other very well. We seem to have nothing in common. I hadn't planned on getting pregnant so many years ago, and it was quite a distressing experience at the time, but as my pregnancy progressed, I started to look forward to becoming a mother, and I was especially thrilled when I found out I was having a little girl. I envisioned pink satin dresses, curls, and imaginary tea parties. I thought about how much fun it would be to have a shopping partner when she grew up, to do each other's hair and make-up, to send her off to homecoming dances in pretty gowns that'd we pick out together at the mall. I hadn't anticipated a little girl who preferred baseballs to dolls, and a teenager who refused to wear dresses under any circumstances and harassed me until I finally relented and let her sign up for the all women's basketball league.

After I hear Jodie's door slam, I grab the stack of mail on the table and start leafing through it while Helga sits at my feet waiting for me to make my way to the pantry and scoop her a cup of dog food. She's such an odd-looking dog. Her mother was a Cocker Spaniel, but no one knows what breed her father was, as the Cocker apparently got knocked up one day after she'd managed to slide herself under her owner's chain link fence. From the looks of Helga, I'd guess her father was a black lab or some other large black dog.

The entire pile of mail turns out to be junk, and I toss every single piece in the garbage. Helga follows me to the kitchen, and I pour some food in her dish. I used to try to pet her when I came through the door, but she always backed away and, a few times, she even tried to bite me. Helga and I really only interact two times a day. She allows me to feed her when I get home from work, and she allows me to take her out for her evening walks. You would think, considering we have a fenced yard, that we could just let her out the back door, and she would do her business and come back inside. But the little princess refuses to do anything but scratch at the door if we put her outside by herself. She insists on being on a leash with one of us attached to it.

Jim, Jodie, and I picked Helga out from a litter of puppies shortly after she was born, but we couldn't actually take her home until she was eight weeks old. When she finally hit her eight-week mark, I was traveling with one of the sales reps in Michigan, and Jim and Jodie went to pick her up without me. She had been alone in the house with the two of them for almost a week when I came back from Michigan, and you would have thought I was the secret police trying to break into the house the day I came home. I thought it'd be such fun to come home to a new puppy, but instead, Helga saw me as the "other woman" trying to make the moves on her man. She wouldn't stop barking and baring her teeth at me. She actually snapped at me when I tried to get into my own bed with her and Jim my first night back. And even now, three years later, she still looks at me with an "Aren't you gone yet?" kind of look. Of course, she's all sweet and wonderful to Jim and sometimes, when she's lying next to him on the sofa and he's stroking her fur, I swear that dog is gloating at me—looking at me like I'm pathetic, like she's got my man. Jim and Jodie had been calling her Millie when they first brought her home, but, the more she ignored me and snapped at me, the more I wanted to give her a name I didn't like. I narrowed it down to Mildred or Helga and finally decided I disliked the name Helga more. I kept referring to her as Helga and, eventually, it just caught on with the rest of the family.

I start flipping through some menus we keep in a file folder by the phone, trying to decide if we should order in or go out for dinner. Unfortunately, I rarely have the time or energy to cook, so most nights we either get delivery or go out to eat. Jim can barely fry an egg and, although I'm fairly adept in the kitchen, I simply would rather spend a little extra cash then lose the time it takes to shop for food, cook it, and clean up after a meal. I used to do it back with Jodie was young and I was a stay-at-home mother, but honestly, I can only think of a handful of times in the recent past that I cooked a meal for my family. I'm thinking of ordering Chinese when I hear Jim come through the front door. Helga immediately abandons her food and rushes toward him.

"Hi precious!" Jim says with zeal to Helga as she dances at his feet and wags her tail. "Hey," he says to me with much less enthusiasm. "How's it going?"

"Good," I respond. "Did you pick up the cookies for me?" Jim works near this wonderful little bakery, and my boss just got back from maternity leave, so I asked him to pick up a selection of cookies for me to take into the office tomorrow and sort of welcome her back.

"Yeah . . . well, not exactly. The bakery was closed when I got out of the office. I stopped in the convenience store next door and got these." He hands me a plastic bag.

I open it up and take a look. "Chips Ahoy!? You got a bag of *Chips Ahoy*?"

"Is that a problem?"

"Yes! It's a *problem*. I can't take my boss a bag of Chips Ahoy as a welcome back gift."

"Why not? They're good. You said you wanted cookies."

"I meant cookies from a *bakery* . . . in a nice white box with gold ribbon," I say with a sigh. I'm trying not to be mad. I know Jim doesn't know any better. To him, a cookie is a cookie whether it's from 7-Eleven or Neiman Marcus. Jim's a pretty simple guy, and sometimes he just doesn't *get it*. Last year he just couldn't understand why I was less than enamored with the new kitchen faucet he bought me for my birthday. He doesn't understand why I get embarrassed when he asks for butter in a nice restaurant when the bread is served with olive oil, or when he asks the waiter for ketchup to put on his grilled salmon. He just doesn't have any interest in, or use for, etiquette and formalities. I try to keep this in mind as I attempt to calm my nerves. He probably thought it really was okay to come home with institutional cookies, but I guess I wonder if the bakery really was closed. Another thing about Jim—he's cheap, and I have to wonder if he saw the price of a dozen cookies at the bakery and decided to bolt and buy the Chips Ahoy just to save a few bucks. Whatever the reason, I guess it doesn't really matter at this point. I'll just have to figure out something else.

"Well, if your boss doesn't want them, I'll take them."

I give him a look, toss the bag on the counter, take a breath, and change the subject. "What do you want to do about dinner? Do you want to order Chinese . . . or a pizza?" I ask.

"How about we go out and grab something? Maybe the deli over at the town center?"

"Sure. You want to holler up to Jodie?"

Eventually we get ourselves together and make it out to Jim's car to head over to the deli. We travel mostly in silence. Jim's listening to the news on NPR, and Jodie has headphones over her ears listening to her MP3 player. I look out the window and then at my family and then out the window again. A part of me wants to scream. When did this happen? When did we become a family that does not communicate with each other? I want Jim to turn off the radio, and I want Jodie to take those stupid headphones off her ears. I want us to have a conversation. It wasn't always like this. There was a time when we actually felt like a family—back when Jodie was little and we were living in a dumpy apartment building in Arlington. It was in a marginal neighborhood just off Columbia Pike. We saw the occasional roach, and the hallways smelled of marijuana every now and then (and one time there was a notice posted asking people not to urinate in the stairwells), but our two-bedroom unit had lots of space, we couldn't beat the rent, and best of all, I could be at my job in the city in about twenty minutes. I remember feeling freer back then. I only worked part-time and didn't spend my life in traffic. I was able to take care of the apartment and cook meals, and I didn't feel so pressed for time like I do now. We used to have energy to do things after work other than just grunt at each other over some undercooked chicken at Boston Market like we do now.

The whole time we were living in the apartment, we were saving up to buy our dream house. We had planned to buy somewhere closer to the city like Falls Church or Alexandria, but when our realtor showed us how much further our money would go in neighborhoods well beyond the Beltway, we got the fever for a new modern home. In one of the close-in suburbs, we could barely afford a fifty-year-old, two-bedroom, one-bath house. In Sterling, we could afford to have a spacious home custom-built to our specifications, which led to extras we had never thought we needed in a house (and really couldn't afford). So what if I'd have to shift from part-time to full-time to afford the granite countertops and cherry cabinets? So what if my commuting time was going to triple? We were going to have a yard (that we never use), and a Jacuzzi tub in the master bath (that we never use), and stainless steel kitchen appliances (that we never use).

When we reach the deli, I pause for a minute before getting out of the car and think about how ironic it is that we sacrificed and saved to afford our dream house, and it was about the time that we moved into said dream house that our lives started to go to hell.

# 4

---

# Nora

"**O**w!" I quickly yelp as Dr. Brock inserts the first needle. The first prick is always the worst—at least it's the one I seem to react to the most. Actually, I think the last few injections are the most painful. I think the needle gets duller with every prick, so Dr. Brock has to press a little harder each time to break the skin.

"Try to relax," he says as he injects the Botox into the muscle between my eyebrows, and I lie back in the recliner, clenching my fists. I'm trying to stay calm, but it just isn't happening. In all the promotional materials they say it feels like a little prick, like a bug bite. Bull shit! That needle fuckin' hurts. The doctor applies some sort of topical anesthetic before starting the injections, but it doesn't seem to help. Sometimes I can actually hear the Botox oozing into my muscles, and I never get used to a needle coming toward my face. It's so creepy, but nobody said looking good was easy. You would think that I'd be used to it by now. This is about my eighth treatment. I come every six months or so to try and keep my frown lines and crows' feet in check. Dr. Brock can usually take care of the area around my eyes with a couple pricks per side and then it's another injection or two into my forehead. I've been seeing Dr. Brock for about a year now. I used to go to Dr. Schulman's Botox party Thursdays over on K Street by the Legal Seafood. I figured I may as well sip some champagne and enjoy some fine cheeses before going under the needle; but my last treatment with Dr. Schulman left me with an upper eyelid droop that lasted for weeks. The day after my treatment I woke up and looked in the mirror to find that my right eyelid was drooping. I remember standing in front of the mirror and trying to raise my eyelid, but nothing happened. I was furious, and let me tell you, you haven't seen angry until you've seen an angry Puerto Rican woman. I frantically called Dr. Schulman, and he said that my falling eyelid was a rare side effect of the Botox and might take weeks to improve. He said this all light and breezy as though only being able to open my eye halfway was no big deal. Well, you better believe I informed him that his botched Botox job was a big deal. I told him he'd better figure out a way to fix my eye, or I was going to Botox his dick. I had a job to go to and dates to keep. How was I going to do any of that looking like someone whose photo should be posted on AwfulPlasticSurgery.com? Unfortunately for Dr. Schulman, I was angry and panicked, which led me to threaten to show up at his office every day and scare away all his patients with my disfigured eye.

Once he calmed me down he told me about some concoction I could get at a health food store that might help the situation and agreed to refund my money. I called in sick to work for a few days and made up some lame story about how I'd been playing with one of my nephews, who'd gotten a little too rambunctious and accidentally poked me in the eye with a pencil. I told my boss that the incident had required minor surgery on my eye, which conveniently explained my absence and the sunglasses I wore constantly for the next couple of weeks until the sagging cleared up.

You'd think the whole debacle would have made me swear off Botox altogether, but it really only prompted me to change doctors, which I had been planning to do anyway just to get away from all the bitchy white Georgetown ladies who showed up at Dr. Schulman's all the time. I was always the only Latina in the bunch and generally the only one on my lunch break from an actual job. All the other women were stay-at-home mothers—at least they called themselves stay-at-home mothers. When you have a live-in nanny to tend to your kids all day and night, can you really call yourself a mother? Those chicas had nannies to take care of their kids, maids to clean their houses, and they had no jobs. What the fuck did they do all day? . . . got Botox injections, I guess.

"You ready for the next one?" Dr. Brock asks, holding up the needle.

"Ready as I'll ever be," I say, bracing myself for another injection. My eyes water, and my nose begins to run as he inserts the needle. I wince a little bit less this time, but I still hate every minute of it. God, getting old sucks! I'll be forty next week, and these Botox shots are only the beginning of my battle plan to keep myself up as well as possible. Sometimes I wish I wasn't such a vain person. I've actually had dreams about it. In the dreams I don't give a rat's ass what I look like. I eat what I want, I blow off the gym, and I save huge amounts of money that would have been spent on beauticians, colorists, manicures, clothes, make-up, weight-loss books, conditioners, creams, the list goes on and on. In the dreams I feel so free, like a huge weight has been lifted off my shoulders. It would be so liberating to give up vanity—I know it would, but I also know there is no way in hell I'll ever do it.

I love being pretty. I've always loved it, and I have no intention of giving it up without a fight. I think I like the attention more than anything. I grew up with five brothers and sisters, so you can imagine the amount of individual attention our parents were able to give us. With them both working full-time and having six of us to contend with, I was left perpetually starved for attention. In fact, I can remember only a handful of days from my entire youth when I felt as though the focus was on me. My parents were good about fawning over each of us individually on our birthdays, but other than that they pretty much "band-aided" whichever one of us was having a crisis and then moved on to the next one. I remember one of my birthdays being particularly special, and that was the day I really got the fever for being pretty. It was my fifteenth birthday and my *quinceanera*. A *quinceanera* is an old Catholic ritual, sort of a coming of age ceremony that presents a Puerto Rican girl to society. Lots of Puerto Rican girls in the U.S. have forsaken the *quinceanera* in favor of the more American Sweet Sixteen celebration, but my sisters and I weren't interested in waiting an additional year to have our special day. In many ways a *quinceanera* is like a wedding . . . only without a groom. My parents weren't wealthy, but unlike the stereotype of New York Puerto Ricans being *frijoles*-eating welfare recipients, they both had good jobs. *Papi* managed the entire maintenance staff for a high-rise office building in Manhattan, and *Mami* was a legal secretary at a law firm on Madison Avenue; accordingly, although money was often tight considering they had six children, they were able to put on fairly elaborate celebrations for me and my two sisters for our respective *quinceaneras*. I had to use my sister's tiara, but my mother bought me my very own dress. It was a beautiful white gown with specks of light blue to match the color of my seven attendants' dresses. I still remember that day as if it were yesterday. I got fawned over from morning to night. I got my hair done at Sabio's, and a make-up artist (actually an Avon-lady-friend of my mother's) came to the house to doll me up. I remember staring in the mirror when my look was complete and feeling absolutely stunning, like I could take on the world.

The ceremony was scheduled to start at two o'clock, but everyone (except the few Anglos who were invited and actually showed up at two o'clock) knew it would be on "Puerto Rican time," and it was almost three by the time I did my walk down the aisle, and boy did I *walk* down that aisle—strutted is more like it, and I loved every minute of it. All eyes were on me. People were smiling at me, and I heard murmurs of, "so pretty," and *"muy bonita,"* and *"toda una señorita,"* and, from that moment on, I was hooked. I felt powerful that day, and I still believe that beauty is power.

After the ceremony, in which I essentially promised to remain a virgin until I was married (a promise I broke about a year later with a cute white guy named Alex who I met while working at the Gap in Brooklyn), we had a reception in a small ballroom at the Ramada Inn in Queens. We served *arroz con pollo* and fried plantains, and a DJ played music while my friends and I danced for hours. It was *my* day, and I adored the spotlight. I loved it so much I didn't want to let it go and here I am, twenty-five years later, still trying to hang on to it.

"Ow!" I say as the doctor hits a sensitive area of my face. "Sorry," I add, apologizing for my outburst.

He laughs. He's not a bad-looking man. I wonder if he thinks I'm attractive. I'm sure he would have ten years ago, but I'm probably only a few years younger than him. He has a wedding band on—probably married to some woman half his age. I hate that about men—especially rich, successful men. They always hook up with women years and years younger than they are. Although I guess I shouldn't be one to point fingers. I had a date with a twenty-seven-year-old personal trainer over the weekend. He's hot as hell, but he's certainly not someone I want to get serious with. Actually, I'm pretty sure I don't want to get serious with anyone. I love being single and dating a variety of men. It wasn't long after my *quinceanera* that I started dating men and moving from one man to the next. I'm a pretty girl—about five-six, a hundred and twenty pounds, shoulder length brown hair, medium brown eyes, and a nice rack if I do say so myself—so I've never had a shortage of suitors, and it always seemed like there were too many men to settle down with just one. If I did settle down, I know I would be afraid someone better suited to me would come along, and I'd always have my eye out for him. Accordingly, I tend to casually date a lot of men, and overall it's been a great way to live. I've dated doctors, congressmen, poets, chefs, out-of-work actors, accountants, you name it. My dates have taken me to some of the finest restaurants in the city and some of worst hole-in-the-wall places you've ever seen. Some had access to private jets, and some couldn't even afford a car. I don't date men for their wealth or because of where they can take me. I date them to have a good time, and I'm a sucker for a cute mug and a hot body. And, no, I don't sleep with all of them. Don't get me wrong—I'm no saint, but I'm not one for giving away the goodies until I've been taken out a few times and treated right.

It's all been good, and I don't regret a single moment of my dating life, but as the big 4-0 approaches, I have to say that I'm getting a little bit scared. How much longer can I command the attention of attractive men? I know I still look good, but looking good at forty is not the same as looking good at twenty. I'm not ready to give up my lifestyle, and if I have to get injections in my face every few months to stay in the game, so be it.

When Dr. Brock finally finishes, I head out of the room toward the reception area, write a five-hundred dollar check, hand it to the receptionist, and leave the office. On the way to the elevator I start my facial exercises—squeezing my eyes shut, opening them, squeezing them shut again . . . crinkling my forehead, then relaxing it, crinkling it again. I do these over and over again. It's supposed to help work the Botox into the muscles, so, in a few days, my facial wrinkles will diminish. I pull out a compact and take a look—sometimes I get a little bruising that I have to cover with concealer, but so far I don't see any discoloration. I'll check again later.

As I press the down button next to the elevator, I wonder how much longer the Botox is going to cut it. Lately, I've been considering going under the knife. In fact, in a couple weeks, my friend Brenda and I are going to a seminar about plastic surgery. I told her I wanted to go just to see what my options are, but I think I've pretty much decided it's time to put up or shut up, and I'll probably end up having something done—now it's a matter of deciding what to have lifted, tucked, or liposucked.

# 5

## Brenda

"Gosh I'm stuffed," I say as I come through the front door with Jim and Jodie behind me.

"That's what happens when you eat meat. It makes you feel all retchey and bloated . . . just another reason to stop murdering animals," Jodie says to me, referring to the club sandwich I just consumed at the deli.

"Is your homework finished?" I ask, ignoring her "murdering animals" comment.

"I've got a couple things to wrap up," Jodie says, plopping down on the sofa and unzipping her backpack. She takes out a notebook and a pen and tosses them onto the coffee table before getting back up to slip a DVD into the player on top of the television.

"Oh Lord . . . not *Xena* again?" I say with a sigh as Jodie presses the play button on the remote control.

"No. It's just some music to play in the background while get some studying done."

"All right. Well, I'm off to bed. Don't stay up too late. Okay?" I ask as I see Melissa Etheridge appear on the TV screen doing an intense rendition of "I'm The Only One."

Isn't that Melissa Etheridge a lesbian? I think to myself. No, maybe it's that woman who looks like a man that I'm thinking of . . . Katie Lang, or K.D. Lang or something like that? Or is it Whitney Houston? I think I heard something about her being gay. No, it is Melissa. I saw something about her marrying her partner on *Oprah*. It rattles me a bit, thinking of Jodie watching *Xena* all the time and now playing a Melissa Etheridge DVD. Sometimes I think Jodie's trying to send me a message by doing these things . . . watching *Xena*, listening to Melissa Etheridge, cutting her hair so short. I think she might be trying to prepare me, laying the ground work to tell me that she's . . . No, no, that's silly. I'm sure there are plenty of straight girls who watch *Xena*, and Lord knows, Jodie listens to plenty of non-lesbian singers. She's always been a bit of a tomboy. I'd thought she would have outgrown it by now, but she's still young. She's only sixteen. I know she thinks she's all grown up, but she's really still a child.

Before I head upstairs I go to the den to smoke a cigarette and then stop by the kitchen for a sip of water, where I find Jim. He's doing what he always does about this time every night—sitting at the kitchen table with a mug of Budweiser, watching CNN and reading *The Washington Post*. Somehow he manages to do both at the same time, and Lord help him if either one isn't at his immediate disposal. Occasionally, when the cable goes out, making CNN unavailable or, every now and then, when the paper doesn't arrive on our doorstep, you'd think oxygen had been removed from the air by how upset he gets to have to go without either one. He's odd that way, and very particular about other things too. He doesn't like anyone to read the paper before him. He likes it in perfect order, so Jodie and I don't dare touch it until he tosses it on the recycling pile in the garage after he's done with it. And it's not only the paper and CNN that Jim obsesses about. He's funny about several things. His car, the interior and exterior, must be immaculate at all times—we keep a shop vacuum in the garage that he uses almost daily. The house could be filthy and he wouldn't bat an eye, but heaven forbid Jodie or I leave a single crumb in his vehicle. He only eats Raisin Bran (Kellogg's . . . never Post . . . there's a difference, apparently) every morning, and if we happen to be out, he drives to the grocery store immediately for a new box. And, ever since he quit smoking, he's very sensitive to smells and any sort of fragrance gives him a headache. We can only use Dial soap, Clean & Clear Face Wash, Almay unscented deodorant, Aveeno unscented shaving cream, and this expensive fragrance-free shampoo and conditioner that I have to buy at Whole Foods in Reston. And I am never (*never ever*, under any circumstances) to wear perfume.

"I'm heading up," I say to Jim, walking up behind him and rubbing his shoulders. "You'll be up soon?"

"Yeah. I'm just going to finish reading the paper."

"Okay. Good night," I say and climb the steps to our bedroom. Before I slip into a nightshirt and get into bed, I take a quick shower and wash my hair. I try to do this most nights before bed (although sometimes I'm just too tired). Jim has never complained, but sometimes I'm afraid my hair smells of cigarette smoke, so I try to wash it out at night. I generally only smoke outside or by a cracked window at home and in the car, so I shouldn't smell too smoky, but I don't want Jim feeling like he's sleeping with a cigarette.

When I finally get into bed, I'm almost giddy with fatigue and the pure joy of being under the covers and able to lay my head on a cushy pillow and drift off to sleep. Sometimes the first thing I think when I get out of bed in the morning is, how long until I can get back under those covers and shut my eyes once again? It's a horrible way to live, I suppose—the highlight of my day being my time in bed—but what can I do? It truly is my favorite part of the day. What does that say about my life—that one of my favorite things to do is sleep? One of my other favorite things is shopping at Target and Wal-Mart. Is that even sadder? I absolutely love to go to those big box stores. Okay, so they're a little bit disheveled, and the lines can be long, but they have so much neat stuff! Every time I go, I leave with a cart full of items I never intended to buy. And I always feel inspired to throw a party. I've found that both Target and Wal-Mart are very good at stocking all sorts of fun things for whatever holiday is on the horizon. If I go before Halloween, I see all sorts of plates and napkins and cake molds of bats and witches, and I want to plan a Halloween party. Before Valentine's Day, I see all those red decorations and pink party favors, and I immediately think about having a Valentine's Day party. Sometimes I even start loading up the cart with all sorts of party goodies, but as I make my way to the check-out stand, I start thinking about all the work involved in being a hostess—the cleaning, and the shopping, and the cooking. Then I start calculating the cost of food and liquor and invitations. And, before you know it, I'm taking all the items out of the cart and laying them on top of a display of laundry detergent or sporting goods.

I say a quick prayer, asking God to bless me and my family, before I turn on my side and close my eyes. About a half hour later I'm barely awake when I hear Jim come into the room and the jingling sound of Helga's dog tags as she trots along behind him. Helga jumps up on the bed while Jim gets undressed, puts her nose to my head, and starts sniffing my hair as if she has no idea who I am, or why I'm in *her* bed. Then she deliberately lies down right smack in the middle of the mattress, sure to keep Jim and me separated—protecting him from that strange woman with the wet hair, who so rudely turned up in her bed.

I pretend to be asleep as Jim gets into bed. If he knows I'm awake, he may start with the touchy-feely stuff—shoving Helga to the other side of the bed and pushing against me. Not that I mind my husband wanting to cuddle with me—I'd actually like that, but Jim only cuddles when he wants it to lead somewhere, and I'm just too tired for any of that business tonight. Actually, I'm too tired for it most nights, and I guess, if I'm being honest, it's more than fatigue at play here. I can't place exactly when it happened, but for some time now, I've had about as much interest in having sex as I do in gathering up the dirty clothes and doing a load of laundry. Neither one is a particularly unpleasant task, but both feel like work, and most of the time I can only be bothered to do either one when I feel like I *have* to. Accordingly, the laundry and sex with Jim only get done about once a week.

If Jim had his way, we'd still be intimate a few times during the week and at least twice on the weekends. That's how it was during the first few years of our marriage. Even when Jodie was a baby and in need of almost constant attention, we still found time. I'm not sure I can say that sex with Jim has ever been "rockets and fireworks" or anything like that, but it did used to be pretty darn good. During the first few years we were together we could barely keep our hands off each other. We both had solid sex drives—we wanted to be together so much that we were never bothered by doing it in the back seat of Jim's Mazda or on the tiny twin bed in my dorm room at GMU. It wasn't unusual for us to go at it first thing in the morning when neither one of us had showered or brushed our teeth. We just wanted to be together, and little things like less-than-fresh breath didn't matter. I wouldn't say we were ever truly adventurous in the bedroom, but we certainly had a healthy sex life. I owned my share of mesh teddies and garters and, at one point, I even had a pair of crotchless panties. I was never a raving beauty queen, but I used to feel much better about my body back when I was in my twenties and teetered between a size eight and a size ten. Back then I felt sexy when I donned skimpy lingerie. There were even occasions when *I* was the one who would initiate sex with Jim. But, little by little, over the course of time, our sex life started to unravel. We slowly started going to bed at different times. We were tired from the demands of careers and commuting and parenthood. And now that I've gotten older and put on some weight, I find it hard to drum up sexy feelings—I actually feel frumpy and silly on the rare occasions that I wear a sexy nightie even though Jim still seems to appreciate it when I do. Several years ago, when I used to picture us making love, I felt sexy and aroused by the vision. Now all I see is a thirty-five-year-old woman with too much natural padding and stretch marks on her stomach being mounted by a balding man with a bit of a beer gut—it's just not a titillating image anymore—it's more like the image high school kids grudgingly have of their parents having sex.

Aside from Jim, I've only been with a couple of other men, and those encounters were so long ago I can hardly remember them. They occurred during my freshman year in college when Jim and I had agreed to break up after high school. I was pledging Zeta Tau Alpha, and there were always mixers and other events with various fraternities on campus, most of which involved heavy drinking. I enjoyed the attention I got from some of the fraternity brothers and, with the help of a little too much Milwaukee's Best or whatever cheap beer was being pumped out of a keg, I relaxed my morals and had a one night stand . . . or two. I'm not proud of it, but compared to most of sorority sisters I was positively saintly. There was Raymond, a Pi Kappa Phi that I met on a Halloween hayride. I agreed to go back to his dorm room after a few too many hot apple ciders spiked with vodka. He was a little nerdy and seemed to have no idea what he was doing in bed. I think I may have been his first lover, but I didn't want to embarrass him by asking him if he was a virgin. He called me once several days after our night together, but, by then, Jim and I had reconnected so I never returned his call. My only other indiscretion was with Louis, a sophomore I met when my sorority went bowling with Sigma Chi. The thing I remember most about him was how tall he was—he was six foot five and had these enormous hands, which were more than twice the size of mine . . . and no, his hands didn't serve as an indication of the size of a certain other body part, which was just average. I really enjoyed the way Louis made me feel physically—next to him I felt petite and feminine. I remember feeling him on top of me with his thick fingers exploring my body. His size just made him feel like a *man*, and it made me feel like a *woman*, but after the sex he informed me that he belonged to the Sigma chapter at Radford University down in southwestern Virginia and was just up visiting for the weekend. We exchanged phone numbers, but I didn't really expect to hear from him, which was good, as I never did.

I remember how inept Raymond was, and I still remember the feel of Louis' hands, but what I recall most about the encounters is how, throughout both of them, I couldn't get my mind off Jim, and what he would think about me being with another man. I thought about how their touch was different from his, how they had different scents and different rhythms to their movements. Jim was my first lover, and we had such a comfort level with each other in and out of the bedroom. My one-night-stands with horny frat boys only made me miss him more and realize how stupid our break-up was. We were young and just starting college—I think we both wanted to try new things and see what else was out there for us without being constrained by a high-school relationship. I was at George Mason University just outside D.C., and Jim was at American University in the city. There was virtually no distance between us, so even though we were officially broken up, we kept reconnecting, enjoying each other's company and the ability we had to just be ourselves around each other. Our paths would cross when we got together with mutual friends from high school, or sometimes we'd just pick up the phone and check in with each other, which often led to us getting together just to "catch up." It was during one of those "reconnecting" periods that Jodie was conceived, and our fate was pretty much sealed.

Jim and I have such a history together and have been together so long it's hard for me to pinpoint when the connection between us started to weaken, particularly with regard to our sex life, or maybe more accurately, with regard to my sex drive (or lack thereof). I feel bad for Jim sometimes. I know he has needs, but sometimes I think he should be grateful we do it once a week. It's gotten so bad that sometimes I have to sneak into the bathroom and use that awful KY jelly just to keep myself lubricated. It's not that I've lost interest in Jim—at least not *just* in Jim. I don't have much of a libido at all. Brad Pitt could walk into my bedroom naked, and I'd be like, "Hey, can you move? You're blocking the TV." I supposed I could see a doctor about it, but I doubt there's anything they can do. As far as I know there is no Viagra for women. I'm hoping it's only a phase, and eventually my sex drive will come back, but tonight, I'm actually thankful that that spiteful dog is sleeping between my husband and me.

# 6

## Nora

So, I'm on my third date with Scott, a guy I met at the bookstore a few weeks ago while looking for some lame-assed book about getting rid of wrinkles. We've just finished dinner, and we're on our way to his place. I'm slowly discovering that he's dumb as a box of hair and has about as much personality as Carson Daley, but, considering his chiseled body and high cheekbones, I'm doing my best to ignore his lack of intellect and charisma. He's twenty-seven with dark hair and light eyes, and the night I met him he had on this T-shirt that hugged his body and showed off a chest to die for.

I was in the Health & Beauty section when I spotted him from the corner of my eye. I looked up from the book I was flipping through to get a better view of him, and he caught me checking him out. He smiled at me, so I smiled back and said, "Hello." He asked me if I'd come across some Atkins cookbook, which led to some conversation about carb-free living and an invitation for a cup of coffee in the adjoining café. We sat in the coffee shop for more than an hour while I listened to him go on and on about his job as a personal trainer, his favorite protein shakes, and the advantages of free weights over Nautilus machines. I barely had a chance to get a word in edgewise but, honestly, I didn't really care. The more he talked, the more I had the opportunity to look at his adorable face. I think I was also a bit taken with the fact that a ripped guy in his twenties was into me.

On our second date I told him I was thirty-three. I'm not sure I can pass for thirty-three, but since men expect women to lie about our ages, I believe that when you do lie, you should *really* lie. I figured if I told him I was thirty-three, he'd probably think I was really thirty-five or so, and I can definitely pass for thirty-five. I know, maybe lying is not the best way to start a relationship, but I'm not terribly interested in starting a relationship with Scott. I mean really, how much am I going to have in common with a gym rat who's more than ten years younger than me? I just want to have some fun with him and then move on.

Now, as we walk up Wilson Boulevard toward his apartment, I've decided that tonight is the night he's going to get lucky. I figure three dates before sleeping with him is respectable. Sometimes I make a man wait longer, but I need to have sex with Scott tonight just to find out if it's worth going on any more dates with him and having to listen to him drivel on about quality protein and the concentric versus the eccentric phases of exercise (yawn!).

It's cold out tonight, so I'm bundled up in my navy blue wool jacket, and Scott keeps rubbing my back with his gloved hand as we hurry along. We're a block or two from his apartment when I hear someone call my name.

"Nora!" I hear coming from behind us, and turn around to see Gretchen Morrow, an administrative assistant from work who's about as nutty as a can of Planters.

"Hi Gretchen," I say, wishing I hadn't turned around and just pretended not to hear her calling. Gretchen and I pretend to tolerate each other since we have to work together, but, truth be known, she really gets on my nerves, and she's less than enamored with me as well, because I refuse to put up with her bullshit. She's lazy and incompetent and always calling in sick with these ridiculous excuses.

"I thought that was you when you passed by," she says and then looks at Scott and back at me. "I didn't know you had a son."

Here she goes with her passive aggressive crap. "Scott is my *date*," I respond. "You remember dates, don't you, Gretchen? Or has it been that long since you've been on one?" I say with a laugh, so she can't quite tell if I'm kidding or not. Okay, so we may as well be meowing at each other, but she started it.

Gretchen gives me a wicked look in return for my comment, but can't seem to think of a comeback. "So where are you guys off to?"

"We just had dinner. So we're heading home." Of course I don't add any information about to whose home we are headed. "And you?"

"I was hanging out at the bookstore down the street, copying down a few recipes I want to try."

I laugh. "Beats buying the cookbook I guess."

"You know it."

"Well, it was fun to run into you," I lie, trying to wrap up this little encounter.

"Yeah. You two have a good night," she says and goes on her way.

"Who was that?" Scott asks.

"A secretary from work."

"Do you two not like each other? I couldn't quite tell from your exchange."

Like I said—dumb as a box of hair. "It's nothing personal. She's just a pain in the ass and gets on my nerves," I respond and get back to hurrying up the sidewalk to get out of the cold. When we finally reach Scott's building we take the elevator up to his apartment.

"So this is it," he says as we come through the door to a one room studio on the third floor of a new high rise in Clarendon, a hoity-toity neighborhood in Arlington, Virginia. He probably pays almost two grand a month for this shoe-box. I look around at the place as I step inside and take in the sterile surroundings typical of a young single man's living space—beige carpet, white walls, no artwork, and a lonely sofa (which I assume opens into a bed) against the window that faces a television with a thirty inch screen. Aside from the sofa and the television the only other pieces of furniture are a small coffee table, a cheap floor lamp, and some sort of universal weight-lifting contraption that sits in one corner of the room.

"Please. Have a seat," he says. "Can I get you anything? I think I have a couple of beers in the fridge."

"Sure. A beer would be fine," I reply, taking off my coat and lowering myself to the sofa. I'm not a big fan of beer, but I doubt very seriously that there's a nice bottle of Shiraz or Pinot Noir floating around in his little galley kitchen.

"Thanks," I say as he hands me a Michelob Ultra and sits down next to me.

"It's low-carb and only has ninety-six calories. It's the only beer I drink. I used to drink Miller Lite, but Michelob has slightly less carbs—"

"Shh," I say, putting my finger to his lips, offering a playful grin. I know we just got here, but he's so damn cute, and if I have to hear another word about carbs or protein or diet plans, I'm going to lose my mind. I move my hand down to his knee, giving it a light squeeze, and he reaches over and grabs my leg. I can feel the weight-lifting calluses on his hands as he slowly rubs up and down, moving his hand up higher on my thigh with each up motion. He reaches in to kiss me, and we wrap our arms around each other. He's all man . . . his body is so solid and hard. All the carb watching and protein consuming may make for boring conversation, but boy what it does for his body!

"You really are beautiful," he says to me, after gently removing his lips from mine.

I smile.

"I'm so glad I ran into you at the bookstore."

"Yeah, me too," I respond, just wanting him to shut up and start kissing me again.

"You know, I never did find the Atkins cookbook I was looking for," he says with a laugh.

"As I recall, you sort of stopped looking for it after we started talking."

"Oh well. I found you. I guess that should be enough."

He leans toward my lips again. As we kiss, his fingers keep moving upwards on my leg, and he eventually slips his hand up my skirt, and I feel his thick thumb lightly massaging my special place. He pulls me closer to him, and I spread my legs as he spreads his fingers. He slips my panties off, and his fingers continue to toy with me. I'm sighing with pleasure, but after a few minutes, I decide it's my turn to offer some gratification. I pull his moist hand away from my crotch and turn to face him. I untuck his shirt and help him slip it off. As he unveils one of the most sculpted chests I've ever seen, I loosen his belt buckle and slip off his pants. He looks utterly amazing in nothing but white athletic socks and a pair of black boxer briefs that show the outline of his hard dick pushing against its constraint. He looks like he should be posing for a billboard in Times Square exactly as he is. I stare at him for a moment and take in his strapping body. I'm so excited, I can't stand it. It feels amazing to look at someone so virile and gorgeous and know that he wants me as much as I want him—it lets me know I've still got it. Bagging a guy like him ten years ago wouldn't have caused me a second thought, but with my fortieth birthday looming around the corner, being with Scott gives me a real boost.

I stand between his legs and nudge them apart, giving myself enough room to get on my knees. As he stretches his feet outwards, I put my face against the hardness in his boxers. I caress his dick through his underwear for a moment or two before I lower them and expose his erect self. I take him in my mouth and move my lips back and forth as he massages my scalp with his fingers. He has a nice smell down there—a hint of a manly scent—unlike *some* men. It's so funny to me the way men talk about women reeking like fish, and then you go down on some of them, and it smells like one of those awful cheese shops in Greenwich Village.

Giving head isn't one of my favorite sexual activities. In fact, I wish, for once in their lives, men had to experience what we go through down there. They should have to try it on a cucumber or a banana or something, and see what it's like to take such a thing in your mouth, try to make sure your teeth don't touch it, and attempt to keep from gagging while some jerk tries to shove it down your throat.

Like I said, performing oral sex isn't the first thing I'd order off the sexual menu, but all seems to be going well until something very odd happens. I'm down there getting things done, when, all of a sudden, Scott slips his cock out of my mouth, pushes it between his thighs, crosses his legs over his whole package, and shoves my face back into his crotch. I'm not sure what to do. Does he want to play some sort of "Find the Penis" game? Everything has been tugged out of the way, and there's nothing but his furry bush left. I can't think of anything else to do, so I gently give it a few kisses.

Scott pulls my head in tighter. "That's it," he says. "Eat my pussy!"

Huh?! I think to myself. Did he just say what I think he said?

As if he read my mind, he says it again. "Yeah, eat my pussy. Eat my man-pussy!"

Okay, if I were a man, I would have officially just lost my erection. Eat his *man-pussy*!? What the fuck is that about!?

I don't know what else to do, so I just keep kissing his pubic hair and doing a little action with my tongue, which is getting sore from the rough texture. I've got my face in this nest of dark hair, and all I can think about is how only a few days ago I was thinking about how much I love my dating life, seeing lots of men, going to different places. But, at the moment, things don't look so rosy. I guess being on your knees eating some *man's* pussy can really put things into perspective.

# 7

# Brenda

"Oh my God!" I say to Nora, who just phoned me from her office to tell me about one of her crazy sexual adventures from the weekend. "So what did you do?"

"I ate his pussy. What else was I going to do?" she responds, as if my question were ridiculous.

"How does one eat a man's . . . wait, you know what . . . I don't think I want to know. So are you going to see him again?"

"Oh God no! I'd like to think of myself as a fairly sexually adventurous person, but I think I have to draw the line at eating man-pussy. I mean if I wanted to eat pussy, I'd become a big ole dyke and cut my hair short and buy a Subaru."

"Don't use that word. I don't like it," I say, the words surprising me as they fall from my lips.

"What word?"

"Dyke. I think it's derogatory," I respond, wondering why I had such a quick reaction to the word even though I guess I already know—I would just hate to think of someone calling Jodie such a word. Not that I think she's a . . . well, you know. But, you know, if she were (even though I'm certain she isn't), I wouldn't want anyone calling her that.

"No no," Nora says. "Dyke isn't disparaging anymore. They used it on *Will & Grace* a while back."

"Well I still don't like it," I say as I see Gretchen poke her head into my office. "Sorry, Nora. I've got to go. You'll be over in a few minutes for the conference call?"

"Yeah," Nora says, and we say good-bye.

"Did you reserve the conference room for noon tomorrow?" I ask Gretchen, gesturing for her to come in and sit down. I've asked her to do it twice already, but with Gretchen you have to confirm and reconfirm everything. Anything you tell her is in one ear and out the other. Some days I feel sorry for her. She serves as the only administrative assistant for six people in the Marketing Department including me and Nora, so I can understand her getting a little frazzled from time to time, but I barely ask her to do anything—it's just not worth it. By the time I deal with the attitude I get from her, the repeated reminders, and the constant checking in on her to make sure she's on top of whatever I asked her to do, I may as well just take care of things myself. Sometimes I wonder if that's her strategy (actually I wonder if it's the strategy of half the people I work with)—to be just *barely* competent enough not to get fired but remain such an exercise in frustration to work with that no one asks her to do anything.

Gretchen nods at me, but it's the sort of nod I'm used to getting from her. It usually means that even though she's says she's on top of something, she actually forgot and will rush out of my office when we're done talking and try to take care of it before I find out it slipped her mind.

"Good," I say, playing along, knowing that I'll have to check the conference room schedule in a couple of hours to make sure it is, in fact, reserved. "Could you order a cake as well?" I ask, wondering if it would just be easier for me to call the Safeway and order the cake myself. I'm trying to put together a little office celebration for Nora's birthday . . . just some cake and punch in the conference room. We don't do much celebrating in the office, but since this is Nora's fortieth, I thought we should acknowledge it with a little party (not that I'd dare mention her actual age to anyone . . . she'd kill me if I did). Plus, it will help break up the day and get us all away from our computer screens for a half hour or so.

"Sure. What kind of cake should I order? There's a bakery over on U Street that has this incredible chocolate buttercream cake. It's a layer of dark chocolate and a layer of white chocolate with chocolate ganache and raspberries. They served something like it at Goldie Hawn's fiftieth birthday party a few years ago, and it was a real hit."

"Well, if the Safeway carries it, feel free to order it. Otherwise get a yellow cake with chocolate frosting. And keep it under thirty dollars." I know I'm supposed to ask about the Goldie Hawn party, which I'm sure Gretchen will tell me she attended when she used to live out in L.A. and was a personal assistant to numerous celebrities. She even claims a brief stint working for Jennifer Lopez with a primary duty of filling in all the craters on Jennifer's ass with some sort of flesh-colored spackle-like substance before her more revealing photo shoots. She tells all sorts of exciting stories about her days in L.A. But, thing about Gretchen is . . . well, she lies—lies like no one I've ever known before. And from what I can tell, most of her lies are for no apparent reason. I can understand someone telling a few fibs to avoid getting into trouble or to make a story a bit more colorful, but Gretchen seems to lie simply for the sport of it. When you first meet her you actually believe some of her stories, but I guess it was about two days after I met her, when she told me that she was instrumental in Geri Halliwell's decision to leave the Spice Girls, that I began questioning everything she told me and so, whenever possible, I try to avoid having to hear about any of it at all.

"Can I get a chocolate cake instead of yellow? Something in the yellow cake exacerbates my condition."

"Sure. That's fine." Like the Goldie Hawn party, I know I'm supposed to ask about Gretchen's "condition." She talks about her "condition" all the time. How her "condition" keeps her up at night, how she mustn't eat anything after eight PM because of her "condition," how the company had to spring for an eight hundred dollar chair at her cubicle because the standard-issue one aggravated her "condition." I've worked with Gretchen for three years and hear about her condition every day, but, to this day, I still have no idea what this condition is, or even if it really exists. I'm not sure anyone in the office knows what it is. Like me, no one dares ask about it—we all fear being held hostage at our desks for hours hearing about the gory details if we venture to inquire about it.

"Scoot along, Gretchen," Nora says as she comes through the doorway of my office. "Brenda and I have a conference call." Nora has no patience for Gretchen and, if she bothers to acknowledge her at all, she basically barks quick orders at her or just plain tells her to go away.

Gretchen gets up from her chair, and, right before she leaves my office, she lets out a quick cough while looking at Nora, "Ahem . . . Forty . . . Ahem," she says under her breath and exits the room.

"Did that big ole bag of crazy say what I think she said?" Nora asks me. "You didn't tell anyone about my birthday did you?"

"No. I didn't hear anything. She was coughing. You know . . . that 'condition' of hers."

Shoot! Now I'm worried that I may have let Nora's age slip while planning the birthday gathering with Gretchen. Although I'm sure Gretchen doesn't need me to tell her Nora's age. Aside from being a pathological liar, Gretchen is also the office busybody and seems to know everything about everyone.

"Yeah . . . her condition is going to be my foot up her ass if she makes any more cracks about my age."

"She didn't say anything. You're paranoid. Just drop it."

"Whatever," Nora sighs. "So how are you doing, chica?" she asks.

"All right. I've still got this little sinus infection, and I can't get in to see the doctor for two weeks."

"Two weeks? Why?"

"I don't know. The receptionist said he doesn't have any openings for two weeks."

"You didn't tell them you have the crap HMO insurance this cheap-assed company covers us with, did you?"

"Of course I told them. It was the first question they asked."

"Chica, you can't tell them your real insurance when you call to schedule an appointment. You have to say you have the PPO option or Blue Cross."

"Lie? And then what happens when I get there?"

"Who cares? I just tell them that I forgot my insurance changed, or just deny ever lying about it in the first place. They're not going to turn you away once you're there with an appointment."

"I don't know, Nora. I'm not a good liar. Besides, I already told them I had an HMO," I say with a sigh. "All I need is a prescription for amoxicillin."

"Well, why didn't you say so," Nora says. "Hand me the phone."

I push the phone in her direction, and she picks up the receiver and dials. "Hi. Can I have the CVS at 1500 K Street, Northwest."

Nora waits a few seconds, presses a button and starts again. "Hello. This is a new prescription for Brenda Harrison. Her phone number is 202/555–1275. She needs amoxicillin, five-hundred milligrams, one PO TID for ten days. No refills. This is Dr. Laura Reyes, and my phone number is 202/555–6895," Nora chirps into the phone with complete confidence.

"There you go. Should be ready for you pick up in an hour or so." she says, hanging up the phone.

"How'd you know how to do that?"

"Please! You can find out how to build a bomb on the Internet, you don't think you can find out how to call in a lousy prescription? It comes in handy when I don't feel like bothering with doctors, but you can't really do it with controlled substances. You have to have a DEA number for those. But, for something benign like amoxicillin, they don't bother to check and make sure the prescription's valid."

"Are you sure? I'm not going to get arrested when I go to pick it up?"

"No," Nora says with a laugh.

"Who's Dr. Reyes, anyway?"

"Some gynecologist I used to see before she broke a speculum while it was still inside my kitty."

I gasp. And, honestly, I'm not sure why. Is it because of the thought of a speculum breaking while inside a woman's . . . well, you know? Or did I gasp because I'm shocked that anyone would share such a story with someone else, not to mention using the word "kitty" to do it? But then this is Nora I'm talking about. She has very few inhibitions.

I'm trying to decide if I really want to hear the details of the speculum incident when my eyes catch sight of the clock, and I remember why Nora really came into my office in the first place.

"Shoot. We'd better log on." I click on the speaker phone and dial into the conference call. Once a week we have a call with the sales vice presidents, our proposal department, and the underwriting folks to go over all the active sales leads.

"So, who's leading the call today?" Nora asks, even though she sits in on these calls every week and the same person has been leading them for the past two or three times.

"Sara Gates."

"Pig-Face Girl?" Nora inquires.

"Well I don't know that she has a pig face, Nora . . ."

"Sara Gates? The head of sales, right?"

"Yes."

"Yeah. Pig-Face Girl," Nora says, conclusively.

"Hello this is Brenda and Nora," I say into the phone as Nora pulls a *People* magazine from a manila folder she brought with her and starts flipping through it. Nora always carries manila folders around the office. They rarely contain anything work-related. She generally uses them to disguise whatever magazine or trashy novel she's reading during work hours. It bugs me how she's able to spend so much of the work day goofing off. It doesn't bother me because I think she's lazy or isn't pulling her weight. In fact, it's sort of the opposite. I'm jealous of her innate ability and competence when it comes to the kinds of projects we do. She gets everything done so quickly and efficiently that she always seems to have extra time on her hands to read magazines or surf the Internet or take on freelance projects. We both handle the same number of assignments, yet Nora takes care of her workload in a fraction of the time it takes me to finish mine. I don't think she's necessarily smarter than I am. I think she's just more decisive. I tend to flip-flop on the structure and look of my presentations and prepare several drafts before I submit a final one to the sales reps. Nora quickly decides the look she's going to go with, does a single draft, and moves on to the next one.

"Hello," responds a voice on the other end. It's Sara Gates, apparently otherwise known as Pig-Face Girl, who usually leads these waste-of-time calls. "We'll get started in another minute or two. We're still waiting on a few others."

"Sounds good," I respond as Nora reaches over and puts my phone on mute.

"We should ask Pig-Face Girl if she's still fucking that young boy in Finance."

"Shhh," I say, always afraid the phone isn't really going to be on mute while Nora's ranting. Truth is Nora's just jealous of Sara, who's a few years younger than her and rumored to be dating the twenty-five-year-old clerk in Finance who processes our expense reports. If anyone is going to be sleeping with the twenty-five-year-old "boy" in Finance, Nora believes it should be her. And my guess is, in a matter of weeks, it probably will be. She'll seduce him to prove to herself that she's more desirable than Sara and then dump the poor fellow before he knows what hit him.

When the call finally gets started I take the phone off mute, and Nora and I look at each other and roll our eyes while the sales vice presidents try to make it sound like they're about to close all their deals. Every time Sara steps in to moderate the call Nora grabs a piece of paper and crumbles it up by the speaker on the phone.

"Is someone rustling paper?" Sara asks.

Of course we reply, "No," with the rest of the callers.

A few minutes later Nora does it again, and I try not to laugh out loud as I grab her hand and try to pull it away from the phone. Some days she's forty going on four.

"Whoever is rustling paper, can you please stop? It's blocking out my voice." Sara tries to sound stern but mostly comes off as pathetic.

I give Nora a look, hoping she'll behave herself, but instead of making noise with paper, as soon as Sara gets rolling again, Nora reaches over and puts my phone on hold and cups her hand over the base, so I can't release the button. A few seconds later she releases it herself, and we can hear the anger in Sara's voice.

"Who put us on hold?" she demands, as if she's speaking to some unruly children. "When you put your phone on hold all we get is your hold music, and no one can hear anything—"

Before Sara can finish Nora hits the hold button again, all the while, laughing likes she's at a comedy show.

"Stop it," I say, prying her hand away from the phone.

"WHO IS DOING THAT? STOP PUTTING YOUR PHONE ON HOLD!" we hear when I hit the hold button to release it.

After everyone on the call denies being the culprit, Nora finally seems content to sit back in her chair and behave, which concerns me. If Nora appears to be behaving there must be trouble brewing. But the call seems to progress without incident for the next twenty minutes or so, and Nora and I are bored to tears listening to the underwriting staff hash out cost issues with the sales force. Then at exactly eleven-forty-five, Nora looks at me and mouths the words, "Three, two, one," and cocks her head, waiting to hear something.

As Jack Turner discusses the fee he'd like to charge one of our potential clients, all of a sudden there is moaning on the line.

"Oh yeah . . . oh yeah . . . hard! Hard! Harder! Harder!" we hear coming though the phone with some twangy music in the background.

"Yeah, fuck me! Come on, what are you? A fucking boy

scout? Can't you fuck me harder than that?" we hear a women's voice calling.

I look over at Nora, who's laughing so hard her eyes are watering. She's trying to keep it quiet, but I can see she wants to howl. Nora did this once before a year or two ago. She gives the dial-in information to a friend and has them call in to the conference call and put the phone up to some cheesy porno movie. I'm sure I'm blushing, and, honestly, I think that's half the reason Nora is acting so mischievous. The other half is, of course, to aggravate Sara.

When Nora's friend hangs up there is dead silence on the line, and even I am smirking a bit at the thought of the looks on everyone's faces as we wait for someone to say something. How do you go back to discussing proposals and sales presentations after such an incident?

"I'm not sure what's going on today," Sara finally speaks up. "We may need to rethink the structure of these calls." As she's speaking, Nora is giving the phone the finger, which really bugs me. I'm sorry, but there is nothing more vulgar to me than a *woman* flipping someone the bird.

Finally, the call seems to get back on track, and I look over at Nora, who is back to flipping through her magazine, and I wonder why it is that we are friends—we are so different. Although she's a few years older than me, she's ten times more attractive and has a totally different set of priorities from my own. She's brash and sassy and sometimes downright lewd. I'm none of those things—I lean toward being reserved and quiet. I don't know of a single other woman that Nora gets along with. She makes no bones about preferring the company of men to other women, but even Blanche Devereaux had Dorothy, Rose, and Sofia. I try to recall if Nora has any other female friends, but none come to mind. Sometimes I think the only reason Nora and I get along so well is because we *are* so different. I think it also has something to do with Nora's insecurities about other women—she sees almost all of us as her competition for attention from men. Maybe with me, she knows she has nothing to worry about. I could certainly never match her in the looks department, and I shudder to think about the kinds of things that might go on in her bedroom—things I couldn't even imagine, let alone participate in. I think she knows I'm very safe. People have always seen me as very safe and non-threatening. I'm not *un*attractive, but I've never had the kind of looks (or the personality for that matter) that would make a woman worry about leaving her man alone with me. I'm about five feet six inches tall with short dark blond hair and blue eyes. I've got full cheeks, a soft nose, and not much of a chin—the kind of face that seems to make people want to confide in me. My body probably isn't any more remarkable than my face. I'm still managing to fit into my size twelve clothes and even squeeze into a size ten in some brands. I don't think I'd be considered fat, but I'd probably qualify as "round" or "full-figured." I've gone through a few phases where I start exercising to try and firm up my body, but they never last more than a few weeks. One time, after a few weeks of doing sit-ups, I actually thought I was beginning to get some definition in my abs. I was sitting on the bed in my bra and panties, putting my socks on, and, for just a second, I thought I was starting to get those little six-pack creases like Janet Jackson or Shania Twain, but then I realized it was just my belly flab bunching up into little rolls.

I look at Nora again, and I wonder what it must be like to be her—to ooze sexuality and put herself out there the way she does. The idea is so foreign to me I can't even imagine it, and I know I could never do it. Sometimes, when I'm stuck in traffic on the way home, I daydream about what it would be like to just take a break, hop a plane somewhere and be someone else for a few days. Wear the clothes no one would expect to see me in, liven up my make-up, have a few too many drinks and dance the night away with some strange man. Not that I don't love my husband and my daughter. It's just that sometimes I think I could use a vacation from them—or maybe I could just use a vacation from me.

# 8

## Brenda

I left work early to pick Jodie up for a dentist appointment, and I'm sitting at a stop light on the way out to Sterling. There's some little old woman in front of me, and the light has turned green, but she doesn't seem to notice. I figure I'll give her another second or two before I give the horn a quick toot to get her moving. But before I know it, the man behind me is wailing on his horn as if the poor woman is about to run down his mother. It's so *nice* how we all spread such good cheer on the highways, I think to myself, hoping the old lady won't think it's me honking at her. I don't see what the big deal is to sit and wait a second or two when someone hasn't noticed that a traffic light has changed. Sometimes when Nora's in the car with me, and we get stuck behind someone like this, she'll actually reach over and press my horn for me once she realizes that I'm not going to do it. I'm in as big a hurry as everyone else, but I hate honking my horn at people. It's just so rude. There's so much hate and bitterness out in the world already. Do we really need to add to it all by pounding on our horns at each other on the highways? I often think how nice it would be if cars were equipped with two horns—your standard issue honker for people to release their rage, and another one that could be recognized as a friendly toot to tell someone a light has changed or to get someone's attention. The way it stands now, whenever you honk your horn, regardless of your intention, it just comes off as rude.

It's only two o'clock, so I manage to make it out to Sterling from the city in less than an hour, and that includes my little pit stop at the pharmacy to pick up my illegal prescription. As I pull into the school driveway it hits me that I forgot to switch cars with Jim for the day. Jodie specifically asked me not to pick her up in the "sniper-mobile," which is what she calls my car. I should really get rid of it, but I can't seem to bring myself to do it. It's a 1990 blue Chevrolet Caprice. Yes, it's almost sixteen years old, but, for the first eight years of its life, it was barely driven at all. It belonged to my grandfather who essentially only drove it to the store and to church, so it was in mint condition when he passed away and willed it to me. He had seven grand-children and chose to give his car to me. That really means something and, accordingly, even as the car has aged and racked up the miles, I haven't been able to bring myself to trade it in. It met my transportation needs quite nicely for years until one day in 2002 a pair of madmen, in the exact same type of car, started terrorizing the Washington, D.C. area—shooting random vic-tims from the trunk of their car in a horrifying series of sniper attacks. Everyone in the Metro area spent weeks afraid to walk around outside or pump gas into their cars; after-school and outside activities were canceled, and it wasn't uncommon to see people bobbing and weaving when they walked away from their cars in shopping center parking lots. It's been almost four years since our entire area was held hostage by these men, but I still get all sorts of looks when I drive my car.

I stop the car in front of the main entrance of the school and see three girls leaning against the wall smoking cigarettes. It's the middle of the day, and I assume classes are still in session. What are they doing outside? And smoking? Can't they at least have the decency to sneak cigarettes in the bathroom or along the side of the school where no one can see them? I take a quick look at them, and they remind me of my high school years. All three of them are petite blondes with salon highlights and trendy clothes. They're the kind of girls I hung out with in high school. I was never really *one* of them with my dark blond hair (with no highlights) and my wide hips, but they were still my friends. I sat at their lunch table and went to their parties. I was part of the popular group—friends with the popular girls. And, actually, I was friends with the popular guys too, but unlike those petite blondes smoking cigarettes in front of the school, I never dated any of them. I was the kind of girl guys were friends with. I was the one my girlfriends could always count on to be single when they were in between relationships. I think that's why I so readily agreed to date Jim when the opportunity presented itself. I was so happy to get some attention . . . any attention from the opposite sex. When I think about it, Jim and I were a lot alike in high school. He also hung with the popular crowd. He was good at sports and friends with the jocks, but like me, he didn't date much. I guess it was his plain boy-next-door looks that kept him from being a hit with girls. Maybe it was only natural that we found each other.

I wait a few more minutes and finally see Jodie emerge from the entryway. She's walking the way she always walks—quickly, with purpose, and with a bit of a scowl on her face. She's on the tall side for girls her age and has a trim body and small breasts that just sort of appeared about four years ago. She keeps her hair very short and doesn't bother to do anything more than wash and comb it. As soon as she passes the group of young dragon ladies, I can tell they're talking trash about her—and not trying to be all that discreet about it either. I shudder to think about how some of the more eccentric members of my class were treated in high school, and I fear that Jodie may be subject to the same kind of ridicule, but then I see her do a one-eighty and walk back toward the bitchy girls. She gets in the face of one of them and shouts something at her. The girl's face goes red, and I can see her cheeks swell up with angst.

That's my girl, I think as the other girl lifts her hands up and seems to apologize for whatever it was she said about my daughter. That's the thing about Jodie—she's tough, and the blonde bimbo was right to fear her. Jodie's strong as an ox and could have (and probably would have) pummeled her to the ground in a matter of seconds if the girl gave her any more lip. I'm proud of her for standing up for herself, but I wish she wouldn't make herself such a target. Does she really have to cut her hair so short and always dress so masculine? Couldn't she tone it down a little bit just to make life easier for herself?

I know she has a little group of friends that she hangs around with but she rarely gets together with them outside of school. She's active in some of the clubs and plays on the softball team in the spring but, unlike me in high school, she doesn't seemed concerned at all with being popular. The phone was practically glued to my ear when I was a teenager, yet Jodie rarely gets calls at home, and when she does, she's on and off in a matter of seconds. It used to worry me that Jodie doesn't have much of a social life, but it doesn't seem to bother her, so I guess it shouldn't bother me either.

"Hi sweetie," I say as she gets in the car. "What was that all about?"

"I don't know. That Barbie doll just doesn't like me."

"Why would she not like you? What's not to like?"

"Just drop it, would you? I took care of it. She knows better than to mess with me."

"All right, all right . . . but I don't understand why she wouldn't like you."

"She's just a bitch. If you don't dress and act like one of her clones, she's gets her little designer panties all in a knot."

I want to suggest to Jodie that maybe she *should* try to dress a little bit more like the other girls. I'm not saying she has to grow her hair to her shoulders, start wearing make-up, and begin toting a knock-off Kate Spade bag, but would it really be such a bad idea to take her current look down a notch or two? Maybe let her hair grow out a little bit and start wearing something other than jeans and T-shirts everyday. I think it would make life easier for her if she'd conform a bit more, but I don't want to say anything and make her feel like I'm ashamed of her. I'm afraid if I suggest ways for her to fit in better at school, she'll think I have a problem with the way she dresses and wears her hair, and I don't. Well, maybe I'd like for her to be more feminine, but I love my daughter regardless of how she acts or dresses or whatever. Besides, Jodie's a lot of things, but she's not stupid. I'm sure she knows that interaction with her peers would be easier if she'd put on a skirt every once in a while and lost the manly haircut, but she chooses to be who she wants to be. I guess I should respect her for that.

"I thought you were going to switch cars with Dad?"

"I know. I'm sorry. I meant to, but I forgot about it this morning," I apologize. "So, how was school?" I ask, and it reminds me of hearing my own mother's voice asking the same question.

"Fine," Jodie replies. It's the same reply every time. You'd think I'd stop asking the question, but I never know what to talk about with her anymore.

"Just fine? Can you tell me anything else about your day?"

"There's not much to tell. I had a history test this morning that I'm sure I aced. We did a really lame experiment in chemistry class with baking soda and vinegar, and, thanks to my dentist appointment, I don't have to sit through poetry class this afternoon. I hate poetry class. It's so damn boring."

"Yeah. I hated poetry too. Half of it doesn't make any sense."

"I know," Jodie says. "The wind meets the sea in a pulse of wickedness," she says dramatically. "I was on the sand with great glee. Dolphins frolicking with pure delight in a cool summer mist," she adds. "See, I made up a poem in a few seconds. Why is what I just said any better or worse than that crap they make us analyze in class?"

"I don't know. Somehow the powers that be just decide what's great poetry and what's not. And that's what you have to study. Like it or not."

"Not," Jodie replies, and I let out a quick laugh. At least we're having a conversation, and she seems to be in a pretty decent mood.

"Well hang in there with it. You're bound to stumble onto a poem or two that you actually like." I crack the car window and reach for my cigarettes.

"Do you have to do that now?" Jodie says. "I don't want to have to sit in the dentist's chair smelling like smoke."

"I've got the window cracked," I say in my defense, putting a cigarette to my lips and lighting it with the lighter.

"When are you going to give that up? It's killing you, and it's not particularly good for me either."

"One of these days, I suppose."

"Yeah, when you're dead of black lung."

"Can we talk about something else?" I ask as we pass by a construction site with a sign that says "Future Home of the Loudon Bible Church," one of those mega churches that advertises on the radio and boasts a few thousand members.

"Oh great," Jodie says, looking out the window. "Just what we need. Another church. Can't they build something useful?"

I know she says these things just to push my buttons, and I should probably ignore her, but, instead, I respond, "Churches are useful, Jodie. They're places for people to worship the Lord—"

"Yeah, worship the Lord and spread hatred for anything that doesn't conform to their hypocritical beliefs."

So here we go again. I have to prod every detail about her school day out of her, but give Jodie the chance to pontificate about the hypocrisy of the religious right or the "pure evil" that is the Republican party, and she could go on for hours.

"There's good and bad in every organization. It doesn't mean churches in general are bad things. You wouldn't want people making sweeping generalizations about you or the groups you support. Shouldn't you offer churches the same courtesy? I've actually been meaning to start going to church again, and I think you should come with me." I *have* been meaning to start going back to St. Timothy's, which is only a couple of miles from our house. I'm not the most religious person on the planet, but I enjoy the quiet time during services and the connection I sometimes feel to something more powerful than me. Of course, we attend services on Christmas Eve and Easter Sunday, but it's been years since I've been a regular Sunday morning worshipper. I get up at five-thirty every morning during the week, and when Sunday rolls around it's all I can do to get out of bed and set up camp in my smoking chair with the Sunday *Post*, my coffee, and, if Jim went and picked them up, a box of Dunkin' Donuts.

"I'm not going to any church to listen to evil people use their stupid Bible to discriminate against people."

"What are you talking about?" I ask, even though I already know.

"Look at the whole gay marriage debate. These people who call themselves Christians are up in arms about gays getting married because the Bible has a passage or two that forbids it. Yet these same people have no problem ignoring passages about the sin of pursuing wealth when they pull up to church in their Mercedes, or what the Bible says about divorce when they sit in the pew with their third husband, or what the Bible says about birth control when they listen to a sermon with a purse full of condoms sitting next to them. I don't know too many church-going women who consider themselves the property of their husband as passages from the Bible say they should be. It's real easy for those hypocrites to strongly enforce things written in the Bible that don't impinge on the way they live, but the moment something said in the Bible affects *their* lifestyle, they disregard it. It's really easy to ignore verses in the Bible that affect the way they want to live their lives and even easier to adhere to the ones that allow them to justify their own bigotry. People don't adopt lifestyles to fit their religious beliefs. They adopt religious beliefs that won't impede their lifestyle."

She says all of this and then takes on that egotistical drawl she uses when she's imitating people. "Oh, I'd really love to help those poor starving kids, but, you know, Jesus came to me in a vision and said I should buy that sofa from Pottery Barn instead," she adds, before readopting her normal voice and continuing on her diatribe. "They're willing to be Christians as long as it doesn't inconvenience them too much. The whole thing makes me sick to my stomach."

So what the hell am I supposed to say to that? It all came spiraling out of her mouth so fast I'm not sure I even understood exactly what she was saying. And whenever I hear the word "gay" I get so frazzled. Of course, just because she's talking about gay marriage doesn't mean that Jodie is . . . you know. She has all sorts of causes, and she may just be rooting for the underdog like she always does, but it still makes me nervous.

I learned early on that Jodie was going to be a daughter who would challenge me. I think I first started to figure it out when she was about three years old and we were at a restaurant about to have lunch. Jodie kept getting up and running around the table, and I decided to make one of those empty threats that parents often make before their kids are old enough to realize we have no intention of carrying them out. I said, "If you don't calm down and sit at the table like a nice girl, we're going to leave before your food comes." Most kids would have sat down and behaved themselves. Jodie's response was, "Fine, let's go." She said it with a gleam in her little toddler eyes that told me she knew I was bluffing, and, even at three, she was going to call me on it. I remember a couple of years later when I told her she couldn't go to her Brownies meeting unless she finished her school work, her response to me was, "Good, I hate Brownies anyway." If I tried telling her that Santa wasn't going to bring her some toy if she didn't behave, she be like, "So? I don't care." She always said these things with such defiance. And here we are, so many years later, and she still speaks her mind at every chance.

"Okay, you've made your point, but it doesn't mean that everyone who goes to church is like that. It's not so black and white. I'm sure there are plenty of people who go to church who are in favor of gays marrying. *I* try to go to church when I can, and *I'm* not against gays marrying." Oh God! Did I just say that? Am I really not against gays marrying? I suppose the idea of gay marriage doesn't really bother me. If two people love each other and want to get married, what do I care if it's two men or two women? But I guess the real reason I said that is because I want to show Jodie that I could handle it if she does turn out to be . . . not that she will . . . or is . . . but, if she is, I want her to know I'm okay with it . . . even though I'm not.

Jodie's quiet and doesn't respond to what I just said. It's an uncomfortable silence, and I find myself silently praying that she doesn't blurt out that she's . . . *that thing,* so I change the subject before our discussion goes in a direction I'm not sure I'm ready for.

"So, back to the poetry thing. Have you had to read any Emily Dickinson? Talk about boring."

# 9

# Nora

So it's my fortieth birthday—my fucking fortieth birthday. *Feliz* fucking *cumpleaños* to me! How the hell can I be forty? I remember when I was twenty and *thirty* sounded old—forty was downright ancient. When I got out of bed this morning all I wanted to do was crawl back under the covers and pretend this day wasn't happening. And when I looked in the mirror I wanted to cry. I look so hard first thing in the morning. I remember when I was young and could hop out of bed, throw my hair in a pony tail and still look fresh and attractive. Now, when I first get up, my face is puffy, and, sometimes, I have to soak it in bowl of ice water just to make myself presentable. And thank God for Lancôme's under eye concealer—before I blend it into the area around my eyes I look like a freakin' raccoon. Once I get my make-up done and my hair pulled together I feel pretty good about the way I look, but the first few minutes right after I wake up I feel like a hag, and it scares me.

Maybe if I had stayed in bed I'd still be thirty-nine. How sad is that? You have to really be old to be wishing to be *thirty-nine.* But instead of hiding out in bed I'm at work on my way down the hall for some stupid meeting about improving our interface with the sales force. I don't have time for this meeting. I have two copies of *Vogue* and the new issue of *Latina* on my desk waiting to be read, I've got some bills to pay online, and I need to call and register for the plastic surgery seminar next week.

When I reach the conference room the door is closed. I figure I must be late, as I am for most meetings, and they've started without me. Once again, I'll have to quietly open the door and slink in and join the meeting, trying to draw as little attention to my tardiness as possible. Jill hasn't said anything about it to me, but lately her looks have been getting a little more intense. I know it shouldn't be that difficult to make it to meetings on time, but I rarely manage to. Maybe it's because I hate meetings so much. Ninety percent of them are a total waste of time— everyone talking just to hear themselves speak, making up all sorts of bullshit to try to make themselves seem much busier than they actually are, or just plain attempting to sound smart and knowledgeable about things they know nothing about.

I turn the handle on the door and as soon as I push it open I hear this loud "Surprise!" coming from the room. Shit! I think to myself as I look around and see most of the department standing around the conference room table. Please tell me this isn't happening!

I give the room a quick once-over and try to be gracious. When my eye finally catches Brenda I see her smiling at me and immediately I know she is responsible for this. I'll kill her. Okay, maybe I'll only maim her for planning the gathering. As long as she didn't tell anyone how old I am, I may let her live.

"You guys!" I say, trying to sound enthusiastic when all I really want to do is crawl under the table like a five-year-old and refuse to come out until I'm young again. "This is so sweet." I give Brenda a quick glare between smiles to let her know she'll pay for this.

"Happy Birthday!" Brenda says, getting up from her chair, pulling out the one next to her, and motioning for me to sit down. As I lower myself into the seat, I tell myself to be strong. I can get through this. Everyone probably thinks I'm turning thirty-five. I'm sure no one will dare ask me how old I am. I've just about convinced myself that maybe this little celebration is not such a bad thing when, without warning, I see it—staring at me from the other end of the table—one of those cheap sheet cakes from the grocery store. And resting on top of it is a candle shaped like a four and another shaped like a zero. No! This can't be! Brenda wouldn't do this to me! She wouldn't tell people how old I am!

I look over at Brenda, and honestly, she looks just as horrified as I feel. Then, when I look back at the cake, I see Gretchen hovering over it with a lit match. She ignites the four, then the zero, and then she looks up at me and smiles—you know, the kind of smile that says, "Take that, you bitch!" So this is what I get for not humoring her when she's talking about how she nursed Tori Spelling through nose job number two, or how she had to massage Pamela Anderson's breasts every day after boob job number three. Fuck! I never should have underestimated the power of an angry secretary.

Gretchen picks up the cake from the table and starts walking toward me with it—those two horrid candles blazing on top of it. Everyone breaks into an office rendition of "Happy Birthday." The little puffs of smoke coming from the tips of the candles cast these little waves on Gretchen's face as she gets closer and closer, and I feel as if the sound of my colleagues singing is coming from some distance away rather than from right there in the room with me. I'm trying to hide my trepidation but, suddenly I feel like I might pass out.

When the cake lands in front of me and the singing stops, I manage to collect myself. I'm about to fiercely blow out the candles in a desperate attempt to make them go away—to make it all go away . . . to make *forty* go away. But as I take in a deep breath, Howard Glick, one of my co-workers from Accounting who shows up to anything that involves free food, scoots this young girl toward me. I know nothing about children (nor do I care to learn), but I guess she's about ten or so. It must be his daughter. I wonder what she's doing with him at the office. I mean this is a place of business, not a frickin' kiddy-camp. I heard something on the radio about schools being closed today from the light snow we had last night, so I guess he didn't want to leave her at home. But couldn't he find a sitter or drop her at the mall for the day or something? I swear, one day, I'm going to bring my cat into work with me and say I couldn't get a sitter for him.

"Do you mind if Haley helps you blow out your candles?" he asks. I see a hopeful look in Haley's eyes, as if it would make her day to help me put out my candles. I want to inform him that, "Yes, I do mind. It's my birthday, and she can blow out candles on her own fucking birthday." But, instead, I pretend not to hear him, take another breath, and finally extinguish those God-awful reminders of what today means. I immediately lift the smoldering candles off the cake and try to get them out of sight. Someone hands me a knife, and I start cutting into the cake. I'll get everyone served and hope that they will be too busy stuffing themselves to notice that I don't have any. Not that I wouldn't love to indulge in big ole hunk of cheap lard-infused birthday cake, but I haven't kept this figure for forty years by giving in to every craving. If only it were a low-carb cheesecake or made from Atkins brownie mix. Then maybe I could have a little sliver.

As I'm lifting slices of cake onto little paper plates and passing them around, I look around at everyone in the room, and my nerves finally start to ease. I may be forty, but after stealing a few glances at the motley crew surrounding me, I conclude that I still look better then everyone in the room. Okay, Lauren Miller, one of the sales rep's assistants, has a better body, but she's in her twenties, and I suspect her boobs are fake. And Britney Jordan, one of our Web designers, does have a pretty face, but let her keep eating slices of cake like she is now—those hips are already starting to swell and she's only thirty or so. All and all, I have to say I'm holding up pretty well, but, if I want to keep my edge, I know what I have to do—I have to take more drastic measures. I bet with a little help from a plastic surgeon I can take five to ten years off this mug and give girls like Lauren and Britney, girls almost half my age, a run for their money. The more I think about it, the more excited I am about the prospect of going under the knife. What a wonderful world we live in, I think to myself as I watch all these people with no self-control stuff themselves with cake, when you can just go to the doctor and get rid of your wrinkles and sags and keep yourself looking young and beautiful almost indefinitely. Yes, plastic surgery is a wonderful thing. How did people ever get by without it?

# 10

## Brenda

"Hey," I say to Jodie. I've just come through the front door, and she's sitting at the kitchen table eating a bowl of cereal. "Sorry I'm late. I fell behind at work today." I feel bad that my daughter is eating a bowl of Frosted Flakes for dinner. It's almost eight o'clock. I'm usually home by six-thirty or seven, but I had to spend almost an hour this afternoon apologizing to Nora for throwing her a little birthday celebration at work. Actually, I don't think she was as upset about the party itself as much as the tell-tale candles Gretchen put on her cake. I assured Nora that I had no intention of telling anyone that she was forty. Gretchen had sneaked the candles on her cake, and, by the time I noticed, it was too late to do anything about it. And, if you ask me, Nora sort of deserved it. I don't like Gretchen any more than anyone else, but would it kill Nora to be remotely pleasant to her? Besides, Nora needs to get over her panic about turning forty. There's nothing she can do about it, and it's really just a number anyway. She looks better than most women half her age; she's one of those women who will have sex appeal into her seventies.

"Where's your father?" I ask.

"He called a couple hours ago. Said he's got to work late."

"He worked late last week." As soon as the words come out of my mouth, I regret saying them in front of Jodie. I don't want her to know that Jim's recent stint of late nights is raising my eyebrow a bit, so I change the subject. "Okay. Well, why don't we head out and have a real dinner somewhere?"

"Nah. This is my second bowl. I'm not really hungry anymore."

"Okay." I step over and open the refrigerator as if some magical gnome may have put a gourmet meal in there since I last looked inside it this morning. Unfortunately, there's little more than some milk and juice and a few condiments on the shelves.

"Things good at school today?" God, I've got to come up with another question.

"Yeah . . . fine."

"Any more lame chemistry experiments?"

"No, we just have lectures the rest of the week."

"How about that history test? Did you get it back?"

"I got a B, which really pisses me off. I should have gotten an A. My answers were correct, but Mr. Higgs just didn't like them. Forgive me if I don't believe all the propaganda the Loudon County school system tries to pass off as history."

Here we go. "What did you say on the test?"

"One question asked about why the U.S. dropped the atomic bomb on Japan during World War II. And we're supposed to say that Truman made the decision to save American lives and quickly end the war, blah, blah, blah. Of course, we had no discussion in class about how the bomb was dropped simply because too much money was spent on it not to use it, how the bomb was dropped to intimidate the Soviet Union, how a second bomb was used before Japan really even had time to react to the first one, how our government killed hundreds of thousands of civilians."

I wonder if what she's saying is true. I honestly have no idea. History wasn't one of my stronger subjects. "Well, you should be able to offer different perspectives, and it shouldn't affect your grade as long as you present the facts. Do you want to me to call the school?" I'm hoping she will say no. I don't like confrontation, and I don't know enough about history to argue Jodie's points.

"No. It wouldn't do any good anyway. People believe what

they want to believe. They want to demonize their enemies and conveniently forget that our government killed hundreds of thousands of innocent people . . . that we enslaved an entire race for generations, that the clothes on our backs are made by children in third-world countries in deplorable conditions, that gays in this country are still officially second-class citizens."

How did we get from history class to gays? I wonder.

"There's nothing you can do," she says and gets up from the table and puts her bowl in the sink and heads toward the family room. I watch her walk away, and I wonder why she thinks about these things. When I was in high school I was worried about my hair and my grades, not kids working in sweatshops or the legitimacy of what was being taught in history class. She gets so worked up over things. I wish she could just relax and go with the flow a little more. Wouldn't life be more enjoyable that way?

When I hear Jodie click on the TV in the other room I go back over to the freezer and open the door. I pull out a Lean Cuisine Shrimp and Angel Hair Pasta, take it out of the box, poke a few holes in the plastic, and pop it in the microwave. I watch it spin around and, when the sauce starts to bubble, I take it out, pull off the plastic, and drop the little plastic tub on the table. I grab a fork and a glass of water and sit down in front of my dinner. The pasta is limp, the shrimp are barely larger than a nickel, and the whole thing looks gooey. I sit there for moment, wondering how I got here—sitting alone at my kitchen table about to force-feed myself a frozen dinner. I'm about to dig in. But, instead, I abruptly get up from the table and toss the whole thing in the trash. Then I grab a bowl and a spoon and pour myself a big serving of Frosted Flakes.

When I'm done with my completely-devoid-of-nutritional-value dinner I settle into the family room with Jodie. She's watching *The O.C.*, which I used to find very odd as it represents everything she hates. She isn't someone you'd expect to watch one of those "pretty white people with problems" shows, but I soon realized she doesn't so much watch the program to be entertained as she does to rip it apart and offer commentary. As for me . . . I guess it reminds of watching *Beverly Hills 90210* back when I was in college.

"Thank God she's pretty," Jodie says as we watch the young woman who plays Marissa attempt to get through a scene without looking like a robot. "A wooden doll would be a better actress."

I laugh. "Yeah, she is a little artificial."

"A little artificial? She's a mannequin," Jodie responds before adding, "And, honestly, would it kill them to add an African American to the cast?"

Jodie goes on like this for most of the show. Pointing out how high school students are played by actors in their twenties, and their parents are played by actors in their thirties. She calls out the actress who had a little too much collagen injected into her lips, and another one, who mysteriously went up a couple of cup sizes since last season. Eventually, I get in on the action and make fun of Peter Gallagher's eyebrows (it's the best thing I could come up with . . . I'm not good at this sort of thing). I love these moments when my daughter and I can just chit-chat about nothing and be together. Although it would be nice if Jim were here too.

I finally get to bed at about ten-thirty, and it's almost midnight when I'm jolted from a shallow sleep as Jim comes in. When he crawls into bed I think I might smell a woman's perfume on him—nothing pungent, just a faint hint of fragrance. Could he really be having an affair? Why would he have an affair with a woman who wears perfume when he insists that I never wear any? I just can't believe that he would do such a thing. He's not the type. No, it's ridiculous, I assure myself, as I try to go back to sleep. There must be a logical explanation.

# 11

## Brenda

"**D**id you put the coat and the briefcase in my office? And turn on my light and my computer?" I ask as I look at my watch and slam the door on the sniper-mobile. It's almost eight-thirty in the morning, and I'm on my cell phone with Nora. I should have been in the office a half hour ago.

"Yeah, it's taken care of," she says. Nora and I keep a spare coat and briefcase at work for just this sort of thing. Usually I'm the one putting the coat and briefcase in Nora's office and turning on *her* lights and *her* computer to make it appear that she's in the office when she's running late, but this time I'm the tardy one.

"Thanks. If Jill's looking for me, tell her you just saw me in the bathroom." I hurry down the dreary steps of the parking garage. I left my coat in the trunk of my car so no one will see me coming into the office with it on, thus giving away my late-ness (another trick I learned from Nora), so I'm freezing as I scurry down the block to the office building. I'm not sure how I overslept. I must have kept hitting the snooze in a daze or something. I don't think I slept very soundly last night. I woke up when Jim got home, and I sort of remember him smelling like perfume. Or was it a dream? Did I dream that he smelled of women's fragrance? Damn, now I'm not even sure if I was really awake when he came home. Even if I was, surely there's a logi-cal explanation. He may have just stepped into an elevator with one of those women who douse themselves with perfume. Sometimes people wear too much perfume, and it ends up attaching itself to other people. One time Gretchen came into my office reeking of some cheap fragrance, and I ended up smelling like her the rest of the day, just from being in her presence.

When I get out of the elevator and head toward my office, I take the long way around to avoid having to pass by Jill's door. I'm not sure why I'm so worried, anyway. This is the first time I've been late in months. Nora comes in late all the time and, half the time, doesn't even bother to explain herself to anyone. But I guess I'm not Nora—I like to be punctual, and somehow I don't feel as though I can get away with the kinds of things Nora can. Men overlook Nora's professional shortcomings because she's sexy, and women overlook them because . . . well, I guess we're all afraid of her.

When I step into my office, Nora's sitting at my desk scribbling a note on a little yellow sticky.

"Hello."

"Chica," she says, looking up. "I was just leaving you a note."

"About?"

"I was going to warn you that there's some new woman in the department. I saw Jill parading her around, making introductions. I caught a glimpse of her . . . some black chick. I don't think I'm going to like her."

"Nora, you can't call people 'black chicks' at the office. Actually, it's probably not a good idea in any part of your life."

"Excuse me . . . some *African-American* chick."

"You only caught a glimpse of her, and you already think you're going to dislike her? Why?"

"I don't know . . . just a feeling."

"What's she look like?" I ask, knowing that she must be younger and/or prettier if Nora dislikes her without even knowing her.

"Oh, I don't know. Bad hair, fake boobs, too much make-up, not very tall. . . ."

Before Nora finishes her list of flaws my phone rings. "Brenda Harrison."

"Hi Brenda. It's Jill. Can you swing by my office? We have a new staff member I'd like for you to meet."

"Sure. I'll be there in a minute. Nora's here with me. Should I ask her to come too?"

"Yes, please," Jill says, and we end the call.

"Jill wants us to come over to her office. I think she's going to introduce us to the new girl," I say to Nora.

"Oh, goodie!" Nora says sarcastically, and we make our way down the hall to Jill's office.

"Oh my God!" I say, my mouth dropping with delight, when I spot Jill's new baby lying quietly in a playpen in the corner of her office.

"My nanny was sick today, and I *had* a few things I just had to take care of, so I figured I'd bring him in with me for a couple of hours," Jill says, as I make a beeline toward the playpen with Nora reluctantly following. I love babies.

"That's neat that he has his own little cage."

"It's a *playpen*, Nora," I say, and turn to Jill. "Can I pick him up?"

"Of course," Jill says, beaming with pride.

"His head is huge," Nora comments as I reach down and lift him up. "Doesn't that mean there's something wrong with a baby? When its head is so big?"

"Nora!" I say. "Babies have big heads. Their heads are disproportionately large compared to an adult's. I'm sure he's fine." I offer an apologetic look to Jill.

"Oh," Nora says before we hear a light knock on Jill's open door.

"Kamille," Jill says. "Please come in. I want to introduce you to our graphic design team, Nora Perez and Brenda Harrison."

Kamille smiles and comes into the office.

"This is our new Quality Improvement Director, Kamille Cooper," Jill says to Nora and me.

"Hello," Kamille says and extends her hand toward Nora.

"I didn't know we were in need of quality improvement," Nora says, shaking Kamille's hand, but addressing Jill. Nora is doing exactly what Nora does best—being bitchy, but not quite bitchy enough that anyone can call her on it.

Before anyone can respond to Nora's comment, I extend my baby-free hand and try to offer a warm smile to Kamille. "Welcome," I say and give her hand a hearty shake. "You have your work cut out for you with this bunch," I add with a laugh and give Nora a quick glare that says "Be nice!" I feel like I'm back at one of my sorority pledge parties, and one of my sisters is being an aloof bitch to the freshman wanting to pledge Zeta Tau Alpha, and I'm running around trying to be nice and make all the pledges feel comfortable. I don't know why I always feel compelled to be the "nice one." I guess it's in my genes or something.

"Thank you," Kamille says. "Your baby is adorable," she adds, smiling at the newborn in my arms as if it's perfectly normal for women to bring their children to work.

"He would belong to me," Jill says and motions for me to hand the baby to her. "No nanny today. I stopped in to take care of a few things and had to bring him with me," she adds, gently taking the baby from me.

"He's adorable," Kamille repeats. She's smiling from ear to ear with youthful energy. She appears to be in her late twenties, and I have to stop myself from laughing when I think of how Nora described her as having bad hair and wearing too much make-up. Kamille actually has a soft and well-coiffed head of relaxed black hair, and her make-up is flawless. Nora may have been right about her boobs being fake, but nonetheless, they are fantastic. She has soft features and a petite frame. She's actually quite stunning, and I'm sure Nora is fuming just looking at her. I don't think Nora realizes that I'm aware of this, but I know she carries a mental inventory of everyone in the department (as she does with everyone in the whole company, everyone on the subway, everyone in the check-out line at the grocery store) and ranks us all according to how attractive we are. And I'm sure Nora takes pride in the fact that she's been at the top of the heap in our department. But with Kamille walking through the door today, she's dropped to number two, and I know she's seething right here in front of us.

"Kamille's on board to help us improve efficiency and the quality of our work. Her position was created as part of the departmental assessment we did in the fall. I finally got approval to fill it a few weeks ago," Jill says.

"That's great," I say. "We need all the help we can get around here."

"I'm sure everyone does a fine job. I think my role will just be to make some refinements and develop some resources to help people do their jobs better," Kamille responds, a smile of gleaming white teeth never leaving her face. "I'm so excited to be here. I know Saunders and Kraff is a top-notch organization, and I look forward to making it an even better one. I hope to improve the value of the work we do here." She sounds like she's trying to sell us something.

Nora rolls her eyes at me, and I almost feel sorry for Kamille. She's only just met Nora, and she's already on her bad side, which is not a pleasant place to be. But somehow I suspect that this Kamille woman doesn't need my sympathy. She strikes me as someone who can take whatever Nora dishes out and serve it right back to her.

"Well, we've got a few more introductions to do before we get Kamille settled," Jill says, which I guess is our cue to skedaddle.

"Okay. It was great meeting you, Kamille," I say. "If you have any questions, feel free to stop by my office. I'm just down the hall."

"Thank you. It was so nice to meet you," Kamille responds to me, before turning to Nora. "And it was a pleasure to meet you too, Nichole."

Before I can stifle it, I let out a quick laugh. As we used to say back when we were kids, *Burn!* Somehow I doubt Kamille actually forgot Nora's name. I was right—she can serve it right back to her.

"Nora," Nora corrects her, raising her eyebrows.

"Oh I'm sorry. Nora's pretty. That's my grandmother's name." *Double burn!*

"Have a good day, ladies," Jill says, probably sensing that things are about to get ugly.

" 'I'm so excited to be here. I know Saunders and Kraff is a top notch organization,' " Nora says in a whiny voice, mimicking Kamille once we're back in my office. "What the fuck was that about?"

"Oh, behave, would you? She was nice. She's young and excited. She can't help it if she isn't jaded yet like the two of us. I bet she actually thinks she can change some things around here. Silly girl."

"Yeah really. She wants to improve 'the value of the work we do.' Doesn't she understand that we're a consulting firm—we don't do anything of value."

I laugh. "Ah, to be young and energetic. She'll learn. Unfortunately for her, she'll learn the hard way. Like when she tries to get our crusty sales reps to do something differently. Remember when we tried to get Jack to use e-mail instead of calling us on the phone constantly?"

"Or when that poor girl from human resources came upstairs and told him he couldn't smoke in his office."

"You mean the girl who was fired the same day?"

"That's the one."

Nora and I laugh, but maybe a part of me does believe we could use some improvements around the office. I mostly enjoy what I do here, but it would be nice to have time to be more creative with our projects. I never would have guessed that'd I'd end up in corporate America—I had really planned to do something in social work or counseling, but everything sort of shifted when I got pregnant. I was a sophomore at George Mason University when the little pregnancy test stick turned blue, and everything changed. I was majoring in Psychology with plans to go to grad school and become a therapist. Everyone came to me with their problems anyway, and I was good at helping them sort through their thoughts and making them feel better. I figured I may as well get paid for something I was good at. I never thought I'd end up in working with computers and graphics programs. It's really something I fell into.

I finished out my sophomore year in college but decided to put higher education on hold for a while to take care of my baby, and that's exactly what I did for six years. I stayed home with Jodie and was a wife and mother while Jim finished school and got a job to support us (with some help from my parents and his). Surprisingly, I enjoyed it. I don't know how mothers with young children manage to work full-time without losing their minds. If I had worked full-time when Jodie was little, I would have been a basket case. It wasn't until Jodie was in school that I felt I could get a job. I had more free time, and we certainly needed the money. The only problem was that I had very little to offer an employer in the way of education or experience. I could type and had basic computer knowledge, so I managed to snag a decent-paying job as a part-time administrative assistant for an Account Executive at a health insurance company. I did a lot of phone answering, typing, and meeting scheduling, but after only a few weeks I started to help her with her presentations. I managed to teach myself how to use Power-Point, and later the company sent me to classes for Photoshop and PageMaker and, as time progressed, I either took classes or taught myself how to use all the major graphics programs. After a year as an assistant, I got a job in the marketing department of the insurance company, developing brochures and annual reports, which eventually led me to my current job at Saunders and Kraff.

I like what I do, but we're so busy most of the time I don't get to be as creative as I'd like to be. When I get a new assignment, I mostly just rework presentations and brochures that I've already done rather than develop new ones. The timelines we have are often so tight there isn't time to develop something from scratch.

Wouldn't it be great if this new Quality Improvement Director were actually able to make a difference? I think to myself. And just as I'm contemplating how nice it would be to have more time to be truly creative with my projects, Nora brings me be back to reality.

"Guess I better head back to my desk. Can you send me that brochure you did for ConAgra? I've only got a couple days to come up with something for the Wachovia account. I figure I can just rework that ConAgra brochure a bit and be done with it."

I find myself wanting to say "no" to Nora—to persuade her that it might actually be fun to be creative and develop a brand-new brochure, but I know she'd just look at me like I'm crazy. "Sure," I say.

"Thanks." As Nora heads back to her office I sit down at my desk and think about this new young woman and wonder what kind of changes she has in store for us. I'm not averse to change, but I will admit, almost any sort does make me nervous. As I begin attaching the brochure I promised to e-mail Nora, I say a silent prayer that nothing too drastic happens, and that this Kamille person doesn't try to shake things up *too* much. I have enough chaos and uncertainty going on at home—I don't need it at work as well.

# 12

## Kamille

It's my second day on the job, and I think I feel more over-whelmed than I ever have in my life. I'm not sure I can imag-ine a more daunting task than finding ways to improve the efficiency of a department I know nothing about. There is so much to learn, so many things to read, so many people to talk to. And I know better than to waste any time before producing results: my job is to improve productivity, which means, that above all else, *I* need to *produce*. I have lots of ideas. I'm going to read over all the company literature as soon as possible. I've already scheduled meetings with several members of the depart-ment to get a feel for what their jobs entail and how things are done in general around here, and I'm currently brainstorming and compiling a random list of things I can do that will produce immediate results. That's the kind of person I am—a "results" person. I want certain things in life, and I'll do whatever I can to make them happen. I plan to approach this job the same way I approach my overall existence, which is to make any necessary changes to bring about improvement.

It was interesting, and a bit unnerving, when Jill took me around to make introductions. I could see people's eyes widen-ing when she told them I was the new Quality Improvement Director and explained that I was hired to improve productivity. Words like "productivity" and "efficiency" always make people nervous, which is understandable—they do tend to get batted around with frequency right before employees are laid off; however, at the moment, I honestly don't believe that my role is to identify members of the department to let go. I was hired to find ways to get things done more quickly, improve the quality of work, and, overall, just improve the ability of the company to sell its services. But I think I'm going to have to really sell the idea that I'm here to make people's lives easier, not to screw them out of a job.

It was especially interesting to be introduced to those two women I met in Jill's office yesterday. That Brenda woman seemed nice enough, but I didn't get a good vibe from Nora. Maybe I'm just imagining things, but I got the feeling she was being bitchy toward me. Not that I'm surprised—attractive women like her think they can get away with anything, and I guess the reality of the situation is that attractive women are given much more leeway when it comes to many of life's challenges. Whatever the case, if she was trying to dish it out to me, I think I did a pretty decent job of handing it right back to her. Of course I knew full well that her name was Nora when I called her Nichole, and my grandmother's name is Daisy—I just told Nora that she shared my grandmother's name to make her feel old. I've spent enough of my life being a doormat to women who think they own the world because of their looks and, quite frankly, I'm done with it. But as much as Nora's chilly reception bothered me, a part of me sort of welcomed it. I know her kind, and women like her tend to be most bitchy to women they feel might threaten them or upstage them in some manner. What a coup that would be—for me to make someone as beautiful as Nora feel insecure. That would mean that I'm making some real progress with the way I look. I'm probably just being silly. Maybe Nora is just someone who doesn't make a good first impression. She couldn't possibly be jealous of someone like me.

Sometimes I think I should try to relax more and not worry about people like Nora, and the impression I make, and maybe I should be a little more willing to accept status quo, but it's just not my nature. I've always been that way. My mother calls me a perfectionist, and maybe I am. But what's wrong with wanting the best? Even as a little girl I hated to lose. How many third graders do you know whose mothers had to force them to go to bed and stop studying their spelling book because they are terrified of missing even one word on the next day's test? All through my school years I was obsessed with succeeding. I had to make the honor roll, I had to win the one-hundred-yard dash, I had to write the winning essay . . . I *had* to find a way to feel good about myself. One of my crunchy friends in Atlanta told me I had an "unhealthy obsession with success." She's known me since I was a little girl, and she knows the struggles that I went through as someone who was, shall we say, "a less than attractive" child. She said my desire to succeed in academics and sports stemmed from low self esteem about the way I look. She concluded that, because I felt unattractive, I was desperate to find other ways to feel good about myself. Maybe she was right, maybe she wasn't. What does it matter anyway—in the end I guess my will to achieve paid off. I went to college on a full scholarship and graduated *cum laude*. But, like my mother has always told me, "it's never enough." I've achieved a lot in my life, and I'm only twenty-nine, but just as when I was a little girl, I somehow still don't feel quite good enough.

# 13

## Nora

"What can I say, I guess I'm one of those metrosexuals," Zack says to me after I compliment him on his highlights. We've just finished having a few drinks and listening to some live music at Flannigan's in Bethesda. Mary Ann Redmond was performing there tonight, and her soulful sounds set a wonderful backdrop for a first date.

"They came out really well," I say, taking in his handsome mug. He has dark blond hair under the subtle highlights, light brown eyes, and a lean but sturdy-looking build. He strikes me as a cross between Ryan Seacrest (without the bug-eyes) and Ryan Phillippe (minus the forehead lump). I'm guessing him to be about thirty-three or so.

I met Zack at a salon on R Street. He was in the chair next to me. I was getting a trim while he was having his hair highlighted. My hairdresser and I were talking about where to find some bargains on designer clothes when Zack chimed in. And he actually did provide some useful information. I had no idea there was a Loehmann's outside the city in Falls Church; and he also gave me a tip on some local discount chain called Syms that's supposed to have some deals.

We chatted back and forth from our chairs for the next few minutes and had some really nice conversation. We talked about discount stores and our shared mistake of going out to Potomac Mills Outlet Mall in Dale City, Virginia with expectations of finding something other than frumpy white people with bad hair and no fashion sense. He also gave me some recommendations on local restaurants and a cheap place to buy home furnishings out in Springfield. It was fun to talk to him—I didn't feel like I had to put up my guard at all, try to be charming and witty, or worry about him seeing me with wet hair that was in the process of being cut. I just relaxed and enjoyed conversing with him because . . . well . . . I assumed he was gay. I mean he was getting his hair highlighted at a salon off Dupont Circle and telling me where to get the best deals on Ralph Lauren overstocks.

I must say I was quite surprised when he walked up to me as I was handing my credit card over to the salon receptionist and asked me out on a date. I wasn't sure I was interested . . . honestly, I'm not sure how I feel about dating a man who quite possibly could be prettier than I am, but I gave him my phone number and figured I'd think about it. He happened to the call the day after my last date with Eat-My-Pussy Scott and, at that point, I was ready to accept a date from anyone as long as it didn't involve him abruptly making his genitals disappear.

"How often do you get your hair highlighted?" I ask.

"Every six weeks or so. I used to feel self-conscious about getting it done, but thankfully there doesn't seem to be much of a stigma involved in men taking care of how we look anymore."

"Yeah. Men should take better care of themselves. Why should women be the only ones subject to all the tortures involved in keeping up appearances, like leg waxing and—"

He cuts me off. "I know. That waxing is a bitch."

"You know about waxing?"

"Sure. I have my chest done and that pesky little patch of back hair just above my waistline," he says as he hands some cash to the bartender to close out our tab. "So. It's only nine-thirty," he adds, looking up from his watch. "Do you want to go back to my place and watch some TV or have another drink or something?"

I know I should say no. This is our first date—I generally don't sleep with guys on the first date. *Really,* I don't! But, despite the highlights and the fashion sense and the waxing, there is something manly about Zack, and after my disastrous evening with Scott, I could really use a night with a handsome man.

"Um . . . sure," I say, and watch him get up from his stool in his Banana Republic three-button blazer and flat-front pinstripe pants. We depart the bar and drive back into the city to his apartment on the third floor of a converted row house off Logan Circle. The place is rather small but exquisitely furnished.

"Are you sure you're straight?" I just come out and ask, as I look around at the Pottery Barn and Crate and Barrel furnishings. "This place is so nicely decorated."

Zack laughs. "Yes. I'm sure I'm straight. In fact, I'd be more than happy to prove it." He puts his arms around my waist and leans in and gives me a quick kiss. "What can I get you to drink?"

"Whatever . . . a glass of wine would be nice."

"Okay," he says, and, as he walks off toward the kitchen, I give the room another look and see a small desk in the corner with a few white ceramic pieces and some jars of paint.

"What's all that?" I ask when he comes back into the living room with two glasses of red wine.

"Just a hobby of mine."

"Painting ceramics?" I ask, realizing that my dismay about his hobby may have come across in my tone.

"Yeah. It relaxes me, and they make great gifts."

Suddenly I have a vision of gaudy ceramic birds and clown heads under my Christmas tree, and I start to wonder if Zack might be a little *too* comfortable with his feminine side. He's a great-looking guy, and I love his flair for clothes and his coiffed head of hair, but *ceramics*? It might be a bit too emasculating.

Zack sits down next to me on a sofa I recognize from the Storehouse catalogue, and clicks on the television. He sits just close enough to me that our thighs are lightly touching. He flips the channels and eventually settles on *The Tonight Show*. We watch Jay Leno do his monologue and eventually move on to interviewing his guests, one of whom happens to be my fellow-Nuyorican, Jennifer Lopez. As she comes out from backstage, I'm relieved to see that she's not dressed like a whore. You never know with her. Sometimes she does us Puerto Rican girls so proud—she can look really refined and tasteful when she wants to. But she also has this tendency to show up to awards shows and other high-profile events in clothes that make her look like a common prostitute, which does nothing for the image of Puerto Rican women. I loved her back when she was in *Selena* (who, by the way, was Mexican, not Puerto Rican), before she became this larger-than-life-celebrity-megastar and started going through marriages like most of us change our underwear.

As the show wraps up with Jennifer singing a song from whatever digitally enhanced CD she's hawking these days, Zack reaches over and puts his arm around me. I respond by snuggling in close to him and putting my head on his chest. By the time *Late Night with Conan O'Brien* comes on the sexual tension in the air is almost palpable, just from us sitting next to each other—that nervous feeling you have when you know that sex is inevitable but don't know who is going to make the first move.

I try to focus on the TV, but my eyes keep catching sight of Zack's little ceramics workshop in the corner. "So you really paint ceramics?" I ask during a commercial break, as if I'm just trying to make conversation.

"Yep," he replies, looking at me with a grin. "Did you really come over here to talk about ceramics?"

I chuckle. "Um . . . no, I guess not."

"I didn't think so." Zack pulls me in closer and starts kissing me. The rub of his five-o'clock shadow against my cheek starts to make up for the ceramics. He pulls me in closer, and I feel his strength, the strength of a man, and he flips me over so that I'm underneath him. His lips meet mine and we kiss while our bodies push against each other. I feel his hard dick against my pelvis and grab his buttocks while he runs his lips over my neck, and I slip my hand under his shirt and feel his smooth chest. He cups my breast through my blouse, and his hand makes its way underneath my slacks down to my panties. A soft moan escapes my lips, and I let my hand fall from his chest to his belt buckle, which I quickly undo.

His head moves from my neck down to my breasts. He starts to mouth my bosom through my blouse. I enjoy the sensation for a few moments before I lift his head to bring it back to my mouth, but as I pull his face away from my chest, I see little cream-colored smudges on my shirt.

"Sorry," he says, noticing the blotches. "It's my concealer. I had a couple blemishes. It's supposed to be smudge-proof."

My eyes involuntarily widen.

"I'll pay for the dry-cleaning," he jokes, thinking my wide-eyed expression was one of annoyance about the stains on my shirt when, in fact, it was more related to my wondering if Zack might just be too much . . . too much *woman* for me. But, before I have a chance to say anything else, Zack again puts his mouth to my neck and starts running his tongue upward toward my earlobe. Oh hell, what's a little make-up? I think, as I lie back and enjoy his attention. I eventually return my hand to his waistband and slip my hand down into his boxers. I'm not surprised to feel the hardness of his erect tool, but I am surprised to feel pubic hair that has been clipped to about a quarter of an inch in length, and when I reach down further, I'm downright startled to find that his balls are shaved bare as a baby's bottom.

"You like?" he asks.

"It's different," I say, and, honestly, I'm not sure if I like it or not. There's something neat and clean about his crotch-work, but, at the same time, it might be a tad much; however, when Zack lowers both my pants and his head and starts working some magic with his tongue, I once again decide to overlook his metrosexual tendencies. I'm sighing with pleasure and running my hands through his thick head of hair when, all of a sudden, I see *them*—the straw that finally breaks the camel's back. With my thighs wrapped around his neck and my hips arched, my eyes lazily roam to the little ledge underneath the top of the coffee table and there they are—little cropped pieces of yarn bundled together in a wrap of plastic. Lying next to them is one of those hook-things that I remember my grandmother using while she watched her Spanish-language soap operas and my grandfather played dominoes in the kitchen. I can deal with the highlighted hair, and the ceramics, and the shaved balls . . . even the make-up. But, I'm sorry, I have to draw the line at latch hook! I can't . . . . I just can't fuck a guy who does *latch hook*! What's next? Embroidery? Knitting? Crotchet? Sitting in front of Telemundo in a house-frock latch-hooking a Santa Claus rug? No! I just can't do it.

"I'm sorry," I say, working my way out from underneath of him. "I just . . . can't do this." I get up from the sofa and pick my slacks up from the floor and step into them.

"What's wrong?"

"It's just too soon," I lie. "You're so attractive . . . hard to resist, but I'm just not that kind of girl," I lie again. "I need more time to get to know you."

He looks at me from the sofa with a bemused expression, his clothes rumpled and half undone. He looks so good, I almost reconsider my exit, but then I see the little pieces of yarn again and know I'm doing the right thing.

"I really am sorry. I'm really not a tease. It's just too soon," I lie yet again and kiss him quickly on the cheek. "I think I should go," I say and make my way toward the front door.

"Are you sure there's nothing else going on?" he asks, getting up from the sofa, looking hurt, rejected.

I can't very well tell him that I'm bothered by almost everything about him—his hair, his hobbies, his shaved body parts, his use of make-up, so all I say is, "No . . . nothing else. Really. I'm just not ready." I touch his arm and give one last look of remorse. I'm about to open the door to leave but I can't help myself—I have to ask him.

"Hey, before I go, can I ask you a question?"

He nods.

"What kind of concealer is that you're wearing?" I know, what a thing to ask under the circumstances, but a chica's got to get her beauty tips where she can.

"It's MAC. It's their Studio Finish Concealer."

"Hmm . . . maybe I'll have to give it a try. I totally couldn't tell you had it on."

"The key is setting it with powder. I like their Select Sheer," he says, and, although I'm grateful for the make-up consultation, I'm also grateful to be getting the hell out of there. A guy who knows more about the MAC product line than I do is just not for me.

"Thanks. It was a silly question I guess." I reach for the doorknob. I'm not sure what else to say so I just offer a quick, "Again, I'm sorry things didn't work out tonight," before opening the door and walking out. I hear the door shut behind me, thankful he didn't persist with wanting an explanation about my change of heart.

As I walk down the steps, I think about how ridiculous I must have seemed, how unconvincing I must have sounded when I said I just wasn't "ready" as if I were some sixteen-year-old virgin instead of a forty-year-old woman who's been around the block her share of times. Lately, it's been one bad date after another. Am I just having a string of bad luck, or are the male-pickings just getting slimmer because I'm getting older? I think about this some more and actually start to have fantasies of finding that one guy—the one guy I could spend the rest of my life with and say good-bye to all the losers. When I get outside a word I haven't thought of in years comes to mind: *jamona*. It's a word I heard my grandmother use from time to time when she was talking trash about some of the women in the neighborhood. I'm not sure if *jamona* is an actual Spanish word or just a Puerto Rican slang term, but I do know what it means. A *jamona* is a woman who isn't married. But, unlike a *señorita*, a *jamona* will *never* get married, either because she's unattractive, or a total *puta* (another word my grandmother would throw around when talking trash) . . . or just because she's *too old*. Thinking of that word, *jamona*, and the way my grandmother looked when she said it, sends chills down my spine. It makes me wonder if I've waited too long—is forty too late to try to find that one special man?

# 14

## Kamille

It's Saturday night, and I'm sorting through my closet trying to find something to wear for my big meeting on Monday. I'm going to have to speak to the entire department and lay out my plans to improve productivity. I'm eyeing various suits and checking out the labels as I peruse them—Dolce & Gabbana, Ellie Tahari, Ellen Tracy, Kay Unger, Diane von Furstenberg. I remember how I felt when I bought each suit—how much I loved buying the designer brands. Each suit was very expensive, but makes me feel special when I put it on, and I need the confidence boost if I'm going to keep my nerves in check at the meeting on Monday.

I need to come across as friendly and helpful, but I also need to let everyone know that I'm not someone they want to cross. The only way I can be effective in this position is if members of the department respect me and my ideas. I keep looking through the suits and finally decide on the beige Dolce & Gabbana. I'll wear it with a white silk blouse. I was thinking of going with the navy blue Ellen Tracy, but decided that it might be a little too conservative.

I feel a little sad to be all alone on a Saturday night with nothing better to do than pick out clothes to wear on Monday. I suppose I could go to a movie by myself or something. Although, seeing as I won't get my first paycheck for another two weeks, I don't really have the cash handy to spend on a ten dollar movie ticket. How sad is that—I'm standing in front of closet full of designer clothes, and I don't have ten freakin' dollars to go to a movie.

I close the closet door, walk over to the window, and look down at the street. I see a few people milling about on the sidewalk and wonder where they're off to. I see two women all hooched-up for a night on the town. I watch them walk down the street in tight jeans and trendy black tops—undoubtedly on their way to some club or party or other hot spot. It makes me miss my friends in Atlanta, or at least how things used to be with my friends in Atlanta, before everything spiraled out of control. I find myself wishing I could tag along with the random strangers I see on the street. I don't even know where they're going, but, wherever it is must be better than being alone on a Saturday night. I've only been in D.C. a few months and haven't really had much time to meet new people. And, to be honest, meeting new people isn't one of my strong points. I push myself to be assertive and outgoing at work but, in reality, I'd probably be considered shy. . . . Yet another thing I need to work on.

I sit on the sofa and click on the television. I peruse the channels, but nothing grabs my attention. There's nothing on TV, and it's too early to go to bed, so I pick up the stack of magazines on the coffee table. Most of them are old copies of *People, Vogue,* or *Glamour*—they're copies that I've saved over the years because some of the models or actresses featured in them moved me in some way.

I open one of the copies of *People*—it's one of their *Fifty Most Beautiful People* issues from a year or two ago. I flip past the white girls: Jennifer Aniston, Drew Barrymore, Scarlett Johansson, and try to find the few token black women featured in the issue. There aren't too many: Halle Berry, Alicia Keys, Sophie Okonedo, Oprah Winfrey, and maybe one or two others. I look at the photo spread of Halle Berry and wonder what it must be like to look like her—to be so insanely perfect that people stop in their tracks just to look at you. Her skin is so soft, her cheekbones are exquisite, and her breasts, which I think might actually be real, are fantastic. What must it be like to have that face and that body? I can't even imagine. I'm sure she has the world at her feet—all beautiful people have the world at their feet.

I browse the photos of the other women and wonder what I'd look like with Alicia Keys' nose, and Sophie Okonedo's sexy eyes, and Oprah Winfrey's bouncy curls. I study the magazine for a few more minutes, then put it down on the table. I lean back on the sofa, close my eyes, and start doing what I do way too often—compiling the "perfect me." I picture myself with Jessica Alba's full-bodied hair, and Beyoncé's hourglass figure. I imagine my face, first with Angela Bassett's nose, and then with Vanessa Williams' nose. I think I like Angela's better. I imagine myself with cheekbones like Janet Jackson, but then I think I might look better with Gabrielle Union's facial features. I relish the thought of breasts like Tyra Banks' or Vivica Fox's. I mix and match the images and find that they start to relax me. Thinking of myself looking like beautiful celebrities almost hypnotizes me, and I feel myself beginning to doze off. With thoughts of perfect noses and voluptuous breasts floating around in my head I fall asleep on the sofa hoping to dream about the "perfect me."

# 15

## Brenda

"Okay . . . so the chica has been here for four days, and she's already hauling us in to a meeting," Nora says to me on our way to the conference room.

"I told you. Youthful energy. She's on the ball. Maybe some of it will spread to us."

"I have plenty of youthful energy, thank you. It's eight o'clock meetings that I don't need." It's funny to see Nora in the office at eight o'clock. She usually slinks in sometime after eight-thirty. Kamille must have really had an effect on her for her to actually show up on time for a meeting. I think Nora may see a bit of herself in Kamille—that's probably why she's a little bit afraid of her.

"You feeling better? How's the sinus thing?" Nora asks as she opens the door to the conference room.

"Much better, thanks to your covert prescription," I respond as we step inside and see that there are only a few seats left at the table. The entire department has actually shown up for a meeting, and we're all on time. I'm not sure I've ever been in a meeting where *everyone* actually showed up, and showed up *on time*. Nora's almost always late, Gretchen often has issues related to her "condition" and doesn't attend, some of the sales reps claim to have conflicting meetings with clients. People usually have a multitude of excuses as to why they can't make it to meetings, but no one seems to be using them today. I guess it has something to do with Kamille confirming the attendance of every single person in the department. We've all been talking about it since we got the meeting notice two days ago. If you didn't accept her request in Outlook, Kamille called and reiterated the importance of her meeting and suggested that we cancel whatever conflict we might have. And, if anyone didn't respond at all (as several of our egotistical sale reps did), she hounded them until she got a response. In the case of Jack Turner, she actually copied an e-mail inquiring about his non-responsiveness to his boss—a great way to get Jack to pay attention to you, but not the best way to win friends when you're new to a department.

At precisely eight o'clock Kamille walks into the conference room in a beige suit, with perfect hair and make-up, carrying a stack of paper. She momentarily looks annoyed that someone has already taken the seat at the head of the table before she lowers herself into another chair.

"Good morning," she says, a smile plastered across her face. "Thanks so much for coming."

"Like we had a choice," Nora says under her breath.

"I'm sorry. Did you say something, Nichole?" Kamille says in Nora's direction.

"*Nora,*" Nora replies sharply. "No, I didn't."

"Okay," Kamille says to Nora before addressing the group again. "Well, again, thanks for coming and welcome to what I hope will be the first of weekly meetings in which we'll get together to discuss our quality improvement initiatives."

I look around and see faces drop. No one is interested in yet *another* weekly meeting. This poor Kamille is becoming less and less popular by the minute.

"I've had the pleasure of meeting all of you and the opportunity to meet one-on-one with several of you to discuss how the department operates, and learn where there might be opportunities for improvement. Jill hired me to help make life easier for everyone in the department so we can get things done more efficiently, and everyone can spend more time with their families."

I see faces drop even more. We've all heard this spiel before, although it's usually said by Saunders and Kraff's consultants when they're meeting with the staff members of one of our client companies—right before they start laying off employees and expect the ones who survive to do more with less.

"Based on my meetings with some of you, and the general observation and research I've been able to do since I started here, I've already come up with a few initiatives which can start us down a path of greater efficiency. We'll meet once a week at this time to discuss how things are going and brainstorm ways to improve how we do things."

As Kamille continues to speak, Nora slips a note in front of me.

*Am I the only one who hears the Wicked Witch of the West's theme music playing in the background?*

I take a quick look at it and try not to laugh while Kamille continues speaking and the group around her becomes increasingly glum. "Some of my plans include instituting a clean desk policy. If we're going to increase efficiency around here, we all need to be organized. I've taken the liberty of ordering several copies of my favorite book on executive organization to be passed around the department and, if anyone needs help keeping their desks in order, I'd be happy to offer some consultation."

Suddenly I have a vision of some trashy woman on *The Jerry Springer Show* yelling, "Oh no she *di-ent!*" She's just told a group of people with years more experience than her, sales vice-presidents; several men who don't like taking *any* assignments from women; and people who have been in the business world longer than she's been alive, that she'd be happy to help them learn how to get organized. Is she crazy?

"I have some guidelines about how to keep an organized office," she says as she passes a stack of papers to the woman on her right. "Please take one and pass them on. I've found them to be very useful." Then she grabs another stack of paper and passes it to the woman on her left. "The next document going around the room is a preprinted log. As you can see, it's divided into fifteen minute intervals. What I'd like everyone to do is start tracking their hours on this form every day—"

"Every day?!" I hear one of my co-workers at the table shriek.

"Yes, every day. I will input all the hours into a spreadsheet, and we'll be able to track how much time we spend doing various activities." Yet another task we have employees of our clients' companies do before one of our consultants recommends whom to lay off.

"Should we log the time it takes us to fill out the log?" Nora asks, once again doing her bitchy-but-not-quite-bitchy-enough-to-call-her-on-it thing.

Kamille simply says, "Yes," and goes on to discuss a few more quality improvement initiatives. As Kamille is speaking I look down and see that Nora's slipped another note in front of me.

*Be afraid! Be very afraid!*

This time I don't have to stifle a laugh. I *am* afraid. Afraid that Kamille is going to make things harder around here for all of us rather than easier, even if we keep our jobs. I look at Nora and know she's wondering how she's going to document her long lunches for Botox shots and the time she spends in her office with the door closed, catching up on magazine reading or working on freelance graphics projects on company time. We spend the next hour listening to Kamille spout off several quality improvement initiatives. Kamille mentions that soon we are going to need encoded swipe cards to track our use of the copiers, that she will be given reports from the IT department that track our use of the Internet, and that the department will now have an actual open door policy, which means everyone must keep their office doors open at all times unless it's absolutely necessary to close them for confidential discussions. She goes on and on about her ideas, all of which are camouflaged under the guise of increasing efficiency, although most of them are designed to make sure we are actually doing our jobs at the office rather than goofing off, and seem to increase the amount work we have to do.

After a few questions, the meeting finally breaks up with most of the attendees muttering under their breath. Kamille had tried to keep smiling and retain her composure throughout the hour, but she obviously noticed the looks of hostility that were directed at her, and a small part of me feels sorry for her. I tell Nora I'll catch up with her later and take a minute to check in with Kamille.

"So how have your first few days been?"

"Very busy," she says with a look that seems grateful for a kind face.

"I can see. You really have a lot of ideas."

"Yeah. I'm not sure how well they were received."

"Oh we'll get used to them. People get a little anxious whenever changes are instituted."

"You think?" she asks, with a hopeful look, wanting to believe what I'm telling her. As she says it, I can now see the fear in her. She held up well during the meeting, but now I can see the young girl in her. What is she? Twenty-eight? Twenty-nine?

She had tried to act like a ruthless businesswoman, but now I see that she's anxious and doesn't like the idea of everyone disliking her.

"Sure," I lie. Unfortunately, people won't get used to it, and some of the real hard-asses in the department will fight her tooth and nail over every little issue. *Poor girl*, I think. She has no idea what's in store for her.

# 16

## Kamille

"I just couldn't take the pressure of Hollywood anymore, you know." These are the words of a creature by the name of Gretchen Morrow, the department's administrative assistant, who claims to have worked for several Hollywood A-listers. "One day you're the cat's meow with top-ten albums and sold-out concerts, and next thing you know, you're sitting between Randy Jackson and Simon Cowell judging a glorified karaoke contest." This was her response when I asked her why she left the glamorous world of Hollywood to come to D.C. to make copies and answer phones for a consulting company.

"Sounds like you did some exciting work," I say, even though I don't really believe her stories about house-sitting for Kate Hudson, or how she had to step in and sing back-up on one of Mariah Carey's albums when one of her real back-up singers lost her voice. I appreciate her stopping by my office to say hello, but I've got a lot of work to do, and I really wish she'd be on her way. "Well, I appreciate you coming by and checking in," I say, trying to politely wrap things up.

"No problem. I'm having a good day today. Some days my condition really acts up and—"

"Well, I'm glad you're feeling good today." I don't mean to be rude by interrupting her, but I fear she'll be sitting in front of my desk all day if I don't get rid of her. "I've really got to get back to work."

"Oh sure, of course," she says, and gets up from the chair. "If you need any help getting settled into your office, let me know. I did some interior design for Bette Midler a few years ago. You'd never believe how disorganized she was. And talk about slobs—"

"Okay, I'll definitely let you know if I need the help," I say, and she finally takes the hint and gets moving. As she disappears down the hall, I put my head in my hands, massage my forehead, and try to decompress from the big meeting. I had just gotten back from it when Gretchen pushed her way in here and started blithering on about nothing. Overall, I think the meeting went pretty well . . . or at least okay. Aside from a smart remark or two from that Nora bitch, people seemed to accept my plans . . . at least no one threw rotten eggs at me or anything. I hope I didn't come on too strong, but if I showed any signs of weakness I may as well just quit now. If other staff members see me as weak, they'll walk all over me, and I'll never get anything accomplished.

I wish I had someone to talk to about how stressed I am by this new job. It would be nice to be able to pick up the phone and vent to a good friend, but I don't really have anyone to call. I haven't been in D.C. long enough to make new friends, and my relationships with my friends in Atlanta are tenuous at best. I'd love to call Tia and tell her all about the meeting and my plans for the department and how bitchy Nora has been to me. But last time I called Tia she said that she thought it was best that we not associate with each other anymore. She's angry with me for a number of reasons, but I think she's most upset about the two thousand dollars I still owe her. People always say that loans among friends are not a good idea, but I didn't really have anywhere else to turn when I asked her to spot me the cash. Of course, I plan to pay her back . . . eventually. I just haven't been able to pay her back according to the timetable on which we had agreed.

I miss Tia and my other girlfriends. I especially miss our regular Friday night get-togethers. Tia, Renée, Theresa, and I would get together almost every Friday night. I met Tia in college; Renée is Tia's cousin, and Theresa was a colleague of mine at my old company in Atlanta. The four of us went out for happy hour one Friday night about five years ago and had such a good time that we agreed to meet the following week, and eventually our Friday night socials became a regular occurrence. We'd usually start at a neighborhood bar for happy hour, have a drink or two there, then head to dinner at a fun restaurant. Sometimes we'd call it quits after dinner, but other times we'd head to a dance club and stay out until the wee hours of the morning. We had such a good time together. We talked about everything: work, the latest movies, fashion, sex, you name it.

I loved hanging out with the girls, but I always had a feeling of inferiority when I was around them—I just couldn't shake it. Tia was tall and thin and gorgeous. Renée had beautiful, naturally straight hair. And Theresa had the smoothest complexion I'd ever seen. I couldn't help but feel like the ugly duckling of the bunch. When the four of us started hanging out I think I was about twenty-four and had just started to really work on improving my appearance. Over the next couple of years I think I made a few strides in making myself look better, but I still didn't feel like I was on a par with the other girls. We usually hung out as a group and stayed together when we went to bars, so it was hard to know which one of us a guy was attracted to when we were approached. But every time we were approached by a man I was always certain he was interested in anyone but me. The girls would tell me that they thought certain guys were really into me, but I just couldn't believe that any of them would prefer me over any one of my friends.

I hated feeling second-best. I think that's one of the reasons I was so determined to improve the way I looked. I thought it would make me feel more confident around my friends and I'd enjoy being with them more. Instead, they began to accuse me of being obsessed with my looks and started talking to me like I was some kind of crazy person, telling me that they were worried about me and how fixated I'd become on the way I look.

About a year before I left Atlanta our Friday night outings began to dwindle. Tia got a promotion that often left her too tired to party on Friday nights, and Theresa got married and her husband didn't like her to go out without him. But I think the main reason we got together less often is because our gatherings started to become tense and, sometimes, downright confrontational. I'd borrowed money from the girls and wasn't able to pay it back as quickly as I'd promised. And I guess I wasn't always honest about what I needed the money for. And, when the girls found out that I'd lied to them, our friendship really took a bad turn.

Thinking about it all makes me sad. I wish I hadn't behaved so poorly, and I wish I had the money to pay them back everything I owe them right now. Repaying their loans wouldn't fix everything, but it would be a start. I miss my friends, and I hate trying to start over in a new city, but I guess I don't have any choice but to make the best of it. With that in mind, I lift my head from my hands and grab the folder sitting in front of me on my desk.

"Make the best of it, girl," I say quietly to myself as I flip the folder open and start going over my notes from the meeting.

# 17

# Brenda

It's finally arrived—the day of the long awaited seminar about plastic surgery. I swear Nora was positively giddy on the way here, and I must admit that I am a bit eager myself to learn all the things modern medicine can do to keep us looking young and fresh.

Nora and I have just walked into a small ballroom at the Hilton off Dupont Circle. There's a man dressed in an impeccable suit sitting at a long table in the front of the room. Nora briefly glances at him. "He's wearing an Armani suit," she whispers before looking under the table. "And Gucci loafers." How she knows the brand of what everyone is wearing I'll never know. It looks like a nice suit to me, but I can't tell the difference between a designer suit and the ones sold at The Men's Warehouse. This gift of Nora's makes me a little self-conscious. Does she know I bought my skirt for twenty-seven dollars at TJ Maxx, or that my blouse came from Target?

Facing the table are about eight rows of folding chairs. Nora and I remove the pink folders, which are lying in all the unoccupied chairs, from two seats toward the back of the room and sit down. We both do a quick flip through the folders and see all sorts of brochures, photographs, and documents about plastic surgery and the doctor who will be presenting today. We see "before" and "after" pictures, drawings of female bodies with dotted lines showing where incisions are made, photos of naked women with their privates obscured by black triangles. All the information is overwhelming, and we both close the folders and start looking around the room as women continue to stream in.

"Check out Turkey Lurkey over there," Nora whispers to me, casting her eyes toward a woman who appears to be about sixty. "I bet she's here to learn about getting that neck lifted."

"Shhh," I say, afraid someone might hear us.

"Gobble gobble," Nora says quickly under her breath.

"Stop!" I say with a laugh.

"What do you say we make bets on what these chicas want to have done?" Nora suggests before diverting her eyes toward another attendee. "See Thunder Thighs over there? I bet she's here to get those babies lipoed."

"Hush," I say, as though I'm talking to a child, and I start looking around the room myself, wondering what brings all these women here. To my surprise, aside from Turkey Lurkey, most of the women are much younger than I expected them to be. It certainly isn't the group of "crusty hags looking to have their soggy breasts heaped up to their shoulders," as Nora had so eloquently predicted.

We sit for another ten minutes before the gentleman at the front of the room clears his throat and starts to speak. "Hello everyone. My name is Dr. Warren Radcliff. Thank you so much for coming. I'm very excited about this opportunity to offer some insight and education about cosmetic surgery and help you decide if having some enhancement done is right for you. If you want to take a moment to open your folders, you'll see a detailed schedule for this series of seminars. Tonight is the first session, and I'll offer two more—one next week, and another two weeks from now. It's my hope that, after you've attended the three sessions, you will be able to make informed decisions about your options as they relate to plastic surgery."

As I'm listening to him speak, it dawns on me that these seminars are probably nothing more than a series of Tupperware parties—you know, when the host demonstrates how everything works with hopes that you will buy something. Or when financial planners offer free presentations about retirement planning or the stock market with hopes that you will sign on with them and buy a mutual fund that will pay them a fat commission. Now I'm skeptical about the real educational value of what we're about to hear, but what choice do I have except to sit here quietly and listen to what he has to say?

After a few more welcoming comments, Dr. Radcliff starts up a laptop computer that projects an animated presentation on a screen behind him.

"Tonight we are going to talk about plastic surgery in general terms," he says as some bulleted points on the evening's agenda appear on the screen. "We'll talk about deciding whether plastic surgery is right for you, setting realistic expectations, the risks and recovery involved with surgery, finding a qualified surgeon, what happens during a consultation, planning for surgery, and the average costs for popular procedures."

As he's talking, Dr. Radcliff is clicking the mouse on the computer and words appear and disappear on the screen. It all reminds me of the sales presentations Nora and I work on every day, which really makes me distrust this whole program. I think about how we are told to leave certain things out of our presentations that prospective clients may not want to see, or how I've had to put things in presentations that I know are not true. I wonder how much this presentation is going to leave out, and if any lies will be flashed up on the screen.

"Next week we will cover more specific information including face-lifts, forehead lifts, eyelid surgery, rhinoplasty, and facial implants. The following week we will discuss breast augmentation, tummy tightening, lifting of the buttocks and thighs, and liposuction. And, of course, after each session I will gladly respond to any questions you may have."

I sit back and continue to listen to what he has to say, but I can't get past how slick he looks with his expensive suit and gelled hair, and, it's hard to tell from the back of the room, but I think he's had a manicure. Oddly, although I have my reservations, I'm finding him likable. He doesn't have that arrogance you find with so many surgeons, and he isn't talking to us like we're idiots.

For the next hour or so, Nora and I listen to Dr. Radcliff talk about how to determine our goals before discussing them with anyone else, recognizing asymmetry, and listening carefully when the doctor tells us the limitations in achieving our cosmetic goals. He goes on to discuss picking a surgeon and talks about getting recommendations from friends or local hospitals and the importance of our physician being certified by the American Board of Plastic Surgery. By the time he's done talking about what happens during a consultation and suggests we take a fifteen-minute break, I'm really warming up to him and, I must say, to the idea of plastic surgery as a whole.

# 18

# Kamille

It's almost nine o'clock at night, and I'm still at work. I've got my head tucked underneath my desk as I look in my trash can. I keep getting an occasional whiff of some foul smell, so I'm checking to make sure the janitorial staff emptied it last night. The receptacle is clear, aside from a few papers I tossed in there earlier today, so I try to forget about it and get back to work.

I can't believe how late it is. This new job is kicking my ass. What have I gotten myself into? There is so much to learn, and I'm wondering if I've tried to take on too much at once. I've put so many initiatives in place to try to improve the efficiency of the department that I'm having trouble keeping on top of all of them. And if that isn't bad enough, I'm sensing that I'm not the most popular person around here. I knew that might be a problem when I took the job, and Jill warned me that people would be resistant to change, but what choice do I have? I need this job. I *really* need this job. Money is so tight lately. If I hadn't landed this position, I'd probably be living in box on Connecticut Avenue.

I'm going over my list of department staff members and checking off who has sent me their weekly logs. You wouldn't think it would be that difficult for people to keep track of how they spend their day on a written log and then send copies of the logs to me at the end of the week, but it's like pulling teeth to get them out of people. That nice Brenda Harrison was the only one who just sent it to me without any prompting. I had to e-mail or phone everyone else to remind them, and I'm still missing two or three. Jack Turner, that obnoxious sales vice-president, didn't turn his in. And that bitchy Nora Perez hasn't sent me hers, either.

I'm about to highlight their names on my list and send them yet another e-mail, when the foul smell hits me again. It's about the tenth time I've become aware of it today. I noticed it faintly this morning, and throughout the day I've been catching a hint of it every so often. But now it seems stronger than it did earlier in the day. It smells like old cheese or rotten eggs. I look around the room with my nose scrunched up to make sure I didn't leave any old food lying around. I even lift up my shoes and look at the soles to make sure I didn't step in any dog droppings. Everything looks clean. Maybe it's something coming through the ventilation system.

I'm about to check one more report before going home when I get this irritated feeling under my breast. It's been a little bothersome for the past day or so, but now it really itches. I reach under my shirt, stick my finger beneath my bra and touch what feels like a welt. It's hard and warm and sore to the touch. I get a little anxious and hurriedly rise from my chair to close my office door. Then I take off my shirt and bra and grab a compact from my purse. Once I've lifted my breast and placed the mirror underneath I see a swollen red area about the size of a silver dollar. I feel the knotted area again and immediately reach for the phone. It's well after business hours, but I need to talk to my doctor now. I dial the number for information, and once I get the receiver to my head the rank stench that I've been smelling all day is so strong I think I might vomit. And that's when I realize that the foul smell has attached itself to my hand—my hand that was touching my breast. The horrid smell is coming from my breast!

# 19

## Brenda

It's almost eleven o'clock by the time I get home from the plastic surgery seminar. It didn't wrap up until nine, and then Nora and I went to a swanky place called 15 Ria for dinner. It was a gorgeous restaurant—white tablecloths and heavy silver, but, like all the restaurants Nora frequents (and her dates pay for), it was way out of my price range. All I had was a glass of wine, a salad, and the grilled salmon and, before I knew it, I was out sixty dollars. But even though I can already hear Jim bitching about it when the credit card statement comes next week, I really enjoyed the evening. It was fun to have a girl's night out and enjoy a meal at a trendy restaurant as though I didn't have my daughter's college fund or a mortgage to worry about. That's what I love about Nora—she's my connection to a life I never really had. I was barely out of high school when I became a wife and mother. I went straight from being supported by my parents to being responsible for a husband and a child. I've never really known a time when money was something to be spent on frivolous things—meals at the latest hot spots, fabulous vacations, designer clothes. Every now and then Nora forces me to indulge. She makes me go to an occasional expensive restaurant or buy the rare designer blouse. Last year she asked me to spend a weekend with her in New York City. I repeatedly said I couldn't spend the money or leave my family for an entire weekend, but she wouldn't take no for answer, and, when I finally relented and decided to go, I had the time of my life. We stayed at the Marriott Marquis on Broadway, right smack in the middle of everything—the blazing signs in Times Square, all the major theaters, the billboards with gorgeous models wearing Calvin Klein and Versace. She took me to meet her family in the Bronx; we had drinks in the revolving lounge on the forty-sixth floor of the hotel and took in the fantastic views of the city; we shopped along Fifth Avenue; and I saw my first Broadway show. For the first time in ages I felt less like a wife and mother and more like an *individual*, and I even managed to stifle most of the pangs of guilt that constantly arose when I thought about the money I was spending or the time away from my family. I was actually sad when it was time to go home—back to the grind. Not that I don't love my family— they're the world to me. But to spend a little time focusing on myself and doing things for me was such a novelty.

I wouldn't give up my family for anything—I just wish I'd had a little more time to get to know and indulge myself before I became a wife and mother. That's why I shudder every time I see these young high school kids or college students sitting together on the same side of the table at McDonald's or The Olive Garden. They think they're in love and, at seventeen or eighteen, that they're ready to start a life together. Like most high-school kids, I assume they're having sex, and I say a silent prayer that they're using birth control *every* time. I don't want those wide-eyed girls staring longingly at their boyfriends to end up with an instant family at eighteen—I don't want them to miss out on all the things that I did. While my friends were going to bars in Georgetown I was nursing a newborn, while they were taking ski trips and doing house shares at Dewey Beach I was changing diapers and pushing a stroller, while they were dating guy after guy I was already with the man I would spend the rest of my life with.

When I come through the front door, I'm surprised to see that Jim is not stretched out on the sofa watching TV, and I immediately head toward the garage to see if his car is there—he drives a late model Nissan, much nicer than the sniper-mobile, so he gets to park in the garage. When I see that the garage is empty, I slam the door before I have a chance to realize what I'm doing. I can't believe he's working late *again*! Or doing whatever the hell it is he's doing *again*. I told him yesterday that I'd be home late, and he said he would make a point of getting home at a reasonable hour to have dinner with Jodie.

After I chug a glass of water in the kitchen and make my way upstairs, I stop by Jodie's room and knock on her door. I hear her stop clicking away on her computer after I knock, and she gets up and opens the door.

"Hi, sweetie. How's it going?" I ask.

"Fine," she says. "Just finishing some homework."

"Where's your father?"

"He called earlier . . . said to tell you he'd be home late. He's still working on some project that has a tight deadline or something."

"Did you have dinner?"

"I had some cereal and a granola bar."

I feel terrible. I was dining at a fine restaurant while my daughter was eating cereal. "I told your father I'd be home late. He was supposed to be here and make sure you had a decent meal." That's it—shift the blame to Jim.

"I wasn't that hungry anyway."

"What do you say we both get up early and have breakfast over at the IHOP tomorrow morning?" I offer, sitting down on her bed.

"Nah. I'm going to be up for a while longer . . . don't think I'll be up for a five A.M. wake-up call," she declines with smile, but I can tell she appreciates the offer.

I smile back at her. "Okay, but I'll make sure you get a decent meal tomorrow night. You have lunch money for school tomorrow?" I give her thirty dollars a week for lunch money and odd expenses but, feeling guilty, I'm now offering to slip her a few extra bucks.

"Yeah. I'm covered." Okay, what kind of teenager turns down money from her parents? When I was Jodie's age I never had enough money, but then Jodie doesn't spend money the way

I did. She isn't into the latest clothes and certainly doesn't spend any money on hair products or make-up. About the only things that seem to interest her are CDs and the occasional DVD of a favorite movie or TV show.

"So what are you working on?" I ask.

"Just trying out some ideas for a fake business I have to start for Economics class."

"A fake business?"

"Yeah. We have to pretend we're starting a business and write up a plan and a start-up budget and everything. I'm trying to think of what type of business to write about."

"How about a pet-sitting business? I pay Rhonda eighty dollars a month just to let Helga out once a day while we're gone."

"Hmmm . . . maybe," Jodie says.

"I think that's a pretty good idea. To have kids think about starting businesses. We never did anything like that in high school."

"I guess. It'll probably end up being a lot of work though."

"Well, don't stay up too late," I say as I get up from the bed and start to walk out of the room. "Good night."

"Good night," she says and closes the door behind me. I'm not sure why she closes her door all the time. If she's only working on some homework, why does she need to keep the door closed? But, then again, she's sixteen, and I guess I kept my bedroom door closed most of the time when I was that age as well.

A few minutes later I'm in my night shirt and under the covers. I'm trying to doze off, but I'm feeling anxious. I'm really starting to wonder about all these late nights Jim is spending at the office. Lately he's had a late night at least once a week, sometimes twice a week. Am I being silly? Of course I'm being silly. People work late. But Jim never used to work late, at least not with this kind of frequency. I don't *really* think he's having an affair. I mean, who would he be having an affair with? Most of his co-workers are men. The only woman he works closely with is his secretary, and she's over sixty and has twelve grandchildren.

As I'm lying on the bed, contemplating my husband's fidelity,

I hear the garage door open. A few moments later I hear Jim come inside and mill about in the kitchen for a little while. He doesn't turn the light on when he finally steps into our bedroom, with Helga following behind him (she doesn't come to bed until Jim does), and I lie on my side with my eyes shut as he gets undressed and slips into bed. Once he's under the covers and on his side, I find myself oddly pushing the dog out of the way and scooting over next to my husband to put my arm around him. I pretend to be in a sleep haze as I do it, acting like I just want to cuddle. But in reality, I've turned into a bloodhound and I start sniffing the air around him, trying to detect any feminine scents. I don't smell any fragrance on him. This reassures me and confirms that I'd been imagining things the other night when I thought I smelled perfume on him. I nuzzle my face against his neck and inhale one more time to make sure I didn't miss anything. Again, there is no hint of anything suspicious but, as I breathe in, I take in the scent of a man after a long day—sort of a musky masculine smell. And, to my surprise, I suddenly feel something that resembles arousal. I take another deep breath and slip my hand under his T-shirt and graze the hair on his chest with my fingers before I start lightly massaging his upper body with my hand. Jim responds to my touch, reaches behind him, and slides his hand down my back and into my panties. For the first time in a long while his touch feels sensual, and I let out a slow sigh. I'm truly amazed at the unexpected rush of passion I'm feeling as I slip my own hand into his boxers and take a firm hold. Most days I couldn't care less if I ever saw my husband's penis again, but tonight as I wrap my fingers around it and feel the hardness, I suddenly crave it—I crave him. I nudge him just enough to let him know I want him to turn over. He quickly sits up and, as he lifts his arms to take his T-shirt off, his scent is so strong it makes me throb. I remove my panties while he lowers his shorts and, once he's completely naked, I pull him on top of me and lift my pelvis to reach him. He kisses me. I kiss him back but then turn my head. Oddly, I'm not in the mood for kissing. I just want sex—pure sex. As he slides inside of me, I continue to thrust my soft place against him, and I realize I'm moaning uncontrollably. I should get up and close the door, but I can't. Right now I can't stop. I feel the moisture accumulating between my legs as I grab my husband's buttocks and push them toward me—wanting him deeper inside me. We find a rhythm, and we rock steadily together. I feel a sensation throughout my whole body that I haven't felt in quite some time. Jim thrusts in and out of me, and when he finally reaches his own climax my body is limp from pleasure and fatigue.

"Where did that come from?" he asks with a grin when it's over.

"I don't know," I say, and I really *don't* know. My sex drive has been almost nonexistent for months and then, out of nowhere, it makes a wild comeback. Maybe my planets are aligned tonight, or maybe Nora slipped something in my wine at dinner. Or maybe the mere possibility that Jim might be having an affair was responsible for the resurrection of my libido. The idea that someone else might be interested in him . . . after him. Maybe it suddenly made him more desirable.

# 20

# Nora

"Get those legs up! Higher! Higher!" I'm calling to my class at the health club. "Keep it going. Keep it going," I encourage from the front of the studio. I'm almost done teaching my sports conditioning class. It brings in a little extra money and helps me stay in shape. Plus, I get to give orders to a lot of hot young men. I don't have any professional fitness training, but the gym agreed to hire me to teach a class as long as I agreed to work on getting my personal trainer certification. Two years later, I haven't bothered, and no one has asked about it. And, if the gym manager were to ask to see my certificate, hell, I'm a graphic artist—I could whip one up on the computer in a few minutes.

Unlike in most of the classes taught at the gym, more than half of the attendees at my sports conditioning class are men. I used to teach a step class on Wednesday nights, but I found it next to impossible to attract any men, or at least any *straight* men, to attend. Most of the time, I had to lead a class full of women and one or two gay men. Aside from a few of the abdominal workout sessions, men seem to find something emasculating about most of the classes offered here—body toning, aerobics, step classes—and very few attend any of them.

I got tired of watching a room full of jiggling breasts and one day, when I was in the reception area at the Red Door Spa waiting to go back for my massage, I took a quick look at one of their brochures and happened to glance at the services they offered men, one of which was a "Sports Facial." Not just a facial, but a *sports* facial. Looking at the brochure made me realize that men can be conned into anything if the word "sports" is attached. Somehow it lets them save face when they engage in activities that might be considered feminine. A facial doesn't sound so girlie when it's called a *sports* facial. Manicures for men suddenly become acceptable when they're called *sports* manicures. Even the most masculine men will wear perfumed deodorants as long as they're called something like Right Guard Sport or Old Spice Pure Sport.

I got to thinking, and it wasn't long before I'd developed the concept for a new class I would offer at the gym. I decided to call it "sports conditioning," and advertised it as a class that would improve the participants' endurance and agility in any sports activity. Keep in mind, I have no training or experience in athletics and don't know a football from a baseball, but for the first class I managed to come up with a series of drills and figured I'd wing it from there. I was hoping that my little marketing scam would draw at least one or two men to the class, but to my surprise and delight, the initial class attracted more men than women, and the whole thing has been going strong for a few months now.

During the first class it struck me as funny how blindly my students would just do what I told them. I'd read about a sports drill where you run from one side of the room to the other, touch a marker, and then run back, so I incorporated it into the class. And, I must say, it was kind of amusing to watch grown men and women run back and forth, and back and forth. As the class progressed, I began to entertain myself by telling the participants to do all sorts of silly things that may or may not have had any athletic value. (How should I know? Like I said, I have no training.) Some days I have them hop around the room. Other days, depending on my mood, I might have them move across the room on all fours, stressing the importance of keeping their legs as straight as possible—not that I have any idea whether the straightness of their legs makes any difference, or even if the exercise has any worth at all, but it makes them look silly, so at least I get a kick out of it.

"Let's do four more rounds," I say as the class moves in a circle around the room, lifting their thighs to their chests and taking long strides. I generally only have them do five rounds of this exercise, but there's a new guy in the class tonight, and I want to get a few more looks at him before we move on to something else. He seems to be in his forties, with a tight body and a thick head of black hair. He's older than most of the people in the class but looks better than half of them—he's the male version of me. Every time he pulls a thigh up to his chest, his shorts tighten around his crotch, and I get a nice outline of what appears to be a generous package. It's amazing how *good* exertion makes men look and how *awful* it makes women look. Guys look manly and virile when they sweat. Women just look haggard. That's one of the reasons I like to push my students— to get the men looking sexy and the women looking tattered. Of course, as the teacher, my responsibility is to lead, not participate, so by the end of class, I still look fresh while the women around me look like they've been rode hard and put away wet . . . and that's just the way I like it.

After I wrap up the class I walk over to my gym bag, and, as I'm taking a long sip from my bottle of water (number six of my eight servings a day), I see the gentleman I'd been eyeing throughout most of the class walking toward me. Shit! Was I too obvious?

"Thanks for the great workout. I don't usually attend any of these classes, but this one sounded interesting."

I get an even better look at him now that he's right next to me, and I'm thankful I now have an excuse to let my eyes linger on his face. He's about six feet tall, with deep brown eyes, wavy black hair, and a hint of an olive complexion. He's one of those men of indeterminate race. He might be a plain old white guy with dark hair, or he could just as easily be Latino or Greek or Middle Eastern. His face, handsome as it is, shows the lines of a man who smiles a lot, and it gives away his age. From his face I'd guess him to be about forty-three, give or take, but he has the body of a twenty-year-old—actually better than most twenty-year-olds. The definition of his chest is evident through his T-shirt, and his stomach is flat enough to fry pancakes on it.

"Thanks," I respond, trying not to let on how enamored I am with him. "I try."

"It shows. Those were some great drills. I'm going to be sore tomorrow."

"Then I've done my job."

"I'm Owen, by the way." He extends his right hand.

"Nora," I reply and shake his sweaty hand.

"Do you teach any other classes here?"

"No. I used to teach a step class but decided to do this one instead."

"Damn. I was hoping you taught a few more. Guess I'll have wait until next week's class to see you again, then."

"I guess," I respond, unable to stifle a grin.

"Okay then. Looking forward to it," he says, before adding, "You know, there so many kids at this gym. It's really nice to find someone my age to chat with."

His age!? I DO NOT look his age! "Um . . . yeah," I say, trying to hide my absolute horror, which I must not have done very well because, before I have a chance to say anything else, he apologizes for his comment.

"Not that you look my age . . . I mean . . . you look fantastic," he says, tripping over his words. "Did I mention I'm twenty-two?" he finally says, hoping a joke will take the scowl off my face.

"That's better," I say, trying to relax, hoping I don't sound all hung up on my age . . . even though I am.

"So, see you next week, then?"

"I'll be here," I say as I watch him head out of the studio. When the door closes behind him I turn and look in one of the many enormous mirrors along the wall. I take a good long look at my face. Do I really look forty? I must. Why would he have said I was his age if I didn't look forty? I see myself in the mirror, wearing a tight leotard and a pair of cotton shorts. Do I look ridiculous in this outfit? I've got the body for it but, like Owen's, does my face give me away? The thought makes me feel sad, and I think I've lost any little bit of hesitation I've had about having cosmetic surgery. It's time to do it. A little nip here, a little tuck there, and no forty-year-old man will be telling me I look *his age*.

# 21

# Kamille

I'm taking a deep breath and trying to relax, but it's hard. How am I supposed to relax when I see my doctor taking a long syringe out of the package?

"I'm going to numb the area with some lidocaine. It's going to be a few pricks," he says. He lifts the paper that was covering my breasts and lowers it to my stomach. Then he grabs the needle and takes a few jabs at the swollen area under my breast. I'm surprised that it doesn't really hurt—usually when a doctor says, "a few pricks," it's code for "this is about to hurt like a bitch."

When the area's sufficiently numb he inserts an even larger needle under my breast. I can't see exactly what he's doing and, although the area is numb, I still have some sensation of him rummaging around down there. It doesn't hurt, but it feels strange, and I'll be grateful when he's done. After a few seconds he removes the syringe and shows it to me.

"That's a lot of fluid."

"Fluid?"

"Pus," he says. "You have quite an infection there. That's what was causing the foul smell." He drops the needle in a hazardous waste container and then starts pressing around the cyst. Even with the lidocaine the pressure of his hands is painful, and he notices my discomfort. "Sorry this is a little uncomfortable. I want to extract as much of the infected fluid as possible. Then we'll put you on an antibiotic and hopefully that will clear it up."

"Hopefully?" I ask.

"I don't think there's anything to worry about." He takes a break from massaging the discharge out of my breast. "I've got most of the fluid out, and a course of antibiotics should take care of the rest; however, there is a slight chance that because the implant is a foreign body inside your chest the antibiotics may not work, and we'd have to remove it. But, like I said, it's highly unlikely."

"Remove the implant!" I shriek. "How am I supposed to explain one of my boobs dropping two cup sizes?"

"It's okay, Ms. Cooper," he says, visibly startled by my outburst. "I really wouldn't worry about it. I doubt very much that it will come to that, and, even if it does, we can replace the implant as soon as the infection heals. But, really, I wouldn't worry about it."

Who the hell is he to tell me not to worry? It's not his chest that will have to be ripped open again if I have to have one of my implants replaced. I don't even know this doctor. I had my breast implants done when I still lived in Atlanta, so I called the surgeon there when I noticed the cyst, and he referred me to this guy, who could be a total quack for all I know.

God! I don't want to have to go through breast enhancement surgery again. But I also have no interest in going back to my real bra size either. I used to wear an A cup. Do you now how ridiculous that is? How many sisters do you know who wear A cups? Some time before I moved to D.C., I finally had all I could take of having white-girl boobs and decided to have breast augmentation surgery. I'm about five-seven, a hundred-and-seventeen pounds, and generally wear a size six. I wasn't interested in looking like Dolly Parton or Queen Latifah, but I wanted something more than the damn mosquito bites God gave me. After consulting with two different surgeons I decided to get a C cup—just some nice prominent tits, nothing extreme. By the time I'd had my breast augmentation done, I'd had some experience with plastic surgery, so I knew what was involved. But any other procedures I'd had paled in comparison to the pain and agony of having my boobs done.

I'll never forget the moment I woke up from the surgery with an ace bandage wrapped from the top of my breasts to my waist and an intense feeling of pressure on my chest. I remember struggling to get into a wheelchair and barely being able to stand up to get into the car to go home a few hours after the procedure. I'll never forget the poor nurse that I snapped at when I finally got settled in the car; I was still woozy from the anesthesia, and she kept pestering me to put my seat belt on. I couldn't bear the thought of even the slightest amount of additional pressure on my chest, but she kept badgering me, and finally I told her to fuck off, or I'd shove the damn seat belt up her ass. I called and apologized the next day, and there certainly wasn't any excuse for my poor behavior, but when you feel like shit your patience only runs so far.

As soon as I got home from the surgery I popped a Vicodin to try to ease the pain and feel less like a Mack truck was parked on my chest. My sister helped me into bed, but it wasn't long before I felt nauseous, and she had to help me to the bathroom. I don't think I can put into words the pain I felt when I had to vomit with my chest so sore—with every heave I was afraid my incisions would burst, and my implants would end up on the bathroom floor. It took several days for the pain to really subside, and the entire recovery process was a miserable time of hurting, sore nipples, stiffness, and sometimes regret for having brought all the pain on myself. And to make matters even worse, right after surgery my new breasts looked terrible, freakishly so. They were swollen and hard and sat too high on my chest. The doctor assured me that they would look great once the healing was complete, but it was discouraging to look at them the first few days after surgery. I had to perform these painful massaging exercises on them to soften them up, and it was more than two weeks after surgery before I could stop wearing that God-awful heavy duty therapeutic bra. It was months before I felt like I had fully recovered from the surgery, and it was a bumpy ride all the way, but, in the end, I didn't have any regrets. I love my boobs now. They look pretty natural even if they do still feel a little bit firmer than the real things. It was definitely worth the agony of the recovery time, but I'll be livid if I have to go through the whole process all over again because of a stupid infection—the pain, the soreness, the special bras, the lost time at work . . . the cost. Oh shit! *The cost!*

Out of the blue, it hits me: I can't afford to have this surgery done again. The procedure cost me over five thousand dollars. How on earth would I come up with that kind of money again? I'm in debt up to my eyeballs. All my concerns about pain and the risks of surgery are now secondary, and the only thing on my mind is the possibility that I will need surgery that I can't afford. What will I do if I need to have the implant replaced and can't come up with the cash to pay for it? Gosh, I don't even want to think about it. The doctor said there was no need to worry, so I guess I shouldn't panic, at least not yet. One way or another I'll find the money if I have to. I've always managed to come up with needed money. If nothing else, I'm a resourceful girl. I may have to do a few things I'd rather not to come up with the funds, but it won't be the first time. If the worst happens, and I need to have surgery again, I'll make it happen.

# 22

## Brenda

I wish I had more interest in sports. I've *always* wished I had more interest in sports. It used to be because I wanted to be able to share Jim's fascination with spending entire Sundays in front of the television watching football game after football game. Living in the D.C. metro area you'd think just watching the Redskins' games would be enough, but it's not. Jim watches all the teams and shouts just as loudly at the TV no matter who's playing. When we were first married I hated all the time he spent watching sports on the weekends. I felt ignored and neglected. We had so little time together between work and taking care of Jodie, I felt like we should be doing something as a family on the weekends. But Jim was (and still is) intent on camping out on the sofa with a large pizza and a few bottles of Budweiser every Sunday. I tried to learn about football and watched a few games with Jim, asking lots of questions, but I never managed to bring myself to care. I couldn't get over the fact that it's nothing more than a bunch of grown men trying to get a ball from one end of the field to another, and finally gave up trying to find any appeal in watching the never-ending series of games. I resigned myself to running errands and getting things done around the house while my husband was occupied by the television.

When Jodie was a toddler she would hang with me. She'd follow along as I did laundry or come with me to the grocery store or the mall. But I think she was about six or seven when she developed her own interest in sports and joined Jim on the sofa. As she got older, they'd shout at the TV together and discuss plays and NFL drafts and individual players' stats. They still watch sports together and have a great time, although Jodie's interest has been leaning more toward watching professional women's sports lately. She watches a lot of women's basketball games and loves women's soccer. I think Mia Hamm is her idol.

Just this year, Jodie became old enough to try out for a local women's basketball league. When I took her to the tryouts I was expecting to see other girls around her age, but the majority of the women were well into their twenties and thirties. Most of the women seemed like your average girls, but a handful of them seemed to have more testosterone running through their veins than my husband, which made me a little wary of letting Jodie try out for one of the teams. I can't explain exactly why, but I was afraid to let her interact with the butch women on a regular basis. *Okay,* I can explain exactly why—Jodie was already such a tomboy, and I didn't want my daughter being around lesbians at such an impressionable age. Do I sound homophobic? I'm not. Really, I'm *not!* I just didn't want my daughter to spend so much time with those women and start to think that the way they live their lives is something she might want to consider. I know Jodie isn't the most feminine of girls, but she's certainly not a, well, you know, one of *those* women, and I just didn't want her getting any ideas. But, in the end, I couldn't bring myself to say no. She really wanted to join the league, and there are so few things that seem to get her excited. At least she'd be out of the house in a social environment.

They haven't had any games yet, but I just caught the end of one of their practices, and I got to watch Jodie on the basketball court. I know about as much about basketball as I do about football, but it was fun to watch her in action. I was actually a little awestruck to see her skillfully maneuver herself around the court, dribbling the ball and making shots. She has always been a little bit awkward and out of place, but she seems to be at home on the basketball court. In fact, she seemed to excel out there. Watching her practice, seeing her self-assured and capable, really made me glad that I let her play on the team.

"You really looked like you knew what you were doing out there," I say. We're in Jim's car on the way home from practice. Knowing I'd be picking Jodie up from the rec center, I'd asked Jim to switch cars with me for the day.

"I do okay."

"You seemed to be doing better than okay." I look over and see her trying to stifle a smile. "You can smile. It's okay to be proud of being good at something."

She lets the smile come out. "Thanks. We have our first game next week." She spears some lettuce with a plastic fork. We've stopped by the McDonald's drive-through on the way home. Jodie has a salad and an apple pie, and I'm trying to eat my hamburger and fries while driving the car. Jim's working late again tonight, so we'd decided to grab a quick fast-food meal on the way home. My intention had been to wait until we got home and eat at the table as though we have a modicum of etiquette, but we were both hungry and ended up digging in on the ride home.

"Great. I'd like to come and watch, and I bet your father would too. I'm glad you're having fun with this. You are enjoying it, aren't you?"

"Yeah. It's cool."

"Meeting some new people?"

"A few. Most of the girls are pretty nice. It's cool that most of them aren't all into lip-stick and capri pants."

"Now what's so wrong with lipstick and capri pants?"

Jodie rolls her eyes and doesn't respond as I turn into the driveway and press the button on the garage door opener. Once the car's inside, Jodie grabs her gym bag and her McDonald's remnants and heads into the house. I'm about to do the same when I notice all the apple pie crumbs Jodie left in the passenger seat. Knowing that I'll have to hear about it next time I ask to switch cars if I don't clean it up, I plug in the shop vacuum we keep in the garage and click it on. I give the seats a quick once-over, and when I lean over to do the floor I catch a glimpse of a little box under the passenger seat. I reach for it, sit up, and open it.

"Yuck!" I say involuntarily. Inside the little jewelry box is a small resin teddy bear on a gold chain. It looks like Jim had gone to a Hallmark store or somewhere and bought the little teddy bear figurine and then taken it to a jeweler. The eyes have been drilled out and replaced with little diamonds, and a tiny sapphire is attached to the belly.

That's so sweet, I think to myself—*hideous,* but sweet. We have an anniversary coming up this weekend, and this must be my gift. I'm pleased that Jim has bought something in advance, and that it took some thought but, honestly, the last thing I need is one more teddy bear from Jim. When I was a little girl my parents started a teddy bear collection for me. From the time I was a baby until I was in my teens they gave me a teddy bear for every Christmas. I do cherish the collection, and I take them down from the attic and put them all under the Christmas tree each year during the holidays, but that's about the extent of my interest in teddy bears—I'm thirty-six years old, for Christ's sake. When Jim learned of the collection I think he assumed I had a passion for everything teddy bear, so he gives me all sorts of teddy bears or gifts with teddy bears emblazoned on them for special occasions. I haven't had the heart to tell him to stop, and I certainly can't do it now, after he's been giving me these types of presents for almost twenty years. I tend to hang on to the nicer teddy bear or teddy bear-inspired gifts he gives me, and the rest I either donate to children's charities or save to give as presents at baby showers.

What am I going to do with this one? I wonder as I close the box and put it back under the seat. I figure I'll have to put in on for a few mornings before work and then take it off in the car on the way to the office. As I push the vacuum cleaner back up against the garage wall, I remind myself that it's the thought that counts and thank God that I found it before he gave it to me, so I can be prepared to pretend I like it.

# 23

# Kamille

I just got home from that damn doctor's office. Can you believe him telling me not to worry? He might have to slice me open, rip out my implant, and then send me home to live with one tiny tit and one big tit until I can have the implant replaced . . . *if* I can have it replaced. We didn't get into any of the specifics about the cost of such a procedure.

I walk over to the sink and pour myself a small glass of water. I filled the antibiotic prescription on the way home, and, as I pull one of the capsules from the brown plastic container, I say a silent prayer that these little pills will work and take care of the infection. After I down the medicine I see the light blinking on my answering machine and hit the play button.

*Beep:* "Yes, Ms. Cooper. This is Lynn calling from Wachovia Visa Collections. I need to speak with you right away. Please call me immediately at—"

I hit the delete button.

*Beep:* "I'm trying to reach Kamille Cooper. My name is Sam. I'm with Mid-Atlantic Collections. Please call me right away about your outstanding balance at—"

Delete again.

*Beep:* "Ms. Cooper, this is Gina calling from Bloomingdales' credit offices. I need to talk to you about your account. Unfortunately, if I don't hear back from you by the end of the week, we will have to forward your case to our collections agency. You can reach me until five o'clock at—"

I delete this message as well. All in all, it's a pretty good day for answering machine messages—only a few calls about outstanding balances. At least no one is threatening to evict me, turn off my electricity, or repossess anything. I've gotten used to all the calls and generally just ignore them until they reach a crisis point. The only time I really pay any attention to them is when they threaten to garnish my wages, cut off my phone, or put me out on the street. It's a terrible way to live, but you have to have priorities. And I'm not going to apologize for my number-one priority, which is looking good. So what if I spent a hundred bucks on a blouse at Nordstrom when I owe Visa more than twenty thousand dollars? Or that I forked over a few hundred greenbacks for hair extensions last month when my rent was two weeks overdue. Paying my bills doesn't make me look good—a Donna Karan silk blouse and hair extensions do.

Glad to have my daily dose of creditors' answering machine messages over with, I take my glass of water into the living room and click on the television, hoping to find something to take my mind off my breast implants. Nothing catches my attention, so I pick up my briefcase and search for a photo Gretchen gave me at work earlier today. It's one of several pictures she'd taken during a little celebration we had for a woman who was leaving the company after three years. I felt silly being there at all, considering I barely knew the woman, but I didn't want to appear anti-social either. I was so busy with work and then preoccupied with the swelling under my boob that I didn't really have a chance to look at the photo, a picture of me standing next to Brenda Harrison, who's been nothing but nice to me since I started at Saunders and Kraff, and Nora Perez, who's been nothing but an aloof bitch to me since I started at Saunders and Kraff.

I turn on the lamp next to the sofa and take a look at the photo. And, as I do every time I look at a picture that I'm in, I zero right in on my own image and start critiquing. My hair looks good and the Garfield & Marks suit I'm sporting in the photo looks quite smart, but something about me looks a tad off. It takes me a moment to place what it is, but eventually, I realize that the problem is my ass—it looks so flat and grossly out of proportion to my breasts. How have I never noticed this before? Maybe I just haven't had many pictures taken showing my side view. I look ridiculous. I work hard to follow a strict meal plan to keep my size-six frame, but I wonder if I've dieted myself out of an ass. I can't be a black woman without an ass. That's the calling card of African-American women. White women may have cornered the market on being petite and having straight hair, but we sisters are supposed to be blessed with voluptuous hindquarters. I can't walk around with an ass like Nicole Kidman. I don't want the brothers talking about frying up an omelet on my flat ass.

Shit! If I didn't have enough to worry about with an infected cyst under my breast, now I have an ironing board behind to contend with as well. There must be some sort of cosmetic procedure to enhance one's buttocks, but if I can't afford to have my breast implant replaced, how am I going to pay to have my ass enhanced?

I walk over to the full length mirror and take a long look at my rear from the side, and I can't get over the fact that I'm just now noticing how deflated it is.

"No, no, no! This will never do," I say to my reflection. Regardless of what happens with my breast, I've got to find a way to fix this pancake of a rear-end of mine.

# 24

# Nora

I'm back at the gym doing a brisk walk on one of the tread-mills. I just ran three miles on the damn thing, and now I'm trying to cool down before I shut off the machine. I've got a sweatshirt tied around my waist—something I started doing a few weeks ago when I noticed a woman on the StairMaster in front of me with a huge sweat spot on the back of her shorts, right along the crack of her ass. I don't think my butt sweats, at least not like that, but I'm not taking any chances. I want any potential dates at the gym to admire my ass, not be afraid that I've got Niagara Falls coming out of it. Not that I'm one of those women who comes to the gym to get dates. I don't reapply my make-up, or do my hair before hitting the gym floor, or wear cutesy little exercise outfits (okay, well maybe my outfits are a little bit cutesy), but I have snagged a fair number of dates by asking sexy men to show "little ole me" how to use some of the equipment. Yes, I know . . . that's the worst. I see other women do it—ask for help around the Nautilus machines or the Hammer Strengths, looking all helpless and confused while they stick out their tits and suck in their tummies, and it makes me want to vomit. But the sad reality is that it's a very effective way to meet men.

As I'm finishing up on the treadmill, I catch sight of one of my former gym boyfriends. He's working on a leg press ma-chine. He's breathing heavily, almost panting, and all these intense expressions are coming over his face as he lifts the weight: his eyes are squeezed shut, and his mouth is open with his tongue pressed against his teeth. I recognize those expressions— they were the same ones I used to see on his face right before he reached a climax in bed. It's funny how similar guys look when they're working out at the gym and when they're having sex— the same tightening of the facial muscles, the same heavy breathing, the same pink cheeks, the same muted grunts coming from their lips. I'm starting to get aroused just watching him. In between sets, he catches my gaze and gives me a quick wave. I wave back. His name is Juan, and we dated for a couple of months. I actually really liked him. He's good-looking, has a decent job, was fun to be around, and not bad in the sack. The only problem was his kids. He has a seven-year-old daughter and five-year-old son. He mentioned them on our first date and said his ex-wife had full custody, and they lived with her in California. He didn't like his kids being so far away, but he didn't want them to be adversely affected by the fight that would ensue if he insisted his ex-wife remain in the area.

I have a thing about dating men with children—I don't do it. It's not that I don't like kids . . . well, maybe it is that I don't like kids. They're so needy and time consuming and, quite frankly, they get on my nerves with their sticky fingers and their Happy Meals and their Lizzie McGuire; however, I decided to give Juan a chance. I liked him and figured his kids couldn't be much of a nuisance if they were on the other side of the country.

Things were going pretty well between us. We went on lots of dates, and I was even considering seeing him exclusively. Then, all hell broke loose. His ex-wife got a job that brought her back to D.C., and, next thing I know, Juan has the kids every other weekend. I tried to be a good sport about it, but after one evening with him and the two rugrats at this positively hellish pizza place by the name of Chuck E. Cheese's, I knew I had to end it. They weren't *horrible* kids. I guess all kids go a little crazy when they're stuffed with pizza and over-stimulated with video games and talking mice, but I don't want to have any kids of my own; why would I want to spend my weekends with someone else's?

The breakup actually went better than most. I think he saw it coming. Maybe it had something to do with the look of horror on my face when his son vomited on my Marc Jacobs pumps. In the end, he appreciated my honesty. I didn't give him the old, "It's not you, it's me," bullshit. I just told him the truth: I prefer cats to children, and I just wasn't ready (nor would I ever be) to play mom to his kids on the weekends. We still see each other at the gym fairly often. At first we'd stop and chat, but now we just kind of smile at each other and wave and leave it at that. I imagine it won't be too much longer before we start pretending we don't see each other at all.

When I finally finish up on the treadmill I grab my things from the locker room and start to make my way toward the exit. As I'm about to walk out, in comes that handsome guy who was chatting me up after my class yesterday. He's looking fine wearing a suit and tie, with a gym bag over his right shoulder.

"Hi," he says. "Nora, right?"

"Yeah . . . ah . . . I'm sorry I have to ask your name again," I lie. I know his name, but I figure he isn't someone who's used to having his name forgotten.

"Owen."

"That's right. How are you?"

"Good. I'd rather be home relaxing than coming here to work out, but you do what you have to do."

"I hear you. I'm glad I have my workout over with for the day."

"Yeah? I'm sorry you're leaving just as I'm getting here."

I smile.

"Maybe we could get together outside of the gym sometime? Grab a bite to eat or something."

I'm about to respond when I notice some blond twenty-something chica pass by and make eyes at Owen, like she's seriously checking him out. Trifling bitch, I think, as she moves on after Owen ignores her. Why is it that older men can always attract women so much younger than them, but older women rarely date younger men? I'm glad that Owen ignored the little hussy, but the fact that she dared make eyes at him while I was standing right in front of her, talking to him, really makes me feel old. She was sending a message—a message that said, "Why waste your time with a dried up old prune, when you can have a fresh young plum?"

"Sure," I say, pretending I didn't notice Ms. Thang checking him out.

"How about next Wednesday? About eight o'clock?"

"That should work. I think I've got a card in here," I say and pull a business card from my purse and hand it to him. "Give me a call, and we can set it up."

"I'll do that," he says with a smile.

"Okay then." I smile back at him, and continue on my way and force myself not to look back and get a last glimpse of him before I go.

"Damn," I say to myself as I put my key in the car door. I forgot that next Wednesday is the second plastic surgery seminar. I suppose I could ask Owen if we could move our date to another night, but then I weigh the options: 1) Listening to medical jargon with a bunch of women wanting their faces pulled tight and the fat sucked out of their bellies. 2) Dinner with one of the best-looking men I've ever met. It seems like a no-brainer. I'll skip the seminar. I don't really need it anymore anyway. I've already made up my mind to have surgery. I read over the materials we were given during the first seminar, and I think I've decided to have my eyes lifted and some cheek implants done. These procedures could take years off my face and hopefully will put a stop to younger floosies, like the one eyeing Owen a few minutes earlier, from thinking they can move in on my men.

# 25

---

# Brenda

"Jim, this is so nice! I must say I'm really impressed," I say to Jim after the hostess seats us at a charming corner table next to the window at Kinkead's, one of the top seafood restaurants in the city—white tablecloths, an expensive wine list, a fabulous menu. It's our anniversary and, although Jim promised to take me somewhere special, I'm surprised we're at such an elegant restaurant. Jim's idea of a "special" restaurant could easily have been Applebee's or Outback Steakhouse. It's so sweet of Jim to take me out to a nice restaurant for our anniversary this year. Last year we ordered Chinese from Hunan Delight, toasted our anniversary with two cans of Diet Coke, and Jim gave me some flowers that were obviously bought from the supermarket.

Looking around the room at all the handsome couples, I'm glad that I took the time to go to the salon this afternoon and get my hair cut and styled. Lisa, my hairdresser of six years, made a big deal over it being my anniversary and wanted to slick back my short hair and add some sort of fake ponytail to it, but I nixed her idea and had her do the usual. I don't like having my hair pulled back. It makes my face look fat, or *fatter* than it does the way I normally wear it. Besides, I wasn't sure where Jim was taking me and, based on his track record, I was afraid I might end up sporting overdone hair while dipping my crab meat in melted butter at Red Lobster. Lisa made such a fuss the whole time she was doing my hair and told me how lucky I was to have been married for sixteen years. She really was excited for me and actually seemed a bit taken aback when she asked me what I was going to wear tonight, and I said, "I have no idea." Her reaction made me realize how long it's been since I've dressed for Jim—you know, really dolled myself up to look nice for him. I rarely bother to really try and put myself together these days, but when I do, it's usually because I'm going somewhere with Nora, or because I have something important going on at work, or because Jim and I have some sort of social event to attend. Lately, whenever I go the extra mile with hair and make-up it's to look nice for friends or, sometimes, people I barely know. When I know Jim is the only person I'm going to be seeing I'm generally quite content to slip on a pair of jeans and a sweatshirt.

It is such a stark contrast from the way I was when we first started dating. I used to spend hours getting ready. I'll never forget the day of our first date. We were seniors at Robinson, and he had asked me to the Homecoming Dance. I had always gone to the school mixers and other social events with my friends, but this was the first time I had an official date to a dance. I spent weeks shopping for just the right dress and the right shoes and the right accessories. The day of the dance I was a nervous wreck the entire time I was getting ready. I remember doing my hair, hating how it turned out, rewashing it, and doing it again. I remember applying my make-up with absolute precision. I remember wanting to look the best I possibly could for him. Now I'm more likely to dress based on what Nora or the other women at work will think rather than based on how my husband would feel.

I tried channeling some of my hairdresser's excitement into my own body, but I'm afraid I wasn't very successful. I'm just not feeling terribly enthused about the whole thing. I was barely motivated this afternoon to stop by the mall on the way home from my hair appointment and pick up a gift for Jim. It's not that I don't love him; I do. It's just that I rarely feel any passion anymore. Aside from that odd burst of sexual energy I had a few nights ago, I rarely feel sexual these days. I can't explain it—why I have next to no sex drive—but I don't. I miss it—having a sex drive, that is. But, at the same time, if it wasn't for the fact that I was married and had obligations to my husband, I'd probably just accept it and forget about sex. If you have no desire to go bungee jumping or write a novel or go to the opera, no one thinks anything of it. You don't want to do it, so you don't do it. But the moment you lose interest in sex, you're seen as some kind of freak, and you must do everything in your power to get your sex drive back. What would be so wrong with not having sex if you don't freakin' feel like having sex?

We're seated for only a few moments when the waiter comes over, welcomes us, and asks if we'd like something from the bar.

"Do you have sweet tea?" Jim asks. I hate when he does that. I'm sorry, but asking for sweet tea at a restaurant anywhere north of Richmond just sounds trashy.

"No. Only regular, I'm afraid," the waiter responds.

"Well, just a Coke for me for now," Jim says, and then I can tell he is about to ask another question. Don't do it! This is an elegant restaurant—please don't do it, I think to myself as I watch.

"Are there free refills on the sodas?"

He did it.

"Actually, no," the waiter says.

"Can you just bring us a couple of glasses of water while we look at the wine list?" I ask, trying to get back into the waiter's good graces, so we don't get second-rate service all night.

"The wine list?" Jim asks me, after the waiter has walked away.

"Yes. It's a special occasion. Wouldn't it be nice to celebrate with a bottle of wine?"

Jim doesn't answer me. He just picks up the leather-bound list and starts to take a look. I want to laugh as I watch him reviewing it as if he knows a Cabernet from Mountain Dew. Jim and I aren't big wine connoisseurs. We usually stick to beers or soda, but on the rare occasions that we come to fine restaurants I usually encourage Jim to share a bottle of wine with me—partly because I really do think a nice bottle of wine adds to the ambiance of a special evening, but also because I must admit that I'm afraid the waiter will think of us as white trash if we order beer with our meals.

"Anything catch your eye?" I ask.

"Oh I don't know. Maybe we can go with the White Zinfandel." Jim points to an entry, which I quickly notice is the cheapest wine on the list.

"How about that Chardonnay," I reply, pointing to another wine on the menu. When I went out to dinner with Nora a few days ago she mentioned something about White Zinfandel being a wine for trashy people who know nothing about wine. Who knew that certain types of wine (well, aside from Boone's Farm) were trashy?

I figure Chardonnay is a good choice since we'll be having seafood. I saw something on TV about how white wine goes with chicken and seafood, and red should be reserved for beef or pasta with tomato-based sauces. I think you're supposed to choose your food first and then pick a wine, but whatever—it all seems like an awful lot of brouhaha for a bottle of what's really just rancid grape juice.

After we order the bottle of wine, a couple of salads, and our entrées, we're left in a bit of a precarious situation—the two of us sitting together alone in a restaurant. I guess we're supposed to have pleasant conversation, but that's not something Jim and I do much of lately. I'm not sure we remember how. Of course we talk over meals together all the time, but most of the time Jodie is there, berating one or both or us for eating meat, we're tired from a long day, and we're just trying to get a little something to eat before we go to bed. Our dinner conversations generally revolve around things in the house that we need to take care of, or how to juggle our schedules to make sure that Jodie gets picked up from basketball practice so one of us is home to let the plumber in. It's not often that we have the occasion to have trivial conversation over a relaxed dinner.

"This really is a beautiful place." I try to the break the silence that has ensued since the waiter left the table. "Where did you hear about it?"

"Ah. . . ." He stumbles for a moment. "Someone at work mentioned it to me. You know, Don. He said he and his wife came here for her birthday and had a really nice time," he continues as the waiter sets down a basket of bread. Jim reaches for a piece, slathers it with butter, and takes a bite.

"It's stale," he says. "At these prices! Bringing us stale bread." He's about to wave the waiter over when I motion for him to stop and take a slice of bread myself. It's some sort of rustic farm bread or something.

"No, I don't think it's stale. I think it's supposed to be like this."

Jim takes another bite. "Really?" he says, and takes yet another bite. "If you say so."

I take a sip of my water and smile at Jim as he's talking and eating his bread. He looks good in his dark wool suit and crisp white shirt. Both of our offices subscribe to a business-casual dress code, so it's rare that either one of us gets dressed up. It's nice to see Jim in a suit and tie. Suits are flattering on him— when he buttons the jacket you hardly notice his beer belly. As I look at him from across the table, I'm having one of those rare moments where I can see the young man in him. I see him as I did when we were in high school. I study his face and look beyond the cheeks that have plumped up over the years, and see the guy who was shaking from nerves the first time he kissed me.

"What?" he says, noticing my smile.

"Nothing," I reply. "I'm just happy to be here." And I *am* happy to be here. It reminds me of a time when things were better between my husband and me. It makes me think of times when I felt more connected to him and our family seemed closer.

He smiles back at me, and I feel like we're connecting in a way we haven't in quite a while, and it sparks a memory of us on an outing more than ten years ago. We were at the National Zoo and Jodie was still young enough for us to push her in a stroller. I barely remember anything about the animals we saw that day. What I do remember is the two of us walking around the park with me pushing Jodie, and Jim walking next to me with his arm around my shoulder. I recall thinking how lucky I was to have such a beautiful family and how good it felt when I was looking at the panda bears and Jim stepped behind me, put his arms around my waist, and pressed his body against mine. We stood there for quite some time, watching the bears, and feeling close to each other. He hasn't stepped behind me and put his arms around my waist like that in years.

Jim and I chat for the next hour over wine, arugula salads, crab cakes, and salmon. The food is wonderful, the wine has given me a little bit of a buzz, and the music in the background has created a relaxing atmosphere. After we order dessert, Jim pulls a small box from his jacket pocket and hands it to me.

"Happy Anniversary."

"Thank you." I'm bracing myself to exude pleasant surprise when I see the awful teddy bear necklace. I open the box and, to my surprise, I actually do feel pleasantly surprised. The box contains a tasteful three stone diamond necklace.

"It's beautiful," I say. "I love it!" I start to remove the jewelry from the box. Once I have the necklace in my hand, I get up from the table and ask Jim to put it on me. I actually quiver as he reaches over my shoulders and places the necklace around my neck. Somehow it makes me feel so special.

By the time we get home from Kinkead's it's after eleven o'clock. We're both tired and Jim heads upstairs to the bedroom while I check in with Jodie and load the dishwasher before heading to bed myself. On the way up the steps, still a little tipsy from the wine, I clutch the necklace around my neck, feeling happy. I'm not sure what happened to the teddy-bear necklace, but I have my suspicions. I mentioned finding it in the car to Nora, and I have to wonder if she intervened, calling Jim and somehow managing to politely suggest he eighty-six the poor little bear with his eyes drilled out and replace it with a diamond necklace. In fact, I bet the suggestion to take me to Kinkead's was hers, too. That would explain why Jim hesitated for a second when I asked him how he'd heard of the restaurant.

"Thank you, Nora," I say under my breath as I walk into the bedroom, pass Jim lying on the bed, and head into the walk-in closet. Since it's our anniversary I put on a silk nightie instead of my usual oversized cotton T-shirt. I'm sure Jim will be expecting sex, and although I'm not really in the mood, I'm not *totally* against the idea. I feel close to him tonight, and I'm grateful that he went out of his way to give me a special evening.

When I get into bed I snuggle up next him and put my arm around his waist. I feel the rhythmic breathing as his belly rises and then settles back down. I can't believe it—he's asleep! He fell asleep on our anniversary and didn't even try to initiate sex. I'd thought for sure I was going to be expected to fulfill my wifely duties tonight and, even though I wasn't particularly looking forward to it, I find myself disappointed that Jim's fallen asleep. Am I not worth staying up for? Have I become that awful in bed that he'd rather just go to sleep? No. I'm making too much of this. He's tired. It's been a long day. All sorts of thoughts are running through my mind, and I ask myself a question that makes my heart palpitate: was tonight a way for my husband to ease his guilt from having an affair? He's never taken me anywhere nearly as nice as Kinkead's for any of our other anniversaries. And, come to think of it, a diamond necklace is one of the most extravagant gifts he's ever given me. Again, I try to tell myself I'm jumping to conclusions. Have I become so jaded that I can't believe that my husband cares about me and just wanted to show me how much he loves me with a nice evening out and a wonderful gift?

I'm too agitated to sleep, so I get out of bed and walk back into the closet and take a look at myself in the full-length mirror. Would I cheat on me? I ask myself as I stare at my reflection. Could I really blame Jim if he were having an affair? Look at me—I'm not exactly Cindy Crawford. I see the weight I've put on since we got married, the hint of cellulite on my thighs, breasts with nipples that point more toward the floor than the wall, the beginnings of crow's feet around my eyes. As I look at myself, I begin to think about the plastic surgery seminar I went to with Nora a few days ago. I never really thought I was the type to get cosmetic surgery, but maybe it's not such a bad idea after all. What a difference it would make if I could get these breasts lifted and looking like they did before nursing a baby and thirty-six years of gravity took their toll on them. A little liposuction on my belly and my thighs might take me down to a size ten. If I felt better about the way I looked, maybe I'd have more of a sex drive, and maybe Jim wouldn't fall asleep on the night of our anniversary.

As it is now, I feel frumpy and self-conscious when I'm having sex. I always want the lights off, and sometimes I hate to be touched. I don't want Jim feeling my squishy belly or the ridged stretch marks from my pregnancy so many years ago (do they ever go away?!). I've realized over the years that sex is as much about the way I feel about myself as it is about how I feel about Jim. I used to think that I only became aroused from looking at Jim, feeling his body against mine, and taking in everything about him that's masculine and strong. Later, I began to realize that I need to feel like I'm turning him on. It got me worked up to know that my naked body, my breasts, and my rear and my . . . my private area were driving him wild. But over the past few years I haven't felt that I could arouse anyone. I know I'm not ugly or anything, and although I could stand to lose several pounds, I don't think I'd qualify as fat, at least not *fat*-fat. I just don't feel good about the way I look, especially without my clothes on. Feeling this way about my body makes it hard for me to feel sexual. Maybe a little surgery is just what I need, maybe if I can whip this body into something I feel better about, I can breathe some life back into my sex drive . . . and back into my marriage.

# 26

# Kamille

I'm sitting on an examining table with my hand under my clothes, feeling my breast, making sure the inflammation is completely gone from the cyst the doctor drained last week. Luckily, the lancing and antibiotics seem to have done the trick, and I don't need to worry about losing my implant for the time being. As I remove my hand and slip it out from under my sweatshirt I hear someone flipping papers outside the door.

"Hello," the doctor says to me after knocking on the door and stepping into the room. "I'm Dr. Klein."

"Kamille Cooper," I say. "Nice to meet you."

"So what can I do for you today, Ms. Cooper?" he says as I study his face, trying to figure out what kind of man he is. His face looks honest and kind and shows the wear of enough years to make me feel comfortable about his level of experience. I do a little research on all of my surgeons before letting them cut on me but, in the end, I've found that when selecting a doctor, I go with my gut and pick the one that makes me feel most comfortable. I also do this thing where I look for pictures of their waiting room online before scheduling an appointment. One thing I've learned about plastic surgeons is that they tend to go all out in decorating their waiting rooms. Some of them are done very tastefully, while others are loud and gaudy. I like to meet with doctors who have tasteful waiting rooms. I figure if they have an aesthetically pleasing waiting room, they must have an eye for beautiful things, which would, in theory, make them a better surgeon and better judge of how to make their patients more beautiful. That's the main reason I chose to see Dr. Klein. I saw a photo of the interior of his office online, and it looked so elegant and classy, which is how I want to look—elegant and classy.

"I saw your ad in *Washingtonian*, and I've been thinking about having a little something done to add some shape to my figure." I guess I could just come out and say I want some implants put in my ass, but it just doesn't sound very dignified.

"What did you have in mind?"

I reach for my purse and take out a page I ripped from *Essence* magazine. I show him a picture of Beyoncé, point to her bottom, and say, "I want that."

Dr. Klein cracks a kind smile and takes a closer look at the photo. "So you're looking for me to enhance your buttocks?"

"Well, make them bigger . . . more pronounced. I don't think they need any lifting or anything. I'm only twenty-nine."

"Hmm," he says. "Would you mind standing up, so I can take a look at the present state of your buttocks?"

I get up from the table and turn around so he can see my ass. "Do I need to lower my pants?"

"Not just yet," he says from behind me. "I can take a closer look later, but at first glance, I'm not sure you're really a candidate. You're not wearing padded underwear, are you?"

"No. Why?" I say immediately, wondering if he somehow saw my credit report before I came in and knows I can't afford this. Or does he assume that because I'm black, I don't have any money?

"Ms. Cooper. I've done many buttock implant surgeries, and most of my patients have a rear-end that looks like yours *after* the surgery. Your current bottom would be considered quite well-proportioned to your body by most standards."

What's this guy talking about!? My ass is as flat as I'd like my abs to be! "That's kind of you to say, but I'm really interested in adding a little more shape."

"Let me tell you a little bit about the procedure, and then maybe you can think about it some more. When a man who makes his living doing surgery tells you that you don't need it, you should really give it some thought."

Jerk! Who is he to tell me what I need and don't need? "Okay."

"To shape the buttock mounds we use a special implant. It's not like a breast implant." His eyes flicker toward my chest as he says this. "Breast implants are filled with fluid. Buttock implants are solid silicone. The surgery only requires one incision overlying the tailbone, but due to the placement of the implants, you can expect a lengthy recovery time. Your buttocks are involved in everything—walking, sitting, lying down. It can be more than a week before you're up and around at all, and several weeks before you can sit comfortably."

The doctor pauses for a moment and seems surprised that I remain unaffected. So I can't sit down for a while? Big deal! I give him a look that says, "And?"

"We'll need to put you under general anesthesia to lift the buttock muscle—"

"I don't want my rear lifted. I just want it more pronounced."

"I understand, but we need to lift the muscle to make a pocket large enough for the implant."

"Oh."

"Once we make the pocket, we insert the implants and examine the area to make sure they look as natural as possible. We'll suture the area with dissolvable stitches and then wrap the area in a bandage that puts pressure over the implants and helps reduce swelling."

"That doesn't sound so bad," I say.

"The procedure is only half the battle. There are several other risks to consider. Like I said, the buttocks are involved in almost everything you do, so the risk of an implant shifting after surgery is higher than with breast implants or, say, chin or cheek implants. There is also the risk of infection. These implants are placed close to the rectal area, which increases the likelihood of severe infection."

"Okay. I think I can live with those risks."

The doctor offers a defeated smile. "Because of the issues involved with this particular surgery, I'm hesitant to perform it on someone who, in my professional opinion, doesn't really need it." He notices me about to interrupt him and adds, "But I will let you make the final determination. After I've had a chance to ask you a few more questions, I'm going to send you home with some literature about the procedure, and I want you to read every word before calling us back to schedule the surgery. Deal?"

I smile. He's getting on my nerves, but you have to respect a surgeon who advises his patients against having surgery. "Deal," I say.

He then picks up my chart and starts looking at the notes made by the intake nurse who met with me when I first came in. "So, you've already had your eyes done and cheek implants inserted, so you have some idea of what's involved with cosmetic surgery."

"Yes," I say. "It was little rough going there for the first few days after surgery, but after that, it wasn't so bad."

"Did you have both procedures done at the same time?"

"Yes," I lie. I actually had them done separately, but he doesn't need to know that. He also doesn't need to know about my lip reduction. The last surgeon I saw didn't notice, so I figure Dr. Klein won't either. And there's a reason I'm wearing the baggy sweatshirt I have on; luckily, so far, he has not asked me to remove it. If he does, he'll surely notice my breast implants and the liposuction I had on my abdomen last year. I've found that if you're honest with doctors about the number of plastic surgeries you've had, it leads to all sorts of needless questions. People seem to have some sort of issue with someone in their twenties wanting to improve upon what God gave them. The last time I offered an honest list of everything I'd had done, this annoying doctor I saw when I still lived in Atlanta suggested I go to counseling, like there was something wrong with my mind.

Yeah, like my mind is the problem. The problem is my body and my face. So what if I've had my lips reduced, my breasts enlarged, liposuction on my abdomen, my ears pinned, facial implants, and my eyes lifted—it's all just a means to an end. And I think I'm almost finished—all I need are these implants in my ass. I thought I'd be done after the breast implants. And I guess I thought I'd be done after the liposuction and the eye job before that, but when I saw how flat my fanny was in the mirror I knew I needed to go under the knife one more time. After this butt job, I'll be done. I'll finally have the look I want, and I can really start living. Well, maybe at some point down the road, I'll get a chin implant, and possibly a tummy tuck, and maybe something done with my calves, but right now I just need to focus on beefing up my ass.

The doctor asks me a few more questions about my past surgeries and my general health, asks me to lower my pants and takes a long look at my rear-end, and then starts to wrap up. "I'll have Jessica, the nurse you saw earlier, bring you the literature we talked about, and she can talk to you about any preoperative tests we need to schedule if you decide to have the procedure."

"Okay," I say. "And what about the cost? How much do ass . . . I'm mean buttock implants, cost?"

"Barbara, at the front desk, can go over all the financial details with you, but you're looking at a cost of about seven thousand dollars when all is said and done."

Fuck! "Do you offer any discounts?" I ask with a laugh, like I'm joking, which I'm not.

He chuckles. "No, I'm afraid not, but we have financing plans that Jessica can go over with you, and we do take credit cards."

"There's nothing I can do to get the cost down?" I ask, trying to show with my eyes that I'll do *anything*. I'm perfectly willing to blow him right here and now if he'll cut the price for me.

He looks a little uncomfortable. "No. Surgery isn't really something to haggle over, Ms. Cooper," he says to me like I'm a five-year-old child. "Think about everything we've talked about and take your time making a decision. Have a good day," he says, and exits the room.

Seven thousand dollars! Where on earth am I going to get seven thousand dollars, I ask myself as I watch the door close behind him. I continue to sit on the table, not quite ready to head out of the office and face the world and the insurmountable task of raising such a large sum of money. I start fidgeting with the ring on my right hand like I always do when I'm anxious. I twist it to the right, then I twist it to the left, then back to the right again. I look down at it and, just as it did when my grandmother gave it to me almost ten years ago, it almost takes my breath away. It's a three-diamond engagement ring, one and a half carats in total. There's a large round-cut diamond in the middle and a smaller one on each side. The diamonds are set on a fourteen carat white gold band. My grandmother wore it as her "engagement ring," and she always called it her "engagement ring," but it wasn't until after she and my grandfather had been married for forty years that he had saved up enough money to buy it for her. She was always so proud of it, and I don't think it left her finger until she gave it to me a few months before she died. She'd left it to me in the will, but when she knew her time was dwindling, she said she wanted to pass it down to me in person. She said she loved me very much and reminded me of all the hard work it took for my grandfather to buy her the ring. Then she took it off her finger and said she wanted me to have it. "A beautiful ring for a beautiful girl," she said as she handed it to me.

I asked her why she decided to skip a generation and leave the ring to me instead of my mother. She said she had already willed the house and her savings to my mother. She also said that even though my father had given my mother a very nice engagement ring of her own, it paled in comparison to hers, and Grandma didn't want to hurt my father's pride by giving his wife a nicer ring than he had given her. I was barely twenty years old at the time, and I was awestruck by her gift. I didn't feel like the beautiful girl my grandmother had said I was, but when I put the ring on, I did feel special, and, even when I look at the ring now, it still makes me feel special.

Looking at the ring, I feel a bond with the matriarch of my family, and that's why I get such chills down my spine at times like these—times when I think about selling it to pay for my plastic surgery.

# 27

## Brenda

This seems so ridiculous—me, coming alone, to the second installment of these plastic surgery seminars that Nora had to drag me to in the beginning. She mentioned something about a date conflicting with the seminar, and how I was off the hook and didn't have to go with her anymore. But when your husband would rather catch some shut-eye than have sex with you on your anniversary, you start to consider options like cosmetic surgery. If you asked me a few weeks ago, I would have said that there was no way I would consider going under the knife for the sake of vanity, but now I'm not so sure. It seems like everyone is doing it.

I got held up at work, so I'm a few minutes late and have to grab a seat in the back of the room. A presentation about face-lifts is already underway, and there's a large sketch of some dour woman's face up on the screen. Certain areas of her face are labeled with words like nasolabial fold, jowl, and platysmal band.

"We perform face-lifts to improve sagging cheeks and reduce the heavy skin fold around either side of the nose and mouth. Face-lifts can also improve a sagging neck," Dr. Radcliff, looking debonair as usual, says while using some kind of laser pointing device to highlight areas of the woman's face. "Now, if I can have a volunteer, I'll demonstrate a few techniques that you can try at home to get an idea of what a face-lift can do for you."

I immediately look at the floor and try to hide behind the person in front of me.

"Oh hell, I'll volunteer," says a full-figured white woman across the aisle from me. She appears to be in her forties, although she's dressed as though she's in her twenties. Her tight skirt ends well above the knee and her silk blouse, aside from a few crisscrosses of thin fabric, is virtually backless (and it's winter!). She's carrying around several extra pounds but, from the way she's dressed and the way she sashays to the front of the room, doesn't seem to be aware of it.

"What's your name?" the doctor asks.

"Jazelle."

"It's nice to meet you, Jazelle. If you'll sit down in this chair, you can be our model this evening."

The woman sits down, and Dr. Radcliff stands behind her. "Now, not that Jazelle in any way needs a face lift—"

"Like hell I don't. Can I get a discount on one for being the class model tonight?" she jokes.

Dr. Radcliff chuckles and places his hands on her cheeks. "All you have to do is look in the mirror and put your hands on your cheeks like this and press the skin up and back," he says as he lifts Jazelle's cheeks back toward her ears. "This will give you an idea of how any folds will be lifted with a face lift."

"You didn't answer my question about the discount," Jazelle teases, prompting a few laughs from the crowd.

"We'll talk later," the doctor says with a laugh. "You can also get an idea of any improvement a face lift will have on your neck, but you'll need two mirrors. Stand sideways against a large wall mirror and then use a smaller hand mirror to view your profile." he adds, placing his fingers on both sides of Jazelle's neck. "Then take your fingers like this and stretch your skin up and back."

It's interesting to watch Dr. Radcliff manipulate Jazelle's face. I immediately want to stand in front of a mirror and try the lifting exercises on myself.

After he thanks Jazelle and she returns to her seat, he resumes the presentation. He shows more slides and then goes over the various face-lift techniques. Who knew there were so many different kinds—subperiosteal face-lifts, skin-only face-lifts, cheek lifts, two-layer face-lifts, endoscopic face-lifts, the list seems to go on and on, and, the more he talks about them, the more confused I get. By the time we take a break my head is befuddled with words like incision, scar, hematoma, facial weakness, and anesthesia, and I find myself craving a cigarette.

I put my coat on and walk through the hotel lobby to get outside. I pass a lounge on the way out, and I'm tempted to step inside and smoke my cigarette in there, rather than brave the cold, but I can see the haze of smoke around the clientele and decide to pass. I don't want all that smoke seeping into my clothes and my hair. I know that sounds strange, coming from a smoker, but since Jim quit, I don't want to come home smelling like an ashtray.

When I get outside I see Jazelle standing by an ashtray puffing away herself.

"Hi," I say once I reach the area and light my own cigarette.

Jazelle smiles. "Hello," she says. "If I hadn't done this for the last twenty-five years, I may not need to be here." She eyes her cigarette. "I think it's responsible for all the fine lines on my face. It makes me laugh when I see anti-smoking commercials that talk about the ill health-effects of smoking. They've got it totally wrong."

"You think?" I ask.

"Sure. All they need is a photo of Lucille Ball when she was young next to one of her after fifty years of smoking . . . or maybe one of Bette Davis. They focus on the lung cancer and the heart disease, when they should be focusing on the brittle hair and the fine lines and the yellow teeth that smoking causes. They try to appeal to people's health concerns when they should be appealing to something people actually care about—vanity."

I laugh. "Yeah, it's a bad habit. I need to quit. It's on my to-do list."

"Mine too," she replies with a shiver. "I walked into a restaurant a few weeks ago and when I got up to the hostess she looked at me and asked how many were in my party. And then do you know what she said to me?"

"What?"

"She said, 'Smoking. Right?' Like she could tell, just from looking at my face, that I smoke. I was horrified," Jazelle says before she smashes her cigarette out in the ashtray and starts rubbing her hands together. "It's freezing out here. Remember back in the day when we could smoke wherever we wanted?"

I want to say that her "back in the day" is different from mine. She's easily five to ten years older than me. "Yeah. I remember when I was a kid, one of my jobs was to put ashtrays all over the house when my parents were about to host a party. Now, you wouldn't dream of willy-nilly smoking inside someone's house."

"I was a bank teller when I was in college, and they used to let me smoke right there at my station while I waited on customers. Those were the days. Now we've been banished to get our nicotine fixes out in the cold," Jazelle says.

We chat for a bit longer about the inflated cost of cigarettes, how we each got started with this nasty habit, trying to light cigarettes on windy days, and Jazelle tells me about a French bistro down the street that doesn't even have a non-smoking section (which is probably illegal). The menu actually says, "Cigars? Cigarettes? *Oui!*" I'm tempted to jot down the name of the restaurant, but I'm sure Jim would never want to go there. He'd be afraid they'd make him eat snails or goat cheese.

We walk back into the hotel together, and, by the time we reach the ballroom, Dr. Radcliff is ready to get started again. As I get settled in my chair I see Jazelle on the other side of the narrow aisle. She turns and smiles at me as she takes off her coat and that's when I notice that she's wearing a necklace—a gold chain with a teddy bear hanging from it—a resin teddy bear with the eyes drilled out and replaced with diamonds, just like the one I found under the seat of Jim's car. I try to smile back at her, but I think I end up offering a more perplexed expression. Could there be more than one of those hideous things?

# 28

# Nora

"Have you been here before?" Owen asks me from across the table.

"Yeah. A time or two."

"Any good?"

"It's great," I lie. We're at Café Asia, a hip Pan-Asian restaurant outside the city. It's a place young attractive people go to sit at the enormous sushi bar or stand around and sip Asian beers. They don't come for nourishment or to quench their thirst, but to see and be seen. On any given night there are at least a couple hundred mostly single patrons in the latest fashions milling about the trendy décor. The scenery of tight bodies and sleek furnishings is so striking, no one seems to mind the mediocre food and spotty service.

"A friend at work suggested it. I've driven by many times, but haven't had a chance to stop in."

"I think you'll like it," I lie again.

"Do you eat out a lot?"

"I wouldn't say *a lot*, but, yeah, I dine out frequently."

"I should have asked you to pick the restaurant then."

I just smile even though I wish he *had* asked me to pick the restaurant. I certainly would not have picked this place—the last thing I need are his eyes wandering toward all the little whores in their Juicy jeans and tight lycra T-shirts that show a hint of their bare stomachs. I could wear clothes like that—my body's in great shape—but you get to a certain age, maybe thirty-five, when it doesn't matter how tight your body is, you just start to look ridiculous in clothes meant for the under-thirty crowd. I haven't stepped foot in an Abercrombie and Fitch or Up Against the Wall in years. I'm actually afraid some sort of alarm might go off as soon as I walk through the door. I can just see the red lights flashing and hear the automated voice saying "FORTY! DO NOT ADMIT! FORTY! DO NOT ADMIT!"

"So, how long have you been working at the gym?'

"A couple of years. I only teach the one class."

"You have another job I guess?"

"No . . . independently wealthy," I joke. "No . . . really I work for a consulting company downtown doing graphic design."

"That's sounds creative."

"It could be, but we're a fairly staid company. Most of the design I do is pretty conservative. But I do a little freelance work on the side, and that can be more interesting."

"That's a shame that you can't be more creative at your steady job."

"Oh well, it pays the bills," I say. "And you? What kind of work do you do?"

"I own my own financial planning business."

"Really? I should have you look over my finances sometime."

"Sure, but I think we can find more interesting things to do than go over your finances."

"I bet we can."

We go on to have a really nice evening. Owen is charming and just looking at him makes me tingle. He has such a kind handsome face. He looks so masculine and honest—like he should be delivering the news on CNN. We talk about our jobs over Thai summer rolls. He tells me about growing up in Pennsylvania while we munch on Tuna Tataki, and I tell him about life in New York City as I eat my Pad Thai. By the time we share a dessert of sticky rice and fresh mango I think I've started to fall for him. There's something different about him compared to the other men I've dated. Maybe it's his maturity or the quiet sense of self-esteem he radiates, but I'm feeling an attraction to him that I haven't really felt before.

As we're walking out of the restaurant, we have to maneuver our way through the crowded bar area. I'm walking behind Owen, and I can't help but wonder where his eyes are going as he walks ahead of me. Is he checking out the twenty-five-year-old whore in the tight black dress sipping an apple martini, or is he staring at the young blonde wearing a Wonderbra sitting at the sushi bar. I don't feel totally out of place among all these young beautiful people. I look good. I'm in great shape. I know a thing or two about the latest fashions. But I can't help but feel like my days at trendy hot spots are numbered.

As we drive home, we make small talk about the restaurant and discuss getting together again some time. I'm enjoying getting to know Owen, but, I must admit, I'm preoccupied with the plastic surgery that I'm now intent on having. How will I choose a doctor? When will I be able to schedule the procedures? How much will it cost? Do I have enough vacation time to cover the recovery period?

When we get to my building, Owen parks the car on the street and insists on walking me up to my condo. There's an awkward silence as we walk down the hall from the elevator, and it reminds me of my dates in high school. There's a nervous energy in the air—an anticipation about what will happen next.

"I really had a nice evening," he says as we reach my door.

"Yeah, me too," I say.

"So, I'll call you?"

"Sure."

There's another awkward moment as I wait for him to kiss me.

"Okay then," he says and leans in toward me. I'm expecting a kiss, but instead, he just gives me a quick hug. I try not to show any looks of disappointment as we separate.

"Good night," he says.

"Good night," I say and turn to put my key in the door, not sure of what to make of the evening. We seemed to have a nice time. Why only a quick hug at the end? Maybe he likes to take things slow. Or maybe he's not interested and didn't want to send any misleading signals. But then why would he have said he would call me? What am I doing? It was only a date. I go on dates all the time and don't give most men a second thought. What is it about this man that's gotten me so worked up, I ask myself as I open the door to my apartment and head inside.

# 29

## Kamille

It's been a few hours since Dr. Klein told me that my buttock enhancement surgery would cost a whopping seven thousand dollars. I was so upset over the impossibility of raising that kind of money any time in the near future that I decided to do something I often do when I want to get my mind off my financial problems—shop. Of course, I don't plan to buy anything. In fact, I *can't* buy anything—those pesky little credit card approval machines have taken care of that. But I thought a few hours spent trying on designer clothes and having a look in the mirror, imagining how great the outfits would look if I could afford to get my butt implants might cheer me up.

I've driven out to The Galleria in McLean, Virginia, probably the most upscale mall in the area—nothing but high-end department stores like Saks and Neiman Marcus, designer boutiques, expensive jewelry stores, and, of course, white people. I always feel like I've stepped into Aryan Nation when I come here. Aside from the people who work in the mall, I only see a handful of other minorities throughout the corridors, and most of them are Asian or Middle Eastern. But, nonetheless, when a sister wants to try on the finest fashions, this is where she has to come. I've heard stories from some other African Americans about being followed around by security personnel when they shop at high-end stores, but I've never had a problem. I get the occasional bitchy sales woman, but I never know if she's being a bitch to me because I'm black or because she's just . . . well . . . a bitch. I never really experienced anything worse than casual indifference—maybe because I look like I belong here. Like today for instance, I'm wearing a Tahari suit with a Charles Nolan silk turtleneck and a pair of Miu Miu pointy-toe flats. The whole ensemble probably cost me about a thousand dollars—a thousand dollars that is now lost in a sea of credit card debt that I have no idea how (or if ) I will ever pay back.

I've just stepped out of the Burberry store where I tried on the cutest pencil skirt with a wool checkered turtleneck. The whole time I was reviewing myself in the outfit in front of the three-way mirror the only I thing I could think about was how much better the skirt would look on me if my behind could fill it out more. Despite my lack of posterior girth, I still loved the ensemble. But considering I have all of seventeen dollars in my wallet until pay day, and the two pieces would have cost me about seven hundred dollars together, there was nothing else I could do but take them off and hand them back to the sales associate. A few years ago, I may have snatched them up and charged them to one of my ailing credit cards, but, unfortunately, all of my cards have cut me off, and I can't seem to get an approval for any new ones.

I don't know exactly when or how things got so out of control . . . well, *maybe* I do. I guess it started about seven years ago, after I had my lip reduction, my first cosmetic surgery procedure. Even as young girl my lips were huge—and not Queen Latifah or Angelina Jolie huge. They were enormous and deformed with the top lip turned upward, showing vast amounts of raw pink tissue, and the bottom lip drooped like a wet rag. I can't remember a time in my childhood when they weren't, at best, the subject of constant inquiry, and, at worst, a prompt for tortuous verbal abuse from other kids. So it really shouldn't be any surprise that having my lips reduced and reshaped was one of the first things I did as a young adult. The recovery was a bit painful but, after the healing period, I was thrilled with my new lips. For the first time since I could remember, I didn't feel as though I looked like a freak.

It's hard to explain the elation of no longer having a deformity. Most people can never understand what's it's like to know that people are staring at you in public, to have people call you names . . . to feel ugly. I felt like I was on top of the world the first few weeks after my reduction. I remember walking through the mall one day. I hadn't really even gone there to shop—I just wanted to enjoy walking around in a public place feeling like a normal person. I was walking through Nordstrom and saw this sexy Jones New York little black dress. It was only about a hundred and fifty dollars, but I was only twenty-two at the time and not making much money, so that was a lot for me. After I tried it on, I had to have it. I can't quite explain it, but buying a designer dress from Nordstrom gave me this special feeling. I felt like I was important as I handed my credit card over to the clerk, and she rang up my purchase and wrapped it with tissue in one of those glossy silver boxes. I'd never been terribly interested in fashion—when you see yourself as unattractive, you don't feel like bothering with clothes shopping. But after my first surgery and initial purchase at Nordstrom I loved the feeling it gave me to buy something nice, to own something nice . . . to wear something nice. And that's when the floodgates opened, the credit card accounts were started, and I began to *spend* some money. I figured that shopping at Nordstrom made me feel so good, why not upgrade to Neiman Marcus and Saks? One-hundred-and-fifty-dollar dresses were soon no longer enough. I felt *more* important, *more* worthy, buying three-hundred- or six-hundred-dollar garments. I loved walking through the opulent stores, looking through the racks, hearing my heels click on the marble floors, having the sales clerks wait on me. Shopping for the clothes, buying them, wearing them—it all made me feel like *somebody,* and I guess it still does.

I was opening charge accounts all over the place—from any department store or bank that would give them to me. The funny thing was that I was buying all these clothes and feeling good about wearing designer labels, but I still didn't feel pretty. I'd look at myself in the mirror in a high-priced David Meister dress or Versace suit, and all I could think about was how it would look better if my breasts were larger or my thighs were thinner. How I'd be more attractive in my Eileen Fisher jacket if my cheekbones were more pronounced. I was on a high after my lip reduction surgery, but it didn't last long. Fixing my lips had made me feel so good—I wasn't a freak anymore—but I wasn't pretty either. It was going to take more than a lip reduction to make me into a beautiful woman. It was only a short time after my first surgery that I was back at the surgeon's office inquiring about another. I had saved for years to pay for my lip surgery (and paid for it in cash) but, during that process, I learned that most plastic surgeons will let you finance your surgery the same way you might finance a new car or a new washing machine. And so it began—my slow descent into debt to pay for plastic surgery and high fashion.

Sitting outside the Burberry store on a bench overlooking the atrium, I'm trying to come up with some way to raise the money for my buttock implants. I could pick up a second job, but that wouldn't be a very expedient way of raising money. I could sell something. But I don't really have anything to sell, except maybe my car, which would be hard to do without. Maybe I could ask for an advance on my salary, I consider, and, as I'm sitting on the bench looking withdrawn and sad, a sharply dressed black man takes a seat next to me.

"Rough day?" he asks with a kind voice.

"Ah . . . . Yeah, sort of." I look him over. He's quite handsome with short-clipped hair and a neatly trimmed goatee. His suit is to die for—probably Hugo Boss or Corneliani. At first I think he must be wealthy. Then I think about myself and the designer suit I'm wearing, and how a church mouse has more money to her name than I do at the present moment. He could be front'n, just like me.

"Care to talk about it?"

I smile. "No. Thanks," I say. "I really should get going," I add, and lift myself from the bench.

"Okay. You have a nice day."

"You too," I respond and start to make my way down the corridor. I guess he was hitting on me. Men seem to do that from time to time. For some odd reason, some of them find me attractive. I think some of them even find me sexy. And maybe, at first glance, I do look pretty to them. I'm assuming that the brother I just left on the bench had an initial attraction to me, but he probably changed his mind when I stood up, and he saw my flat ass. It would be nice to go out on a date with a man . . . to be intimate with a man, but I'm just not ready. I don't feel right about myself yet. Of course, I've *been* with men. It's not like I'm a virgin or something. I didn't really have any boyfriends in high school, but I dated some in college. I went to the University of Georgia in Athens, about an hour outside of Atlanta. My scholarship covered my room and board, so I was able to live on campus my entire four years there. I had been a bit of a recluse in high school and spent most of those days trying to draw as little attention to myself as possible. When I left for college I swore to myself that I was going to be more outgoing. I didn't want to spend another four years fading into the woodwork. I was still self-conscious about my lips, but by the time I graduated high school my peers had matured a bit, most of the adolescent teasing had stopped, and my self-esteem started to improve, if only slightly.

I got lucky and ended up with a wonderful college roommate. Her name was Addie. She was from Savannah and a complete extrovert, which ended up being really good for me. I joined a few campus groups to try and make some friends, but it was really Addie who gave me an "in" to an actual social life. There was always someone in our dorm room—someone Addie had met during class or in the cafeteria or just in the hallway. She had a multitude of social invitations to choose from every weekend and always insisted that I come along with her. Thanks to Addie, I went to parties and barbeques and dances, and I met new people from all over the country. I'll always be thankful to her for helping to pull me out of my shell, but there is one thing I will never forgive her for: labeling me with a nickname that stuck with me for my entire college career. One night we were at a party, we had all been drinking, and, out of the blue, she called me "Lips." I'll never forget it—she was standing next to me about to walk outside to the keg and said, "Hey 'Lips,' you want another beer?" I know she was just being silly; she had nicknames for everyone. She called our friend Paula, "Chaka" because she had big hair like Chaka Khan, she called our friend Denise, "Neesey-Nose" because she had a big nose, and she even labeled herself "Nappy" as her hair could often be out of control. Her intention wasn't to hurt my feelings, and I'm sure she never had any idea how self-conscious I was about my lips, but it still threw me for loop when she said it—it took me back to being a kid and hearing all the evil taunts. And the worse thing about it was that the nickname stuck—before I knew it, it was like Kamille was no longer my name. Everyone just called me Lips, like it was a cute nickname. I guess I eventually got used to it, but I never liked it, and there were times when I just wanted to scream, "My name is *Kamille*! Stop calling me Lips!" No one seemed to realize that it bothered me, and if I protested, people would realize how insecure I was, so I always kept myself in check.

In addition to inviting me along on all her outings, Addie made it her personal mission to find me a boyfriend. She was cute and had a nice figure so there was always a hardy supply of college boys looking to take her out, more than she could handle, really. She was more than happy to send some of her admirers my way, and to my surprise, many of them didn't seem to mind being punted off to me. I wanted to believe that the guys she set me up with really liked me and were attracted to me, but I had a hard time convincing myself that they were anything more than horny twenty-year-olds who would take what ever they could get if it meant getting laid. I met a lot of guys through Addie and had a few brief relationships, but it wasn't until I met Kent Marshall during my senior year that I had my first serious boyfriend. We met at a party and seemed to hit it off right away. He wasn't the best-looking guy I'd ever seen, and he was overweight, but he had the nicest smile, and we just seemed to click for some reason. I really liked him, so I figured I try to stretch things out a bit and not sleep with him right away, like I did with many of the guys I met in college (hey, college guys weren't the only ones who got horny). When I finally did sleep with him after a few weeks of dating, I was honestly a bit surprised when he still pursued a relationship with me. I was so used to guys disappearing after I gave up the goods that his continued interest took me by surprise.

Over the next few months we continued to date and things started to get more serious. We spent several nights together during the week and always spent the weekends together. I started to develop a comfort level with Kent and finally started to believe that a man could actually like me and be attracted to me. We were still together by the time we graduated and, although we never talked about it, I don't think getting engaged was out of the realm of possibility. But following graduation everything changed—everything changed because of one thing . . . one procedure—I had surgery on my lips to have them shaped and reduced.

I worked part-time jobs throughout my four years in school and had been putting away money every two weeks to save for the surgery. I never told anyone about my plans, but I spent many hours researching the procedure, looking up doctors, and estimating the cost of a lip reduction. It wasn't until days before the surgery that I told anyone, including Kent, about my plans to go under the knife, and their reactions made me realize that I had done a much better job of camouflaging my low self-esteem than I thought. Everyone was surprised by my decision and seemed to have no idea that I was at all bothered by the way I looked.

Kent was supportive and went with my mother and me to the hospital the day of my surgery and was sure to visit and bring me magazines and videos when I was recuperating. I really appreciated his commitment to me and I guess, in some way, I really did love him, but once the healing process was over and, for the first time in my life, I felt like I looked normal, I began to yearn for freedom from Kent. I felt like a new person, and to be honest . . . I hate to admit this, but I think I decided that, now that I wasn't a freak, maybe I could do better than Kent. It was only a couple months after my surgery that Kent and I broke up, and I was single again. At first I thought I would immediately start dating again, but even though I felt that my appearance was greatly improved, I still didn't feel like I was complete. I didn't think I was hideous anymore, but I didn't think I was pretty either. Subconsciously, I think I made a decision that I wasn't going to seriously re-enter the dating pool until I felt like I was "finished." And I guess I'm still in a holding pattern now. I'm not ready to seek out a boyfriend or a husband. Some men do seem to find me alluring, but I need to feel beautiful myself before I'll be comfortable getting close to a man, and I think I'm almost there. If only I could come up with the money to have my backside enhanced. Maybe then I'll be ready.

# 30

# Brenda

The seminar has finally wrapped up and throughout most of the second half I found myself unable to pay attention as Dr. Radcliff did a presentation on forehead lifts, eyelid surgery, rhinoplasty, and facial implants. I sat through most of the discussion in a daze, preoccupied with that necklace I saw around Jazelle's neck. I kept trying to visualize what the one I found in Jim's car looked like—the exact color of the bear, the placement of the sapphire on its belly . . . or was it a rhinestone? I kept telling myself how silly I was being. For all I know there's an entire rack of those necklaces at Target or Wal-mart. Sometimes, really ugly things are considered stylish. As I sat through the presentation, I thought of all the hideous things women have worn just because they were in style—I thought about leg-warmers and parachute pants and poet shirts and acid wash jeans. Maybe tacky teddy bear necklaces are all the rage like those yellow Lance Armstrong bracelets I used to see so many people wearing. I mean *really?* What are the chances of that necklace having been given to her by my . . . I can't even think it. It's just too ridiculous! My husband is not having an. . . . He can't be involved with. . . . I'm being so silly. The whole idea is clearly insane!

I follow Jazelle out of the ballroom and through the wide hallway toward the exit. When I get outside I see her about to light another cigarette. On any other night I would have waited until I got to my car to light up, but I'm too damn curious about the necklace, so I walk over and join her.

"Hey," I say, trying to look friendly.

"Hi. So what did you think of tonight's presentation?"

"I enjoyed it. I'm not sure I'm really up to having anything done just yet, but it was informative."

"Yeah. I'm still deciding myself. I'd love to get some of this fat sucked out." She pats her belly and then her cheeks. "And it'd be nice to have my eyes done. But, you know, I'm afraid. Suppose he messes up, and I end up looking like Marie Osmond or Patrick Swayze . . . like I'm in chronic state of surprise."

I laugh. "Yeah that would be a bit scary," I reply, before eyeing the necklace. "That necklace you have on, it's quite unique."

"Oh, this thing?" She chuckles. "I kind of wore it as joke today. I wanted to show some friends at work what awful taste the guy I'm seeing has in jewelry. Isn't it the ugliest thing you've ever seen?"

"I don't know. It's kind of cute. So your boyfriend gave it to you?" I prod.

"Yeah . . . well he's not really my boyfriend . . . more like a . . . a *gentleman* friend. It's complicated."

"Really?"

"Yeah. He's married. We just have a little thing going on the side," she says with no detectable shame whatsoever.

My heart starts to thump after hearing what she just said. What kind of person tells a complete stranger that she's having an affair with a married man?

"This is so awful," she says. "This necklace was actually a gift for his wife. It was their anniversary. Can you believe he wanted to give *this thing* to his wife for their anniversary?"

I try to smile as I feel my pulse racing and my hands starting to tremble. "For their anniversary? Really?" is all I can manage to say.

"Yeah. He showed it to me, and I was like 'no, sweetie, you can't show up to your anniversary dinner with some tacky-assed teddy bear on a chain.' I helped him pick out something much nicer for her—a little three stone diamond necklace from a jeweler near his office."

As soon as the words come out of her mouth I clutch the collar of my coat to be sure to hide the very necklace she is referring too. "That's interesting that you would help him pick out something for his wife," I say, trying to hide my distress.

"Not really. I don't have it in for her. She's the one who has to put up with him on a regular basis. I figure she deserved a decent anniversary. Can you believe that in addition to this piece of crap necklace, he had planned to take her to The Olive Garden to celebrate?"

"The Olive Garden?"

"Yeah. I nixed that idea as well. I told him he better take her someplace nice. And do you know what he said? He said 'Well, what about Chili's?' *Chili's!?* I mean does this man have *any* class? I think that's one of the things I like about him—he's so clueless. I ended up having to give him some suggestions of a few nice places to go."

I can't believe she used the same word to describe my husband as I have for almost twenty years. I can't believe this woman standing before me was responsible for the necklace I received on my anniversary. I can't believe she was responsible for the restaurant that I received it in. I can't believe she's having an affair with my husband!

# 31

# Brenda

I'm on my way home from the seminar. I'm in the sniper-mobile puffing away on a cigarette. I'm still shaking, and I can feel my heart pounding inside my chest. I'm not sure what I'm feeling. Is it sadness or rage? Or is it mostly shock? My husband is cheating on me! How can my husband be cheating on me? I thought he was a good man, an honest man. How can this be happening?!

I'm on the Interstate heading toward Sterling when the hodge-podge of thoughts running through my head is interrupted by a long wail on a horn while a car passes me on the right and the driver gives me an angry glare. I look down at the speedometer and see that I'm going twenty-five miles an hour in the left lane of a major highway. I shift over to the right lane and step on the gas.

You read about this stuff and see it on soap operas and HBO, but you never really think it will happen to you. The signs have been there—all the late nights "at work," the hint of perfume I smelled on Jim a couple of weeks ago, him falling asleep as soon as we got home from our anniversary dinner . . . an anniversary dinner that was just a charade. My husband's lover had planned the entire evening. She picked out my gift and took my teddy bear necklace for herself. I keep getting these flashes in my head of the teddy bear necklace draped over Jazelle's bosom. I see it nestled in her middle-aged cleavage with its little diamond eyes staring at me. And, then, out of the blue, it's no longer the necklace I see between her breasts—it's my husband, his head nuzzled in her chest. I see them naked together, their bodies tangled around each other. The vision makes me sick, and I instantly feel nauseous.

"Oh no!" I cry out as I pull over onto the shoulder and hurry out of the car. I rush over to the grassy area next to the highway and before I know what's happening, my stomach fiercely contracts, and I vomit on the side of the road. With my eyes watering and the taste of bile in my mouth, I stand on the side of Interstate 66 with car after car whizzing by me, their red taillights a blur in my teary eyes. And I stand there and I stand there and I stand there until, like a burst of energy, I feel my face tighten and my mouth drop. My knees feel weak, I let myself drop to the ground, and I cry. I cry so hard my whole body shakes.

"How did this happen?" I call out breathlessly. "How did this happen!?" I can't stop the rush of thoughts: Am I that awful? Do I look that haggard that my husband has to cheat on me? Am I that bad in bed? I'm sitting on the side of the road, paralyzed by a feeling I can't put into words. I've stopped crying, but I can't seem to do anything but sit on the side of the road and stare at the ground. I don't want to move. I don't want to go home. I don't want to face this! I want to do what I've been doing for months—ignoring the whole thing and pretending that everything is okay.

I'm still in a trance when someone in a passing car hits his brakes and pulls off the road in front of my car. I see the taillights backing up toward me, and I'm not even scared. I think a part of me actually hopes that a murderer will jump out of the car and put me out of my misery. I sit there and watch as an older gentleman gets out of his vehicle and walks over toward me.

"Are you okay?" he asks with kind eyes.

I wipe my eyes and quickly get up from the ground. "Yes . . . yes, I'm fine. I had to stop to. . . ." I don't know what to say. How do I explain sitting hopelessly on the side of an interstate highway. "Thank you for stopping . . . thanks for your concern. Really . . . I'm fine," I say as I walk back to my car.

"Are you sure?" he asks as I open the door.

I'm so NOT fine. "Yes. Thank you." I get inside, and offer a clumsy wave before I pull back on the freeway. I wipe my eyes again and try to make sense of everything. I try to figure out how this happened, and what I'm going to do about it, but I can't be logical. All I can think about is my husband with that woman, and, the more I think about it, the more anger starts to boil inside me. How could Jim do this me? How could he do this to our family? We have a daughter and a house and a life! That bastard! I'll destroy him—destroy him!

By the time I pull into the driveway, I'm ripe with rage and disgust. I don't even care that our daughter is home. I'm going to blast through the front door and confront him. When I come into the house Jim is on the sofa watching television and, for a moment, I just look at him, knowing that I will never see him the same way again. Then I walk in front of him and click off the TV. I look at him again, about to burst, about to tell him off—to tell him that I know about his whore. I'm about to scream, but when I open my mouth, all I can say is, "It's late. Let's go to bed."

Jim looks at me with a perplexed expression. "You okay?" he asks.

"Yeah . . . just tired." I walk past him toward the steps. When I get upstairs I change into a nightshirt and crawl into bed. When Jim comes into the bedroom my back is facing his side of the mattress. I listen to him get undressed—the sound of his watch hitting the top of the dresser, his belt buckle clinking undone, the rustle of him slipping out of his pants. These bed-time sounds used to reassure me—they made me feel safe and comfortable. Now they just make me sick—now that they belong to someone other than me. I feel the mattress jiggle as he climbs into bed, and my body tightens. If he touches me, I think I will scream and, for once, I'm glad that that stupid dog has hopped up onto the bed and lain down between us, creating a welcome barrier.

I'm on my side, and I hear Jim's breathing and the occasional snort from Helga's nose. I stare at the digital clock on the nightstand, watching as 11:22 flips to 11:23.

Why didn't I confront him? Why didn't I say anything about Jazelle and his affair? On the way home I was set to go off on him—to tell him that I know what a dirty bastard he is, to tell him how disgusted I am, to tell him how much I want to beat him to a pulp. But when I walked into the house and saw him lying on the sofa, it hit me that there was one thing I was not ready to tell him—I was not prepared to tell him that I want a divorce. Jim and I share a life together—maybe it's humdrum and bland, but we've been together for almost twenty years. We have Jodie and a house and friends . . . even this God-awful dog. The idea of being a thirty-six-year-old single mother terrifies me. I have no way of knowing what Jim's reaction would have been if I had confronted him. Maybe he would have begged for my forgiveness, or maybe he would have been glad that I found out, so that it would finally be out in the open, and he could get out of our marriage. Wouldn't it be easy for him to run off with Jazelle and leave me alone to raise a daughter? Isn't that what men want—to be free of family obligations?

I can't help but wonder what my role in all of this was. Did I bring Jim's affair on myself? I certainly haven't been the most attentive wife in the world, but I'm just as attentive to him as he is to me. We're both busy, and we're so tired by the time we get home from work, we barely have energy to eat dinner and veg-out in front of the TV. I know our sex life hasn't been the greatest lately, but we're intimate at least once a week—that's not so bad for a busy working couple who've been married for sixteen years . . . is it? Maybe it's the way I look. Have I let myself go that much? Lord knows I've put on weight over the years, but so has Jim, although everyone knows we live in a society where it is more acceptable for men to let themselves go than for women. We're supposed to put up with ever-expanding beer bellies, but men are not as tolerant of their women's bodies going to hell.

I start to think of these plastic surgery lectures I've been going to, and, once again, I wonder if maybe surgery would be an answer for me. Would Jim lose this need to sleep with another woman if I lost some of this fat around my midsection? If I had my breasts lifted? Maybe I could get my face freshened up a little bit. From the slides the doctor showed us at the seminar, cheeks implants could take years off my face.

As I try to fall asleep just to escape the pain I'm feeling, I begin to picture how I would look after some liposuction, some cheek implants, maybe a forehead lift. Would Jim stop seeing Jazelle, if I get myself into better shape? Would he lose this need to break our marriage vows if I had some plastic surgery?

I hear Jim breathing next to me and suddenly, as he often does, he starts to snore. He usually only snores when he's lying on his back, so when he starts with the annoying sounds I generally jostle him awake and ask him to lie on his side. But right now, as I lie beside him, I can't bear the thought of touching him. So I just listen to the sound of a buzz saw coming from his nose, a noise that usually only irritates me, but now, on this night, I find it infuriating. And, before I know what I'm doing, I turn my head and yell, "Stop it!"

Jim jerks and opens his eyes. "What?" he says to me in a bit of daze.

I collect myself. "You were snoring. Turn on your side," I say calmly.

Jim turns over and shuts his eyes, oblivious to my unease. I, on the other hand, continue to stare into the darkness, unable to clear my mind. I think about so many things. Why did Jim do this? What did I do to deserve this? How will this affect our daughter? What does he do when he's with Jazelle? I think about so many things, but mostly, I wonder what I'm going to do now that I know the truth—what, in God's name, am I going to do?

# 32

# Nora

I'm sitting in a soft leather chair in Dr. Radcliff's waiting room. I've filled out some paperwork, and now I'm just looking around. I've never seen a doctor's waiting room like this before. There are shiny hardwood floors, leather chairs, artwork highlighted with soft spot lights, some sort of textured beige paint on the walls, and fresh flowers to the side of the reception counter. There's one other patient in the room with me, and I wonder if she's trying to figure out what I'm here for—the same thing I'm wondering about her. She's hard to figure out. She's a little younger than me, and I can't find any obvious imperfections. Her face looks youthful, her nose is well-proportioned to her face, and her body looks fit as well. Maybe she's already had something done, and she's here for a follow-up appointment.

I'm about to pick up a magazine when I hear a door open and see Dr. Radcliff poke his head into the waiting room.

"Ms. Perez?"

"That's me," I say as I get up and walk toward him.

"Nice to meet you," he says, extending his hand. "I'm Dr. Radcliff." He gestures for me to follow him down the hallway.

"I know. I was at one of your seminars."

"You were? Wonderful. I'm glad you decided to come in for a consultation," he says, closing the door to the examining room. "Please have a seat."

I sit down and wait while he reviews my paperwork. I look at him while he's reading. He looks just as dapper as he did at the seminar. I don't usually get nervous around men, but for some reason, my stomach is in knots. There's something very surreal about coming into a doctor's office to inquire about having major surgery for the sake of vanity.

Dr. Radcliff appears to be in his early forties, which I find comforting. I'm glad he's older than me, even if only by a little bit. It doesn't seem like it was that long ago when I could just expect that any professional I dealt with would be older than I am. It used to be that whenever I met with a lawyer or a doctor or a chiropractor, they were always my senior. But, more and more, I've been finding them to be younger than I am. Last month, when I went to complete the final paperwork to refinance my condo, I just assumed the mortgage broker would be older than me, and, honestly, I was somewhat taken aback when I was greeted by a guy who was still in his twenties. I went to see a new dentist a few weeks ago, and she was barely over thirty. It's just weird. I guess it's one of the reasons I'm here.

"So you're in good health?" he asks, closing my file.

"Yes."

"No current medications?"

"Nope."

"And you're not allergic to any drugs?"

"No."

"Okay," he says and takes a seat himself, "so what brings you in today?"

I wrote down the procedures I was interested in on the paperwork, and, for some reason, I wish he would bring them up rather than making me say what I want out loud. "Well, I found your presentation interesting, and I've been doing some research on my own. I thought I might benefit from having some work on my eyes and maybe some cheek implants, but I don't want to overdo it." I feel ridiculous telling him that I want my eyes lifted and cheeks plumped up. It sounds so vain and selfish—wanting to spend thousands of dollars to take a few years off my face when people in the world are starving. Maybe I am vain and selfish. Actually, I *know* I'm vain and selfish, but a chica's got to do what a chica's got to do.

"Let's talk about the eyes first. What is it you're looking to change about them?"

"The lid area has gotten a little baggy over the years," I say, before touching the area below my eyes. "And there's a little puffiness down here I'd like to get rid of."

"Can you close your eyes for me?" he asks.

I shut my eyes, and then I feel him pinching the skin of my upper eyelid. Then he starts pressing on my eye through the closed lid.

"Okay," he says, and I open my eyes, "I can remove some of the extra skin with blepharoplasty."

"Blepharoplasty?"

"Just a medical term for eyelid surgery," he says, before adding, "And we can remove some of the fat under your eyes to reduce the puffiness. For the upper eyelids we'll make an incision along the natural crease in your lid, and it will pretty much be undetectable once it heals. To remove some of the fat from the lower lid, I can make an incision on the inside of the eyelid, so there's no chance of visible scarring."

I nod as he continues talking. "There are some risks involved, and I'll give you detailed literature on all the procedures you're interested in, but we do everything we can to minimize any risks. There's a small possibility of having visual disturbances, which, if it happens, is usually temporary. Sometimes patients have issues with dry eyes, and, very rarely, patients may have trouble closing their eyes. There's a tiny . . . *miniscule* chance of blindness—"

"Blindness!?"

"It's very rare . . . very, very rare. It occurs in less than one in ten thousand patients, but it is a risk that you need to be aware of. When we remove fat from underneath your eye, bleeding can occur behind the eyeball and push it outward, which creates pressure on the retina—that's what can cause blindness. But, I'll tell you, I've probably done about a thousand of these procedures, and this has never happened to one of my patients."

"Okay," I say, finding his words somewhat reassuring. "Do you have to knock me out to do the surgery?"

He laughs. "Well we don't *knock out* our patients for any surgery. We can do eyelid surgery under sedation anesthesia, which doesn't put you in the same type of deep sleep as general anesthesia and has less risk. But if you decide to have additional procedures, we may have to opt for the general anesthesia."

"How about the recovery period?"

"Eyelid surgery doesn't usually cause extreme discomfort. We'll give you a prescription for any pain. Of course, you'll have some swelling and redness and possibly some bruising, but after a couple of weeks you can usually hide any lingering effects with make-up until you're completely healed, which usually takes three to six weeks."

I go on to ask several more questions and, quite frankly, I'm amazed at how patient Dr. Radcliff is with me. He responds to all my inquiries and seems to be taking his time, which is not something I'm used to from doctors. Most of them are always in such a rush. Maybe when you don't have to deal with insurance companies and HMOs you actually have time to spend with your patients.

After he's given me the lowdown on the eyelid surgery we move on to the cheek implants. He tells me all about this procedure, including the risks, and even shows me an actual implant. Apparently, he can use the same incision made to suck the fat from underneath my eye to insert the cheek implants. He goes over everything and, once again, answers a bunch of questions, which really makes me feel comfortable with him as a surgeon. I've already thoroughly checked him out. I called the Agency for Healthcare Administration to check on his license, and I also checked on his malpractice history, using a doctor background investigation service on the Web. Everything came back okay, so I was fairly confident in him as surgeon to begin with, but it's such an added bonus to have someone that I can talk to, and who I know will answer my questions.

I think we're about to wrap up when he asks, "Do you have any interest in me straightening out your nose?"

"My nose?"

"Yes. I only noticed it because that's what I do for living. It's very subtle."

"Hmmm." My nose was broken when I was born and has listed just a hint to the right ever since. It's so slight I only notice it myself when I really study my face in the mirror, but, nonetheless, it might not be such a bad idea to have it corrected. "What would that involve?" I ask, and Dr. Radcliff settles in to give me yet another procedural overview. It must be mind-numbing to describe these surgeries over and over again, but you wouldn't know it from the way he's talking. He doesn't act as if he's put out or as if he's doing me a favor by spending time with me. Seems a shame that I'm actually surprised when a doctor doesn't act like it's my privilege to be receiving his services.

After all is said and done I've acquired a wealth of knowledge about eyelid surgery, cheek implants, and nose jobs. Dr. Radcliff does a brief examination, suggests that I take my time, think about what we talked about, and then call to schedule the procedures at a later date. But, I don't take his advice. After I've thanked him and said good-bye I walk right out to the receptionist and schedule my surgery.

# 33

## Brenda

"Jesus Christ! Would you *shut up!*" I yell at Helga, who's been barking incessantly since I got home from work. I'm sitting at the kitchen table, and she's over at the French doors yapping toward the backyard. There's nothing out there but, as usual, that doesn't make any difference to Helga. She's still barking like some invaders are marching across the patio. I'm always reading about how dogs are supposed to be good for their owners—they help them live longer and lower their blood pressure. Why did I manage to get the only dog that does nothing but increase my stress level?

I have the laptop in front of me, and I'm trying to pay a few bills online, but it's hard to focus with Helga yelping at the back door. I suppose I can't blame my lack of concentration on the dog—it was only yesterday that I found out about Jim's affair, and I've had trouble thinking of anything else ever since. My mind teems with all these thoughts, and I have no idea how to deal with the situation. Part of me wishes I had exploded in front of him when I got home last night so it would all be out in the open, and we could deal with it. But another part of me is glad that I restrained myself. What if I *had* brought it up, and he had asked me for a divorce? What if he had said he was leaving? What would I have done then?

I hit the dropdown menu on the computer screen and scroll through to find the link to my bank's Web site. As I'm searching,

I see some long, involved URL with the words "mail," and "ya-hoo," and "login" mixed in the hodgepodge that makes up the complete Web address. I don't recognize it, so I go ahead and click on it. A log-in page for *Yahoo! Mail* comes up. And the user-name field has been auto completed. It says JamesHarrison1970, my husband's name and his birth year. I'm not even halfway through asking myself why Jim would open a *Yahoo!* e-mail ac-count when we already have e-mail through our cable Internet provider when I realize the answer. He wants a separate account with which to communicate with his whore.

I start frantically typing passwords into the password field, trying to get into the account. I try his birthday, and the last four digits of our phone number, and his mother's maiden name, but nothing works.

"Damn it!" I yell, and pound on the key board. I want to start crying. I just can't take it. I can't take my husband having an affair. I can't take him being a liar. I can't take him being so sneaky as to open up a new e-mail account. And I certainly can't take this damn dog ranting at the back door!

I try to compose myself, get up from the table, and walk over to the refrigerator. "Come here, Helga," I say, once I open the refrigerator door. She generally won't come when I call her, but if she thinks there's a chance she'll get food out of the deal, she usually complies.

"Yum! Cheese," I say to Helga as I take the plastic off a slice of American cheese. Then I walk over to the other side of the kitchen, open the cabinet, and take out a package of Benadryl while Helga wags her tail at my feet in anticipation of her treat. I open the package, wrap a single tablet in the piece of cheese, and feed it to the dog. She gobbles it down and heads back to the door to continue her barking tirade, which, with the help of a drowsiness-inducing antihistamine, should be over in about fifteen minutes. Thank God!

I go back to the computer and try some more passwords. I try my name, our daughter's name, my maiden name. Nothing works. Then I turn and look at the stupid dog, who's still trying her best to get on my last nerve, and it hits me—I type in the word "Helga" and, next thing you know, I have access to Jim's inbox, which of course, I click on and open. There's only one message, and it's from DCJazzyJazelle. I can feel my mouth going dry as I click on it.

Sorry you couldn't make it the other night. But I understand that things happen in our situation. I miss you!
Hugs,
Jazelle

As I read the words, benign as they are, I can feel my ears get hot and my eyes start to water.

"What's the matter?"

I look up from the screen, and Jodie is standing on the kitchen threshold. I didn't hear her come down the stairs.

"Nothing," I say, trying to switch gears and straighten up. "Ah . . . Nora sent me an e-mail about . . . ah . . . about these kids in Africa. And it just got to me . . . you know," I lie, forcing my face into a neutral expression.

"You're so emotional," Jodie says with a kind laugh. "If only Rwanda and the Congo sat on a bunch of oil reserves. Then George Bush and his band of crackpot Christians could pretend to give a crap about the suffering of children and the tyranny over there. But then I guess they'd just heap naked Rwandans on top of each other and intimidate them with vicious dogs instead of the Iraqis."

"What?" I ask. I heard words coming out of her mouth, but my mind was elsewhere.

"Nothing," she says. "You almost ready to go?"

"Go?"

"Yeah. It's Thursday. Basketball practice?"

"Oh yeah. I forgot. Let me get my purse." I get up from the table, actually thankful for the momentary diversion from my preoccupation with Jim and Jazelle.

"Can I drive?" Jodie asks me.

"I guess," I say, trying to hide my apprehension. Jodie got her learner's permit last month, so she's always eager to be behind the wheel. We head out to the car and get inside.

"When are you going to get rid of this thing?" she asks as she takes the keys from me and starts the car.

"Um . . . what?" I say, still distracted.

"What's the matter? You've been walking around in a stupor since you got home from work."

"Nothing. Work is just busy, and I guess it's distracting me." I resign myself to putting on a brave face for my daughter's sake. "But enough about that. What's going on with you? How are things at school?' There I go with the school question again.

"Fine," she says as we head out of the neighborhood.

"The speed limit is twenty-five through here."

"I know," she says as we approach a stop sign where our residential street meets a main road.

"You have to make sure you come to a complete stop at stop signs, Jodie. You rolled through that one."

"I did not. I stopped."

"Not *completely*. You can get a ticket if you don't stop completely."

"So, I'm still trying to come up with an idea for a business to start for Economics class." Jodie is doing what she always does when I start telling her how to drive—she's changing the subject, which I guess isn't such a bad thing. At least we're communicating.

"Have you thought of anything yet?"

"I was thinking that I could shoplift a bunch of stuff from Target and then sell it on eBay." She turns and looks at me with a grin. "I'm *kidding*. Jeesh, you're so serious all the time," she says with a laugh. She's always enjoyed saying things to get under my skin. "Not that it'd be hard, though. They make all their employees wear those bright red shirts. You can see them coming out of the corner of your eye from a mile away, which gives you plenty of time to slip a CD or pair of socks into your pocket."

"Jodie, please tell me you don't shoplift from Target."

She laughs. "You're so easy," she says, still laughing. "I was also thinking that maybe I could whore out some of those Barbie doll wannabees in my class. They're all sluts anyway. They may as well get paid for it, and I could take a cut of their fees."

She looks at me for a reaction, and I have an odd urge not to play the prude. "Hmm. I think twenty percent is the going rate for pimps these days. Be sure you charge at least that much," I say, much to my surprise and hers.

Jodie laughs some more, and then I laugh too, but my general anxiousness gets the best of me, and I have to ask. "You were kidding, right?"

Jodie looks disappointed that my brief moment of freewheeling is already over. "Yes, Mom. I'm kidding," she says as we pull into the parking lot at the rec center. Jodie puts the car in park, grabs her bag from the back seat, and starts to get out of the car.

"Pick you up at nine?"

"Okay," she says.

"Love you," I say just before the door slams shut.

I slide over to the driver's side, and, as I watch Jodie walk into the building, I feel very alone. The car is quiet and cold. For a moment, I sit behind the steering wheel and stare out the window. I can't help but think of the e-mail from Jazelle sitting up on the screen of the computer. I knew it was happening. I knew my husband had broken our trust. But, somehow, seeing it in writing makes it so much more real. My husband is an adulterer. Jazelle is the other women. And I'm . . . well, I don't know what the hell I am anymore.

# 34

## Kamille

"No, Mama. I'm not calling for money. I was just calling to see how you and Daddy are doing," I lie into the phone. I was calling for money, but I can tell from the tone in my mother's voice that's there's no point in asking.

"Good. Cause you know me and your daddy ain't got nothin' left to give you, child." My mother's an educated woman. She teaches third grade at an elementary school outside Atlanta, but she starts talking like Missy Elliott, saying things like "ain't," and "nothin'," and "child" when she's trying to sound tough or teach me a lesson.

"I know. I know. Can't I just call to say hello?" I respond, wishing that Daddy had answered the phone. He may not have been willing to wire me any cash either, but he would have been much less accusing.

"Sure you can. It's just that you *never* do," she replies, back to sounding like her normal self.

"Well I'm starting."

"I'm glad to hear that." Her tone softens. "How are things in D.C.?"

"Good. My new job is working out really well. I love my new apartment." All lies. Everyone hates me at work, and I hate this raggedy-assed apartment. The only reason I rented it was because it was the one place that would approve me to be a tenant due to my poor credit scores. I really didn't have much choice. I needed to get out of Atlanta, and D.C. was the only city in which my old company had another office for me to transfer to. Things had gotten bad in Atlanta before I left . . . really bad. I'd managed to alienate most of my friends, and my parents were barely speaking to me. If people didn't have it in for me because I owed them money, they were on my case about having surgery, as if they have any right to be all up in my business.

My friends and family were supportive of me when I had my lips done, and when I went back in a few months later to have my ears pinned and cheek implants put in, they were still okay with it. But reactions started to get a bit chillier when I mentioned I was having abdomen liposuction some time later. No one said anything *really* negative. I just got a lot of raised eyebrows, and my mother expressed some concern that maybe I was taking "this surgery thing" too far. So you can see why I kept it to myself when I decided to have some work done on my eyes. The one person I informed about it was my friend Tia, and the only reason I told her was because I needed someone to pick me up and take me home. I tried to keep the surgery from my mother, but we lived near each other, and it was rare that we went more than a few days at a time without seeing each other. She knew something was up when I hadn't been by the house in over a week. She took it upon herself to check up on me, and when she stopped by I was still recovering, and there was no hiding what I had done. My eyelids always looked droopy to me, and I think one drooped a bit more than the other. I had them lifted, so I would look more alert and more attractive, but I guess I thought that the change might be subtle enough that my mother wouldn't be able to pinpoint exactly what was different about me when I finally revealed myself to her after the surgery.

When she realized that I had had more work done, she was furious. And I guess I can't blame her. Not only had I kept the surgery from her, it didn't take her long to figure out that the three thousand dollars I "needed" to borrow from her and Daddy wasn't for a graduate course. She swore she would never loan me any money again and, once she calmed down, she started pestering me about getting some counseling and berating me for taking chances with my health for the sake of looking good.

Obviously, I couldn't go back to my parents for money when I decided to get my teeth capped. I had never really thought about getting anything done to my teeth. Honestly, they weren't really in bad shape. They were fairly straight and reasonably white, but when I saw all the stuff that could be done to improve them on shows like *Extreme Makeover* and *The Swan* I couldn't help myself. By this time, my credit cards were really starting to push their maximums and, with my parents having cut me off, I didn't have much choice but to look to my friends to loan me the money. And, honestly, I did plan to pay them back . . . I *do* plan to pay them back, but you start to test your friends' patience when you owe them hundreds or thousands of dollars and they see you showing up to a social event in a new designer dress.

By the time I decided to have my breasts done, I was running out of relationships that weren't tainted by outstanding loans. Not to mention that my mama went off on me like a bat out of hell when she found out I was getting implants. I listened to her rant and rave for more than hour about the risks of breast implants, the cost, how it was demeaning to women—especially *black* women. Things in Atlanta had reached a boiling point, and I knew I had to get out of there before it got any worse, so I applied for a transfer to D.C. Unfortunately, only three months after I got here, my company downsized by twenty percent, and I was let go with a pathetic severance package. Luckily, I landed on my feet at Saunders and Kraff only a few weeks later. But even with steady, high-paying employment, I have no idea how I will come up with the money to pay for my buttock implants.

"Good," Mama says. "I'm happy that things are working out up there. I hope you're more settled there and more . . ." she flounders for a moment, ". . . more *together*. And that you don't feel such a need to change yourself . . . the way you look."

"I am, Mama. I'm very happy," I say. "Can I talk to Daddy?"

"Sure," she says. "Love you," she adds. Then she lowers the phone.

"Now, don't you be givin' that girl no money," I hear her say to Daddy before she hands him the phone. It's comforting to know that it's not just me she starts talking all common to when she's trying to sound intimidating.

# 35

## Brenda

I'm sitting in the back of the ballroom at the Hilton for the third and final plastic surgery forum. I think tonight's topics are breast augmentation and liposuction. As I sit here, my eyes keep darting toward the door to see when *she* walks in. It's been a week since I found out that my husband has been unfaithful. I've been sitting on this information for seven days, and I've yet to tell a soul about it. The night I found out, I was certain I would go straight home and confront Jim—see what he had to say for himself. But when I came through the door and saw him lying on the sofa watching the news, something changed. I remember flicking off the television. I remember being about to burst with anger and betrayal, but after I turned the TV off and saw the bemused look in his eyes, I lost my nerve. I was suddenly terrified. I realized that if I told him I knew about his affair, my life would change forever—my life, his life, our daughter's life would all change forever. Everything I was about to say about him cheating on me, about our marriage vows, about the pain and disgust I was feeling was swallowed down the back of my throat.

This past week has been a nightmare. Knowing something like this . . . being on edge for seven days straight can really start to weigh on a person. It's so hard to live with a man you don't even want to look at—to wonder where his hands have been, his arms, his lips. When he calls me to tell me he's working late, I wonder if she's sitting there next to him. Is she nuzzling his neck while he talks on the phone? Are they naked together while he tells me that he's overwhelmed at the office and won't be home until late?

I've been telling everyone that I don't feel well . . . that I have the flu, to try and explain my general withdrawal and unease. Jim actually tried to initiate sex with me over the weekend. It was about eight-thirty on Sunday morning. He woke me up by curling up next to me and trying to spoon me. When I felt his hardness against my backside I felt nauseous. When he put his hand under my night shirt and touched my breast I felt every muscle in my body tighten with revulsion, and I quickly grabbed his hand and moved it away, telling him that I wasn't feeling well. I can't believe his audacity. He's sleeping with his whore during the week and then has the nerve to try and have sex with me on the weekend. I'm honestly not sure I can ever have sex with him again. I don't even like to look at him. All I see is a liar and a cheater . . . someone stained with the residue of another woman.

It's strange really—that I'm so deadly afraid of losing a man I can't even stand to look at. But I really am scared of what might happen if I tell him I know about Jazelle. What if he leaves me for Jazelle? What if Jodie has to be one of those girls who only sees her father on the weekends? What if I'm left as a single mother? I'm not ready to give up on my family. There's a part of me that still loves Jim and wants our marriage to work. And I can't get past wondering how much of Jim's infidelity is my fault. I haven't exactly been a temptress in the bedroom—oh, who am I kidding, my husband has practically had to beg for once-weekly sex with me for more than a year . . . *mediocre* once-weekly sex.

I still have no idea what I'm going to do, but for some reason, I felt compelled to come here tonight . . . and not to learn about tummy tucks and liposuction. I wanted to come tonight to see Jazelle again. I *have* to see her again—this woman my husband is sleeping with. I'm not sure what I think I can gain from this, but I have this need to see her. Maybe I can figure out what is attracting Jim to her. Maybe I can figure out what she has that I haven't got.

It's just about time for the seminar to get started when Jazelle makes her grand entrance. I watch her come through the door, and I can feel a lump swelling in my throat as she walks down the aisle and takes a seat. I find myself looking her over like I've never viewed another woman before. I can't help but notice every detail of her appearance—her chin-length brown hair that could use a better conditioner and maybe a hair iron, her eyebrows that are in need of waxing, the loud red polish on her fingernails, her breasts, her waist, her calves . . . her thighs, her clothes, her make-up. She isn't exactly what I'd call pretty, and she's definitely carrying a few more extra pounds than I am. She has a tight skirt on that stops a few inches above her knees and a snug blouse with the first three buttons left undone. Her clothes are not appropriate for her figure or her age. I can hear Nora making fun of her—how the tight skirt only highlights the hint of a belly that's hanging over her waistline, and how the low-cut blouse does nothing more than draw attention to her aging breasts.

I sit through the first half of the session barely paying attention to anything the doctor has to say. At the moment we're supposed to be learning all about liposuction. Dr. Radcliff is showing us a liposuction rod and explaining how it's used to remove fat cells. There's a photo of a woman's bare ass up on the screen, and a rod is shoved in the lower half of one cheek. Three weeks ago an image like this would have seemed too explicit and would have made me wince, but now I'm barely bothered to look at it. After three weeks of talk and images of surgery I've become much less unnerved by the whole thing. It's starting to seem like something women just do—like getting our hair done or having a manicure.

Throughout the presentation I can't help but stare at Jazelle and, at one point, she notices me looking and gives me a quick smile. I try to smile back at her, but I'm not sure if it's a smile or a grimace I offer. I'm dreading talking to her, but when it's finally time for the break I grab my coat, scurry out of the room behind her, and follow her to the hotel exit.

By the time I get outside she already has a cigarette lit and is sitting on bench to the left of the doorway.

"Mind if I join you?"

"Of course not."

I sit down and pull out my own pack of cigarettes. As I put the cigarette to my lips, she leans in with her lighter and offers me a light. "Thanks."

"I'm sorry. Did you tell me your name last week?" Jazelle asks.

"Um . . . I'm not sure. I'm Bren . . . Myrtle." I say. *Myrtle?* Where the hell did that come from? If I was going to pick a phony name, couldn't I select one that doesn't make me sound like a ninety-year-old woman? I was about to offer my real name, but I decided that I didn't want her to know my real name. I don't want her to mention meeting a Brenda to Jim.

"Myrtle. That's an original name. Very strong. I like it. I'm Jazelle."

Yeah, I know *who you are.* "Yes, I remember." I'm trying to mimic her friendly tone, even though I'm so nervous I'm afraid I'm shaking. "So, no teddy bear necklace tonight?" It's not as cold as it was last week, and she hasn't buttoned her coat.

"No. I think Mr. Teddy Bear is in retirement indefinitely," she says and laughs. "Although it still sitting on my dresser . . . makes me laugh every time I see it. Jim's such a goofball."

"Jim?" I ask, as if I don't know who she's talking about. It's surreal to hear my husband's name come out of her mouth.

"Jim's the man I'm seeing. He's a sweetie, but kind of clueless. He's sort of in need of a *Queer Eye for the Straight Guy* makeover," she says and chuckles. "I'd love to see what Carson Kressley would have to say about that teddy bear necklace."

I try to laugh with her although I'm not sure who Carson is. I've heard of *Queer Eye* but I've never seen an episode. I probably should know who he is. I'm only thirty-six. I shouldn't be as out of touch with pop-culture as I am. Jodie is always on my case about it. The other night she was watching something on cable, and there was this *creature* on the screen. She was nearly naked and made up like a hooker from head to toe. Jodie couldn't believe I didn't know who she was. Jodie said her name was Lil' Kim. Well, let me tell you, there was nothing *lil'* about her bazumbas. And could she have been wearing any less clothing? I wear more in the shower than she was wearing on national television. I wanted to tell Jodie to turn it off, but I found myself so fascinated with the way Lil' Kim was so blatantly sexual, I ended up sitting down and watching, too. I wasn't sure at first why the show captured my attention, but eventually I realized that it was because Lil' Kim is the antithesis of me. She's comfortable with everything that makes me uncomfortable.

"Oh, one of those types," I say, trying to keep the conversation going.

"Yeah. It's kind of cute actually . . . how goofy he is. There's something manly about it I guess."

"Really?"

"Yeah. He's a great guy. But enough about him. What about you, Myrtle? Are you married?"

"Ah, no," I say, before realizing that Jazelle may have already spotted my wedding band. "I mean yes," I add with a nervous laugh.

"Happily?"

"Oh, I don't know. I guess." As the words come out, I instantly feel like crying, and my face starts to twitch, the way your face does when you're trying to suppress tears.

"Are you okay?" Jazelle asks with a genuine look of concern.

"Yeah," I say, managing to keep it together. "It's been a long day. I'm just tired."

"I hear you. So what kind of work do you do, Myrtle?"

"I'm a graphic artist for a consulting company."

"That sounds so interesting!" Jazelle says with excitement. "Do you enjoy it?"

"It's all right," I say, unable to match her enthusiasm for my job.

"I'm sure it's very demanding."

"Yeah, it can be."

"So, you design brochures and things?"

"Yeah, and a lot of sales presentations and Web sites."

"How did you learn to do that?"

"I just picked it up as I went along. I started in the workforce as an administrative assistant and kept picking up skills as I went along."

"Wow. That's awesome. You should be very proud."

Huh . . . maybe I should. "Oh it's nothing really," I say, and I realize that for a brief moment, maybe five seconds, I wasn't thinking about Jim and his affair. I was just thinking about myself and being involved in telling someone about my work. I had been afraid it would be hard to make conversation with Jazelle, but we continue to talk for some time with Jazelle leading most of the exchange. As we talk, I become aware of what a man might see in her. She's not a beauty queen, but there's something beyond her looks that makes her attractive—the expressive way she uses her hands, the interest she takes in me, her smile.

On the way back to the ballroom, I ask Jazelle if she might like to have coffee somewhere when the second half of the presentation is over, and she agrees. The more we talk, the more I realize that Jazelle has a way of making people feel comfortable and valued. Is that all she's doing for my husband? Making him feel comfortable and valued? I'm not sure, but I intend to find out.

# 36

# Nora

"That was really fun. I haven't been on ice skates in years," Owen says to me. We're sitting on a bench next to the skating rink at the Sculpture Garden, sipping hot chocolate. Owen called earlier in the week to make plans to get together. We talked about doing the typical dinner and a movie thing, but I suggested ice skating as an alternative. I guess I wanted us to have a date that would show what good shape I'm in, and something about ice skating feels youthful and invigorating. I wanted Owen to see that I'm active and enjoy spending time outdoors even when it's barely above freezing.

"I'm glad you enjoyed it. I try to get to the rink at least once or twice before the season is over. My sisters and I used to take the subway into Manhattan and hit the rink at Rockefeller Center when we were teenagers. We always went at least once during the holidays. That's what made it feel like Christmas to me—ice skating under the big tree at Rockefeller Center."

"So that's why you're such a great skater—unlike my bungling self."

"You did pretty well," I lie. He was a mess out on the rink, which ended up working in my favor. He kept having to grab hold of me to stay upright. I think the experience raised the comfort level between us. We laughed a lot out there on the rink and had some nice conversation once Owen began to get the hang of skating. And I don't think it hurt that I purposely stumbled a couple times so I didn't show him up too much. I know that's pathetic—to pretend you're less good at something so you don't threaten someone's masculinity—but a chica's got to do what a chica's got to do. And, okay, I'll admit that I was pretending to lose my balance when I grabbed hold of him a couple times. I've been ice skating since I was a little girl—I haven't really wavered on ice skates since I was five, but it gave me an excuse to latch on to those gorgeous arms of his.

"I think I was starting to get the hang of it. We'll have to come back again, so I can get some more practice, and you don't feel like you have to pretend to fall to make me feel better," he says with a grin.

Busted! "Why I have no idea what you're talking about," I say in one of those annoying Southern women accents. "So I guess my acting skills need some improvement?"

"Yeah, it was cute of you to indulge me. But really, it's not necessary."

"That's good to know." I'm liking this man more and more by the minute.

"I grew up with three sisters. Believe me, I have no problem with women being better at some things than I am."

I laugh. "Three sisters eh? I grew up with two sisters . . . and three brothers."

"Now that's a big family. Your parents must have really had their hands full."

"Yeah, they did, but it worked out for the most part," I say, even though I'm not really sure it did. My siblings and I grew up happy and healthy enough I guess, but my parents having "their hands full" is a bit of an understatement. Their lives revolved around raising kids. They had virtually no time to themselves for more than twenty years. I know they didn't really intend to have six children, but they had this silly Catholic hang-up about using birth control. It wasn't until my youngest sister, Eva, was born that they sat down and had a long talk with their priest, who, thankfully, had a modicum of common sense, and basically said it was okay for them to use birth control. They certainly loved us, and I'm sure they never regretted having any of us, but, sometimes, I would look at my mother and feel sorry for her. If she wasn't working at her job, she was doing house-work, or clipping coupons to try to make the family budget stretch a little bit farther. My grandmother lived nearby and would come and stay with us a fair amount, so Mami could go shopping by herself or get her hair cut, but that was really the only time she had to be alone. I think about her life often, and I think it's one of the reasons I'm so NOT interested in having children. What's weird is I'm the only one of my siblings who doesn't have children. I have a total of thirteen nieces and nephews, which, honestly is one of the reasons I moved to D.C. I was tired of my brothers and sisters coming over with their kids, who would always wreak havoc on my apartment. And sometimes, my sister Rachel would just drop her kids off at my place and expect me to watch them. I needed to get away from it all, so I started looking for jobs in Boston and D.C. and even-tually landed my current job at Saunders and Kraff. It's nice to be in D.C. It's far enough away from family drama and all those kids, but close enough that can I go home and visit fairly regu-larly (usually just long enough to remind myself why I moved away).

"Well, you seem to have turned out very well."

"That's sweet of you to say."

"You about ready to head to the car? I think I've had enough of the cold for a while."

"Sure." We get up and start walking toward the street. We're only a few steps away from the bench when he grabs my hand, and we walk to the car like a couple of teenagers at Coney Island, and I feel something in my stomach, like a knot or butter-flies. It's weird—I haven't felt this way about a man in ages. I don't know if it's something about the way he looks, or the kindness in his eyes, or the masculine strength I feel coming from him—or maybe following my rash of horrid dates, I'm just in desperate need of someone like Owen—someone with a quiet charm and a secure nature.

He drives me back to my condo, and I tell him he can drop me off as parking in the neighborhood is hard to come by, but he insists on finding a space and walking me up.

"I really had a nice time," he says when we reach my door. Then he leans in and kisses me. We wrap our arms around each other, have a nice, long embrace, and I can feel myself melting into him. I want to ask him inside, but I'm feeling something different for this guy, and I don't want to rush things. "I hope we can get together again soon."

"Sure," I say and then I remember—I'm supposed to have my surgery next week. Then I'll need at least three weeks, maybe more, before I'm going to be able to see him again. As I think about this, I'm not sure I can stand to go three weeks without seeing him. "Give me a call," I add, trying to think of how I can explain being unavailable for three weeks. I may have to say that I'm going to be out of town. Maybe I can make up something about work or a death in the family. I certainly can't tell him I'm having plastic surgery—he'll think I'm old and falling apart.

"I certainly will," he says and lingers for a moment, staring at me. "Good night," he says, maybe disappointed that I didn't ask him in.

"Good night." I watch him walk down the hall for a second or two before going inside. As I close the door behind me, I think about what his reaction will be when he sees me after my procedures—after I've been nipped and tucked. If he's enamored with me now, I can't wait to see his reaction once I'm refreshed and rejuvenated.

# 37

## Brenda

"You want to grab that table over there?" Jazelle asks me after we come through the door of a coffee shop a few blocks from the hotel.

"Sure," I say, and we make our way over to a small table in the corner.

"I'm so glad you asked me for coffee. I got divorced three years ago, and sometimes I hate to go straight home to an empty house, especially in the winter," Jazelle says, before a waiter steps in and asks what we would like to order.

"A decaf with cream for me."

"I'll take the same," Jazelle says before adding, "And, hey, bring us one of those S'mores trays."

"S'mores tray?" I ask as the waiter heads back to the counter.

"Yeah. They bring you this Sterno flame with chocolate and graham crackers and marshmallows, and you can make your own S'mores. It's fun."

"Neat." My mouth starts watering as I hear the words chocolate and graham crackers and marshmallows. I haven't had a S'more since I was a kid. Not to mention that I haven't eaten dinner, and it's after ten o'clock.

"I stop in here every now and then after work and wait out the traffic before going home."

"That's not a bad idea."

The waiter appears with two cups of coffee and a wooden

tray loaded with the makings for S'mores and a little burner in the middle. He sets the cream down on the table and lights the burner with a lighter.

"Please, help yourself," Jazelle says, gesturing toward the tray.

Like you have with my husband? "Thanks." I stab a marshmallow with a wooden skewer and hold it over the flame.

"So what are you doing at that seminar, Myrtle? You're way too young to be considering any kind of surgery."

"That's sweet of you to say, but I could certainly use a little help turning the clock back a few years."

"Nonsense. You're very pretty," she says and, the way she says it, it almost makes me believe her. I wonder if she talks to Jim this way—telling him how handsome he is and how young he looks.

"What about you? You don't look like you need to have anything done either," I lie, just like she did to me. Truth is, she's got fine lines on her face, could certainly use a tummy tuck, and, I bet you, when that bra comes off her boobs are almost down to her navel.

"I wish that were true. I'll be forty-four this summer, and time has taken its toll. I look back at pictures of me from ten, twenty years ago, and I just want some of the way I looked then back, you know. I'm not expecting to look twenty-five, but if I could look like a refreshed forty-year-old that would be fine by me."

I figure this is about the best segue I'm going to get to turn the conversation toward my husband, so here I go. "Is any of this for that boyfriend of yours who gave you that necklace we talked about last week?" I ask, realizing that the relative calm I was starting to feel around Jazelle is boiling back up to unease at the mention of my husband. I hope it's not showing on my face.

"Maybe a little. He's almost ten years younger than I am, so it would be nice to look a bit younger."

"How did you meet him?"

"Gosh. It was sometime before Thanksgiving. I had taken a

day off and was shopping at the Dulles Town Center out past Reston and stopped into a Subway on the way home, for lunch. I was standing there watching the counter lady smash my bread with one hand as she sliced it open with the other. Don't you hate how they do that? I don't know why I go to Subway all the time—it's so nasty. But anyway, he was standing next to me. I had the Italian BMT and he ordered the . . ."

A meatball sub with cheese, I think to myself before the words come out of Jazelle's mouth. Jim always orders a meatball sub with cheese.

". . . meatball sub with cheese," Jazelle finishes. "I commented that his sub looked good as the woman made it in front of us and wondered out loud if I should have gotten that instead of the BMT. We kind of laughed together, and that was the end of it, or so I thought. A few minutes later he was looking around the place for somewhere to sit. It was right smack in the middle of the lunch rush, and I had taken the last empty table. He looked so lost standing there with his tray, so I said he was welcome to share my table."

As she's saying this, I can picture Jim in Subway, looking around with a meatball sub on his tray. I can even see the look on his face—that boyish expression of a lost little kid that comes across his face when he doesn't quite know what to do with himself.

"So we sat there and ate our subs and had some nice conversation. I really didn't mean for it to be anything more than that, but the more we talked, the more we started to connect, you know."

I nod my head.

"At first I did most of the talking. I got the sense that he didn't have the best social skills on the planet, so I tried to make him feel comfortable. But then I asked him a few questions and once he got rolling he was actually quite chatty and . . ." Jazelle says, stopping herself mid-sentence. "I'm sorry. I'm going on and on. This is probably way more than you want to know."

"No, not at all."

"Really? It actually feels kind of good to talk about him with someone. I haven't told anyone else about Jim. You know how people can judge. The only reason I told you is because I didn't think I'd see you anymore once the seminars were over. It's not like I set out to date a married man. It just happened."

"Did he tell you right away he was married?"

"No, but I saw the wedding band on his finger. It wasn't like he was trying to hide it. I know I should have gotten up from the table when I was done, thanked him for keeping me company over lunch, and been on my way, but I haven't met a decent man since my divorce. I guess I just enjoyed some male company, so I gave him my phone number before I left and, surprise, surprise, he actually called a few days later."

I think about what she said—how she hadn't told anyone else about her affair for fear of their reaction, so I chose my words carefully. I need her to believe that I won't judge her if I want her to continue feeding me information. "Sounds like it's a bit of a rollercoaster ride—like it's complicated."

"Yeah, it is. I hope you don't think I'm a bad person. I mean, really, I have no intention of being a home-wrecker, but at the same time, if his home life was so great he wouldn't have called me."

"Do you know anything about his wife?"

"Strangely, we never talk about her. My guess is she's not very attentive. Now, don't get me wrong, we have some pretty hot times in the bedroom, but more than anything, I think he likes talking to me and having me take an interest in him and what he's doing. When I ask about his work or his childhood he lights up and goes on and on. I think, more than anything, he's just starved for attention. The other day he was telling me about this promotion he's up for at work. I swear he went on about it for at least a half hour. . . ."

Jazelle continues talking, but I start to zone out. Promotion? What promotion? Why does Jazelle know more about my husband's life than I do? Then it hits me. She knows more about his life because *she* bothered to ask about it.

# 38

# Kamille

I'm going over my finances . . . well, some of my finances—really only the bills that have to be paid to avoid dire consequences like my power or phone being turned off—trying to figure out some way to come up with the cash for my surgery. I bring in about three thousand a month after taxes, and I've concluded that I have about seventeen hundred dollars a month in essential expenses like my rent, my phone bill, my electric bill, food, etc. If I pay only essential bills, that will leave me with thirteen hundred dollars a month, and it would take me only five months to save the money for the procedure. Of course, this would mean that I'd ignore all nonessential bills like car insurance, cable television, and my long-overdue credit card payments, which have mostly been forwarded to various collection agencies. That's also assuming that I'm able to keep my spending in check and actually put some of my salary aside, which is easier said than done. Yesterday, I spent the last of my cash on a pair of earrings a street vendor was selling outside my office building. I knew I had no business buying them. The fifteen dollars they cost me was all I had left until pay day. But they were so pretty, and I figured I could scrounge something out of my refrigerator or pantry to eat for the next two days. Unfortunately, when I looked in the refrigerator I realized all I had were some old condiments, a half-dozen expired eggs, and some slices of American cheese that had hardened around the edges.

I ended up on my hands and knees last night rolling some change I'd collected in a glass jar on my dresser. I wound up with six rolls of pennies, a roll of nickels, two rolls of dimes and a few quarters (not enough to make a roll), which gave me a whopping total of eighteen dollars and seventy-five cents. I used the money to buy a loaf of bread, some peanut butter and jelly, a few pieces of fruit, and some baby carrots. I spent the leftover money on a bottle of nail polish. The food got me through the rest of week, and as I sit here, snacking on the last of the carrots, I'm so relieved that pay day is tomorrow.

Brenda actually extended a lunch invitation to me this afternoon. She's the only person at the office who has made an effort to be nice to me, so I felt terrible turning her down, saying I had too much work to do. I hope she didn't think I was rude. I couldn't very well say I was too poor to go out to lunch. I doubt she'd have believed me anyway. I was wearing a six-hundred-dollar Nanette Lepore suit when she asked me. The same suit I stained (and can't afford to get dry cleaned) when jelly dripped from my sandwich while I was eating it. Until I get paid tomorrow, I can't even afford to buy a bottle of club soda to try and get the stain out! Although, I guess club soda would be considered a non-essential expense, and I should forgo it to allow me to set aside more money for my butt implants.

The more I think about trying to pay for my surgery, the more anxious I get. Much as I'd like to think that I can, odds are I won't be able to put aside enough money to have it anytime in the foreseeable future. And who knows what other things might come up that I'll have to funnel money toward. Suppose I get another one of those threatening letters from a lawyer like I did a few months ago. It came on such stately high-quality stationary but bore the nastiest words. The letter was about a debt I owed to a department store. I've been receiving notices and phone calls about it for more than a year, which, of course, I've ignored. I mean, it was unsecured debt—there was nothing they could really do about it, except harass me with mailings (which I eventually started throwing away before I even opened them) or phone calls (which my answering machine handled for me). Or at least I *thought* that was all they could do. But, apparently, according to the law firm of Jacobs and Rosen, they could have taken me to court and seized my assets. At first I wasn't that worried about it—unless they wanted to bleed my closet of designer labels or rip my breast implants out of my body, besides a five-year-old Honda, I didn't really have much for them to seize. But, they also claimed that they could garnish my wages and mentioned something about my employer receiving some sort of Garnishee Summons to tell them to withhold my money and how much to withhold—how embarrassing that would be!

Luckily, the debt was only slightly over a thousand dollars, and I was able to pay it off before matters went any further. But that was just one of so many debts, and now I'm concerned that other creditors will sic lawyers on me as well. Like I said, there really isn't much for them to take in terms of assets but, if other creditors get wind of my salary at Saunders and Kraff, Lord knows what I could be in for. The stress of it all is so overwhelming. My heart starts to beat faster when I flip through the mail and see all the letters from collectors and pray that there are none in heavy linen-wove envelopes with law firm return addresses. I despise seeing the blinking light on my answering machine, knowing that ninety-nine percent of the calls are going to be from collectors. And, lately, I'm afraid to answer the door. No collectors have come here yet, but I fear that day isn't too far off. It's an awful way to live, and sometimes I can't believe what a financial mess I've made for myself, but, at the same time, I keep spending. Some money comes in and it goes right back out again. But what else can I do? I certainly can't walk around indefinitely with a flat rear-end. One way or another, I'm going to have to find a way to pay for my surgery. There must be a hundred ways to make money quickly. According to late-night infomercials, you can make hundreds of thousands of dollars through all sorts of schemes—only problem is that most of them are probably only making money for the person who made the infomercial. Maybe I could start a gift basket business, or walk dogs in the morning before work, or sell Mary Kay . . . not bad ideas really, but none of them is going to earn me seven thousand dollars in a short period of time.

I wish I had something to sell, but I really only have two things of any value left: my car and my grandmother's engagement ring. I'm not really interested in relying on public transportation to get around the city, and I just can't bear the thought of parting with my grandmother's ring, which I realize I've been unconsciously fidgeting with as I think.

I had the ring appraised a few years ago. I told myself I was getting the appraisal just for the sake of information, but I guess I really wanted to know how much I could get for it if I ever broke down and decided to sell it. I took it to a jeweler in Atlanta who said that the intense sparkle of the diamonds was due to the high-quality cut of the stones. He also said that the diamonds had a high clarity grade and assessed the ring to be worth about five thousand dollars.

I look at the ring and see the diamonds glittering and the band shining. It reminds me of my grandmother and the way her eyes lit up any time someone took note of her ring. It was her prized possession, and she entrusted me with it. What kind of person would I be if I sold it to pay for a plump ass? No, selling the ring is not an option.

"Back to the drawing board," I say to myself, and start picturing myself making gift baskets and walking dogs. It's almost a funny image—me in one of my tailored suits and high-heeled Manolos walking a couple of cocker spaniels. It really should be a funny image, but to me, it really isn't. Actually, it's quite sad.

# 39

## Brenda

I'm sitting out in the car in front of my house, smoking a cigarette. I've just gotten home from the final installment of the
plastic surgery forums and my outing with Jazelle. I just can't
bring myself to go inside. It's pushing midnight, but I'm sure Jim
will still be up, lounging in front of the TV, and honestly, I don't
even want to look at him.

After my conversation with Jazelle, I feel even more violated
than I did before. It was one thing to learn that Jim was having
sex with another women, but to find out they have a relationship as well—that they enjoy each other's company outside of
the bedroom—it makes me feel so sad and beaten. I'm not sure
why their in-depth conversations bother me more than the sex,
but somehow the thought of the two of them chatting and
laughing over dinner seems much more intimate then the idea of
them naked in bed together. There's something more threatening
about it as well. Maybe I felt a little safer when I thought it was
just about sex. I could convince myself that this thing with
Jazelle was a passing fling. Now that I know the details, I'm
more frightened then ever, and I have these visions of coming
home and finding that Jim has cleared out his closet and run off
with her. The thoughts make me panicky, and I wonder if I need
to worry about the money in our joint accounts or the credit
cards in both our names. No, I reassure myself. Jim wouldn't
take our money and disappear. He's not that kind of man. He

wouldn't do that to me, and he certainly wouldn't do that to his daughter. But then again, a few weeks ago I didn't think he'd cheat on me, either.

I sit in the car for another five minutes or so and smoke another cigarette. When I smash it out in the ashtray I count to three and force myself to open the car door and head toward the house. When I get inside, Jim is at the kitchen table, reading the newspaper.

"Hey," he says.

"Hi," I say back to him, looking at him, elbows on the table, an empty bottle of Budweiser next to the newspaper. He looks so trustworthy and innocent, like he should be doing a commercial for Craftsman tools or L.L. Bean. Who would guess that he was an adulterer?

"How was the seminar?"

"It was fine. Learned all about liposuction."

"Hope you're not thinking of doing anything like that," he says with a smile.

"No. I told you, I just go to keep Nora company." I never told him that Nora stopped attending the presentations after the first session.

"You and Nora go out afterward?"

"Ah . . . yeah . . . to a little diner up the street from the hotel." I'm about to say good night and head upstairs to assume my "don't even *think* about us having sex" position (the one where I lie on my side of the bed as close to the edge as possible with my back facing Jim) when something inside me prompts me to pull out a chair and sit down at the table with Jim.

"So, how was your day?" I ask him.

"Fine. Same old. Same old."

"Really?"

"Well, actually, I've been meaning to tell you. I think I might be up for a promotion. George Watson, one of our lead project managers, is moving to Maine. His wife got a job in Portland, so he's leaving the company next month. I talked with my boss about taking over for George, and he seems very open to the idea. Of course, I'll have to formally apply, but I think I'm pretty much a shoo-in for the job. It would mean a nice raise."

"Oh, that's fantastic!" I say with enthusiasm, and I'm not sure if I'm excited about his pending promotion or the fact that Jazelle no longer knows something that I didn't. "You so deserve it. You do such a great job there."

Jim grins. "Thanks."

"George? I think I met him at your company Christmas party. He had the gray hair and the wife who wouldn't stop talking."

"Yeah, that was him. Remember his wife going on and on about the stomach flu she'd had a few days earlier?"

"Oh, God, yes. And you said you'd had a bug as well, and she asked if you'd had the 'explosive diarrhea,' too?'"

Jim laughs. "I think that's the first time I heard the words 'explosive diarrhea' said over cocktails at a holiday party. The things people will talk about."

"Oh, you have no idea. You remember Gretchen, our departmental admin from Hell? You should hear some of the doozies she comes up with when she wants the day off from work."

"The one with the mysterious *condition*?"

"That's the one. She was out sick again today. This time because Freckles, her dog that none of us are sure actually exists, ate an entire bag of Hershey's Miniatures and was strapped to an IV at the animal hospital."

"Must be a very ingenious dog to get the bag open and then unwrap all those individual candy bars."

We both laugh, and suddenly I realize that this is one of the best conversations we've had in quite some time. And all it took was sitting down with him and asking a question or two instead of coming into the house in my usual workday daze, grabbing something to eat, and maybe watching TV before going to bed.

We talk a bit more, and, when I finally say good night and head upstairs, I'm hopeful that I can save my marriage. I learned something from Jazelle this evening—that my husband is starved for attention and intelligent conversation. That we've been leaving our marriage on autopilot for way too long. I wonder what other insights I might be able to tap by getting to know Jazelle. When I come to Jodie's room, I'm about to stick my head in the doorway and see how her day was, when I hear her talking. The door is slightly ajar, and, through the crack I can see her speaking on a cell phone. When did Jodie get a cell phone? And, more important, whom is she talking to at midnight?

# 40

# Nora

It's just after eight in the morning, and I'm standing in line at Starbucks to get my morning caffeine fix. The line is about seven people deep and seems to be moving even slower than usual . . . and there's some government employee in front of me who reeks of Old Spice. At least, I assume he's a government employee. He's wearing cheap khaki pants with sneakers, a striped tie, and the epitome of middle-aged male civil servant fashion, a cotton-poly blend short-sleeve dress shirt—he's either a government worker or a mattress salesman.

I don't know why I, or any of us, put up with this crap—waiting in line every morning for the privilege of spending three bucks on a cup of coffee. I should brew my own in the coffee maker before I leave for work, but I guess I'm too lazy. Every morning I walk from my condo on Connecticut Avenue to my office on K Street. It's a total of seven blocks, and I pass three Starbucks on the way. How can I not stop into at least one of them?

I need my coffee especially bad this morning. I had this horrid dream last night. I'm not sure what sparked it, but I think it may have had something do with my upcoming surgery. I dreamt that men could actually come into a grocery store and buy women. We were on the shelves, displayed like boxes of cake mix or cans of soda. I looked across the aisle from the shelf on which I was displayed and saw all these young women, mostly in their twenties, standing next to neatly organized bottles of salad dressing and condiments. They were sticking out their boobs and tossing their hair as men perused the aisles. Then I looked around on my own shelf and saw other women in their forties. We seemed to be in a state of disorder, and, upon further inspection, I saw that we were displayed along with dented cans of fruit and day-old bagels. The sign underneath the younger women said "Premium Goods. Priced as Marked." I wanted to see what the sign underneath the other older women and me said, so I got down on my belly, crawled to the edge of the shelf, and stuck my head over the edge to read the sign displayed below us. I was horrified to see that it said "Bargain Bin: Priced as Marked. Please be advised some items are due to expire soon." All I remember after that was screaming at the top of my lungs, "No! I don't belong in the bargain bin!" I was actually yelling the word "No!" when I jolted out of the dream and woke up in a cold sweat.

I couldn't fall back to sleep after the nightmare, so essentially I've been up since four o'clock this morning, lying in bed thinking about being displayed in a bargain bin like a Justin Guarini album or Vanna White's autobiography. Needless to say, I'm in a bit of a crabby mood due to lack of sleep, and there is a kid over at the counter that holds the napkins and stirrers and such, who is totally getting on my nerves. He's quite small, but he's managed to climb up on a stool and is wreaking havoc with the display. After pressing on the tops of the creamers and watching the liquid pour out onto the counter and make a mess, he starts getting his probably-unwashed hands all over the stirrers and randomly starts pulling napkins from the canisters. I'm wondering where his mother is, and why the bitch had a child she can't be bothered to keep out of trouble when I see a man walk over to the counter and lift the young boy off the stool.

"Come on, Billy. Let's get you to daycare," he says.

I immediately recognize the voice of the man, and, when he turns around with the boy resting on his hip, I'm startled to see that the voice, and the *boy*, belong to Owen. I'm not sure exactly why, but I turn to the side and try to hide behind government-worker-man, so Owen doesn't see me as he passes by. Maybe I'm afraid he'll see the look on my face—the look that says, "Shit . . . he's got a fucking kid."

Despite my efforts, Owen does see me. "Nora. Hi," he says with obvious unease.

"Hi, Owen. How are you?" I say, trying to hide my own anxiousness.

"Good . . . fine." He seems to stumble for a moment, before looking at the boy he's carrying and then looking back at me. "Ah . . . this is Billy."

"Hi, Billy," I say, trying to muster a smile. The child glares at me and offers no response. I think children sense that I don't like them. "Billy's your . . . ?"

"My son," Owen says, clearly embarrassed that he hasn't told me about him.

"Well, it's a pleasure to meet you, Billy." I try to sound up-beat, but the kid sees right through me and sticks his tongue out.

"Daddy, let's go."

"Okay, just a sec," Owen says to the boy.

"Now!" Billy demands.

"I really do have to go. I've got to get him to the sitter's and then head to work. Can we talk later?"

"Okay," I say, part of me wanting to just say, "No." I'm so not interested in getting involved with a man who has a child, especially one so young, but I must say I am curious about the whole thing. Where is this boy's mother? How involved is Owen in caring for Billy? Why did he not tell me about his son?

"Thanks," he says. "Say good-bye to Nora," he instructs his son.

"No!" Billy says defiantly.

"Bye, Billy," I say, still forcing a smile.

"Bye," Owen says.

As I watch him exit the store, I can't help but wonder what kind of mess I've wandered into. I really like this guy, but a *kid?*

I don't want to have any kids of my own. I certainly don't want to have to deal with his. Lord, what if he has more than one? Suppose he has a whole stable full of them?

"Fuck," I mutter under my breath as I finally get up to the counter. I guess it's too early for a stiff drink, so Starbucks' strongest cup of coffee will have to do.

# 41

## Kamille

"I've been so busy lately, as I'm sure you saw on my weekly tracking report," Gretchen says to me. "It's been hard to keep up, you know; my condition has been acting up, and then Freckles was in doggie intensive care for two days, due to the Hershey Miniatures incident, but he's doing better now."

"Good to know, Gretchen," I say. I'm not even sure why she's at this meeting. After she attended the first Quality Improvement Roundtable (that's what I've been calling my weekly meetings) three weeks ago, I decided to excuse all the admin staff from future meetings just to get rid of her. She did nothing but distract everyone at the first meeting with the story about how she used to work at Versace and knows, without a doubt, that Donatella Versace is, in fact, a man. Or I guess I should say that Gretchen knows, without a doubt, that Donatella had been, in fact, a man. According to Gretchen, Donatella is actually dead and they just pump her cadaver full of embalming fluid every day and prop her up in a chair at various fashion shows, thus explaining her corpse-like appearance. She says things like this with a completely straight face, and everyone around her nods and pretends to believe what she's saying. It's like working in the Twilight Zone. I'm not sure who is more deranged—Gretchen with her wild tales, or the rest of us for pretending to believe them. Whatever the case, I don't have the time for, or any interest in, her absurd stories.

"Thanks for the update, Gretchen," I add.

"But I'm not—"

"Nora?" I say, nodding my head in Nora's direction and cutting off Gretchen. I don't care if she isn't finished. I can't bear the thought of listening to any more of her nonsense.

"I guess I've been busy as well. All the extra work you've created around here has been keeping us all busy," she says, taking an obvious dig at me in front of the whole department. From the very beginning this Nora chick has rubbed me the wrong way.

"Well, my hope, *Nora,*" I say, with an emphasis on her name (an emphasis that I hope says "Don't fuck with me, heifer, or you'll be sorry!"), "is that the tasks I've assigned to each of you will eventually help make all your jobs easier. I know it's a lot of work right now, but once we get my initiatives underway, we'll be able to get things done more efficiently." Oh, it's *on*, Bitch! "How are you doing organizing all the past sales presentations on the shared network?"

Nora reluctantly starts to give me an actual update on the project—a project that should take all of about three hours but for which she requested three weeks. She's totally playin' my ass about how she's working on organizing the files when I bet she hasn't done any of it. I can't help but dislike her—and not just because she's been rude to me from day one. I also dislike her because she's so attractive. I guess I'm jealous. I see the way people treat her, the way one of the sales reps pulled out her chair before she sat down at the meeting, the way people in the office cater to her and laugh at her foul jokes. I wish people treated me that way. I think that's my ultimate dream, and really my ultimate plan—to be treated like a princess because of the way I look. And I think I'm inching closer to the dream of achieving the perfect look. I just need those buttock implants, and then maybe I'll actually be pretty like Nora. Then maybe I'll finally be able to stop feeling like that little girl who used to get teased in the hallways at school. Maybe I can finally forget about those horrible names the other kids used to call me, and put them behind me. I think I was five or six the first time I remember it happening—the first time someone made fun of me because of my lips. The kids would call me Blubber Lips and make jokes about me inflating them with an air pump every day, or ask me if a swarm of bees had stung me right on the kisser. It was traumatizing and now, more than twenty years later, thinking about all the names I was called can still bring a tear to my eye.

I had been saving money all through college, and when I graduated, one of the first things I did was look into having plastic surgery on my lips. I researched the procedure and saw a couple of different doctors before I finally decided to have it done. I was a nervous wreck the days before the procedure, but it ended up not being that bad. I was only in surgery for about an hour and a half and the incisions were inside my lips so there wasn't really any scarring. I had some pain and swelling, but it didn't last that long. It only took a week or so for the swelling to go down, and, when it did, the change in my appearance was unbelievable. I can't even describe how it made me feel—to no longer look like a freak. My lips looked natural and subtle. People could start looking at my eyes when they talked to me instead of my lips. Little kids didn't stare at me anymore and ask their mothers what was wrong with me. Plastic surgery did such wonders for my lips, I began to wonder what it could do for my eyes and my breasts and my stomach. Before my lip reduction I just wanted to be presentable. I just didn't want to feel like a freak anymore. But after my surgery I didn't just want to be presentable anymore. I wanted to be pretty . . . beautiful, in fact. And I decided that I was going to do whatever it took to become pretty. I wanted everything that I had been deprived of my whole life because of the way I looked, and now, I'm almost there. Surgery has given me the lips I want, the breasts I want, the waist line I want . . . the eyes, the cheeks. Now I just need the butt I want, and I'm going to figure out a way to get it.

Nora was the last one I needed an update from for this week's meeting, so when she's finished I thank everyone for their time and remind them to turn in their tracking logs. Everyone gets up from the table and starts to head out of the room, many with less-than-pleased looks on their faces. I know I'm not the most popular person in the office. People don't like change, and they resent the reports that I require from them. But I have a job to do and, Lord knows, I need the money.

"How are you doing, Kamille?" Brenda asks as everyone else jets out of the room.

"Oh. I'm fine. I wish everyone felt a little better about some of the things I'm trying to do around here."

"Don't worry about this bunch. We're not happy unless we're unhappy," she says. "Maybe it would help to take things a little bit slower instead of trying to do so many things at once."

"Maybe you're right," I say, appreciating her concern as she offers a smile and then exits the room. She probably is right. I probably am trying to do too much too fast, but there's a reason I'm trying to get so much accomplished in a short period. I need to have something to show for my brief time with the company. I need to have some solid accomplishments to present to my boss when I ask her for an advance on my salary to pay for my butt job.

I just can't bring myself to sell my grandmother's ring, and the idea of selling my car is almost as loathsome. I figure the only other option I have is to see if the company will grant me an advance. I know it's unlikely, especially since I've only been here for a few weeks, but maybe if I come up with a good story about why I need the money, upper management will have pity on me and cough up the cash.

I hate the idea of having to go to my boss and ask for money—I hate the idea of asking anyone for money. It's just such an awkward situation. People immediately tense up as soon as they sense that you might be inquiring about a loan. I think of the times I've asked my parents for loans, and I see their shoulders tensed and their apprehensive faces staring at me. I also think about the times when my friends avoided me because they knew I might ask them for money. All I had to do was ask one of my friends for a little help and, next thing I knew, word was all over town that "Kamille was on one of her 'fishing expeditions.' " They didn't think I knew about it, but my friends would call and warn each other when I "was on the prowl," and suddenly all I would get was answering machines and voicemail when I called any of them. I think some of them installed Caller-ID for the sheer purpose of avoiding my phone calls even though I generally don't ask for loans over the phone. It's more unnerving than chatting by phone or e-mail, but I almost always make financial requests in person. I've found that people find it much harder to turn you down if you're right there with them, face to face. I've also found that you *never* ask for loans via e-mail. The problem with e-mail is that is gives people way too much time to react. When you talk to people on the phone or speak with them in person they have to offer some kind of answer immediately, but when you send them an e-mail they can take as long as they want to respond, which gives them plenty of time to come up with a plethora of valid excuses as to why they'd "love to help you," but they "just can't right now."

As I get up from my chair and head back to my office, I try to tell myself that asking for an advance on my salary won't be any big deal. I'll just pop into Jill's office, remind her of everything I've accomplished since I joined the company, and come up with a really good story for why I need the advance. I'll hate every minute of the interaction—I'll hate the humiliation of asking someone for money, I'll hate lying about why I need it, I'll hate the look that's sure to come across her face when I make the request, but I won't hate any of it as much as I hate walking around with a flat ass.

# 42

## Nora

"I'm sorry I won't get to see you for three weeks," Owen says to me over dinner. We're at a happening Caribbean restaurant called Ortanique on Eleventh Street. The menu has a few items that remind me of the kind of Puerto Rican food that's so readily available in New York. I think the abundance of good Puerto Rican food is what I miss most about living in New York City. I can't tell you the number of Friday nights I spent with family at Jimmy's Bronx Café over killer *paella*, and I so miss the *pasteles* at Casa Adela and Old San Juan Café. You can't find good Puerto Rican food in D.C.—at least I haven't been able to. There isn't a huge number of Puerto Ricans in D.C. like there is in New York. Most of the Latinos I've met since I moved down here are from Central America: El Salvador and Guatemala.

I miss how easy it was to get things like *kenepas*, a favorite Puerto Rican fruit, or *mavi*, a pungent juice that's made from the bark of ironwood trees, in New York City. But I guess in some ways, maybe it's for the best that Puerto Rican food is hard to come by here—most of it wouldn't be on this damn Atkins diet I've been following, anyway.

"Yeah. Me too. But I'm looking forward to spending time with my sister and the new baby," I lie. None of my sisters has had a new baby in more than three years, and if one of them had, you could bet that I'd be running as far in the other direction as possible. But I told Owen that I was traveling back to the

Bronx to stay with my sister and help her with her new baby for a few weeks rather than admit to the fact that I'll really be spending the next three weeks recovering from cosmetic surgery.

It's funny that I'd make up an explanation that involves helping my sister out with her kids when one of main reasons I left New York was to get away from all my nieces and nephews. I love them . . . I *do*. There's just *so many* of them, and my siblings seem to let them run wild. I got tired of kid-proofing my apartment before they came over or cowering in silence behind the door, pretending not to be there, when I saw one of my brothers or sisters through the peephole with a litter of kids behind them. And as much as I miss the Puerto Rican community in New York, I *so* do *not* miss the way Puerto Ricans fucking bring their kids with them everywhere they go—parties, receptions, weddings. Any event that a Wasp crowd would expect to be adults-only is teeming with children when it involves Puerto Ricans, and quite frankly, it gets on my nerves. Maybe I'm too Anglo-fied, but this is mainland America. I wish my Puerto Rican brothers and sisters would get with the program and hire a damn babysitter once and a while.

"That's sweet of you. Maybe when the baby's a little older your sister can come down for a visit, and I can meet her and the baby."

Crap! I'm so used to not thinking very far into the future with most of the men I date, I hadn't thought about Owen being around long enough to find out that there really isn't any new baby. "It's . . . I mean *she* isn't really a *new* baby. My niece is three years old." I hesitate a moment and try to think of what else to say in an effort to weasel my way out of my previous lie in case Owen is actually around for a while and finds out there is no new baby. "She's just the last child any of my siblings have had, so I always refer to her as the new baby. I don't get to see her or any of my nieces and nephews much, so I decided to take a three-week block and really spend some quality time with them." It's almost scary how easily the lies just fly off my tongue.

"I think that's great." Owen looks down at the table nervously, and then starts again. "I'm glad to hear you like spending time with kids. You know . . . with Billy and all. I'm sorry I didn't tell you about him when we first met. I guess I wanted you to see me as a man before you thought of me as a father and all that entails. Does that make any sense?"

"Sure. Although I do wish you had told me . . . just so I wasn't so surprised when I ran into you and Billy at Starbucks."

"I'm sorry. I was going to tell you. I was waiting for the right moment. Does it change anything? My having a four-year-old son?"

"No, no. Of course not," I lie, and then, before I know what I'm saying, I blurt out, "Do you have him full time?"

"Yes. My ex-wife and I divorced when Billy was only seven months old. She's an aspiring singer and was on the road all the time trying to catch her big break. It didn't leave much time for Billy and me. She's still chasing her dream and hanging around smoky nightclubs. Traveling through the country in dirty vans with a bunch of band members is no life for a little boy. There was really no question about who would get full custody of Billy after the divorce."

"Is his mother involved in his life at all?"

"A little. She sees him when she's in town every couple of months. She loves him, but she loves her music more."

"That's a shame."

"Not really. Billy and I make out pretty well. I enjoy having him."

What a wonderful man this is, I think to myself. He's kind and loving and gorgeous and a devoted father. I'll admit that when I met Billy at the coffee shop I had pretty much decided I needed to end it with Owen. I'm just not interested in raising someone else's child, and, when you date a man with a kid, in reality, you end up dating both of them—they're a package deal. But there is something . . . well, really, *so many* things about Owen that just won't allow me to let him go. I feel something for this man and part of me feels like I would be a fool to end it with him over his son. And yet another part of me feels like I would be a fool to think this relationship has any chance at all.

I don't generally get so attached to men. Most of the time, I see them as diversions or playthings. I enjoy their company for a while, see the inside of some nice restaurants or nightclubs, and have a little fun in the bedroom. Then I send them on their way when another man comes along who interests me. I guess I'm sort of like a child myself that way. We quickly get bored with our toys and want them replaced with new ones. I seem to move from man to man the same way a little girl dumps her Barbie Dream House in favor of an Easy Bake Oven. But, as I look at Owen across the table, I can't help but feel the desire for something more permanent with him. Much as I might try, I just can't see him as a plaything. He seems to have too much . . . gosh, I don't know how to put it . . . he just seems to have too much *value* as a person. He has too much to offer to be seen the way I look at most men, which is essentially as a commodity to be used for my own benefit. I guess part of the reason I look at men that way is because I believe that most of the men I've dated have looked at me that way. I don't feel like a commodity to Owen. I haven't known him long enough to be sure, but I don't think he's the kind of person that would treat anyone that way. Feeling this way about a man is such a novelty to me. It's strange and exciting, but mostly, it's scary—my God, is it scary.

# 43

## Nora

"Nervous?" Brenda asks me.

"Yeah," I say. We're sitting in a waiting room at Washington Hospital Center. The day of my procedures has finally arrived. I'm excited for the surgery, and the way I'm going to look once I've recovered, but I can't help but worry about what could go wrong. Suppose I come out looking all nip-tucky like Melanie Griffith or Nicolette Sheridan. Suppose the doctor hits a nerve, and my eyelids droop for the rest of my life? What if I get some awful infection and die?

"It's not too late to back out, you know."

"What? Are you kidding me? I've researched the doctor and the procedures. I've agonized over exactly what to have done. I opened a new credit card to pay for the surgery. I've made up vacation plans to explain why I'll be out from work, and I told Owen I was going to New York to visit family to explain why I can't see him. We're sitting here in the hospital. The operating room has been booked. Oh, no! There is no backing out now," I say to Brenda, repeating all the things I've been telling myself to keep from running out the door screaming and never looking back.

"Okay," she says. "Anything I can do to help you relax?"

"No, but thanks for offering. And for bringing me here and agreeing to pick me up and look after me when I get out of surgery."

"It's my pleasure. I'm happy to do it."

I look at Brenda, and I'm so thankful to have her as a friend. I don't have many friends. Actually, aside from my sisters, Brenda is really my only female friend. I know lots of men but making women friends has never really been a priority for me. It's funny how I know so many men, but it's my one girlfriend who's here by my side when I need her. Of course, I have my family up in New York, but Brenda is the only person nearby who I can count on, and she has her own family to think about. It's a little scary to think about that—how alone I am. I have no husband and no kids and, up until recently, I liked it that way, but turning forty and having this surgery is making me rethink things. When I scheduled the procedure, the secretary told me that I must have someone come to the hospital when the surgery is over and take me home, and it could not be a cab driver or a car service. It had to be a friend or family member. Of course, Brenda came to mind immediately. But it was scary and unsettling to wonder what I would have done if she hadn't been available. I don't really have anyone else in my life who I would have felt comfortable asking.

"You're so lucky, Brenda. To have a husband and a daughter . . . a family."

"You think?" she asks, as if I don't really mean it.

"Yeah. It's times like these that I wonder if I shouldn't have settled down at some point, gotten married, had a couple of kids."

"Really?"

"Oh, I don't know. It's probably the pre-surgery jitters talking. But I've been thinking more about getting older, and how it'd be nice to have a son or daughter . . . and I guess maybe a husband too. I worry sometimes about who's going to look after me when I'm old and gray." As I listen to myself speak, I realize how selfish I sound—like the only reason I'd want to have children is so I don't end up in some nursing home sitting in my own urine for hours at a time. But, then again, that's why I've never wanted kids—because I know I'm too selfish for them. I don't want to be one of those mothers who pops out a kid then resents all the time and money and work it takes to raise them properly. My mother had very few nice things because all of our family's money was sucked up by her six kids. She never seemed bitter, but if it were me, every time I had to pay a pediatrician bill or dole out some cash for ballet lessons instead of paying off my Pottery Barn or Saks bill, I'd be at least a little bit resentful. Does that make me a bad person? I don't think so. I'd be a bad person if I recognized this about myself and then went and had kids anyway.

"It's not too late. Plenty of women are having kids in their forties these days. But raising children is no easy task," Brenda says to me.

"Yeah, I know. Did you see Jill the other day?" I say, referring to our boss. "When she came into the office with her baby? I was so horrified. He spit up on her, and the baby spew went right down her blouse, and I don't think she even noticed. If she did, she just ignored it. I can't imagine walking around with barf on my chest all day."

"It wasn't barf. It was a little spit-up. Babies do that," Brenda says with a laugh just as a nurse comes out, calls my name, and tells me to follow her.

Brenda and I both stand up, and she gives me a hug. "I'll be right here," she says.

"Thanks again for doing this for me," I say, and follow the nurse down a long hall to a small dressing room. She asks me a few questions, confirms the procedures that I'm scheduled for, and writes a couple things down in my chart. Then she hands me a hospital gown in a plastic package, tells me to slip it on, lock any valuables in the locker next to me, and open the curtain when I'm done. She isn't nasty or anything, but she's rather cold and methodical, like she's on autopilot—not exactly the kind of person you want around you before you go under the knife. As she steps outside the cubby and draws the curtain, I can't help but wonder if she treats all her patients this way, or just the narcissistic plastic surgery patients who don't deserve any compassion. I imagine her going back to her station and telling the other nurses about the vain middle-aged woman trying to regain her youth.

When I've undressed and covered myself with the gown, I open the curtain. A few minutes later, the same sullen nurse comes back and tells me to follow her. I walk behind her, and she leads me to a large room with six or seven hospital gurneys lined up next to each other with curtains as partitions. All the beds I pass are empty at the moment except for one, which holds an elderly woman who appears to be asleep. The nurse directs me toward one of the beds, and I sit down on the edge. She tells me that this is the pre-op area, and that my doctor and the anesthesiologist will be by as soon as they can.

I want to ask her for a magazine or something to occupy myself with until the doctors come, but I'm oddly bashful. I have this strange fear that she will lash out at me for making any requests—that she'll tell me that she has actual sick patients who need tending to and can't play nursemaid to some aging Jennifer Lopez wannabee. So, I sit on the bed and wait and think. Brenda's words come back to me: "It's not too late to back out, you know," I hear her saying in my head. Once again, I'm about to start thinking about all of the things that could go wrong, but instead I force myself to think of all of the things that can go right. How much better and more refreshed I'll look. How my nose will no longer have that little crook no one else has ever noticed but which has always bothered me. How my cheeks will be full and youthful, and my eyes will no longer look heavy and tired.

I'm trying to picture the new me when Dr. Radcliff shows up at my side. Unlike the nurse, he is upbeat and gracious. He's already dressed in surgical scrubs. Without his designer suit, and with his hair covered by a surgical cap, he looks much older than he did in the past. At first, I'd pegged him to be in his early forties, but now I'm adding ten years to that. His leap in age, and presumably experience, is reassuring to me. He gives me a quick pep talk about how smoothly everything should go and then hands me three little pieces of paper.

"Here are three prescriptions. Do you have someone here with you?"

"Yes, my friend is out in the waiting room."

"Good, if you'd like, I'll have someone take them out to her, and she can run and get them filled while you're in surgery. You're not going to be in any mood to stop at the drug store on the way home from here."

"Okay," I say, his words making me more nervous.

"One is for pain. One is an anti-inflammatory. The other is a suppository for nausea."

"A what?"

"A suppository. Unfortunately, with rhinoplasty, you're going to be swallowing a lot of blood, and it's going to make you nauseous."

Swallowing a lot of blood!? He didn't say anything about that when I had my consult. "Can't you give me a pill?" I'm not terribly enthused with the idea of shoving anything up my ass.

"I could. But it's very doubtful that you would be able to keep it down. If you use the suppository for nausea, you'll be more likely to keep the pain and anti-inflammatory pills down."

I nod my head, still a bit annoyed that the first time I hear about swallowing blood and throwing it back up and suppositories is when I'm in a hospital gown, about to go into the operating room.

He seems to notice my apprehension. "Don't worry. Everything is going to go fine."

I offer a feeble smile, and he goes on to explain a few more things about the surgery. Then he says that he'll meet me in the operating room, and makes his way through the curtain wrapped around my bed.

It's not long after he's gone that another middle-aged man approaches and introduces himself as Dr. Jordan, my anesthesiologist. He tells me a little bit about what general anesthesia is, and how he's going to administer it to me. He tells me to lie back and relax while he inserts an IV into my wrist. I feel a pinch, no worse than a Botox injection, as he sticks me with the needle.

"That wasn't so bad?"

"No."

"Okay, I'm going to hook up the IV to your anesthesia," he says. "Now I want you to count backwards from one hundred. Okay?"

"Now?" I ask, and he nods his head. "One hundred, ninety-nine, ninety-eight, ninety-seven . . ."

# 44

## Kamille

"Are things okay?" Jill asks me soon after I close her office door and sit down in front of her desk. I'm sure she's wondering why I asked to meet with her today.

"Yes. Everything is fine. It's just that it's been almost a month since I started with the company, and I thought you might like to have an update on how things are going."

"That would be great."

"Honestly, I think I've made a huge amount of progress in a very short time." I hand her a pile of paper. "These are the minutes from the Quality Improvement Roundtables that I lead every week, if you'd like to take a look at them later."

"Thanks," she says and sets them aside. I bet they go straight into the trash can as soon as I walk out of her office.

"And here's a written summary of my accomplishments." I hand her yet more paper. "When you have a chance to take a look at it you'll see that I've managed to get time tracking sheets from every employee in the department, and I've begun tallying the number of total department hours spent on various initiatives. I have the whole project in an Excel spreadsheet and, as soon as I have more data, I'll give you a full report. I've worked with the sales force to develop a standard template for all of our sales presentations and create a certain look for all our presentations . . . sort of like a brand. Here is a sample of what we've developed." Yes, more paper. "I've created a style guide as well.

It's based on the Associated Press Stylebook. I'm going to train all our proposal writers on it, so their writing is consistent across all of our proposals. Here is the prototype." More paper. "I have the graphic arts department reorganizing all the sales presentations on the network, so anyone in the department can easily access them, although Nora is taking longer to accomplish this than I had hoped." Okay, a slight dig at Nora. She's pretty—she's deserves it.

Jill looks at me with amazement. I'm sure she's surprised that someone in the department is actually productive and doing her job, something that can be rare in corporate America these days. I go on to tell her about some other projects I'm spearheading and load her up with reports and other documents. I don't expect her to read much, if any of it, but that doesn't stop me from handing them over to her. It's been my experience that you need to show people something for them to believe that you've actually accomplished something. Spoken words are meaningless. Written words are everything.

"Wow, Kamille. You've really been on the ball. I'm impressed. I'll take some time this week to look over these reports."

"Thanks." I pause for a moment and take a deep breath. "Actually, one of the reasons I wanted to present everything to you is to show my commitment to this job and the company."

"Well, I'd say you've succeeded in doing that."

"I'm glad you feel that way because I want to run something by you . . . ask you something."

"Sure."

"I'm in a bit of a financial bind. My mother needs surgery, a hysterectomy, and she doesn't have any insurance and can't afford to pay for it," I lie. "I really want to see that she has the treatment she needs, but I don't have the money to pay for the surgery either. I was wondering if there's any chance of getting an advance on my salary to help her out."

Jill instantly becomes uneasy. "What about Medicaid? Does she qualify?"

Shit! I didn't think about that. "No. She's employed and manages to get by on her salary, but she doesn't have any insurance or savings to cover the surgery. It's going to cost seven thousand dollars."

"Don't public hospitals have to provide necessary surgery whether the patient can pay for it or not?"

Double shit! I really should have thought this excuse through better. "Well, it's not emergency surgery. So they could make her wait for months before scheduling it. And she's in a lot of pain." Do women who need hysterectomies have pain? I have no idea.

"Hmm," Jill says and looks down at her desk. "I sympathize with your situation, but you've only been with the company for a few weeks. I just don't think there's any way I could convince senior management to advance that kind of money to a new employee. I'm not sure they'd do it for any employee, regardless of their tenure."

"Are you sure?" I can hear the desperation in my voice. I need those butt implants. I NEED them!

"I'm really sorry, Kamille. You've done some great work. But seven thousand dollars? I'm sure it's out of the question. There's just nothing I can do. Do you have any credit cards, or can you take out a loan from a bank?"

"I can't get that kind of credit," I say, trying to keep tears from dripping from my eyes.

"I'm really sorry, Kamille. I wish I could help. Really, I do."

"Okay," I say, getting up from the chair, wanting to get out of there before I break down. "Thanks for listening," I add and open the door to leave. I walk back to my office with my head down, and as soon as I get to my desk, I lose it. I start crying into my hands. All I want is to be pretty! Is that really so much to ask? All I want is an ass that doesn't look like a board. What's seven thousand dollars to a multi-million dollar consulting firm?

I sulk in my misery for a few more minutes. When I'm finally able to collect myself, wipe my eyes and blow my nose, I sit back in my chair and try to attack the problem at hand. How else can I raise the money to have the surgery? I think and I think, and, finally, I reach a conclusion. I have no choice but to sell my grandmother's ring.

# 45

## Nora

"Ms. Perez? Ms. Perez?" I hear my third grade teacher calling. She always calls us by our last names. I like that about her—it makes me feel grown-up. I'm playing on the swing set, and she's yelling for me to come back into the school. But I don't want to go back into the school, I'm thinking as I ignore her on the swing. School's boring.

"Ms. Perez?" I hear again and then I'm awake, and I realize I'm not on any swing set. I'm lying on a stretcher. I try to open my eyes, but they feel like they're glued shut. I strain again and manage to lift my lids enough to make out the nurse standing over me. "How are you doing?" she asks. She looks distorted and hazy.

I look at her, and it takes a second for me to realize where I am, and what has just happened. I feel as though a truck has run over my face. My head is throbbing, and I feel this intense sense of pressure on my cheeks. I can't breathe out of my nose, and my mouth is as dry as a cotton field.

"Having some pain," I try to say, but it comes out very weak and hoarse.

"That's to be expected, but Dr. Radcliff said everything went perfectly."

I want to say that it doesn't feel like everything went perfectly, but I don't have the energy to try and speak again. I can't even force my eyes open anymore. I just let them shut and I lie there in agony.

"I'll check back with you in a little bit. Get some rest for now," she says and walks away.

A few minutes later I feel something warm dripping down my face and over my chin. In a daze, I try to wipe it away with my hands. I struggle to open my eyes, which seem to be well on their way to swelling completely shut, and see the bloodstains on my hand.

"Nurse," I try to call from the bed, but my voice is weak, and no one hears me. "Nurse!" I call again, but it still comes out as little more than a whimper. I feel more blood dripping down my face and see it staining the sheets. I start feeling around the bed and find something that feels like a TV remote control. I start pressing it and pressing it and, as I do, I feel the blood start to collect in my mouth. I try not to swallow it, but eventually there's too much, and I let it go down my throat. Finally, the nurse comes back.

"It's okay," she says as if having blood gushing from your nose is a normal occurrence. "Don't swallow it. Spit it out in here." She hands me a little kidney-shaped plastic basin. "I'll be right back," she adds and then reappears a few seconds later with latex gloves on her hands and starts wiping my face with gauze, every stroke feels like sandpaper being rubbed against my wounds. Then she hands me a stack of gauze and tells me to use it to catch any more blood dripping from my nose.

The bed is adjusted so that I'm slightly sitting up. I'm holding the gauze up to my nose and spitting a heinous-looking fluid into the little plastic bowl when I see Brenda approaching.

"They finally let me back here," she says, her smile quickly fading. Through my swollen eyes I see a brief look of horror on her face. She tries to hide it, but I can see that my appearance unnerves her.

"Do I look that awful?"

"Ah . . . no . . . you don't look so bad."

"Liar," I say and try to crack a smile, but it makes my face hurt even more, so I stop.

Brenda offers a nervous laugh. "Does it feel as bad as it . . . I mean, are you feeling okay?"

"It hurts. It really hurts," I say, wanting to cry. I don't want to upset Brenda, but more importantly, I'm not sure I'm allowed to cry.

"The nurse said you should be able to go home in a few hours. Is there anything I can get you?" Brenda asks. I bet she really wants me to ask for something, so she has an excuse to get away and stop having to look at me.

"No. I'll be all right," I say, but I'm not really sure that I will. The pain is terrible, and they say it's not at its worst immediately following the surgery. God! Can it get worse than this?

"Okay. Why don't I go back into the waiting room and let you get some rest."

"Can you stay here for a little while?" I ask, hearing the desperation, the fear, in my weak voice.

"Of course," she says and grabs my hand. "As long as you want me too."

I'm so glad she's here—that she's holding my hand and reassuring me. I feel so vulnerable and helpless and scared. "Thank you, Brenda," I say. "Really. Thanks so much," I add, as I shut my eyes and try to go sleep.

# 46

# Kamille

Here I am again, twisting my grandmother's ring on my right finger like I always do when I'm anxious. I've never been in a pawn shop before. I've done a lot of things to get money in the past, but I guess I have all sorts of preconceived notions about pawn shops and did my best to avoid them. This time I've decided to give the whole pawning thing a chance. If I out-right sell the ring to a jeweler or some random person then it's gone for good, but if I go through a pawn shop, at least there's a chance that I'll be able to get it back.

As I walk through the door of Rose's Pawn Shop on Seventh Street, I'm surprised by the looks of the place. It's not seedy-looking at all. It's clean with fresh carpeting and well organized shelves and glass cases. As I'm standing there taking in the watches and jewelry and cameras and DVD players, a large middle-aged woman with long frizzy hair steps out from the back.

"May I help you?" she asks.

"Um . . . yeah," I say as I approach the counter. "I'm interested in pawning something." I'm not sure why I don't just come out and say that I want to pawn my ring, but I guess if I say it out loud it will mean that I'm actually doing it—I'm actually selling my grandmother's ring.

"What would you like to pawn, darlin?"

I'm quiet for a moment. Then I look down at the ring and

pull it from my finger. "This ring," I say, and show it to her. She reaches to take it from my fingers, and I hesitate for a second or two before letting it go. As she holds the ring up to a lamp, I can see the diamonds reflecting the light, and I find myself wanting to look away.

"This isn't a recent purchase, is it? This ring must be at least twenty years old."

"Yeah. It was my gran . . ." I pause. "Yes, it is old." I can't tell her it's my grandmother's. What would she think about someone who pawns their grandmother's engagement ring, a family heirloom, for quick cash?

I watch her as she continues to examine the ring with a microscope and some other equipment I don't recognize. Honestly, I don't even like her touching it. I hate watching a stranger handle my grandmother's ring like it's just some metal and stone article that has nothing but monetary value.

"These are quality diamonds," she says when she's done evaluating the ring. "I can give you a loan of two thousand dollars on it."

"Two thousand dollars? I have it on good authority that the ring is worth at least five thousand."

"Darlin', what the ring is worth and what I can loan you for it are two different things. Should I write up a ticket or not?"

I want to say, "Not!" Two thousand dollars won't even cover a third of the cost of my surgery, but at least it would be a healthy start. I'll find a way to raise the rest, and I'll find a way to keep making payments on the loan so I can eventually get the ring back. I look at the woman behind the counter and then down at the ring. And finally I say, "Yes."

"I'll need some identification," she says to me, and I can see my hands shaking as I open my purse and reach for my wallet. As I hand her my license, I try to reassure myself that I will be able to pay off the loan and get the ring back. As she's filling out the ticket, she rattles off some information about interest and fees and pay-back schedules, but I'm not really listening. I'm just staring at the ring sitting on the counter. In some strange way, I feel like it's staring back at me, and I can't take my eyes off of it. Then, without a word, I reach for the ring, put it back on my finger and hurry out the door without looking back. I scurry to my car and hop inside. As soon as I get the door closed, I let the tears stream down my face.

"How did I get into this mess!?" I shout out loud. "I'm so sorry!" I say to no one, or maybe I'm saying it to everyone. "I'm *so* sorry," I say again as my body shakes with grief and shame. Maybe I'm saying that I'm sorry to my grandmother for even thinking of pawning her ring—a ring my grandfather worked for forty years to pay for. Maybe I'm saying I'm sorry to my parents for lying to them about needing money to pursue my education when I really used the money for plastic surgery. Maybe I'm apologizing to all my friends in Atlanta for ruining our relationships over loans that went sour. Maybe I'm just saying that I'm sorry to myself for making such a financial mess out of my life.

I sit behind the wheel and just let it all come out for a few more minutes. Then I look up and catch a glimpse of myself in the rearview mirror, and all I can say is, "What a mess you've made, Kamille Cooper. What an unholy mess!"

When I finally get myself together I put the key in the ignition and start to back out of the parking space. I feel terrible for almost selling my grandmother's ring, but now that I've collected myself, I'm back to wondering how I'm going to pay to have my backside enhanced. But I guess I already know the answer. If I can't part with the ring, I'll have to sell the only material thing I have left of any value—my car.

# 47

---

# Brenda

When I finally pull into the driveway it's after midnight. The nurses let me take Nora home at about two o'clock this afternoon, and I've been over at her place all evening. She hired a nurse to stay with her the first night after her surgery, but I didn't feel right leaving right after we got there. I just wanted to stay and show my support even if the nurse was there to tend to her needs. Nora mostly slept while I was there, so I ended up reading the paper and watching TV the bulk of the time, which really wasn't such a bad way to spend an evening. I didn't end up leaving until after eleven o'clock, when I gave her a gentle hug and told her I'd be by to check on her before work in the morning.

She woke up from time to time, asking for pain medication or for help to get to the bathroom. By the time we'd gotten to her apartment, her eyes had swollen completely shut, and she needed me to lead her to the bathroom. She looked so pathetic. I was expecting her to look rough after the surgery, but she'd looked much worse than I had anticipated. There were no pictures of women with bruised and swollen faces puking up blood during the slide show at the plastic surgery forums. No one said you might wake up so weak and hoarse that you can barely communicate with anyone. There weren't any photos of noses stuffed with packing or patients wincing in pain as nurses wiped blood off their faces.

As I walk into my house, I think about how lately I've been entertaining the idea of having some plastic surgery myself. But after seeing Nora, I'm not sure I can bear it. It would be so nice to look a little younger, a little fresher, a little thinner. I think it might help me feel more confident and sexy, but, as I learned today, it comes at a price, and I'm not talking about just a dollar amount. You also pay with pain . . . lots of pain; bruises, pain, swelling, pain, blood . . . did I mention pain? It seems like an awful lot to go through to erase a few years from your face or take an inch off your waistline.

I never really thought of myself as the kind of person who would have plastic surgery. And I certainly never thought that it would be something I'd be considering at thirty-six years old. But I also hadn't planned on my husband taking a mistress.

The house is quiet as I walk up the stairs. You'd think that worthless dog would at least offer a yip or something when someone comes into the house after midnight, but I'm sure she's snuggled up next to my husband. When I get upstairs the hallway is dark, but I see light coming from under Jodie's door. I'm about to knock when I hear her speaking. I figure she must be on her cell phone again and wonder who she'd be talking to this late when I hear another female voice coming from inside the room.

"Hello," I say, and knock on the door.

Jodie opens the door, and I see a pretty girl, about the same age as Jodie, sitting on her bed. "Hi," Jodie says.

"How's it going?" I ask Jodie and then look in the direction of the blonde.

"Fine," she says and sees me looking at her friend. "This is Kylie, a friend from school."

"Hi, Kylie. It's nice to meet you."

"Ah . . . yeah. You too," Kylie says.

"What are you guys doing up so late? You have school tomorrow."

"Just working on a school project."

"Oh. I see," I say, even though I don't feel as though I am being told the truth. I'm sensing that I walked in on more than a late-night study session. "Well. It's late. I think you girls should call it a night. Do you need a ride home?" I ask Kylie.

"No. My car's out front," she says, and starts collecting her things.

"Okay then. Good night, girls." I walk down the hall to the bedroom wondering what is going on. Jodie rarely brings friends from school home, and this Kylie girl is certainly not someone I'd expect Jodie to be friends with. I think about how Kylie is the kind of girl that Jodie would refer to as a Barbie doll, and then it hits me—if I'm not mistaken, Kylie is the girl who was muttering snide comments about Jodie the day I picked her up from school to go to the dentist. Of course, I can't be sure. I only saw that girl briefly, and Lord knows there are probably a bevvy of bleach-blondes running around Dominion High School. But even if Kylie is not the same girl, something just isn't kosher about the two of them hanging out together.

After I take a quick shower, I slip on a night shirt and head toward the bed. Jim is sound asleep, snoring like a hibernating bear, with the dog lying next to him. As I quietly climb into bed, Helga lifts her head, and I see her big brown eyes glisten in the darkness. She gives me a look like, "Oh, you again," and lowers her head back to the mattress. I shuffle under the covers, turn on my side, and listen to the sound of Jim snoring. It makes me think of a time, so many years ago, when I'd nudge him awake and tell him that he was snoring, sometimes even when he wasn't, just so I had an excuse to have him turn on his side and so I could cuddle up next to him and spoon him. Part of me wouldn't mind doing that right now, but another part of me won't even let myself entertain the thought. How can I seek intimacy with him when I know that he's sleeping with another woman? Why would I even want to?

I lie next to him and listen to the sounds coming from his nose, and I find myself wondering if he ever snores when he's with *her*. Do they ever fall asleep together? Is snoring just another thing about him that she finds "cute?" I can feel the goose-bumps forming on my arms as I think of the two of them together—Jim and Jazelle lying next to each other the same way

Jim and I are now. The more I think about it, the more Jim's snoring starts to infuriate me—the same way it did the night I found out about his affair with Jazelle. The rustle of the inhalation and the different pitch and crackle of the exhalation—it's like he's mocking me somehow with his noises, like his snoring is one more thing I'm supposed to overlook.

The noise of his breath starts to radiate in my head and before I know what I'm doing I smack him on the stomach yelling, "Stop it! Stop it!" Then I pull my knees in toward my chest and kick him with both feet, thrusting him onto the floor. I hear a clunk as he hits the ground and see Helga jump to her feet.

I watch as Jim lifts himself from the ground. "Are you okay?" he says to me, startled, but groggy at the same time. "You pushed me out of bed," he adds, as if I don't realize what I did. "I think you were having a bad dream or night terrors or something," he says as he climbs back into bed and moves in close to me.

"Yes, that must have been it," I lie, while Jim puts his arm around me and tries to comfort me.

"It was just a bad dream. Relax and go back to sleep," he says, and I rest on the bed with his arm across my stomach, and think how much I wish it was just a bad dream—that this whole mess my marriage has become was really just a bad dream.

# 48

---

# Brenda

"Let me ask you something," the well-dressed woman in the leather chair across from me asks, before adding, "Now don't be offended by this question. I'm your therapist, and you're paying me to help you, so I have to ask it."

"Okay," I say.

"Exactly when did you say, 'To hell with it all', when did you decide to just give up?"

"What do you mean?" I ask.

"Look at you," she says to me. "You have this short wash-and-wear haircut. You don't have any make-up on. You've let your body go. You clothes are dowdy . . . honestly, I've seen nuns with more sex appeal." She holds a mirror up to my face. "Look at yourself. Lord, I'd cheat on you too."

I sit there aghast for a moment before responding. "But I'm busy. I don't have time for all of that. I have a daughter and a full-time job and spend half my life in traffic. I'm busy," I say again, and I find myself still saying, "I'm busy," as my eyes suddenly shoot open, and I quickly sit up in bed. The horrid therapy session was just a dream, but I can still hear the nasty therapist's words—telling me how dowdy I look, insinuating that it's my fault that my husband has strayed.

I glance at the clock. It's almost five-thirty in the morning. I turn and take a quick look at my sleeping husband and that stupid dog nestled up against him before getting out of bed and heading downstairs.

A few minutes later I'm sitting in my smoking chair puffing away on a Marlboro Light between sips of coffee. I'm at that point in the morning where everything that is going on in my life is coming to mind. When I first get out of bed in the morning I don't necessarily remember all the craziness that has become my life. It takes a minute or two before I remember that my husband is having an affair, or that I have an hour-and-a-half commute into the city ahead of me, and that I have so many concerns about my daughter. But sooner or later it all comes rushing back and, in typical Wasp fashion, I've been doing my best not to think about any of it. It's hard, but I've had years of practice at ignoring things that upset me. You'd be surprised how good one can get at such a thing. In fact, yesterday I was so caught up in taking care of Nora after her surgery that I barely thought about my husband being intimate with another woman. But now that I've gotten some rest, and the sun is starting to come out, it's all coming back to me.

I take another puff from my cigarette, inhale it deep into my lungs, and watch the smoke stream into the air as I exhale. I've been smoking more lately. My pack-a-day routine has become more like a pack and a half. I know it's a nasty habit, but it helps to calm my nerves, and my nerves have needed a lot of calming these days. Lately, I feel like I'm living in some sort of netherworld or like I'm starring in a Lifetime movie called something like *Her Husband's Betrayal* or *The Silent Wife: The Brenda Harrison Story*. I never thought I'd be the type of woman who would just put up with her husband's infidelity and go on like nothing's happening. Although I guess that's not exactly what I'm doing. In fact, I have plans to meet Jazelle for lunch today. I'm not exactly sure what I intend to gain from seeing her again. I guess I just hope that I can learn something from her—learn how to hang on to my husband and get her out of our lives.

When I finish my cigarette I shut the window I had cracked

open by the ashtray, stop by the kitchen to drop my coffee mug in the sink, and then head upstairs. On my way to the bathroom I see Jim is still sound asleep. He actually looks innocent lying there with his eyes closed. I watch him and see his stomach moving in and out, and I still feel love for him. I'm so sad that our marriage has crumbled into this mess—that I've let it happen, that he let it happen—but I do still feel love for him.

I move on to the sink, and when I've washed my face, I take a long look in the mirror. Even after seeing how horrid Nora looked after her surgery and the pain that she was in, I can't help but wonder what a little plastic surgery would do for me. Would it help me compete with women like Jazelle? Would an eye-lift improve my appearance? Maybe cheek implants—would they knock off a few years?

I'm brushing my teeth when Jim steps into the bathroom behind me.

"Hey," he says.

"Morning." As I watch him in the mirror, I catch sight of his underwear and immediately notice that Old Navy is not on the waistband. All of Jim's underwear is from Old Navy . . . or at least it used to be. I try not to be obvious as I strain to see that $2^{(x)}$ist is emblazoned on the elastic. What the hell does that mean? $2^{(x)}$ist? How do you even say that? Why does Jim's underwear have some sort of mathematical equation on it? I can't believe that, in all the years we've been married, he hasn't bought himself a single pair of underwear, but the moment he starts fornicating with some whore he goes out and buys some designer briefs I don't even know how to pronounce.

Once again I'm starting to silently fume like Bree Van De Kamp on *Desperate Housewives*. I stand at the sink, wondering how much more of this I can take as Jim walks over to the shower and starts the water. Then he takes off his T-shirt and slips out of his underwear. As he steps into the shower I see that his rear-end looks red and irritated.

"What happened to you?"

"Hmm?" he asks.

"Your butt's all red."

"Huh? Oh . . . yeah. I slipped on a patch of ice in the parking lot at work . . . fell flat on my ass."

"Really? Gosh, I'll be glad when winter is over."

"Me too," he says and puts his head under the water.

I watch him massage some shampoo into his hair and, out of the blue, I have one of my sex-drive reappearances. I see Jim soaping up his naked body in the shower, and I have this odd urge—well, odd for me—to join him in the shower. To take off my own clothes, slip into the shower behind him, and press my naked body against his. What if I joined him under the water and gave Jazelle a run for her money? I start to feel flushed as I think about it. But I couldn't possibly do such a thing. I haven't done anything like that in ten years. He'd think I'd gone mad. Jim and I don't do things like that.

What could possibly be causing these sudden surges of libido I've been having lately? It must have something to do with jealousy or with not realizing what you have until someone comes along and takes it away from you. I watch him in the mirror and, for the first time in what seems like forever, I see Jim as a handsome sexy man: bulging belly, thinning hair, and all. I remember when I was kid and I had this rabbit-fur jacket that my parents gave me for Christmas. I wore it once or twice but never really liked it that much. It hung in my closet for months until, one day, my friend Amanda from next door asked if she could wear it. I said yes and that night we went to the roller-stating rink, and a couple of other kids told her how much they liked her coat. The more people complimented her on it, the more she seemed to shine with it on . . . and the more I hated the fact that she was wearing *my* coat, and I wanted it back. What had I been thinking—letting her wear it? It was mine, and it was actually much prettier than I had originally thought. Has the same thing happened with my husband? Is Jim the adult version of my rabbit-fur coat? Is he so much more attractive to me now because someone else has him?

# 49

## Kamille

It's early in the morning, and I'm standing next to my car on Georgia Avenue in the city. I had garage parking when I first moved into my building a few months ago, but I fell behind on the rent and, although they haven't been able to evict me, they did cut off my access to the parking garage. I've got the rent paid up for now, but those fools in the leasing office still haven't reset the pass that lets me into the garage. In my short time here I've learned about two major advantages of living in D.C: 1) the city has extremely renter-friendly laws on the books, so you can go months without paying your rent without any real threat of eviction, and 2) that I can, if I have to, get by without a car. The public transportation system is not the best, but it will get me to work and around the city, to my doctor and hair appointments and such.

I'm eyeing strangers as they walk by, wondering if any of them is Roy Williams, a used car dealer who called me last night about buying my car exactly thirty minutes after I put up the ad on the Internet. It's a 2001 Honda Accord that I managed to buy before my credit went completely to hell. And, believe it or not, I actually paid it off a few months ago. I've found you can skate around credit card debt and even stall with the rent but, funny thing about car loans—if you don't keep up with the payments, those fuckers come and take your car. The bank threatened to repossess the car on numerous occasions, but I always managed to come up with payment money in the nick of time. Of course, it was always at the expense of my electric bill not getting paid, or my phone being cut off, or a number of angry calls from department store creditors. But, before I lived in D.C., I lived and worked in Atlanta. There was no way I could do anything in Atlanta—get to work, run errands, whatever— without a car, so, one way or another, I always managed to keep the Honda in my driveway and off the back of a tow truck bound for the repo lot.

It's cold outside, and I use my gloved fingers to hold the collar of my coat tightly around my neck. It's a sad day for me—to sell the only thing of any real value that I own. But, at the same time, I desperately hope that this Roy Williams and I can make a deal. According to Edmunds.com, the car is worth seven thousand dollars, the exact amount I need to pay for my new ass. Mr. Williams seemed eager to deal. My ad had barely been posted on the Internet when he called and inquired about the car, and he even agreed to meet me before work to take a look at it.

I'm concerned about getting around without a car, but I'm more concerned about continuing to live with Calista Flockhart's ass. It's going to be a big change—having to take public transportation everywhere, but it will be worth it, and I'll be more attractive and more attractive people make more money, so I'll be able to buy a new car sometime soon. Once I have the butt implants I'll be able to catch up on some other bills and start to pay down some of this debt. Or maybe I'll just declare bankruptcy and be done with it all. I wish I hadn't gotten myself into this financial mess, but I look at most of the money I've spent as an investment—an investment in myself and the way I look. People take out mortgages for hundreds of thousands of dollars to buy homes and, the last time I checked, the type of home you own makes little difference in the way people treat you, the way people look at you, and the way you feel when you look in the mirror. If I had been born beautiful, I wouldn't need to spend so much money turning my face and my body into something presentable. But, unfortunately, I wasn't born beautiful. I was born with disfigured lips, nappy hair, a sunken face, small boobs, and a flat ass. I've needed every surgical procedure, hair extension, and cosmetic product I've ever purchased. We live in a society where being beautiful is everything, and I'm almost there. *Really*, I'm almost there. I just need the cash for this last procedure, and then I'll be done . . . for a while, anyway.

I'm really starting to get cold when I see an older black man approach from the corner. He's probably in his fifties, with very short hair, and wearing a long navy blue wool coat.

"Kamille Cooper?" he asks.

"Yes," I say, my mouth slightly numb from the cold.

"How are you?"

"Good. Thank you."

"Is this the car?"

"Yep," I say and open the driver's side door. "It's in great condition. It only has sixty-five thousand miles on it."

He pokes his head around the interior and then climbs inside and sits in the driver's seat. He looks all around and eventually leans over and takes a look in the backseat. "Can I start it up?"

"Sure." I hand him the key. Maybe I shouldn't have done that. For all I know he's a car thief, but he's looks honest enough and is dressed professionally—I saw a tie peeking out from his overcoat. He starts the car and listens to the engine hum for a few seconds. Then he pulls the hood release and gets out of the car to take a look at the engine. After giving the motor a quick once-over he walks around the car and takes a close look at all four tires.

"Do you mind if I take it for a drive around the block?"

"Um . . . no," I say. "I'll ride with you." I'm not sure that it's the best idea for me to get in my own car with a strange man, but I certainly can't let him take it without me, and I don't suppose I can expect someone to buy a car without test-driving it. The street is crowded with cars, and the sidewalks are busy with morning commuters walking to office buildings or Metro stops. If he tries anything, I can scream out the window.

We take an uneventful ride for about fifteen minutes and pull over back where we started from. The heater has finally started to blow hot air, so we stay in the car to discuss business.

"I can give you five thousand dollars for it," he says.

"Five thousand dollars? No way!"

He grins, like he didn't expect this kind of reaction. "Okay. I can do six thousand, but no higher."

Six thousand is not enough. I'd love to have the car sold this morning, but where am I going to get the other thousand dollars needed for my surgery? "Mr. Williams, I did my research, and I know this car is worth at least seven thousand dollars."

He smiles again. "You may get seven thousand dollars for it . . . if you want to keep showing it and paying for your ad to run on the Internet. Yeah, if you have the time, you *may* be able to get seven thousand, but I'm offering you six thousand for it right now."

Shit! My desperation must show in my face. Maybe I shouldn't have agreed to meet him so early in the morning—it probably made me seem too eager. But I *am* eager. I need the money, but I need more than what he's offering me.

"I'm afraid I'll have to pass." I reach over, turn the ignition off, and take the keys. I click the door handle open, and I'm about to get out of the car when he pipes up.

"All right, all right. Sixty-five hundred. That's my absolute final offer."

I close the door. I'm about to take it—surely I can come up with the additional five-hundred dollars, but something stops me—it's the thought of how long it will take me to come up with the additional money. My next ten paychecks are essentially earmarked to keep the Capital One pirates from crashing through my front door.

"Mr. Williams, this car is worth seven thousand dollars and that's what I want for it. Take it or leave it."

He laughs at me like I'm some kind of stubborn schoolgirl. "I like a woman who plays hardball," he says. "It's kind of sexy."

"Seven thousand dollars, Mr. Williams. Do we have a deal?"

"Okay. I'll give you seven thousand dollars, but you need to sweeten the deal—throw in a little something extra on top of the car."

"Like what?" I ask.

His eyes take a quick scan from my head to my breasts, down to my lap. "If I'm going to pay you five hundred dollars more, I want you to make it worth my while . . . if you know what I mean."

It takes a minute for what he's implying to register in my mind, but when it does, I can't believe I'm not telling him to get out of my car, to stop looking at me like I'm a piece of meat, to get his perverted face away from me. That's what I should be thinking. But, instead, I find myself weighing his offer. How bad could it be to give him a little sugar for a brief while? Then I'd have all the money I need to pay for my surgery.

"Seven thousand dollars," he says. "That's what I'm offering for the car and just a brief . . . shall we say . . . *rendezvous* . . . an intimate rendezvous."

I look at him. He looks like a puppy begging at the table, hoping his owner will drop him a piece of steak.

"That's my offer," he says. "Take it or leave it."

I turn my head and look out the window. My eyes meet the backside of a woman on her way to work. She's wearing a short leather jacket and a tight wool skirt. Her ass goes on for days. I take a moment to stare at her perfect derriere—the kind of ass I want for myself.

"So? We have a deal?"

I turn my head back to face him. "You bring me a cashier's check for seven thousand dollars, and, yes, we have a deal."

# 50

## Brenda

I'm sitting in a booth by myself at Reeve's, a diner on G Street, waiting for Jazelle to show up and join me. I'm exhausted. I didn't get to bed until late last night, and it's been a busy morning. I had to stop by Nora's place on the way to work and check in on her, and I'm also covering her projects while she's out of the office. She looked better than she did yesterday, and her voice was starting to come back, but she was still terribly swollen and in a lot of pain. She only hired the nurse to stay with her for the first night after surgery, so I'll need to stop by there after work and keep checking in on her throughout the week.

Nervous about having another meeting with Jazelle, I find myself anxiously fidgeting with the straw in my iced tea. Trying to relax, I look around at the waitresses in the restaurant. I'm not sure why, but for some reason, virtually every waitress in the place is a black woman over seventy years old. They move around pretty well for women their age, and, because they remind you of your grandmother, you tend to forgive and forget (and still leave a nice tip) when they give you white bread instead of wheat, or never bring the cream you want for your coffee, or hover over you and make sure you sign your credit card receipt before they'll step away from the table. It also helps that they make the best chicken salad around, and that Reeve's is one of the few places where you can get a slice of fresh strawberry pie. I actually see a slice of that famous pie go by in the hands of an elderly waitress, but I find that it barely stirs my appetite at all. I must really be distressed if strawberry pie is of little interest to me.

I'm not sure why I'm so nervous. I've already done this quasi-interrogation thing with Jazelle once before—that night last week when we went for coffee and S'mores after the plastic surgery thing. I think I managed to appear fairly relaxed during our last encounter. I can do it again. Sure I can, I think to myself as I see Jazelle come down the steps into the diner. I watch her come over to the table and try to study the way she moves without being too obvious. She doesn't walk as much as she swaggers or sashays. She has her coat on her arm, and she's wearing a short skirt and what Nora calls a "boob shirt," a turtleneck that's so tight it leaves nothing to the imagination. And she has heels on. I'm guessing they're at least two and half inches high. In fact, as best as I can recall, she's worn heels every time I've seen her. I wonder how she walks around the city all day on those little spikes.

I'm clear across the other side of the restaurant, so I have plenty of time to take her in as she approaches the table. I don't want to stare too long, so I divert my eyes around the room, and, when I do, I notice a gentleman or two checking her out— checking her out! She's older than I am and heavier than I am, and men are checking her out. I can't remember the last time I felt like a strange man was giving me a once-over.

"Hey there, Myrtle," she says, and slides into the booth across from me.

"Hi. I'm glad you could make it."

"Yeah. Me too."

"So how have you been?"

"Oh, just fine. Busy as a beaver. How about you? Have you scheduled any plastic surgery yet?" she asks with a laugh.

"No. Not yet. I'm still batting around the idea, but I haven't made any definite decisions."

"Yeah. Me either. I think I might start with something a little less invasive . . . maybe get a chemical peel or something."

"Hmm . . . maybe I should look into that."

"Oh, please! You don't need a thing. I don't know what you were doing at the seminar to begin with. You look barely over thirty-five."

I'm not sure what to say to this. I *am* barely over thirty five. Couldn't she say I look barely over twenty-five or even thirty? "I guess we all need all the help we can get."

"That's for sure. I'm learning that the hard way. If I had known how hard it would be to be over forty and single, I'm not sure I would have divorced my husband."

"Really?"

"Yeah. I've been divorced now for three years, and the only companionship I've been able to find is a married man."

"Oh yes. You said something about him the last time we got together," I mention, appearing almost disinterested. "What was his name again?"

"Jim."

"You didn't tell me much about him last week. What's he like?"

"He's a real sweetie. I only get to see him a couple times a week. You know, with the wife and all. And he has a teenage daughter too."

"That's got to be a difficult situation."

"It is. But I enjoy our time together. And the sex! Oh my God! The sex!"

I can't believe it's barely lunchtime and this woman, who I hardly know, is telling me about her sex life. I see her face light up just *talking* about sex with Jim. My face doesn't look like that when I'm *having* sex with Jim. "That good?"

"Oh yes! I think it's the married thing. He doesn't talk about his wife, but I get the feeling she's pretty frigid. I think he's been sexually repressed for a long time with her. I'm the recipient of all that pent-up sexual energy."

*Frigid*!? I'm *frigid*!? "Really?" I hope the heat I'm feeling in my face isn't showing.

"Yes. His wife buys him this crap underwear from Old Navy, so last week I bought him some of those $2^{(x)}$ist designer briefs, and you would of thought I had just bought him a Rolex. I just do little things for him that his wife can't be bothered to do."

"I see," I say, thinking of Jim in that very underwear this morning. Apparently it's pronounced "to exist." Who knew?

"Last night we did this thing," she says and pauses for a moment, looks around to make sure no one is eavesdropping and lowers her voice. "We did this little S&M thing. He wanted me to spank him with my hair brush. It was wild."

"Spank him?" I say, and my mind flashes back to this morning in the bathroom when Jim was walking into the shower and I noticed the inflammation on his rear-end. He said he had slipped on the ice and fell on his butt.

"Yeah. I think he gets the vanilla stuff from his wife, so I've been trying to jazz things up," she says as a waitress finally approaches our table to take our order. I listen as Jazelle tells the server what she wants for lunch. I'm looking at her, but the only thing I can see is a vision of my husband. He's naked and on his knees like a dog with Jazelle kneeling beside him, swatting his rear with a hair brush. I order a chicken salad sandwich for myself, but I know I won't be able to eat it. All I can think about is a hair brush and my husband's ass and the sound of her swatting him.

After the waitress leaves, Jazelle excuses herself to go to the restroom. I watch her walk toward the bathroom in her short skirt and tight shirt. And then I look down at myself in my knee-length gray wool skirt and baggy navy blue blouse. I look back at her sauntering on those high heels and look down at my own feet—at the plain black flats I have on them. I'm frigid, I think to myself. I'm a frigid bitch. I've done this to myself . . . to Jim. I forced him into the bed of another woman.

I feel tears start to well up in my eyes, and I realize that I can't bear the thought of hearing any more about my husband and Jazelle. I don't even want to look at her again. I just want to go home, slip the dog a Benadryl, crawl under the covers, and sleep. I want to escape the pain.

"You okay?" Jazelle asks when she returns to the table.

"Yeah . . . yeah, sure," I say. "But, you know . . . when you were in the bathroom I got a call on my cell phone. Something's come up . . . an emergency. I have to go," I say distractedly. "I'm sorry. I really have to go." I get up from the table and leave without another word.

I walk out of the restaurant and onto the sidewalk. It's quite cold outside, but I can't seem to muster the focus it would require for me to put my coat on. Frankly, I'm surprised I remembered to grab it from the booth before I took off and just left Jazelle sitting at the table. As I march down the sidewalk, I find myself taking in all the faces of the people passing by. I look at them, and there isn't a single one of them with whom I would not change places. I see a young girl, probably twenty-years-old, with a petite frame and rich brown hair, and I wish I were her. I see two men in overalls pushing a cart loaded with construction supplies down the sidewalk, and I wish I was them. I see an elderly woman with a bad wig and a cane, wearing a fur coat, and I wish I was her. I wish I was any of them. I don't care about what kind of life they have, how much money they make, the status of their health. It doesn't matter—none of them could possibly be feeling the kind of pain that I'm feeling now.

I keep walking until I see an empty bench. When I reach it, I let myself collapse onto it. I sit on the bench and look straight ahead, wishing I could just disintegrate into thin air, but then I think of how convenient that would be for Jim and Jazelle. Wouldn't it be nice for both of them if I just disappeared—if the frigid bitch just got out of the way?

I'm lost in thought when a taxi driver whales on his horn and snaps me out of my daze. I look at my watch, and much as I'd like to just go home and hide from the world, I know I have to go back to work. With Nora out of the office recuperating from her surgery there is way too much work to be done for me to be able to blow off the rest of day. So I do what I always do, which is suck it up and keep on going. I take a deep breath and pull myself from the bench and head back to the office.

# 51

# Kamille

"Hi, Mr. Williams," I say as I'm walking down the hall-way toward the door to my apartment where he is ea-gerly waiting. I can feel myself filling up with angst and dread as I continue down the hall. I thought we might just take care of business this morning, but Mr. Williams said it would take a couple hours for him to get the check, so we agreed it would be a better idea to meet back at my place during my lunch break.

"Hello. Please, call me Roy," he says when I reach him.

"Do you have the cashier's check?"

"Yes. Right here." He pats his shirt pocket. "Shall we go in-side and seal the deal?"

I take a deep breath and swallow. "Yes . . . yes, of course."

We step inside my apartment and, strange as it sounds, I'm embarrassed for Mr. Williams to see it. He's a seedy used car salesman who's paying me for sex, but I'm still embarrassed that he now knows that my living space is of a much lower caliber than my clothes and hair and accessories.

"Would you like anything to drink?" I ask, which really is a silly question, considering I don't think I have anything to drink other than water from the tap, which I hope hasn't been cut off.

"No, thanks. I have a one o'clock meeting, so can we get on with it?"

"Sure . . . I guess so." The knot in my stomach grows larger as he starts to unbutton the cuff of his shirt. "Wait!" I say, stalling, not sure if I can go through with this.

He looks at me with wide eyes. "Yes?"

"Um . . . the check. I'd like to see it."

"Sure." He pulls the check from his pocket and hands it to me. I give it a quick once-over, and it looks legit. It's the exact amount I'll need to pay for my new ass. As much as I dread the thought of going to bed with Mr. Williams, I'm more afraid of spending the rest of my life with my flat rear-end.

"Looks good." I set the check on top of my desk and walk over toward him. I can do this, I think to myself. I'm not going to like it, but I can do it.

He sits down on the sofa. "Do you mind if I take off my shoes?"

"No. Please . . . go ahead." I join him on the sofa.

"You're so beautiful," he says. "I've never made this kind of offer to any other customer."

"Thank you." Maybe he does think I'm beautiful. What does he know? He's probably one of those guys who thinks any woman who's under eighty and doesn't have any warts is beautiful.

He touches my knee, looks at me for a moment, and then leans in and starts kissing me. I immediately want to vomit as I feel him pushing his tongue against my lips, trying to shove it in my mouth. I know I should part my lips and let his tongue inside, but I can't bear the thought of it. He's not a *hideous*-looking man—just your average middle-aged Joe, but he repulses me. I try to return his kisses, but I can feel my body cringing as his lips move to the side of my head, to the area below my ear. I reluctantly hold his head, trying to feign interest, while he devours my neck.

Mr. Williams eventually retreats from my neck long enough to undo the buttons on my blouse as I lie back with my eyes shut, trying to appear as if I'm lost in the throes of passion. When what I'm really doing is trying to pretend that he's Usher or Mekhi Phifer. But Usher or Mekhi wouldn't smell like Aqua

Velva. Usher or Mekhi wouldn't be slobbering all over me like a Rottweiler attacking a T-bone steak.

I slip out of my shirt and, just to speed up the process and get this whole mess over with as soon as possible, I go ahead and undo and remove my bra myself. Mr. Williams begins to caress my breasts with his hands, which are still cold from being out-side a few minutes earlier—or has my heat been turned off again? Mr. Williams looks at my chest with a greedy smile. This is silly I know, but I'm actually proud to show my tits to Mr. Williams. After all, I paid a fortune for them—in money, time, and a painful recovery—and they are quite spectacular since the surgery. They're perky and round and voluptuous—so much better than those pathetic mammary glands God gave me. Mr. Williams begins to work on my nipples with his tongue, the sen-sation much duller than before I had the surgery. As he goes at my boobs with his fingers and his mouth, I place my hands on his shoulders and grip them tightly. I still want this over with as quickly as possible but, I will admit, I've found myself starting to enjoy the attention. The intense way he's consuming me, and the fervor of his breathing, lets me know that my breasts are beautiful and captivating, and the thought is what keeps me going as he reaches behind me and unzips my skirt. I just need to get through this, I think to myself. And when it's over I'll have the money to make my buttocks as beautiful as my breasts.

# 52

# Nora

"Why did I do this to myself," I mumble as I roll over in bed. The pain and the agony have been much worse than I expected—much worse than I was told to expect by Dr. Radcliff. Every time I think of him standing in front of the room during the seminar on plastic surgery, I just want to pull off one of his Gucci loafers and shove it up his ass. As I'm writhing in pain, I picture myself saying, "Oh don't worry about the pain from the shoe up your ass, Dr. Radcliff. It should subside over the next few days. Try to keep your mind off of it. I'm sorry if I led you to believe that a shoe up your ass would involve only minimal discomfort, but, you know, everyone has a different tolerance for pain," which is pretty much what he told me when I complained of the pain I've had since surgery.

Thank God the incessant vomiting has finally subsided. For the first two days all I did was throw up blood. Brenda even made a little bed for me on the bathroom floor with my comforter and some pillows as it just took too much energy to repeatedly make my way to the bathroom from the bed.

Even though I still can't breathe through my nose and the throbbing in my head is still intense, I will admit to feeling somewhat better then I have since the surgery three days ago. I can now open my eyes without the aid of my fingers; the swelling in my cheeks has gone down a bit; and my nose is no longer gushing blood at regular intervals. Don't get me wrong— I still feel like hell, but at least I'm seeing signs of improvement.

I reach over for one of my pain pills, swallow it with a cup of water, and maneuver myself back under the covers. I'm trying to fall back to sleep. The Percocet helps relieve some of the pain, but the only true escape has been sleep. I'm lying there with my eyes shut hoping sleep will come soon when the phone rings, and I have to carefully lean toward the night stand, as gently as possibly, and reach for the phone.

"Hello."

"Hey. It's me. Owen."

I'm silent for a moment, not sure what to do. I lied to him last week and said I was going to New York for a few weeks. My first impulse is to hang up the phone, but it's too late. He already knows I'm home. "Ah . . . hi."

"I was going to leave a message on your voice mail at work, but someone answered your line and said you were home recovering from surgery."

"What!? Who said that?" My voice is suddenly stronger than it's been since the procedures. The only person who knows about my surgery is Brenda, and I can't imagine she would tell someone.

"I think she said her name was Gretchen."

That nosy bitch! How'd she find out about my surgery?

"She didn't say what kind of surgery. Nothing serious, I hope."

"No, nothing serious," I say. "Listen I'm really tired right now. Can I call you later?"

"Sure. But how about letting us in first? Billy and I are at your front door. When I heard you were sick, I thought I'd pick up a few things for you and drop them by."

My heart starts pounding, causing my head to throb so hard I think I might pass out. There is no way he can see me like this. *I* can't even stand to see me like this. "Now's not a good time, Owen. I'm sorry."

"Oh come on. It'll only take a moment," he says, and then I hear him talking to someone else. I assume it's Billy, but it turns out to be one of my neighbors. "Your neighbor let us into the building, we'll be up in a jiffy," he says and hangs up the phone.

"Fuck! Fuck! Fuck!" I say and hurry over to the mirror. A minute ago I could barely roll over in bed, and now I'm racing toward the mirror like a woman on a mission.

"*Ay Dios mío!*" I say out loud as I catch sight of myself. My eyes and cheeks are bruised and swollen. There's a bandage over the splint on my nose, and the stitches are still in my eyelids. No amount of make-up is going to make a dent in the mess that my face has become, and I doubt I could stand the pain of applying it anyway. I haven't taken a shower or washed my hair in days. I look like one of those photos of an abused woman shown in court, or a picture of someone who's been in a terrible car accident. A car accident! I think to myself. Yes, a car accident.

I grab a brush, and I'm about to push it through my hair but then, figuring it's pointless, I toss it back on the dresser just in time to hear Owen's knock on my door. With my adrenaline burst fading, I hobble over to the door, brace myself for his reaction to my appearance, and turn the knob.

"Hi." I wait to see his face contort into a look of horror.

"Hi," he says, more with a look of concern than anything else. "What happened?"

"I was on my way to the airport to leave for New York, you know, like I talked about last week, and I had a car accident."

"Oh my God! Are you okay?"

"I will be. My face hit the windshield and broke my nose and really messed up my face. It really looks horrible, I know, but the doctors fixed everything. It's just a matter of the swelling and bruising going away now."

"That's terrible," he says, and that's when I notice Billy at his feet, clutching Owen's leg for dear life. I was so busy trying to gage Owen's reaction to my disfigured face, that I hadn't noticed Billy standing next to him. Owen may not have a look of horror on his face, but Billy is staring up at me as if I'm Satan himself.

"Hi, Billy," I say. "Don't be afraid. I'm just healing from an accident."

My words seem to be of little comfort to him. He continues to stare at me as he tightens his grip on his father's leg.

"Say hi to Nora," Owen says to Billy, picking him up and resting him on his hip. Billy turns and buries his face in Owen's neck.

"Sorry. He's shy."

"That's okay. I'd be afraid of me, too, the way I look at the moment."

"Can we come in?"

"Of course." I move to the side, just now realizing that I haven't invited them in. They follow me into the living room and Owen, with Billy on his lap, joins me as I sit on the sofa.

"We won't stay long. I'm parked illegally out front. I just thought I'd stop by and see how you're doing and drop off a few things." He sets a grocery bag on the coffee table and pulls out some magazines, a jar of soup, and some ginger ale.

"That's very sweet of you." I'm honestly touched.

"No problem." He pauses and really takes a look at my face. "Gosh, you really got banged up. Did you hit another car or . . . ?"

"Yes . . . well . . . no, they hit me. So I'm told anyway. Honestly, I don't remember what happened. Apparently that's not uncommon after a traumatic accident." I figure that if I say I don't remember the accident, I won't have to come up with any details about it.

"I hope you're suing."

I try to offer a little chuckle. It hurts too much to smile. "We'll see," I say as I see Billy turning his head toward me, his fear fading into curiosity.

"Why's her face *bwue*?" he asks Owen.

Owen looks at me with an apologetic glance and then back at his son. "She was in a car accident. Sometimes people's skin turns blue and swells up when they have accidents. It's nothing to be afraid of.

"Does it *hort*?" This time Billy's question is directed toward me.

"Well . . . yeah, Billy. I guess it does. But it won't for too much longer. I'm healing."

"I had a *bwue* spot on head once when I fell against the coffee table."

"You did?"

"Yep, but it went away."

"I'm glad." I'm just happy that he isn't wincing in terror at the sight of me anymore.

"So your *bwue* spots should go away too," he says to me, then turns back to Owen. "Right, Daddy?"

"Sure," Owen smiles at me. "She'll be as good as new in no time," he adds and then turns his head toward the window behind the sofa. "Shit!" he blurts out.

"That's a bad word," Billy scolds.

"They're towing my car." Owen lifts Billy off his lap and gets up. "Stay here, Billy," he says before turning to me. "I'll be right back."

I watch him quickly walk away and out the door before Billy really has a chance to react to being left with Medusa. As the door closes behind Owen, I look at Billy. He's standing at the far end of the sofa staring back at me. When I look at him I can't help but feel a pang of jealousy. His skin is so soft, and there's not a wrinkle on his face. What I would do to have his skin.

"It's okay. Owen . . . I mean your daddy, will be right back. Why don't you sit back down?"

He just stares at me.

"Okay," I say, taking a look out the window. "Look at the window. In another minute or two you'll see your father out there." Billy does as I say, and it isn't long before we see Owen talking animatedly with a tow truck driver. "There he is. He'll be right back. You want me to turn the TV on? Some cartoons or something?"

"SpongeBob?"

"Huh?"

"Is SpongeBob on?"

What the fuck is a SpongeBob? Sounds like some new form of birth control. "Um . . . I'm not sure. We can check." I get up to look for the remote control, and as I'm tossing around a couple of magazines, I suddenly feel something in the back of my throat, making me want to gag.

"I'll be right back," I say to Billy and move toward the bathroom as fast as a person with a throbbing head can. When I get inside the bathroom I can hardly breathe—something is lodged in my throat. I rush to the mirror and try to see the inside of my mouth, but there isn't enough light. I reach inside and shove my finger toward my throat, but I can't seem to get a hold of anything. I panic and scurry back out into the living room.

"Billy! Billy!" I shout while trying to gasp for the little bit of air that seems to be getting past whatever is blocking my throat. I go up to him and get down on my knees. "Look inside my mouth, Billy. Do you see anything in the back?" I ask, opening my mouth, too frenzied to realize what a ridiculous position I am in.

Billy does as he is told. "*Oooks* like cotton."

Cotton? Oh shit, I think. It's the packing from my nose. It's fallen down into my throat, and it's blocking much of my airway. I reach my fingers toward the back of my mouth again, but I can't seem to get a hold of anything. Instantly I have a vision of Owen walking back into the apartment and finding his son standing over my dead body. The paramedics will come, but it will be too late. I can see it now—the cause of death written on my death certificate will be "the pursuit of vanity."

I'm struggling to grab hold of the debris in the back of my throat when Billy pulls my hand away and reaches in my mouth and grabs hold of the packing and starts pulling it out. I suppose it hurts, but it's all happening so quickly, and I'm so alarmed, that I don't even notice. A few seconds later my airway is clear, and Billy is standing in front of me with a small mound of stained packing in his hands.

I take a deep breath, thankful for every ounce of air going into my lungs, and then I give Billy a big hug. "Thank you, Billy," I say and hold him tightly.

"Ow," he says, and I release my grip on him.

"Sorry." I pull back and grab the waste from his hands. "Do you need some PediaCare?"

"Some what?"

"PediaCare. That's what daddy gives me when I don't feel good."

"No, thanks. Let's get you into the bathroom and wash your hands."

He follows me to the bathroom, and I turn on the faucet and pick up the soap dispenser. "I can do it *myself*," he says, taking the soap dispenser from my hands. I watch him as he lathers up his hands and rinses them under the faucet. Stubborn little guy, I think to myself. I feel myself wanting to smile, but smiling still hurts so I suppress it. Funny that he just cleared my airway for me, but I still assume that he needs help washing his hands. I guess I've always seen kids as this cesspool of need. But standing here watching Billy, and knowing what he did for me, I'm wondering if maybe I have it all wrong—or at least a little bit wrong. Maybe dating a guy with a kid isn't such a bad idea after all.

Billy is hauled up in front of a show he informed me is called *Blue's Clues,* and I'm just getting off the phone with Dr. Radcliff's office, when Owen comes back through the door.

"I had to pay the jerk fifty dollars to keep him from towing my car. We should all become tow truck drivers. It must be very lucrative when you add in the bribery factor. . . ." He's about to go on with his tow truck rant when he notices me holding a tissue to my nose and leaning my head back.

"Are you okay?"

"Yeah. I had a little incident with the packing in my nose while you were out. It came loose and lodged in the back of my throat."

"Oh my God!"

"It's all right. Your son came to my rescue and helped me get it out."

"Really?" Owen turns and looks at Billy, who can't be bothered to take his eyes off the television.

"Yeah. Don't worry. He's washed his hands."

"Do you need to go to the emergency room or the doctor's office?"

When Dr. Radcliff's receptionist told me I should come in

right away instead of waiting for my planned follow-up appointment tomorrow, I said I would try. But I'm not sure I'm up to driving, and I certainly have no intention of being seen on public transportation.

"Yeah. I'll head back to the doctor's office later today."

"Shouldn't you go now?"

"I'll go soon."

"Why don't you let me take you? Billy's nanny took a personal day, so I have the whole day off. It wouldn't be any trouble."

I had planned to see if Brenda could run me over there, but I guess it really doesn't make sense to bother her at work when I have someone already willing to take me.

"Are you sure?" I ask Owen, and as the words come out of my mouth, my mind is already working on an excuse for why he'd be taking me to a cosmetic surgeon's office. I'm thinking of telling him that it's routine for plastic surgeons to treat accident victims, but then I decide 'to hell with it,' I like this guy, and I'm starting to like his son. If I plan to make anything out of this relationship maybe I should begin by stopping the lies.

"Of course," Owen says back to me.

"I'd really appreciate that, but I guess it forces me to come clean about something."

"What? Your plastic surgery?" he says with a grin.

"How did you know?'

"The stitches around your eyes, I had the same ones when I had my eyes lifted last year. It was sort of a tip-off."

"You had your eyes done?"

"Sure. I was like you at first. I wanted to keep it all hush-hush, but the more I thought about it, the more I realized there was nothing to be embarrassed about. I'm not ashamed of going to the gym to stay fit or watching my diet to keep my weight in check. Why should I be embarrassed that I had a little surgery on my eyes to try to look better?"

"I don't know. I guess you shouldn't," I respond, and I don't say it out loud, but, to myself I think, I guess I shouldn't either.

# 53

# Kamille

I'm sitting at my desk, trying to get some work done, but all I want to do is take a shower . . . take *another* shower. I've taken upwards of twenty since I slept with Mr. Williams two days ago, but I still don't feel clean. I know it's impossible, but I still smell him on me, and the scent, whether imagined or real, makes me sick. I've done some loathsome things for money, but this really tops the list. I keep trying to tell myself that it's the *end* that's important, not the *means* used to get there. I simply did what I had to do to get what I need. If I hadn't agreed to sleep with Mr. Williams, I'd be months away from having the cash to pay for my surgery.

I try to force myself to put it out of my mind, but I keep getting these horrible flashbacks. I think of him on top of me, his hot breath in my face, his rounded belly pressing against me. The only way I was able to get through the experience was to think about how I would look once I have my implants. I tried to take myself to another place, imagining myself on the beach in the Bahamas wearing a bikini that my ass would actually fill out. I thought about how the men on the beach, men quite unlike Mr. Williams, would look at me with desire. I remember trying to feel the heat from the sun on my lotioned body while I lay on the beach with the waves crashing against the shore.

Why is it that I was able to get through the encounter by focusing my mind on something else, but, now that it's over, I can't get the memory of it out of my head. I always seem to work up the nerve to do what's necessary when it comes to obtaining money, but after my actions are completed, I can't seem to escape the guilt. Sleeping with Mr. Williams may be the most unsavory thing I've done to pay for my quest for beauty, but it's certainly not the only thing. I remember having similar feelings of shame when I shoplifted four cashmere sweaters from Bloomingdale's. The process was easy—I didn't look around to see if anyone was watching, I didn't try to sneak the sweaters into a large purse, I didn't dash out of the store once I had them in my possession. I just gathered them up and casually strolled out of the store with them as if what I was doing was perfectly legit. And no one so much as batted an eye. I did the same thing several more times at other stores, but I didn't get the high you often hear of shoplifters feeling—the satisfaction of knowing you're getting away with something. *Stealing* didn't compare with the high I got from *paying* for expensive clothes—handing my credit card to the sales clerk, making her think that I could afford to buy my purchases—that I was "somebody." Ironically, I occasionally used the money I received from selling stolen clothes on eBay to go back to the stores and buy the same garments I had previously stolen. Why didn't I wear the stolen clothes? Because I wanted the thrill of buying them. Besides, somehow it was okay to resell stolen garments to losers on eBay, but I didn't want the ill-gotten clothes on my own back.

I'd probably still be at it if I hadn't gotten caught walking out of Macy's with a silk blouse. I was doing my thing—just idly walking out of the store with my bounty in hand when a sales clerk stopped me, and asked why no one gave me a bag for my purchase. I responded by looking terribly embarrassed and said that I was in a daze, having had a hard day, and hadn't noticed that I still had the blouse in my hand. I handed it back to her, apologized again, and quickly went on my way before she had a chance to really react any further. It was a pretty benign encounter, but it was enough to scare me into quitting the shoplifting business.

I know it was wrong to steal, but, at the same time, it wasn't as though I was stealing from a little old lady or something. These were big department stores where everything was over-priced. It wasn't like I was hurting anyone—that's how I managed to shield myself from the guilt of shoplifting, by convincing my-self that I wasn't hurting anyone. But this approach isn't really cutting it when I try to apply it to my having sex with Mr. Williams. I wasn't hurting anyone by having sex for money. We had a deal, and we both came out of the situation with something we wanted. He got his freak on, and I got the cash I needed to pay for my implants. But if no one got hurt, why do I feel so scathed?

I guess at this point it really doesn't matter anyway. What's done is done and, regardless of how I got it, I now have the money I need to have my surgery. So I guess all I have to do now is pick up the phone and schedule it.

# 54

## Brenda

I've been back in my office for a few minutes now although I'm thinking that maybe I should be in the bathroom. I feel like I could vomit at any minute. I can't get the vision of Jazelle spanking my husband out of my mind. My brain has even added cheesy porn music to the film that won't stop running in my head. I wish I could make it stop—I wish I could make all of it stop!

The exhaustion is catching up with me—the fatigue of living a lie, pretending that I don't know that my husband is cheating on me. I'm tired of thinking about it and analyzing it . . . tired of trying to figure out how it all went so wrong, tired of feeling sorry for myself. I'm not sure how much longer I can do this. In the beginning I suppose I thought that if I ignored it or wished it away, it would all somehow fizzle out on its own—my husband would realize what a mistake he'd made and end his affair. Then, when I happened upon Jazelle, I started to believe that, by getting to know her, I could learn what attracted my husband to her and use the information to get rid of her. And, now . . . now I don't know what to think. The only thing I've learned from Jazelle is that my husband has a thing for being spanked with a hair brush.

I'm staring blankly at my computer screen when I hear a knock. I look up and see Kamille standing in my doorway.

"Hey. Do you have a minute?"

"Sure." I take a deep breath, thankful for an interruption of the vision of a hair brush slamming against my husband's rear-end.

"How are you?"

"Good," I lie. "You?"

"Hanging in there."

"Great. You're doing some great work around here—helping us all get organized," I lie again. In reality she's been a royal pain in the ass. I had to stay two hours late yesterday to re-file some of our presentations on the server so that the filing system would meet with her approval even though Nora was supposed to do it before she took leave for her surgery.

"Thanks. I think you're the only one who thinks so. I haven't gotten the warmest reception since I started here."

"People will come around. If they keep complaining, just tell them not to worry—our jobs are probably going to be shipped to India in a year or two anyway, and they won't have to be bothered by any of it," I say with a laugh, although I fear my words are not out of the realm of possibility.

Kamille smiles. "You're really the only person that has made any effort at all to be nice to me."

"Oh, that can't be true."

"I don't know. People have been pretty lukewarm, and I think Nora hates my guts."

"No, she doesn't. Nora just has a strong personality. Give her some time."

"Maybe," she says and hesitates for a moment. "Can I ask you a favor?"

"Sure."

"You're the only one in the office I feel even remotely comfortable asking this of."

"Okay," I say, my curiosity piqued.

"I'm having some elective surgery in a couple of weeks, and they require that someone pick you up and take you home, and I just moved here a few months ago and don't really know anyone in the area . . ."

"You don't need to say another word. I'd be happy to pick

you up," I say, and I *am* happy to help, but it does seem like an odd request coming from someone I barely know. "It's nothing serious, I hope."

"No, just something I need to take care of."

"Okay, well let me know the details, and I'll put it on my calendar."

"Thank you, Brenda." She gets up to leave. "I really appreciate it."

"No problem." I watch her exit my office. Here we go again, I think to myself. Didn't I just do this for Nora? Although I'm sure Kamille isn't having plastic surgery—she's far too young and far too pretty. I really do hope it's nothing serious. She didn't seem interested in volunteering the details of the surgery, so I didn't pry. Maybe it's a female thing or a tonsillectomy or something.

I look back at my blank computer screen and wonder what it is about me that says "mother hen." Why do people always come to me when they need help? I don't mind helping—in fact, I guess I like it, but sometimes there's a fine line between being a giving person and being a doormat. I want to help, I want to give, but I don't want to be walked on either . . . at least, not the way my husband is walking on me.

# 55

## Nora

When Owen, Billy, and I reach the fourth floor of the office building, we step out of the elevator and head down the hall and look for a door marked "Private," which is the door the receptionist told me to use when I called about coming back into the office. She said they have a separate waiting area for post-op patients. She added that it was private and I would feel more comfortable there, but my guess is that the separate area is not about my comfort level at all—it's about them not wanting any of their initial consultation patients to see how God awful they are going to look if they choose to go through with having surgery. To put it mildly, I look like hell! I have a splint on my nose and bandages wrapped around my face. The area under my eyes is black and blue, and my entire face is swollen like a blowfish. And, yes, it feels just as bad as it looks, if not more so.

"Never again, never again," I mumble to Owen as we enter the office. I've been saying that since I woke up from surgery three days ago.

I step over to the little tinted window and wait for the secretary to greet me. When she slides the window open I can see that the room I'm in is on the opposite side of the reception desk from the general waiting room, and I almost want to laugh at the measures they take to assure that their new patients don't see how bad they are going to look a few days after their procedures. I'm surprised they didn't ask me to walk down the hall with a bag over my head in case I ran into anyone on the way in. I guess I can't blame them, though. If I had seen someone like me in the waiting area when I came for my first visit with Dr. Radcliff, I'm sure I would have given my surgery a lot more thought before agreeing to go through with it.

After I check in the three of us sit down and wait. I look around and see that this waiting room is nowhere near as nicely appointed as the other one. It's quite small with flat institutional carpeting and typical doctor's office furniture—a far cry from the hardwood floors and leather sofas in the main waiting area.

"Do you want me to go back with you?" Owen asks.

"Oh, thanks, but I don't think that's necessary. Besides, Lord knows what they have in store for me. It could get ugly, and Billy certainly doesn't need to see anything like that."

"Like what?" Billy wants to know.

Owen looks at me and smiles. "Nothing for you to be concerned about," he says to his son. "Why don't you get your coloring book out of you backpack and color Nora a picture."

"Okay," Billy says, unzipping his bag. Owen and I sit in silence for a few more minutes until an assistant calls me. I follow her down the hall to an examining room and sit down. A few minutes later Dr. Radcliff comes in with one of his big smiles.

"Hello there!" he says, his chipper voice getting on my nerves. "How are you doing?"

"Not so good. Feeling a tad bit better then I did, but the pain is still pretty intense."

"You're taking your medications?"

"Yes."

"Good, good. Well, the worst few days are over, and things will keep improving for you."

"I hope so," I say as he sits down on the stool next to me, gets close to my face, and admires his handiwork.

"Your eyes are healing nicely." He pulls his head back, and starts to take off the bandages on my face. Once he has them removed, he lifts the splint and starts to examine my nose and my cheeks.

"Everything looks perfect," he says after a few minutes of

poking and prodding. Would you like to see it with the bandages off?"

"Yes," I say, not really sure that I do.

He hands me a mirror, and I take a look. And it's a scary sight. Through the swelling and the blue patches under my eyes I can see that the bend in my nose is gone, but that's really the only improvement I can find at this point. My face is still too disfigured to get a sense of what kind of difference the eye surgery or the cheek implants are going to make once I'm healed.

While I look at myself in the mirror, I'm inwardly shouting, "Never again, never again!"

Dr. Radcliff looks at me and smiles (I'm getting a little tired of his smiles). "Don't worry. You are going to look fantastic once you've healed." He takes the mirror from my hand, and grabs some sort of wooden stick with a Q-tip-like swab on the end. It looks to be about as long as a standard ruler.

"Now this might be a bit uncomfortable," he says, and I immediately tense up.

He brings one of the tools to my nostrils.

"You're not going to put that up my nose?" I say in a panic.

"Try to relax, and we can get this over with as soon as possible. I need to clear out some of the mucus and clots." He puts one hand on my forehead and starts to insert the chopstick-like thing into my nose. As the stick goes deeper and deeper, and he starts twisting it, I grab the chair arms and involuntarily lift my buttocks off the seat. It hurts! Fuck! Does it hurt! I want to grab his arm and make him stop, but I'm afraid he might puncture my nose if I jerk his hand away. I force myself to remain still and tolerate the pain. As I feel myself gagging as the stick goes deeper, I wonder why I've never seen a doctor shove a long wooden stick up anyone's nose on *Dr. 90210* or *Extreme Makeover* or *The Swan*.

"And we're done," he says when he's finally finished impaling my nostrils. I can feel my entire body relax as the instrument comes out, and I let out a huge breath of relief that it's over. "That's probably the worst part of the whole procedure. You're now over the biggest humps," he adds, before going on to cover a few more things about my recovery, taking the stitches out from around my eyes, and sending me on my way with a couple more prescriptions. As I walk down the hall to meet up with Owen and Billy and go home, this time I say it out loud, "Never again. Never again. . . ."

# 56

# Brenda

So here I am again, dropping off another friend to have surgery. Kamille still hasn't told me exactly what kind of surgery she is having, but the plate on the door we just walked through says Clover and Klein Cosmetic Surgery. Unlike Nora, who had her procedures in a hospital, it appears that Kamille is going to have her surgery, whatever it may be, right here in the doctor's office.

"Thanks again for bringing me here," Kamille says after she checks in with the receptionist, and we sit down in the waiting area.

"No problem," I say, which isn't true. I had to get up at four o'clock this morning to pick her up at five-thirty and get to the doctor's office by six. "You're going to have your surgery here in the office?"

"Yes, they have a whole surgical suite here. It's just like a hospital operating room."

"That's good to know."

"You don't have to stay. I'll be fine if you want to get on to work."

"I'm fine. I don't need to be in the office until eight. I may as well stay and keep you company until they call you in."

Kamille looks at me. "You're so sweet to help me out. I mean . . . we barely know each other."

"It's not a big deal. I'm really just giving you a ride and offering some support. I'm sure it's hard to be new in town and not have any family or friends in the immediate area."

"Yes it is. Especially at times like these when you need a little help." She flounders for a moment, and then continues. "It's also been nice of you to not ask about the kind of surgery I'm having, but I guess the cat's out of the bag now."

"What do you mean?"

"Well, we're in a plastic surgeon's office."

"Yeah, I did figure that out," I say with a grin. "But that doesn't mean I know what you're having done. Well, I know it's plastic surgery of some sort, but that's it. It's really none of my business," I say, even though I am curious. She's such a beautiful young woman. I can't imagine what she would want to change about herself.

"I had to sign a HIPAA release for them to discuss my discharge with you when you pick me up, so you're going to find out sooner or later that I'm having . . ." Her voice trails off for a moment as if she's embarrassed to talk about it. "I'm having my buttocks enhanced."

"Really?" I say. "What on earth for?" The question comes out involuntarily. I've never taken a close look at Kamille's backside, but I'm quite certain it's not in need of any enhancement.

"It's just so flat."

I'm not sure what to say. I don't feel that now, mere moments before she is about to go under the knife, is the time to convince her that she doesn't need surgery. "You think?" I ask.

"Well, yes. Don't you?"

"Ah . . . well, no, actually I think your butt looks just fine the way it is."

"That's nice of you to say. If only it were true."

I'm about to protest further when a nurse comes out.

"Kamille Cooper?" she says in our direction

"Yes," Kamille responds and eagerly stands up. It's odd how relaxed Kamille seems about the whole thing. Nora was quite anxious before her surgery, but Kamille doesn't seem nervous at all.

"Are you ready?"

"You bet," Kamille says.

"Are you going to pick her up after the surgery?" the nurse asks me.

"Yes," Kamille answers for me. "This is Brenda. She has to work today, but she'll be coming to fetch me when I'm ready to leave."

"Nice to meet you, Brenda," the nurse says to me. "If you can wait a few minutes, I'll take Kamille back, and she can get changed. Then I can bring her personal effects out for you to take with you, and you can bring them back when you pick her up. That way we don't have to worry about locking them up or them getting lost."

"Sure," I say to the nurse and then turn to Kamille. "Good luck," I tell her and give her a quick hug. I watch her follow the nurse out of waiting room and take a real look at her behind— not a thing in the world wrong with it. It's not huge, but it seems like a nice enough derriere to me.

As I sit back down in the chair and wait for the nurse to come back out with Kamille's things, I wonder if it might be me soon—the one going back with the nurse to have cosmetic surgery. My God, if women like Kamille—gorgeous and in her in twenties—are having plastic surgery, then it certainly isn't too early for me. Would it really make any difference, though? I wonder. Would anything about my life actually change if a surgeon shaved a few years off my face? I guess I won't know until I have it done—when and if. But I'm getting desperate, and desperate times call for desperate measures.

# 57

## Nora

I'm standing in front of the mirror giving my face a hard look. It's been three weeks since my surgery. The bruising is gone, but there is still some swelling, which is a bit of a problem as I have to go back to work today. I've used every bit of sick and vacation leave that I have. I suppose I could claim to still be sick and take a few more days, but I can't really afford to take leave without pay, and poor Brenda has been covering much of my workload while I've been out. I'm sure she's ready for me to come back. Besides, I doubt a few more days are going to make a huge difference in the residual swelling. It could take weeks or months for all the swelling to completely go away. I guess I'm going to have to bite the bullet and hope no one notices the swelling at work. Although I don't think anyone would have the balls to ask me about it anyway—except for Gretchen, that is, and she'll probably do it in the middle of a meeting, so she could put me on the spot in front of a large group.

Looking in the mirror, I can see that the tiny crook in my nose is gone, which is really nice, but it was barely noticeable before, anyway. And I'm only noticing a minor improvement in my looks from the eye-lift and cheek implants. Once the swelling is completely gone I'm sure everything will look better, and I guess, in a way, it's good that my face doesn't look drastically different. I figure a subtle improvement is better than looking like someone is standing behind me pulling my hair. If nothing else, at least I don't have that too-tight look like Joan van Ark or Marie Osmond.

As I keep looking at my reflection from different angles, I can't help but wonder if it was really worth it. When I look at my adjusted nose all I can I think about is being in the recovery room with blood pouring down my throat. Even now, three weeks later, I'm constantly walking around with a tissue in my hand to wipe the unending drainage of clear fluid that dribbles down my nostrils. When I look at my eyes, it's hard not to think about having to lift them open with my fingers to be able to see or feeling my way to the bathroom because it was too painful to pry them open with my fingers right after surgery. I can see an improvement, but, the more I think about it, the more I think I might be done with plastic surgery. I'm just not sure it was worth the financial expense, and the time off from work, and, most importantly, the pain and just the general state of sheer misery I was in the first few days following the procedures. Who knows, maybe I'll feel differently once my face has completely healed or a few years down the line when my breasts are down to my navel, or my thighs start rubbing together when I walk.

Owen's whole reaction to the catastrophe that was my face when he stopped by a couple of weeks ago is also making me wonder about whether all this surgery was necessary. A part of me thought that, once he saw me all puffy and purple, that I'd never hear from him again. But he's been a real trooper. He didn't seem mad when I told him that I had made up my plans to visit New York City—he understood that I was embarrassed to tell him about my surgery. He has stopped by a second time and has called almost every day to see how I'm doing. I'm so used to the guys I date being totally superficial that it's surprising when a man actually sticks by you when you're not at your best. I almost feel ashamed that I had planned to dump him just because he had a kid, a kid who came to my aid when I needed it most.

I'm thinking about Owen and Billy when I start sorting through the mail, and I come across a card in a green envelope with a child's handwriting. I immediately open it up. It's a folded piece of construction paper with big flowers drawn on the front. When I open it up it reads:

> *I hope that your nose is better and that you can breathe.*
> *Love, Billy*

It's only a few simple words but, all of a sudden, I feel my eyes start to water. I've never had a good rapport with kids, and this card from Billy is really affecting me. I look at it again, and I just start to cry.

# 58

---

# Brenda

I'm pulling into the parking garage after leaving Kamille at the surgical center. I felt like I should have stayed while she was in surgery, but I already took a day off when Nora had her procedures, and all I did was sit around a waiting room. There really isn't any point in my missing another day's work to be holed up in the lobby of a surgical center. I'm sure the nurse will call me when Kamille is ready to be picked up.

It was only six-thirty when they took Kamille back, and I don't really need to be in the office until eight, so I decided to stop in a coffee shop down the street from the surgical center and treat myself to a breakfast of eggs, bacon, and toast and, I must say, it was mighty good. I'm always in such a rush in the morning that breakfast generally consists of cereal or some random piece of fruit that I scarf down in the car while sitting in traffic. It was a delight to relax and read the paper over a greasy breakfast, for once.

It's about eight when I step out of the car. As I push the door shut, I see a passerby look at the back of my car and frown at me. I'm used to the sniper-mobile getting some negative attention, but this woman really seems to be giving me an ugly look. In fact, on the way in to the city this morning I sensed that another motorist at a stop light next to me was snarling at me as well. Maybe I'm imagining things, I think to myself as I walk away from the car. Then, as I often do, I turn around to make sure I shut my headlights off or that I'm not sticking out of the parking lines, and I see a bumper sticker on the back of my car. It reads: *YOUR Bible Should Not Be MY Problem!*

"Jodie!" I say aloud and scurry back over to the car. I get down on my knees and try to get my fingernail under the edge of bumper sticker. I manage to lift it and slowly pull it off the car, crumple it up, and take it over to the trash can. I'm not sure if this is Jodie's idea of a joke, or if she really is trying to make some sort of point. I'm going to need to sit down and talk to her about this tonight. It's not like I'm an avid churchgoer myself, but I believe in God and Jesus and all that. At least, I guess I do. I mean, really, what's the harm in believing? I'm perfectly willing to let Jodie develop her own religious beliefs as long she tries to be a good person, but I certainly can't have her defacing my car with confrontational bumper stickers.

I'm trying to think of how to approach the subject with Jodie as I walk into the building and get onto the elevator. By the time I reach my office I barely have a moment to sit down and flick my computer on when my phone rings.

"Brenda Harrison."

"Hi Brenda. It's Gretchen." She talking in that phony hoarse, listless voice she uses whenever she calls in sick.

"Hi Gretchen," I reply, wishing I had let the call roll into voicemail. Lord knows what kind of drama I'm in store for. Gretchen never just has a cold or the flu. It's always some sort of bizarre illness or wacky accident.

"Do you know where Jill is? I'm going to be late today, so I tried to call her, but she's not answering, and her voicemail isn't picking up."

"I don't think she's in yet."

"Could you tell her that I'm going to be late?"

"Sure," I say, hoping that I can get off the phone without getting any further details.

"I'm at the doctor's office, and he is has to run some tests. He thinks I might have West Nile virus."

"West Nile virus? Isn't that really rare? Don't you get that from mosquitoes?"

"Yeah."

"It's *winter*???" I don't know why I'm questioning her. It will only lead to more outlandish excuses, but I just can't help myself.

"I know, isn't that weird?"

I have a thousand questions for Gretchen. If she were really having symptoms of West Nile virus, wouldn't she be more than just *late* for work? Wouldn't she be deathly ill? I guess these are the same questions I had for her last year when she thought she had bubonic plague. Fortunately, my second line starts to ring, so I have the perfect excuse to end the call. "Gretchen, I've got to get that. I'll tell Jill you're going to be running late. Feel better," I say and press the button to answer my other call. "Brenda Harrison."

"Yes. Hello, Ms. Harrison. This is Dr. Klein. I'm Kamille Cooper's surgeon. She was scheduled to have a procedure today."

"Yes."

"She listed you as her emergency contact."

"She did?" I say, wondering what's going on.

"Yes, Ms. Cooper had a severe reaction to the anesthesia shortly after we put her under. Her heart stopped beating, and we had to resuscitate her on the operating table. We were able to get her pulse back, and she wasn't deprived of oxygen for a dangerously long time, but the extent of damage, if any, isn't clear yet."

"Oh, my God!"

"She's been transferred by ambulance to Washington Hospital Center. She's still unconscious, but we're hopeful that she will awaken soon."

"Oh, my God!" I say again.

"I'm sorry I can't offer any more information. But we are hopeful that she will pull through this."

"*Hopeful* that she will pull through this!?" I ask. "Is there a chance she won't?"

The doctor is quiet for a moment. "I'm afraid there is a chance, but like I said, we are hopeful that she'll make it."

I'm breathing heavily. "What do I do?" I ask the doctor. "I barely know Kamille. I just agreed to take her and pick her up from her surgery. We've only been working together for a short time."

"Do you have the names of any of her family members?"

"No," I respond and think for a moment. "Her purse! I have her purse in my car. I'll have to look through it, and see if there's any contact information."

"Okay. Again, I'm sorry I don't have any more information. We'll know more about her condition after some tests are run at the hospital."

"Do you know what room she's in at the hospital?"

"No, not off-hand. I'm sure they can tell you at the hospital and give you directions or anything else you need."

"All right," I say. "Thank you for calling." Yeah, thank you for calling and telling me that someone I barely know, but am somehow responsible for, has almost dropped dead.

# 59

## Nora

"Where's Brenda?" I ask Jill in the hallway, having just poked my head in Brenda's office door. It's my first day back at work, and I wanted to stop in and catch up with her.

"She had to leave and take care of something."

"Really? Okay. I guess I'll meet up with her when she's gets back," I add, eyeing Jill's expression for any reaction to my new face.

"She's wasn't sure if she'd be back today. She may not be in until tomorrow. She said she'd give me a call in a couple of hours and let me know. So," she adds, switching gears. "How was your time off? I hope everything went well."

She hopes everything went well? What does she mean by that? Does she know about my surgery? Somehow Gretchen knew, so half the office probably knows by now. "It was fine. Things went well," I say, not bothering to offer any further details. I figure it's easier that way. If people know that I had plastic surgery, then so be it, but I'm certainly not going to advertise the experience to everyone.

"Well, I'm glad you're back. Things have been busy."

"Thanks." I still can't tell if she notices the change in my face. My eyes do look a bit more youthful and alert, and my cheeks are fuller, but the residual swelling is still hiding the final effects.

"I guess I'd better get back to my office and start sorting through e-mails and phone messages."

"Okay," she replies with no mention of my how I look or any unusual stares or expressions that would make me think she notices anything is different about me at all. As I walk toward my office, I'm a little annoyed. When I stopped by the break room I chatted with two other co-workers for a few minutes, who didn't seem to notice, either. I'm about to reach my office when I see Gretchen coming toward me.

"Welcome back, Nora!" she says with a big phony smile.

"Thank you, Gretchen."

"Did you have a nice time off?"

"Oh, it was busy," I reply. I know she knows about my surgery (God knows how . . . nosy bitch), or she at least knows that I had some kind of surgery, because she told Owen as much when he tried to leave me a message on my work voice mail.

"I bet," she says. "You look well. The time off must have done you good."

"Thanks. How are you?"

"Not so good. I had to go to the doctor's office this morning. He thought I might have West Nile virus, but it turned out that it was just my condition acting up again."

"Hmm," I respond. "Well I'm sort of busy. First day back and all. I'd better get to work." That was polite, wasn't it? I don't want to have to listen to any stories about West Nile virus.

"Okay. I should get to work too, but, hey, let me ask you something," she says. "What do you think of these slacks?" She motions toward her pants.

"They look nice . . . you look nice," I lie. As usual, she has too much make-up on and her hair teased up too high—she looks like a New Jersey Mall Chick.

"Thanks! The pants are new. You don't think they're too *tight*, do you?" she says with quite an emphasis on the word "tight."

Be nice! "No. They look great."

"I'm not sure. I really think they might be too *tight*. I may need to get a bigger size. I mean, I could barely get my shirt *tucked* in this morning. I had to keep *pulling* on it and *pulling* on it."

Passive-aggressive little wench! I want to tell her that it's the size of her fat ass that's the problem, not the size of her jeans, but she obviously knows about my surgery. If I get nasty with her, she'll be even more likely to spread my business all over the office. "Well, I think they look very nice. They flatter your figure." Then I think about what Owen said about there being nothing shameful about having plastic surgery. "I got a few new pieces of clothing during my time off as well. I had a little plastic surgery while I was out and I thought it would be nice to have some new clothes to go with my new look."

Oh, my God! For the first time ever, Gretchen Morrow is speechless! She looks at me blankly as if she's not sure how to react. It's obvious she was trying to push my buttons. But now that I've been open about my surgery, she doesn't have that power anymore. All she can muster is a weak, "Really?"

"Yep. I had my eyes and nose done and got some cheek implants," I say, and then I hear my phone ringing from just outside my office. "Guess I'd better get that."

"Okay," Gretchen says, still looking perplexed, and moves on down the hall.

"This is Nora," I say after I pick up the phone.

"Hey. It's Owen. How's the first day back?"

"Oh . . . so far so good, I guess."

"That's good to hear. I wanted to check in with you about Wednesday. Are we still on?" Owen had called yesterday, and we made plans to get together.

"Sure. I should be able to get out of here by five or so. Pick me up at seven?"

"Sounds like a plan. I'll make sure the sitter gets to my house by six. That should give me enough time to get to your place by seven."

"Don't worry about the sitter, Owen," I respond, and I can hardly believe what I'm about to say. "Why don't you bring Billy along? It will be nice to see him again. We can go to some kid-friendly place."

"Like Chuck E. Cheese's?" Owen asks.

"Oh my God, no!" I blurt out before I have chance to censor myself, visions of screaming kids playing video games running through my head. "No . . . I mean, you know, just not someplace too fancy."

Owen laughs, "Baby steps," he says.

"What?"

"Nothing."

"No. What did you mean by that? Baby steps?"

"Nothing. I just appreciate you making an effort with Billy. It was silly of me to think you'd be ready for a place like Chuck E. Cheese's. But maybe you'll get there."

"Don't hold your breath," I say with laugh.

"I wouldn't dream of it. So, we'll see you at seven?"

"Absolutely." I hang up the phone, and I'm surprised to realize that I really am looking forward to spending time with Owen *and* Billy. My God! What's happening to me? First I'm honest about my surgery with Gretchen, and then I'm eagerly anticipating an evening with a four-year-old. Maybe I took a few too many painkillers when I was recovering from my surgery.

# 60

## Brenda

I almost feel like a burglar or someone on a covert operation as I stick the key into Kamille's front door. After I got off the phone with her doctor I rummaged through her purse to see if I could find any contact information for a family member or a close friend, but I came up empty. I even did a brief search of her office and her rolodex, but I didn't have any luck there either. I figured the only thing I could really do was swing by her apartment and try to find someone to call. Maybe she'd have her mother on speed dial, or a rolodex or address book lying around. Someone—someone closer to her than me—needs to know what happened.

I have to try a couple of different keys, but I eventually get the door open and step inside. Honestly, I'm a little surprised by her living space. Her building is an old high rise in a bit of a scary neighborhood off Georgia Avenue, and her unit is tiny. It's a one room studio with a small kitchen and little furniture. It's all very strange—she's a Director at Saunders and Kraff, just one rung down the ladder from vice president. She must make a nice salary. Why would she live in such a meager place? The carpet is worn. There's a small sofa against the wall, facing a little television set. And there's a bed and a big dresser by the window and a beat-up desk in the corner. That's pretty much the extent of the apartment's furnishings. There's no artwork on the wall—not even a tacky print from Bed Bath & Beyond or Pier 1.

I must be in the right place. I know this is her building—I picked her up out front this morning. I got the apartment number off her driver's license, and her key fit the door, but I can't imagine her living here. Women who look like Kamille—who wear designer clothes and flawless make-up and are just plain beautiful—don't live in places like this.

I figure the desk is the best place to start, so I head in that direction and take a seat. I look at the phone, but there's nothing written next to any of the speed dial buttons, so I pick it up and just press the first button. She must not have them programmed since nothing happens. I just continue to get a dial tone. There's no rolodex on the desk, so I open the top drawer and look for a personal phone book, but I don't find anything but some envelopes, old stationary, and some paper clips. I move on to the next drawer and find a manila folder fat with papers. It must be several inches thick.

I pull it out of the drawer and place it on the desk. I flip the cover over and, in front of the pile of papers, is a photo of chubby young black woman. She looks to be about twenty years old. She has a flat chest and short curly hair, but the most pronounced feature of the young woman is her enormous lips. It's hard to tell from the picture, but they look like they might have some sort of deformity to them—not like a cleft, but it looks like they're turned up at the edges. At first, I think it might be Kamille's younger sister or another relative, but something about the eyes of the girl in the photo tell me that it's a picture of Kamille, a very different-looking Kamille. I flip the photo over to see if it's dated, but all I find is the word "YUCK!" written on the back.

I start rifling through the folder and see that it's full of doctor's receipts and pre-op instructions. I come across more photos . . . before and after pictures. There's one of a pair of small breasts and another of a pair of larger breasts. They're photos of Kamille taken from the neck down with certain areas of her body circled in black marker. There are magazine cutouts of Beyoncé and Halle Berry and Tyra Banks. There are papers related to discharge instructions for after surgery and stacks of receipts for hair extensions and chemical peels and Botox injections. There's a collection of bills from hospitals and doctor's offices that would make Suze Orman speechless. There must be nearly a hundred thousand dollars worth of bills and receipts.

After a few more minutes I can't look at it all anymore. It's too overwhelming and way too much information for me to handle about someone I don't really know that well. I close the folder and sit back in the chair. What am I supposed to do with all this? I wonder to myself. I'm in awe, and I'm trying to digest everything I've seen and figure out what to do with such personal information about someone I barely know—someone who obviously needs a lot of help—if she lives to see tomorrow.

# 61

# Brenda

*I* *so* hate hospitals! I hate the way they smell. I hate walking down the halls and seeing the fragile patients with tubes shoved up their noses, and the sound of the machines keeping people alive. I hate the shiny white floors and carts full of cleaning supplies or patient meals.

I'm making my way down the hall to the intensive care unit. When I reach the doors, I pick up the phone and tell the nurse I'm here to see Kamille. She tells me to hold on for a moment and then comes to the door and lets me in.

"She's doing much better," the nurse says to me as she walks me to her room. "She's awake, and the doctors seem to think she'll be okay."

I feel the tension in my body—the tension that I've felt since Kamille's doctor first called me—finally let up. "Oh. Thank God!" I say with a big sigh of relief.

"This is her room," the nurse says and leaves me to walk in alone. Kamille is lying with her eyes closed, but she must sense me in the room because she opens her eyes and looks at me as I come toward her.

"Hey there," I say, trying to sound as upbeat as I can as I take hold of her hand. "The doctors say you're going to be okay."

Kamille nods softly. "Thanks for coming." Her voice is weak and raspy, but it's good to see her awake and not attached to life-support.

"Of course," I reply. "Is there someone I can call for you? I couldn't find any information about your family."

"No. I don't want to worry anyone."

"Are you sure? Don't you think they would want to know," I ask, but then I realize that I shouldn't make assumptions about people and their families. I have no idea what kind of relationship Kamille has with her family.

"Yes. Thank you," she says.

"Okay. Is there anything else I can do for you or get for you?"

Kamille barely shakes her head in response to my question, and I realize how weak she still is.

"Okay. Well you get some rest. Close your eyes and take it easy, and I'll sit with you for a bit." I'm not sure what else to do. As far as I know, no one else even knows she's in here, and I don't want to leave her all alone, so I sit there and hold her hand and watch her drift off to sleep. She looks so different from the Kamille I see at the office. At work she's always so put together and confident—every hair in place, perfect clothes, an air of competence. Now she looks fragile, like a little girl who needs someone to give her a hug and take care of her.

I think about how she ended up in this state, how she almost died for the sake of a fuller rear-end. I feel like a madwoman for even considering having plastic surgery myself. It's so clear now. Seeing Kamille lying in a hospital bed has made me realize that I just don't want to go down that road. I think of all the procedures she has had and how none of them have made her happy. She just keeps getting more, and her obsession with beauty has almost cost her her life. Life is too fragile, too precious . . . too brief to risk it for a tighter face or perkier boobs. As I watch over Kamille, I come to these realizations about plastic surgery. But, as I look at her with her eyes shut and her head slumped on a pillow, I realize something else—I realize that, not only is life too short to go under the knife for the sake of vanity, it's too short for me to spend it in this bizarre world I've created for myself, pretending that I don't know that my husband is having an affair. I'm suddenly very frightened by how my husband's infidelity is becoming a normal part of life. Even scarier is my ability to pretend I know nothing about it. Looking at Kamille, I'm reminded of the limited time we have on the planet, and, just now, I'm terrified to know that I could quite possibly spend the rest of my days looking the other way, acting as if everything between me and my husband is okay. *The rest of my life!* I can't let that happen. I can't! It's time to forget about having plastic surgery and, much as I've been hiding from the issue, it's time to confront Jim about his affair with Jazelle.

# 62

# Brenda

It's about nine o'clock at night, and I just got home from visiting with Kamille at the hospital.

"Hello," I call out as I walk in the door. I didn't see Jim's car in the garage, so I'm not sure if Jodie's home or if she's out with him.

"Yeah," Jodie calls from upstairs.

"I'm home," I say, as if it's not obvious.

"Okay," she calls back. "Dad's working late."

Of course he is. "Did you eat?"

"Yeah. I had some pizza."

Apparently, she has no intention of coming downstairs, and I'm tired of us exchanging shouts, so I make my way to the steps. When I reach the top Jodie is just outside her bedroom, and so is that Kylie girl who was here a few weeks ago. Before they realize I'm there, I catch a glimpse of Kylie handing Jodie some cash.

"Hello," I say, and they both seem startled to see me.

"Hi," Jodie says. "Kylie was just leaving."

"Yeah," Kylie says and makes a quick bee-line past me. "Good night," she adds on her way out the door.

"So what's going on? What were you two up to?" I ask, trying to sound as if I'm just asking a breezy question.

"Nothing. Just hanging out . . . getting some homework done and stuff."

"Why was she giving you money?"

"I gave her a few bucks for lunch, and she was just paying me back. What's with all the questions?"

"Just curious. It's just seems odd that I've seen her over here twice. I never heard you mention Kylie, and she seems like one of those girl's you'd call a 'Barbie doll.' "

"We were assigned to be partners for our Economics class project, and I've gotten to know her. She's not so bad. Kind of flighty and self-involved, but, whatever."

"Oh . . . well . . . good." I was about to say that I was glad she had made a friend, but I heard the words in my head before I spoke them out loud, and it would have sounded as though I thought Jodie didn't have any friends at all. "So how are things? Sorry I got home so late. I had to visit a co-worker in the hospital."

"Fine. Nothing new. What happened to your co-worker?"

"She was having surgery, and I guess there were some complications, but she seems to be doing fine."

"You've been getting home late a lot . . . almost as much as dad. Are you having an affair too?"

*Too!?* "What?" I try to pretend that her words haven't frazzled me although I'm certain my face has gone bright red. "What do you mean, *too?*"

"Mom, I know you can be a little dense, but even you're not *that* dense." She's saying all of this as if she telling me it's going to be partly cloudy with a light breeze and a chance of rain tomorrow.

"What are you talking about?" I continue to plead ignorance. I can't believe that my daughter knows about her father's affair.

"How much longer are you going to pretend you don't know about it, Mom? Indefinitely? Forever?"

"Stop talking like that!" I blurt out. "Where's this coming from?"

"Mom, Dad works late at least two nights a week now. He used to work late once every few months. He disappears on these mysterious errands on the weekends. Even *I* smelled the perfume on him when he came home a few weeks ago. What's it they say? 'If it walks like a duck and quacks like a duck. . . .' "

I don't know how to respond to what she's telling me. How foolish could I be—to think that she wouldn't notice Jim's behavior and have her own doubts and suspicions. It never occurred to me that Jodie would be noticing all the clues as well. This is *so* not a conversation I want to have with my daughter. "You're being silly," I say, and I know she knows I'm lying. "Even if there was something to worry about, it would be between me and your father and have nothing to do with you."

"If you say so," she says and rolls her eyes at me.

"I'm going to soak in the tub for a while and hit the bed." I'm trying to change the subject and nix this conversation about my husband's infidelity.

"Okay."

"Don't stay up too late."

"I won't."

"Good night." I head out of the room. Once I'm out her door I walk with urgency to my own room and close the door. I sit down on the bed and try to calm my breathing. I can't let this go on anymore. It was so silly of me to be so clueless and think that none of this was affecting my daughter. She can't grow up seeing her father cheat on her mother. And worse, she can't grow up watching her mother putting up with it as if it's just another annoying habit like snoring or chewing with his mouth open. I'll need to arrange for Jodie to be out of the house, and I'll have to do it—I'll have to confront Jim about his affair, and he'll have to make a decision. Is it going to be Jazelle? Or is it going to be me and his daughter?

# 63

## Nora

"You've really healed nicely. You look great. If I ever decide to go under the knife again, I think I'll go to your surgeon instead of the one I went to last time," Owen says to me over coffee. We're sitting in the café at a bookstore. We just sat on the floor for an hour with Billy, so he could participate in their story hour. And, actually, it wasn't the worst way to spend an hour. The woman who read the stories was so animated and enthusiastic I found myself being entertained by the tales of bunnies who live in little huts and make jelly beans and the story about the wiener dog who solves mysteries.

"Under the knife?" Billy asks, looking up from the coloring book they handed out with a small box of crayons after the reading.

"Don't worry. Daddy's not going 'under the knife' anytime soon," Owen says to Billy.

"I'm with you there. I think my plastic surgery days are over for quite some time." I'm not sure I'll *never* have anything done again, but, now that I know the reality of the recovery period, I will think much longer and harder before signing up to be cut on again. Now that the swelling and bruising are gone, and the pain and vomiting have ceased, I guess I can say that my fresher look was worth it, but I certainly didn't feel that way when I was in the midst of healing from the procedures. And I was surprised to learn on my last visit to Dr. Radcliff that we will not know the final results of my surgery for months. He said my work may not settle into its absolutely permanent look for quite some time, particularly with regard to my rhinoplasty. The final results for my nose job could take more than a year.

"Well, you really do look great. Not that you needed to have anything done in the first place."

"That's sweet of you to say."

"I mean it. You're a beautiful woman, Nora. On the outside *and* the inside."

"You're going to make me blush."

"What's *bwush*?" Billy asks.

"It's when you make someone feel silly, and it causes their face to turn red."

"*Wed!* Neat," he says. "Daddy, make her *bwush*! Make her *bwush*! I want to see her face turn *wed*."

I laugh. "Well it doesn't turn red so much as a little bit pink."

"Oh," he says with a sigh, disappointed.

"I bet I can make you blush." I give his tummy a little tickle. He starts giggling. Then, of course, Owen and I start giggling.

"You're really good with him," Owen says to me.

Huh? That's something I never thought I'd hear someone say. "Really?"

"Sure. You've really grown on him. I think he was a little bit timid around you at first. But since the day we came over after your surgery, he seems much more comfortable around you."

"Nothing like pulling gauze out of someone's throat to bring you closer together," I say with a grin.

"Do you *wike* my picture?" Billy asks, holding up his coloring book.

"I think it's very pretty. If you pull it out, I'll put it up on my refrigerator." Did I just say that?

"Okay!" Billy responds, as if I made his day. "Wait . . . wait! Let me color another one. I'll do a better job this time since you're going to put it on your *wefrizerator*."

"That would be nice. Thank you, Billy." As I look on while Billy colors, I can sense Owen watching me, enjoying that I'm getting along with his son. And I'll admit that *I'm* enjoying getting along with his son. I don't know where this relationship with Owen and Billy is going to go, but I've decided to give it my best shot. I don't think I'm ready to be a mother right now, but, as far as I know, no one has asked me to. I'll get to know Owen better, and I'll get to know Billy better, and we'll just have to see what happens. Billy's a good kid, and at least he's old enough that there won't be any of that diaper-changing business—yuck! We may not make it, but at least I will have learned something about children and about myself. Although, I guess I've already learned a few things. I *can* enjoy being around children, and maybe the sacrifices you make for them produce their own rewards.

When I'm with Owen and Billy I have these strange feelings that maybe it isn't that big a deal if my Pottery Barn sofa gets a stain on it, or if my make-up isn't perfect because I was running late getting a kid dressed for school . . . or that a ripped-out page of Billy's coloring book displayed on my fridge doesn't go with the décor in my kitchen. I just feel good when I'm around them. I wonder if this is the way my mother felt around my father and all her children. Maybe we gave her enough happiness that she didn't need a slim figure, perfect furniture, and grand vacations. As much as my mother's life seemed overburdened to me, she always seemed happy. Who knows . . . maybe I've got a little of my mother in me after all.

# 64

# Kamille

"Hey!" Brenda says to me as she comes into my room at the hospital. "You ready to get out of here?"

"More than you know." I've been stuck in this place for three days. How ridiculous is that? To leave the hospital after three days and not have my frickin' butt implants!

"How are you feeling?"

"Pretty good actually. Ready to go home."

"I bet," Brenda says. "Well, you look great."

"Thanks." I accept the compliment even though I don't believe it. I'd look great if that stupid doctor hadn't aborted my surgery. So my heart stopped beating for a few seconds. They revived me, didn't they? I'm still annoyed that they didn't continue on with the surgery after they got my pulse back. And if they think I'm paying one red cent for anything related to this debacle they are sadly mistaken. Maybe I'll agree not to sue if Dr. Klein does my butt implants for free.

"I signed all the papers already, so I think I'm free to go. If we hurry we can sneak out of here before the nurse shows up with a wheelchair."

"Okay." Brenda walks with me out of the hospital room, and there's an uncomfortable silence as we step inside the elevator. I feel so silly asking for her help like this. I barely know her at all, but there was no one else to ask. And of everyone at the office, she's the only one that I could even think of asking. I wish they didn't make someone pick you up after surgery. It's always such a pain to find someone and it also gets them all up in your business. I don't see why I can't just take a cab home from my procedures anyway.

When we get to the car Brenda opens the door for me like I'm some kind of cripple. No one seems to realize that I didn't really have surgery. I was just put under anesthesia for a brief time. I don't have any incisions or swelling or bruising or pain and, most important, I don't have my fucking butt implants.

"You really do look great, especially considering what you've been through," Brenda says after we get settled in the car, and she starts to make her way out of the parking garage.

"That's nice of you to say. You're such a sweet person. I can't tell you how much I appreciate you helping me. It felt odd to ask someone who I don't know very well for such a personal favor."

"Don't worry about it. I'm happy to help," she says, and then hesitates for a moment. "You know, when the doctor called and told me that your surgery had taken a bad turn I wasn't sure what to do. I guess I felt like I needed to let someone close to you know what happened."

"You didn't call my mother, did you?" I say too quickly to hide the panic in my voice.

"No, no," she reassures me. "I didn't call anyone, I couldn't— I couldn't find anyone to call. I checked around your desk at the office, but when I couldn't find any contact information I didn't know what else to do, so I went to your apartment and let myself in."

"You went to my apartment?"

"Yes. I'm sorry if I invaded your privacy, but your condition sounded very serious and, like you said, we don't know each other that well. I felt like I had to get in touch with one of your family members. I thought you might have your mother or a sister or someone programmed into your phone, or a personal phone book in your desk or something."

"You looked in my desk?" I ask, trying not to sound accusatory. Brenda is a nice woman, and she is really helping me out here, but I can't stand the thought of her rifling through my personal things.

"Yes. Again, please accept my apology for going through your things, but I didn't know what else to do."

"It's okay," I lie.

"I never did find anyone to call but . . ." Her voice trails off.

"But what?"

"Kamille, I came across this big folder with all sorts of receipts and summaries for . . . well . . . for *a lot* of surgery."

Oh, good Lord! Here we go again. I'm going to have to listen to someone else tell me I'm addicted to plastic surgery, or that I need professional help. "Oh that's just a few records I've hung on to for some work I've had done," I say, looking out the window as I speak.

"Maybe this is none of my business—"

I cut her off. "Yeah, maybe it isn't." I just blurt it out. And then I see this hurt expression on her face. "I'm sorry. I didn't mean to sound snippy. It's a little embarrassing talking about having plastic surgery. I can see how someone might look at the file that you found and think I went a little overboard, but you have to realize that those procedures have been spread out over a few years. It's not like I get something done every day."

"I didn't mean to imply anything. I was just concerned. You're so young and so beautiful. I guess I was shocked to learn that you still think it's necessary to have plastic surgery. You do know what an attractive woman you are, don't you?"

I let out a quick laugh. "That's sweet of you to say. You sound like my mother. She always told me how beautiful I was even when I was younger and had deformed lips. She'd tell me how pretty I was, but the kids at school told me an entirely different story. Did you see the picture of me when I was younger?"

"I guess I did come across it."

"Hideous, wasn't it? Ugliest thing you ever saw?"

"No, not at all. I thought the girl in the picture was cute."

"It's nice of you to lie, Brenda, but I know how tore up I looked, and I know what I look like now."

"Gorgeous?"

"Hardly. I know I'm not as heinous as I was when I was twenty-two, but I still have a ways to go."

"To go? What are you going toward?"

"Oh, I don't know," I lie. I'm going toward being beautiful (and I'll get there one day), but I really just want to end this conversation. "Can we let it go? It's really not a big deal."

"Not a big deal. You almost died, Kamille! You almost died!" she says to me, taking her eyes off the road and looking at me for a response.

I don't have one to give her, so she diverts her eyes back to the road ahead and keeps driving while I think about what she said. I almost died—I almost died having surgery to make my ass more voluptuous. A part of me can see how ridiculous it was to risk my life to have a butt like Beyoncé, but another part knows what it takes to make it in the world, and looking good is very important. We take risks every day. Sitting in this moving car right now is a risk.

"Can we please not talk about this anymore?" I ask.

"Okay, we can stop talking about it," she says. "For now."

# 65

## Brenda

*REMEMBER WHEN "CHRISTIAN VALUES" MEANT HELP-ING THE POOR AND THE HUNGRY RATHER THAN HATING GAYS AND BANNING ABORTION?*

That's what the button on Jodie's shirt says. The button isn't very big, so I have to get up close to read it. "Hmm, that's a lot to squeeze onto one little button," is all I say. My guess is that's she wearing it just to get a rise out of me, so I decide not to comment any further on it.

"You ready to go?" I ask. I've just gotten home from collecting Kamille from the hospital, and Jodie and I are about to leave to meet Jim for dinner. I called him earlier and told him to meet us at Ruby Tuesday at seven-thirty. He said he had to work late. I told him that was fine, but I still wanted him to meet us for dinner. I told him that I wanted us to have a meal as a family tonight, and he would just have to take a break and go back to work after dinner. He must have sensed that I meant business because he didn't argue with me. I don't know where I got the balls to demand that he have dinner with us tonight, but I think it had something to do with my conversation with Kamille. I didn't realize it until I left her at her apartment, but when we were in the car, I actually initiated a confrontation—me! I was worried about all the surgeries she'd had and, as uncomfortable as I knew it would be, I brought up the topic anyway. And guess what happened? Not much of anything. She was a little bit terse, but that was about it. No one got violently angry, no one's head exploded, no one hates me. I brought the subject out in the open, and, now, maybe she and I can start to have some more conversations about it and try to attack the problem. She wasn't willing to be forthcoming about it yet, but I think I've at least started a dialogue with her. I did what I thought I needed to do. In fact, I took it a step further and told Nora about Kamille's situation and asked her if she'd speak to her. As much as they rub each other the wrong way, I suspect that Nora will be able to relate to Kamille better than I can when it comes to issues of beauty and plastic surgery. People expect me to tell them they are pretty, but, when such a compliment comes from Nora, Kamille might actually believe it.

"Yeah," Jodie responds. "Let me grab my coat."

She fetches her jacket, and we head out to the car. I was so horrified by the comments Jodie made the other night—about Jim having an affair. I know the three of us sitting down for a meal together isn't going to put her mind at ease, but you have to start somewhere. I want to make sure she knows we are still a family. . . . Whatever happens, we are still a family.

"How was school today?" I ask as we head up the highway.

"Fine."

"You and Kylie working on your school project?" I inquire. I can't help but be curious about her friendship with Kylie. It just doesn't make sense to me and, frankly, it has me a little bit worried. Kylie is everything Jodie hates about people, and their little money exchange raised a few hairs on the back of my neck. The two of them together just reminded me of Ellen DeGeneres and Portia de Rossi. Jodie is sort of tomboyish like Ellen, and that Kylie is very prissy and feminine like Portia, who by the way, I was stunned to find out is a lesbian—who knew lesbians could be so pretty? Anyway, I know I'm being ridiculous—I'm sure they're just friends.

"Yep."

"You two are really friends?" I say. It just sort of comes out.

"Why is that so hard to believe? Do you think she's too good for me?"

"No! Of course not. She just doesn't strike me as someone you would be interested in hanging around with."

"Why is that?"

"Because she's one of those girls you are always saying are plastic . . . at least she seems that way."

"She is plastic, but she's okay I guess. I don't really have any choice but to be nice to her. We have to work together for the rest of the semester."

"Well that's a good attitude, I guess," I say as we pull up to the restaurant.

When we get inside Jim is already seated at a table. We walk over, and he stands up to greet us. We say hello, and I give him a quick peck on the lips. I rarely greet my husband this way, but I want Jodie to see that things are okay—even though they are *so not* okay.

"How's it going?"

"Fine," I say . . . the same response Jodie gave me when I asked her how school was.

"And what's new with you, Jo?" he asks Jodie as we sit down.

"Not much," she says and starts feeling inside the pockets of her jacket as she takes it off. "Crap! I can't find my cell phone."

"Can we not use the word "crap" at the dinner table?"

"I think I may have left it at school. Can we go by the school on the way home, so I can pick it up?"

"I don't know. What do you need it for?"

"Nothing," she says a tad too defensively. "I'd just like to have it."

"If you need to talk to someone you can use my cell or, heaven forbid, the land line at the house."

"Can we just go by the school and pick it up?"

"No. I'm not going all the way over to the school tonight," I insist. "I don't know why your father bought that thing for you anyway," I say, giving Jim a look. "What does a sixteen-year-old girl need a cell phone for?" The school really isn't that far, but this urgency about her cell phone is concerning me. Why is a girl with virtually no social life so eager to get her cell phone?

"Dad, can you take me?"

"Sorry, Jo. I've got to go back to work tonight."

"Oh *really?*" Jodie says, rolling her eyes before giving me a look.

"Jodie, would you drop it?" I interject quickly. I'm a little afraid Jodie might start questioning Jim about working late, so I change the subject as fast as I can. "Let's just figure out what we want to order, and we can talk about the cell phone later."

Thankfully, before Jodie can protest, the waiter arrives at our table and takes our drink order. Jodie and I opt for iced teas while Jim asks the waiter for a glass of water with lemon. When the waiter departs, Jodie and Jim open their menus and start looking over the entrées. I'm about to peruse my own menu, but, instead, I feel compelled to sit back and look at my husband and my daughter. I watch them reading about grilled chicken breasts and cheeseburgers and take in what might be our last meal together before I confront Jim about his affair. There's no telling what life will be like, once that happens.

After our drinks arrive, and we place our orders, I sit at the table in a daze. I try to make some conversation, but my mind is running wild with thoughts and fears. I barely notice Jim squeezing multiple lemon wedges into his glass of water and then dumping in a packet of sugar—his way of scamming a free glass of lemonade rather than paying the whopping dollar-ninety-nine that it would cost to order off the menu.

Our entrées arrive quickly, and we eat mostly in silence. I'm sitting there, over a plate of Sonora Chicken, contemplating when and how to have my dreaded conversation with Jim when I notice him looking distractedly over my shoulder toward the salad bar. I turn around and see Jazelle standing there with a heaping plate of greens, staring back at our table. I'm too shocked to turn away quickly, and I'm certain that she sees me. When I face the table I see Jim's face is as red as a cooked lobster. I can tell he's trying to remain collected, but the anxiety is showing. He's probably praying that she doesn't come over to the table. Or does he actually want her to come over? Maybe he really wants it all out in the open, to be free of the secrecy and the sneaking around. Whatever his preference, Jazelle never comes over to the table, but that doesn't stop Jim's hand from trembling as he reaches for his water glass. I'm so busy watching Jim's reaction that it takes a moment before I feel the heat in my own face and notice my own limbs shaking. Jim looks at me, and I look at him, and I can tell that he now knows that I *know*.

Neither Jim nor I eat another bite, but we wait for Jodie to finish her salad before paying the check and getting up from the table.

"Have a good night," he says with a fake smile on our way out to the cars. "I'm heading back to the office. I should be home in a few hours."

"Okay," I say, on the verge of tears. I just can't take this any longer. The only reason I'm holding it together is that I don't want to have a breakdown in front of my daughter in the parking lot of a greasy chain restaurant. I don't want her to witness the things I have to say to Jim.

"So can we go by the school and get my phone?"

"No."

"Oh come on. It's only a few minutes out of the way."

I don't respond to her insistence. I'm afraid if I speak, I'll lose it, and I don't want Jodie to see me like that.

"So? Are we going by the school?"

"No! End of discussion," I manage to snap.

"Are you okay?"

"I'm fine," I say, pursing my lips, trying to take control of my facial muscles and hold back tears.

"If you say so," Jodie says and turns and looks out the window.

# 66

# Kamille

I guess I have to go to work tomorrow, I think as I sit on the sofa watching a rerun of *Girlfriends* on UPN. I had arranged to take two weeks off, leave without pay of course, to recover from my surgery but, so far, I've only used four days. Despite the fact that I supposedly briefly died on the operating table, I'm fine now, and I obviously can't afford to take any unnecessary unpaid leave.

I'm about to flip the channel with I hear someone knocking on my door. As much as I appreciate Brenda trying to offer her support, I so do not need her rolling up into my apartment to lecture me. I thought I had gotten away from all the unsolicited advice when I left Atlanta. I'm certainly not interested in going down that road again here in D.C.

I look through the peep-hole and see the outline of a small woman with dark hair. I don't recognize her, but she looks harmless enough, so I open the door.

"Nora," I say. I'm sure my surprise is showing in my face.

"Hi, Kamille. How are you?"

"Um . . . fine. What are you doing here?" I didn't mean to be so blunt, but the question came out before I could stifle it.

"May I come in?" she asks, avoiding my question.

"Yeah . . . yeah, sure," I say and open the door wider and step to the side. "Please. Have a seat. Can I get you anything?" I ask, my anxiety about her visit rising with every minute.

"No, thanks."

"So what can I do for you, Nora?" I didn't mean it to, but I think that came out sounding bitchy.

"I'm sure I'm the last person you expected to see outside your door."

I just raise my eyebrows.

"To be honest, Brenda asked me to stop by."

"Brenda? Why?"

"Please don't be mad at her, but she told me a little bit about your . . . um . . . your situation."

"My *situation*?"

"She's concerned. You know Brenda. She's always worried about everyone. She told me that you've had *a lot* of plastic surgery, Kamille."

I stand up. "Thank you for coming by, Nora, but this really isn't any of your business."

"No. You're right. It's not any of my business. Brenda just thought . . . well, she thinks that you don't see yourself as attractive, that you didn't believe her when she told you how beautiful you were. She seemed to think you'd believe it if it came from me."

"What!?" I say with a nervous laugh.

"She knows what a vain bitch I am," Nora says, with her own nervous laugh. "And she knows . . . well, she knows. . . . This is hard to say. She knows the reason that I may have been less than pleasant with you since you started at Saunders and Kraff."

"You? Less than pleasant? *Never*." I relax my stance somewhat and sit back down on the sofa.

"Please. I've been a total bitch."

"Oh, I wouldn't say a *total* bitch. Maybe just a little bit . . . shall we say . . . *salty*."

"The reason I haven't been the nicest person to you is that I'm jealous as all get-out."

"What! Why?"

"Because you're fucking gorgeous! You have a perfect body

and perfect hair and ideal facial features. And your clothes! Chica, those clothes are fierce!"

I laugh. "You are totally playin' me."

"I wish I was. I was the prettiest girl in the office until you came along."

"You think I'm prettier than you? You've got to be joking."

"Kamille, I went and had my own plastic surgery just to keep up."

"What?"

"Well. Not *just* to keep up. I've been thinking about it for a long time."

Now that's she's mentioned it, I can see that something is different about her. I knew she had been out of the office for a few weeks. And, since she wasn't due back until after I left for my own surgery, this is the first time I've seen her in quite some time.

"What did you have done?"

"My eyes, my nose, and I had some implants put in my cheeks."

"Hmm," I say, studying her face. "Your doctor did a nice job." I want to ask for his name and contact information, but I guess now is not the time.

"Thanks."

"Sure." I find myself wanting to tell her about my own eye surgery, and my own cheek implants, and get some advice from her in case I ever decide to have my nose done, but I'm afraid to bring it up, so I simply try to conclude the conversation and maybe get her on her way.

"It really was nice of you to come by, but I assure you, I'm fine."

"From what Brenda told me, you're not fine, Kamille. I now know all that goes with plastic surgery—the pain, the long recovery, the cost, the lost time from work. Someone who looks like you, at your age, doesn't go through all that over and over again if there isn't a problem."

"Really, Nora. It was nice of you to stop by, but I think it best that you leave now."

Nora gets up from the sofa. "Okay. I'll go, but I hope you'll think about what I said."

"I will," I lie, and I'm about to get up from the sofa to walk her out, but I feel strangely paralyzed, like I really do not want her to leave.

"I hope so," Nora says, putting her purse over her shoulder and turning to leave. She's halfway to the door when she turns and sees me still sitting on the sofa looking down at the floor. I can feel her looking at me, but she isn't saying anything. She's just standing there waiting for me to say something, and the silence is deafening. I keep looking down, and I think about how I just want to look good . . . feel good. I want to be pretty. I want to stop looking at women like Nora, wishing that I was them. Is that really such an odd thing to want? I've felt ugly most of my life. How could I not? I was barely out of diapers when I became known as . . . I don't even want to think about it. It makes me too sad. I'm trying to suppress the memory. I'm trying so hard not to think about it, but it becomes too much, and I burst.

"They called me Blubber Lips!" I cry out. "I was just a little girl, and they called me Blubber Lips!" I feel the tears coming to my eyes. I can hear the chanting as if it were yesterday—the kids on the playground shouting, "Blubber Lips, Blubber Lips, Blubber Blubber Flubber Lips!"

Nora comes back to the sofa and sits down next to me.

"Do you have any idea what that's like? That name stuck with me through high school. And in college my friends just called me Lips. I was known around campus as *Lips*. People would call my dorm room and ask to speak to *Lips*! I didn't make a fuss about it back then. I just laughed it off, but I hated it. I just wanted to look normal. That's all I still want. To look normal!"

"Oh, chica," Nora says, taking me in her arms. "You do look normal. You look beautiful."

I weep into her shoulder.

"This is such a 'Brenda' thing to say, but, you have to realize that no amount of surgery is going to fix the way you feel about yourself. Only you can do that."

I hear what she is saying. It's nothing I haven't heard before but, for some reason, this time it's starting to make sense. Maybe because it's coming from someone like Nora, or maybe because, for the first time in my life, I admitted to someone how painful it was to be called names and to be made fun of. I've never told anyone, *anyone*, about how hurtful it was to be called Blubber Lips when I was a kid or Lips when I was in college. It was such a release to get the words out . . . to let someone know the pain I was feeling . . . *am* feeling.

"I'm sorry. God, I'm so embarrassed." I pull away from her and lean back on the sofa. I *am* embarrassed by my outburst but, at the same time, I have this almost insuppressible urge to share more. I want to tell her about all my surgeries, about my out-of-control debt, about how I prostituted myself to pay for my last procedure. But it's too much—it's too much to share with someone I didn't even like a few minutes ago.

"Don't be. This is what you need, what we all need. We keep too much bottled up."

I try to smile and wipe my eyes. We talk a few minutes more before I thank her again for coming and walk her out. As I shut the door behind her, I really am thankful that she came by. And not because she told me I was beautiful and don't need surgery. I'm thankful because she made me realize the power of getting my feelings and my past out in the open. I decided not to share any more intimate details about my life with Nora, but she made me realize how much I could benefit from finding someone to talk to about everything I've been through . . . everything I'm going through. She made me realize that I do need some help.

I walk over to the phone, pick up the receiver, and dial.

"Hi Mama," I say. "I'm not calling for money. This has nothing to do with money, but I need your help. Will you help me, Mama?" I ask, my voice breaking up as tears start to come to my eyes.

"Sure, baby. Tell Mama what's going on."

# 67

---

# Brenda

As soon as I got home I went straight up the steps to my bedroom. I told Jodie that I had a headache and was going to bed early. I'm sitting on the bed, and I'm frozen. I can't believe we ran into Jazelle at the restaurant. I can't believe that Jim's illicit lover was standing a few feet from my daughter—from my family! But mostly, after such a close call, I can't believe that Jim would still claim that he had to go back to work. I wanted to attack him right there in the parking lot: tell him to go run to his whore, but not to be surprised if he couldn't get in the house when he came home. I wanted to get it out in the open right there in front of the restaurant, but I couldn't do such a thing in front of my daughter.

I sit lost in my thoughts for sometime before I'm able to move my body from the bed. I decide that I need a nice stiff drink, something to calm my nerves before Jim gets home and I have it out with him. I step out of the bedroom and into the hall. On my way toward the stairs I can hear the muffled sound of Jodie on the phone through her closed bedroom door. I put my ear to the door to see if I can make out anything she's saying. I know it's wrong. I shouldn't be spying on my daughter, but I have to know what's going on between her and Kylie. I can't hear anything comprehensible with my ear pressed to the door, so I tiptoe back to my room, press the mute button on the phone keypad, and pick up the extension.

"What do you think we can charge?" I hear Kylie's voice on the other end of the phone.

"For you? I don't know . . . a hundred dollars an hour maybe."

"You think we should charge by the hour? Or just per job?"

"Definitely by the hour. We have no idea how long each job will last."

"Should we charge a hundred for Melissa too?"

"I guess so."

"That's fine, but I don't think anyone is going to pay that much for her. She's got all those freckles, and she's a little overweight."

Upon hearing this, I immediately put down the phone and barge into Jodie's room. I grab the receiver from her ear and hang it up while Kylie is still talking.

"What the hell is going on?"

"Huh?" Jodie looks at me, perplexed. "What do you mean?"

"What are you and Kylie up to?"

"Nothing."

"Don't 'nothing' me, young lady!" I say in a tone I don't think I've used with Jodie since she was a little girl. "You're going to tell me what's going on, and you're going to tell me now!"

Jodie starts laughing.

"This is funny to you?"

"Sorry. I just haven't seen you fired-up about anything in a long time," she says.

"Jodie," I say, and then I stop and take a deep breath. "Are you prostituting your classmates?"

Jodie's laugh intensifies.

"What? What is so funny?" I ask.

"You are. Prostituting my classmates? Have you gone mad?" She's still laughing at me.

"I was listening in on your conversation, Jodie. I heard you talking about charging a hundred dollars for Kylie and some other girl."

"You were listening in on my phone call?" Jodie asks with an accusatory look on her face.

"Yes, and I want to know what's going on."

"What's going on is that I was talking with Kylie about how much we should charge for modeling activities. My project for Economics class? Remember?"

I just look at her.

"Kylie and I decided to write up a business plan for a teen modeling agency. Actually, it was her idea. She has this hare-brained idea that it will help her prepare for a career in modeling after she graduates. We figured we'd need a Web site for the business, and we were talking about how much we'd charge for modeling jobs. We were going to use photos of Kylie and this other girl, Melissa, on the Web site. It's not even a real business, *Mother*. But we figured we'd get a better grade if we went ahead and developed a Web site anyway."

I sit down on her bed and lower my head in shame. Not only did I invade my daughter's privacy, but I accused her of being a pimp. "I don't know what to say. Things have been a little upside-down lately."

"You jump to the strangest conclusions, Mom."

"It wasn't *that* strange. You were talking about whoring out your classmates in the car a few weeks ago, and then I see you guys exchanging money, and then I find you on the phone with a girl you used to hate, talking about how much you would charge for her."

"I told you she owed me some lunch money. If you had concerns about us, why didn't you just ask me?"

I look away from her for a moment. I don't know the answer to her question.

"If you're curious about something, you can ask me, Mother. I know you've been running around thinking I'm a lesbian for the better part of the year. I think you even thought me and Kylie had a thing going."

"What? I have not!" I lie.

"Oh please, Mom. You're like a nervous little mouse anytime

I turn *Xena* on, or when you see me around one of those butch girls at basketball practice. I see your face go red every time I mention anything about gay rights."

"Well . . . maybe I've been wondering a little."

"I'm not a lesbian, Mother. Just because I think gay people deserve to be treated as equal citizens of their own country doesn't make me gay. I know I'm not the girliest thing in the world, but not wearing uncomfortable dresses and stupid make-up doesn't make me gay, either."

"It doesn't matter to me if you are . . . you know . . . gay. It wouldn't change anything."

Jodie laughs. "If I were gay, Mother, I'd tell you. Unlike you, I don't believe in ignoring reality."

"What's that supposed to mean?"

"Do you ever wonder why I'm so outspoken? Why I try to live my life on my own terms?"

I remain silent for a minute and think about what she just asked me. "I'm not sure. I think I've spent more time wondering why you don't try to conform."

"I love you, Mom, and I think you're a really good person. But, God! Sometimes you are such a wuss. You just let things *happen* around you. You never stand up for yourself, you never say what you feel, and it's . . . well, it's a little bit sad. And I just don't want to be like that myself."

I just sit there and listen to what she has to say.

"I've been running around doing things to get a rise out of you forever. I've been wearing my anti-Christian buttons, I put that Bible bumper sticker on your car, I paused a scene of *Xena* when Xena and Gabrielle were bathing together when I knew you were looking, I even confronted you about Dad's bullshit. And nothing. Nothing! You ignore everything and just hope it will go away."

"Why would you do those things? Why would you pause a scene like that on the TV?"

"Because I knew you'd been thinking that I'm gay, and I was just curious how much it would take for you to actually, heaven forbid, ask me about it. At first it was kind of fun to do things to get under your skin, but the more I did it, it got to be kind of sad."

I'm still silent, and for a few moments, I sit on the edge of the bed and try to digest everything my daughter said to me. "You're right, Jodie. It is a little bit sad . . . maybe a lot sad. If I had questions, I should have just asked them. And believe it or not, that's what I'm going to start doing," I say before I pause for moment. "Jodie, I want to hear whatever you want to tell me. You're my daughter, and I love you for who you are. In fact, I actually admire you."

She looks at me with a surprised expression.

"You do things your way. All through high school I tried to conform as much as possible. Hell, I still do it today. You, on the other hand, are determined to be who you are regardless of the consequences. You're very brave. I respect that immensely."

I see a smile wanting to break through on her face, but I can tell she's suppressing it. "It's okay, you can smile," I say. "It's getting late. We'll talk more tomorrow." I get up from the bed and give her a hug. "You know I love you. We really need to open the lines of communication between us." I'm about to walk out the door when I turn around. "You know that I . . . both your father and I, will always love you and support you no matter what you are or do or whatever. You need to know that you can tell us anything. You don't need to keep anything from us."

"Okay," she says.

"Okay," I say back to her, and leave the room.

# 68

## Brenda

How did my entire life—my entire family—fall to pieces, I wonder as I lie on the bed staring up at the ceiling. My husband is probably sleeping with another woman right now, and my daughter thinks I'm a . . . what did she call me? A wuss . . . my daughter thinks I'm a wuss. I'm beyond crying at this point. I'm just in a state of . . . God! I don't even know what kind of state I'm in. I'm not sure I was ever one of those little girls who spent a huge amount of time sitting around dreaming about what her grown-up life was going to be like, but I certainly never envisioned any of this.

I don't understand where it all went wrong. Other women work full-time and have long commutes and bills and all sorts of issues to contend with, and they still have happy families. Why can't I? I know this didn't happen overnight. It took years for our family to evolve into its current state.

I'm on top of the covers, lost in thought when I hear my cell phone ring. I pick it up and look at the caller ID. It's Jazelle. What does *she* want, I think as I stare at the little screen on the phone. I know she saw me looking at her at the restaurant—we made eye-contact. But why would she be calling me?

I take a breath, click the "talk" button on the phone, and put it to my ear. "Hello."

"So, you're Brenda, not Myrtle," Jazelle says on the other end of the phone.

I don't say anything. I have no idea what to say.

"What's going on here, Brenda? What's all this about? Why have you been befriending me?"

"I'm sorry," I say. "Everything got so complicated—" I cut myself off. "Why am I apologizing to *you*? You're the one who's been *fucking* my husband!" Did I just use the f-word?

There's a long silence on the other end of the phone before Jazelle speaks. "I don't know what to say to that, Brenda."

"Why don't you just say 'Yes. Yes, I am fucking your husband.'" There I go again with the f-word.

"Is that really want you want to hear from me?"

"I don't know that I want to hear anything from you. I don't really have anything to say to you! I have no idea why you're calling me."

"I'm calling you . . . well . . . because I like you, Brenda. And you need to know something."

"What?" I say flatly.

"It wasn't a coincidence that I saw you at the restaurant. Jim told me where he was meeting his wife and daughter, and I wanted to see what his family looked like. I can't explain why, but I figured there wouldn't be any harm done. How was I to know that *you* would turn out to be his wife?"

"That's the something I have to know?"

"No. There's more. After you and your daughter left Jim came back into the restaurant and talked to me. He ended it with me."

She waits for me to respond, but I don't. I'm silent on my end of the phone.

"He said that running into me while he was with his family made him realize what he was risking, and he just couldn't risk losing you or your daughter."

"Well, then. That just fixes everything," I say, surprised by the sarcasm in my voice.

"Look, Brenda, I'm not interested in breaking up your marriage. That was never my intention. I was lonely, and Jim gave me some attention. It was nice. I never wanted to hurt anyone."

"It didn't quite work out that way, now did it?"

"No, it didn't. But, listen to me, Brenda. Jim was in tears here. He was frantic. He doesn't want to lose you. He doesn't want to give up his family."

I think about what she said, and I wonder if it's too late, if he's already lost us.

"I'm sorry, Brenda. I really am. I really did enjoy spending time with you and, I know you won't believe this, but I do hope that you and Jim work things out. I didn't tell him that we've met. He doesn't know that I know you."

I don't know what to say. I can't bring myself to say "thank you," so I just extend my silence.

"Good bye, Brenda," Jazelle says, waits for a moment to see if I'm going to say anything, which I don't, and hangs up.

# 69

## Brenda

It's about ten-thirty or so, and I'm sitting in my smoking chair, puffing on a Marlboro Light, thinking about how my family has fallen to pieces around me, and how I've stood by for years as it slowly happened. All sorts of things are running through my mind. I've realized I need to take action. I need to make a change. I can't live in this netherworld where I ignore the things in my life that are not to my liking and keep living like everything is okay. Signs that my family life was crumbling have been there for years. My marriage with Jim has been going downhill for quite some time, and Jim and I both seem to have had this apathy about it. It was probably ten years ago that we stopped kissing each other goodbye, and about the same amount of time since we stopped greeting each other with a kiss. It was some time before that when we stopped cuddling together on the sofa when we watched TV—it was just more comfortable for me to lie on the sofa and for him to sit in the chair. Eventually, we became bored with each other and listening to the radio in the car seemed a better alternative then the effort of conversation. Slowly, everything unraveled—our intimacy, our conversations, our sex life, until we reached a point—the point where we are now—that intimacy between us is almost awkward and unnatural. It makes me sad and angry—angry at myself, but angry at Jim, too, that neither of us bothered to address the slow demise of our marriage. His affair with Jazelle didn't end our marriage. It was just another symptom of our real problem. We never stepped in to save our marriage. We never talked about the disconnect between us. We just tiptoed around it like it was a grouchy old man—something better to leave unengaged rather than risk the consequences of stirring it up.

A part of me is dreading Jim coming home, but another part of me is eager with anticipation. There is no dodging the conversation that needs to happen tonight. I'd like to wait until Jodie is out of the house, but I can't put this off any longer. I'm thinking about how I might initiate the discussion when I hear the garage door open. I continue to sit in the chair, knowing Jim will see me through the doorway that opens to the kitchen when he walks in.

"Hi, sweetheart," he says as he comes through the side door into the kitchen. Not to me, of course. He's talking to Helga and gives her a quick pat on the head before looking up and seeing me in the den.

"Hi," he says, startled. "What are you doing up?"

"Waiting for you."

"Really?"

"Yep," I say, feeling an unexpected and odd sense of power. I feel like I'm in control. I don't elaborate beyond the simple "yep" I just gave him. I decide to make him squirm and keep asking me questions.

"So what's up?" he asks, trying to act as though he's not nervous, but I can see it in his eyes. Something happened, something clicked, when our eyes met at the restaurant after we saw Jazelle. I could tell that he knew that I knew that something wasn't right. Maybe he doesn't know for sure that I'm aware of his affair, but he definitely knows something is up, and I can see that he's scared. And, as unkind as it may be, I'm finding some comfort in the fact that he's frazzled—it means he must care . . . he must care at least a little bit.

He's looking at me with these nervous eyes and tense shoulders, and I blurt out, "I want to sell the house."

"What?"

"I want to sell the house," I say again, realizing, as they come out of my mouth, that the words sound right—like selling the house is really something I want to do.

"Why?"

"Because we need to start somewhere."

"Start what?"

"Start putting our family back together."

Jim looks at me, speechless. We're both quiet for what feels like an eternity. We look at each other and study each other's expressions. I stare at him—his eyes, his cheeks, his lips—and realize that it's the first time in so long that I've really looked at my husband's face. I see him every day—I've seen him every day for years, and I've just now realized that I had forgotten what he looked like. It's been years since I noticed the ridges in his forehead, the fullness in his cheeks, the sparkle in his blue eyes. I see him every day, but I haven't really *looked* at him in forever. The thought brings tears to my eyes and, oddly, I don't try to stifle them. I just let them flow. What would my mother, Queen of the Hide-Your-Emotions-Wasps, think?

"What's the matter?" he says, coming closer to me but not touching me.

I continue to weep and don't answer his question.

"What is it?" he asks.

I slowly manage to rein in my blubbering in hopes of responding to his question, but I don't know what to say. How do I answer his question? What is it? It's so many things. Where do I begin? How do I put years of shoving issues under the rug into a few words?

"I'm ashamed," I finally say. "I'm ashamed of myself . . . of us, for letting things get so bad."

"Letting what things get so bad?"

"Oh, for Christ's sake, Jim! You know what I'm talking about! For once, can we not beat around the bush and lay it on the table. Us! You and me and Jodie! Our family! That's what's gotten so bad. We're like a family of pod-people operating on autopilot."

Jim looks at me, waiting for me to say more, so I wipe my eyes and continue. "I want us to be a family again. I want us to have conversations. I want us to enjoy each other's company. I want us to have a meal at our table every now and then. I want my husband to kiss me good-bye before he leaves the house. I want . . ." I'm about to say it, that I want a husband that doesn't have affairs. I'm about to. Really I am, but, instead, all that comes out is, "I want a husband who doesn't call to tell me he's working late three times a week." That's the best I can do. I've just berated him for beating around the bush, and there I go confronting my husband about his affair in code. "Do you want that Jim? Do you want a real marriage and a real family?"

"Of course."

"Really? Because I can't take all the blame for the state of our family. We're in this marriage *together*. We're Jodie's parents *together*." My words surprise me, but I know in my heart that they're true—our lives didn't become so mundane because of my actions alone. "I'm willing to take some of the responsibility for state of our marriage, but I'm not the only one who let apathy take over. We both did, and it's going to take both of us to fix it . . . if it's fixable."

"Of course it's fixable," he says and sits down on the floor and puts his hand on my leg.

"I really want to work on this. I can't go on anymore the way things have been. I'm just a few cigarettes away from a complete meltdown as it is."

Jim laughs. "That's what attracted me to you in the first place."

"What?"

"Your sense of humor. I loved . . . love that about you."

I offer a glimmer of a smile. "I need to know that we are going to work on our marriage. The way things have been . . . especially the way things have been lately with all the late nights you've been working. I need to know that it's over. And that you're not going back to doing that."

"It's over . . . no more late nights," he says, more than happy to converse using this code system I've developed for discussing his affair. "I promise. You and Jodie are very important to me. You're everything, and I don't want to lose you two. I'm so sorry. God, I'm so sorry," he says, and I see that I'm not the only one with tears escaping my eyes. "I'm so sorry," he says again and touches my face with both hands.

"I'm sorry too," I say. I'm not the one who committed adultery, but I am sorry. I'm sorry all this happened. I'm sorry that I didn't take a stand sooner. I'm sorry that I pretended not to know about his affair.

"We're going to work on this," he says. "And we're going to get it right. I promise." He leans in and gives me a hug. "I promise," he repeats with conviction and squeezes me tight. For the first time in ages I feel like he's really holding me, like he wants to be as close to me as he can. I can feel his fear of losing me. I hug him back and feel something rush through my body, a feeling of security and hopefulness that I haven't had in years. For the first time in so long I feel a connection with my husband. We have so much to work out and so much to put behind us, but I have a sense that we are both willing to make the effort, that we both want to save our family, and I recognize the power of hope.

# Epilogue

## Brenda

A couple of weeks ago I went to Target, and I raided the seasonal party supply section. I picked up the cutest pink plates and napkins and plastic flatware, a cake mold shaped like a bunny, yellow icing and pastel-colored sprinkles, a darling little strand of lights shaped like marshmallow Peeps, little tealight candle holders with bright spring floral designs, and loads of other goodies. And do you know what? For the first time ever, I actually took all the supplies to the register and bought them. Because this time, I didn't give in to all my misgivings about having a party. I let the thoughts of money and time and aggravation just roll off my back like a summer rain. This time I decided to go through with it—I decided to throw the damn party.

I sent out invitations inviting all our friends and family and co-workers to my "Welcome Spring Bash," and now there are upwards of fifty people milling about our house and our backyard. Jim's grilling hotdogs and hamburgers outside in the lovely April weather, and I've spent the last few days preparing a veritable feast of comfort foods—potato salad, ambrosia, homemade baked beans, coleslaw, fresh baked rolls, and I even concocted a punch made with ginger-ale and sherbet, the kind we always used to have at gatherings when I was a kid.

Everyone seems to be having a good time. Even Jodie, after a little prodding from me, invited a few of her classmates to come and hang out. I think there might even be a little something going on between her and a young man she introduced to me as Tyler. It's hard to tell, but they seem to keep pairing off within the group, and Jodie did something that almost resembled giggling around him. He's not someone I would have been interested in when I was in high school—he's skinny as a rail with long shaggy hair and lanky arms and legs—but it's nice to see Jodie hanging out with friends—if she's happy, I'm happy.

"You got anything to kick this punch up a notch or two?" Nora asks me as I refill one of the platters on the dining room table.

"Like?"

"You know . . . a little sompin-sompin. Vodka? Rum?"

I laugh. "Sure. There's some liquor on the counter in the kitchen. Take your pick."

I watch Nora walk into the kitchen, spike her glass of punch with a heaping shot of vodka and walk back toward Owen and Billy. When she reaches the two of them I see her pick up Billy, rest him on her hip, and take him outside to get a hotdog. Now that's not an image I ever expected to see, but things seem to be working out for her and "her boys," as she calls them. I never thought I'd see her take such an interest in any male who hadn't yet hit puberty, but she seems happy with the whole deal. The other day we were talking at work, and she said she "had the perfect thing going." She had a great man whom she enjoyed being with. And she was finding some joy in being involved with a child. But, in many ways, she's still the same old Nora. When I asked her what she liked best about Billy, her reply was, "That it was some other woman's figure that got ruined in the process of bringing him into the world."

Kamille is here as well. I can see her through the back door sitting on a lawn chair. Gretchen is sitting next to her, no doubt boring poor Kamille to tears with some story about George Clooney or Whitney Houston. I'm still worried about her, but I have high hopes that she's getting her act together. She's still a little guarded about her situation, but she has told me that she's in counseling and being treated for something called Body

Dysmorphic Disorder. And if nothing else, she's at least agreed to hold off on any more surgery for "the time-being." I'm getting to know her better as time goes by, and she's actually quite likable once you get past the overzealous Quality Improvement Director we deal with at the office. She's even grown on Nora. Kamille, Nora, and I have become almost like the *Sex and the City* girls, getting together after work about once a week and having drinks and talking trash about everyone in the office.

"How's it going?" Jim says to me as he sets a plate of burgers on the table.

"Good. Everything seems to be going well," I reply and as I say this, I realize that my words cover much more than just the current party. Everything does seem to be going well. It's been more than a month since I had it out with Jim about his affair and our marriage in general, and I can honestly say that everything we talked about that fateful night after we happened upon Jazelle at Ruby Tuesday, we have taken to heart. We are both making an effort to save our marriage. Jim even agreed to see a marriage counselor with me. Well, I didn't actually present the idea of seeing a counselor as something he had an option of "agreeing" or "not agreeing" to. One thing I've realized, like it or not, is that I've gained the upper hand in our marriage. Jim needs my forgiveness and my commitment, which has made me more assertive in what I ask of him. I know you shouldn't look at a relationship in terms of who wields the power, but at the moment, I really am that person. Jim realized that he did not want to lose me and Jodie, and he knows that he needs to make some changes if that isn't going to happen. But, rest assured, I plan to use my powers for good—one example being my insistence that we start counseling, so we can have someone who is impartial help us rebuild our relationship and make sure we stay on track. Our current therapist insists that Jim and I have a date night at least once a week in which we do something as a couple. A few days ago we actually went and played miniature golf over at a course in Vienna and had the most wonderful time. Our therapist also suggested that we eat at least two meals a week at the dining room table with our daughter. That may not seem like much, but for a family that has been grabbing meals on the run for years, it's a good place to start the process of re-connecting.

All in all, things are on the upswing. I believe that Jim and I are being honest with each other—*completely honest* with each other for the first time in years. We've stopped conversing about his affair in code, and, with the help of our counselor, we've had some in-depth conversations about why he strayed, and why I foolishly tolerated it. I'm not stupid, I know I'm not responsible for his infidelity, but I also realize that I do share some of the blame for letting our marriage drift into a sea of indifference. And now we both finally understand that communicating with each other is more important than anything if we are going to keep our relationship alive.

An odd side-effect of all this communication has been a welcome return of my libido. It's just a hunch, but I think I needed some *emotional* intimacy before I could feel a desire for *physical* intimacy. And now that Jim and I are both working to tell each other how we are feeling and making an honest effort to spend time together, our sex life is better than it has been in quite some time.

"Aren't you glad we didn't sell the house," Jim says as we look around and see our friends and family milling about. The night I confronted Jim about his affair I really did think that selling the house was one way to get our family back on track, but now I realize that the house was never the problem. Although I will admit to still wanting to put it on the market as soon as Jodie graduates from high school. I'd love to have a smaller place that's closer to work, so I can spend more time doing things I enjoy rather than spending so many hours in my car.

"Yeah. I guess I am," I reply, and suddenly I start hearing my new theme song in my head. When Jim and I started therapy, for some reason, all I could think about was an *Ally McBeal* episode when Ally went to see a counselor played by Tracey Ullman, and she tells Ally that she must pick a theme song that she can sing to herself when she starts feeling blue. I think Ally picked the song "Tell Him" by the Exciters. Well, I decided to steal my theme song from *The Mary Tyler Moore Show* and use "Love is All Around." And right now, with my husband standing next to me, I'm having one of those moments when I hear the song playing in my head; I imagine that I'm standing in the town square throwing my hat in the air, and I think to myself, You're going to make it after all.